Ann,

Thank you for your support!

Diana Taylor Hart

Moving On

By

Diana Taylor Hart

Copyright © 2013 Diana Taylor Hart

All rights reserved.

ISBN-10: 1481985663

EAN-13: 9781481985666

Library of Congress Control Number: 2013900911
CreateSpace Independent Publishing Platform
North Charleston, South Carolina

To my parents and husband for caring and
To the parents and teachers who care about children

Acknowledgments

I want to thank Jo, Grace, Angela, Jen, Barb, Patty, Susan, Sheri, and John for their support and helping make my dream come true. I also want to thank my editor, Catherine J. Rourke, for making me a better writer and Dara Fowler for creating an amazing book cover.

Table of Contents

Main Characters

Family and Household Members

Samantha Cabot Samuels, aka Sam – main character
Thomas Ryan – Sam's love interest; chief deputy county attorney
Maxie Samuels – Sam's deceased daughter
Peter Samuels – Sam's deceased husband
Henry and Marge Samuels – Peter's parents and Sam's in-laws
Doc Jake Simpson – Henry Samuels' cousin and a veterinarian
John and Annie Ryan – Thomas' parents [Judge Ryan]
Michael and Becca Cabot – Sam's deceased parents
Max and Cate Cabot – Sam's paternal grandparents
Sarah Stein – Sam's cousin
Louisa and Aaron Stein – Sam's maternal grandparents
Maria and Pepé Martinez – Sam's housekeeper and gardener

Central Characters

Dr. Bill Austin – school district superintendent
DeMorgan Beaker – Sam's former student
Ronald Jasper Beaker III, aka RJ – real estate developer
Ruth Beaker – school board president
William Bennett – Sam's former student
Cindy Cameron – finance director's assistant
Lois Cameron – finance director's secretary
Blanche Campbell – school secretary
Jane Fuller – new district finance director
James Hill – Sam's former student
Darrell Jefferson – former principal of Madison Elementary School
Mario Lopez – Sam's former student
Ray Lopez – a fourth-grade teacher
Ben Machado – head of the University Hospital ER Department
Paul Mendoza – acting school superintendent
Fred Monti – county attorney
Jack Peterson – sheriff
Carlo Santini – FBI agent
Gina Spinelli – third-grade teacher
Patty Steward – president of the teachers association
Rob Stone – school district security guard
Ned Tomer – head of school district security

Monday

August 15

Monday: 4:30 A.M. at Home

I needed to make a good impression on my first day as principal of Madison Elementary School. Unfortunately, I was a bundle of nerves. A mortifying nightmare had disrupted any possibility of restful sleep—there I stood, addressing the staff, completely nude! Rolling over, I climbed out of bed in a semi daze. Quietly, I made my way down the wide hallway to Maxie's bedroom. Bear, my golden retriever, followed close behind.

We stood in the doorway, silently looking in. It had been three long months since my five-year-old daughter died, and I was beginning to wonder whether this gripping pain would ever subside. Some days were worse than others. Maxie's night light glowed faintly in the corner, emitting dim rays across the room. Her favorite Teddy bear lay on the bed just where she had always kept him.

Walking over to the bed, I picked up the old frayed bear from her menagerie of stuffed animals and held him gently in my arms. Maxie always hated sleeping in the dark without him.

Bear waited for a moment before entering the room, but now he stood next to me, sniffing the covers. He turned his head, touched my leg with his cold nose, and whimpered.

"She's in heaven with her daddy, Bear," I whispered, gently patting his head. I placed the Teddy bear back on her bed. I moved to the window and opened the soft yellow shades to let the sunlight in. This had been my morning ritual since her birth. Feeling blue as I stood there gazing out the window, I thought of Maxie. I could almost see my little girl beaming, looking out the window into a dark, velvety dawn and witnessing the sun's rays beginning to rise over Arizona's majestic mountains.

Slowly, I turned away from the window and looked around the room. The hand-painted scenes of Winnie the Pooh still evoked warm memories. Maxie's favorite was when Pooh got stuck in Rabbit's doorway. Thomas and I had painted that image next to the toy chest where she spent most of her time playing and laughing.

I picked up a large, stuffed version of Tigger and sat down in my rocking-chair. As Bear watched me from Maxie's bed, I cradled Tigger as if he were real. Slowly, I began rocking him gently back and forth, clutching him for dear life. Tears flowed as I prayed for the inner strength to face the day ahead.

The phone rang, piercing the stillness of the moment. I quickly picked up the receiver from the small table next to the chair.

"Good morning," I sniffled, wiping the tears away.

"My lady," Thomas greeted me warmly. "How are you doing?"

"I'm fine," I replied softly, thinking back to the first time I met Thomas Ryan ten years earlier. In my innocence then, as a seventeen-year-old freshman at the University of Arizona and still grieving my parents' sudden death, I was terrified by the intensity of my feelings for him. He had remained in my life even though I married Peter Samuels, his childhood friend, instead.

Thomas served as Maxie's godfather and became my rock when she was diagnosed with leukemia shortly after Peter was killed in a plane crash. In this devastating time, he held me together through one trauma right after another. It was during her chemotherapy treatments that I realized I was deeply in love with him and that he had always been in love with me.

My thoughts drifted back to the present as we talked about the day ahead. He was going to appear in court on several matters, as part of his usual routine working at the county attorney's office. At the end of our conversation, he wished me good luck on my first day as principal.

I returned Tigger to his chair and left him staring out the window.

Bear followed me to the kitchen, where I fixed his breakfast and then made my coffee. A hazelnut aroma filled the room while he noisily chomped down his food. From time to time, Bear looked over at me, wagging his tail. After finishing his breakfast, he approached the doggie door with caution, sniffing the air. Then he charged through the flap to chase two rabbits nibbling grass in the back yard.

I stood by the sink with a cup of coffee, watching the rabbits scamper easily through the view-fence, leaving Bear behind barking anxiously. He stood his ground, pacing back and forth, waiting for their return. He wanted to play but, apparently, they didn't. Laughing aloud, I broke the unbearable silence that was choking my home.

I placed the empty cup in the dishwasher. The funny thing was that I really didn't like coffee any more, but the habit felt comforting and I could rely on it every morning. My housekeeper would come by later and watch over Bear while I went to work.

I returned to the master bedroom, thinking about what I needed to accomplish. Dr. Austin, the school district's superintendent, had charged me with the difficult task of changing Madison's culture.

I showered, used a flat iron to straighten my unruly, chin-length auburn hair, applied a little blush to my cheeks and dark mascara to my olive-green eyes, and finally added gold earrings. Skimming through my closet, I selected a green georgette blouse and dark brown trousers with matching peep-toe pumps. Once dressed, my size-eight clothes hung loosely over my five-foot-seven frame.

Still feeling a little nervous, I felt the adrenaline flowing as I played with my bangs again. All I wanted was for the day to go well. Seconds later, I gave up trying to tame the impossible bangs and settled on just being me.

As I left, I glanced at the full-length mirror and was surprised. Here I was, Samantha Cabot Samuels: I looked cool, collected, and professional. Today was a new day. There was no time for tears or regrets. I had to move on since I was starting a new life.

Monday: 8:10 A.M. at Madison Elementary School

My first day as principal was not turning out the way I had planned. I stood outside my office, horrified at the scene I'd discovered earlier this morning. I was still clutching the paper bag that the night custodian had given me to stop hyperventilating.

I looked up at the new sheriff. Jack Peterson was Thomas' commanding officer in the Marines. He had been appointed eight months ago after the previous sheriff had died in a fiery car crash. When I spoke to the tall, heavy-set man, my voice quavered. "I can't believe this! Dr. Austin was my friend."

"Ms. Samuels, I am aware of that," conceded Sheriff Peterson patiently, noticing but not commenting about the paper bag. He'd been briefed by Deputy Allen that I had been very upset when I found the school superintendent's body.

We stared at Dr. Austin's corpse sprawled across my desk. He had been an intense fifty-five-year-old man and an imposing figure.

Unfortunately, his death had created an odious stench. We stood there for another awkward moment before I realized that the air-conditioning system was beginning to work and, hopefully, the horrible smell would start to dissipate.

Overheated, Sheriff Peterson removed his hat, revealing peppered gray hair. He escorted me to the computer lab, where we were able to sit down. This depressing room was used by every child in the building and its appearance was not particularly conducive to learning. The district had barred the exterior windows for security reasons but, unfortunately, it left its occupants feeling imprisoned in their "classroom jail."

The sheriff frowned slightly, taking in the lab's dismal environment. Without making a comment, he turned his deep-set blue eyes directly on me, ready to begin his interrogation. "For the record, what is your full name, Ms. Samuels?"

"Samantha Cabot Samuels," I stated just above a whisper, beginning to shudder.

"And your age?" he asked routinely.

"I'm twenty-seven," I replied truthfully, as he looked up and scrutinized my face. Everyone thought I looked younger than my age, so I always dressed in simple, elegant clothes, hoping they would make me look professional.

"When did you come to the Old Pueblo?" he asked, referring to the city's name.

"I came here ten years ago after my parents' death," I disclosed, seeing his puzzled expression and quickly adding, "to attend the University of Arizona."

"Now, Ms. Samuels, can you tell me when you left home this morning?" He remained silent while I gathered my thoughts.

"I left around five-thirty so I could get to school early. I wanted to make sure everything was in order so, if there were problems, I would have time to take care of the issues."

"Did you stop anywhere?"

"Yes, I stopped at a bakery and purchased an assortment of pastries for the meeting. Then I drove to school. The custodians and I arrived about six-thirty. They helped me carry in the food and supplies into the teachers' lounge."

"What is their schedule for this week?"

"For now, both custodians are working the day shift until classes begin on Monday."

"What happened next?"

"We began setting up in the teachers' lounge for the orientation meeting. While the custodians brought in chairs, I set out the refreshments on the counter and then made orange juice and coffee. Afterwards, I distributed the notebooks and pens while they brought in a large portable blackboard and fastened sheets of newsprint on the front of it."

"How long were they gone?"

"About three-to-five minutes at most."

"What happened after they returned?" he asked in a nonchalant tone.

"We had coffee and discussed our summer vacations. Then, I thanked them for their help, and they went back to work. I checked on a few things in the main office before finding Dr. Austin's body. Then I immediately dialed 911."

At this point, the sheriff wrote down a few reminders: "Electrostat linoleum—the office floor. Take the custodians' and Samuels' shoes—photographs for comparison."

After years of reading my students' writing upside down, I could easily discern his notes.

"Why would Dr. Austin be here?"

"We had a seven-thirty appointment to go over today's agenda. Other than that, I don't know why he was here."

"What did you do when you entered the main office?"

"I checked my box for messages and the answering machine on Blanche's desk."

"Who is Blanche?"

"Blanche Campbell is the school secretary," I answered.

"Were there any phone messages?"

"Yes, but after listening to them, none of them required an immediate response."

"Did you erase any of these messages?"

"No, I left Blanche a note concerning the calls on her desk."

"What did you do then?"

"I walked down the short hallway to my office and opened the door."

"Let me stop you here. Did you smell anything before going into your office?"

"Yes. I thought something was rotting in the refrigerator."

"Why would you think that?" he mused, lifting one eyebrow.

"We experienced a power outage last week due to a summer storm, so I thought it might have happened again over the weekend."

"Where is this refrigerator located?"

"In my office."

"Was the door to your office locked?"

"No," I replied. "It was closed."

"When you entered your office, what was the first thing you noticed?"

"The stench—and then I saw Dr. Austin's body lying on my desk."

"Did you think he was dead?" he pressed, narrowing his eyes.

"No. At first, I thought he was ill. So I approached him, asking if he was all right. When he didn't respond, I knew something was terribly wrong."

"Did you see anything else?"

"Yes. I noticed a knife sticking out of his back. There was dried blood spattered on the desk and the floor."

"Did you touch anything?"

"No. I backed out of the room, trying not to disturb anything, and closed the door. Then I went to the master switch in the main office and rang the emergency bell."

"Then what?" he demanded.

"I dialed 911 using my cell phone. As I spoke to the police dispatcher, the custodians arrived. They stood quietly outside the main office door and listened to my end of the conversation."

"When did the first officer show up?"

"Just as I was ending the call," I said. "He checked Dr. Austin for any signs of life and secured the office."

"Did you and the custodians talk amongst yourselves?"

"Yes, but not about Dr. Austin. I was hyperventilating, and they were concerned," I disclosed, suddenly, feeling a burning sensation on my face. "The night custodian went to get me a paper bag from the lounge."

"What happened next?"

"The paramedics arrived and pronounced Dr. Austin dead."

"When did the detective arrive?"

"She arrived about ten minutes later and separated us in different areas of the cafeteria. Afterwards, she made a few phone calls using her cell in the hallway. I assumed that she was contacting you, the coroner, and the deputy county attorney on-call. Then, she took our initial statements." I couldn't think of anything else to add, so I remained silent.

The sheriff sat quietly reviewing his notes and then drew a quick sketch of the crime scene from memory. He rubbed his chin. "When was the last time you saw Dr. Austin alive?"

"Friday morning," I replied. "We met at his office, which is located in the district's Administration Building."

"What was the meeting about?"

"We went over a list of items for my first faculty meeting."

"What time was the meeting scheduled?"

"Today at nine o'clock."

"What did you discuss in your meeting with Dr. Austin?"

"We reviewed our goals for Madison. We also discussed the changes I would be announcing at the staff meeting today."

"How long did the meeting last?" he peppered.

"Approximately two hours."

"What did you do next?"

"I came back here and worked on several reports until three. After that, I caught a flight to San Diego for a friend's wedding."

"When did you return?"

"Late last night," I stated, catching a glimpse of his slight frown. "My flight was delayed because of a severe thunderstorm, so I arrived home about one this morning."

"How long have you known Dr. Austin?"

"I've known . . ." I started to say, but stopped abruptly. I was still coming to grips with the fact that he was dead. I looked down for a split-second at the paper bag and then looked directly at the sheriff. "I mean, I knew Bill for about seven years."

"Tell me about how you met him and about your working relationship."

"His wife introduced me to Dr. Austin. She was my supervising professor when I did my student-teaching at Madison. As to our working relationship, I would say he was more my mentor. He encouraged me to continue with my education by getting my master's degree, my reading endorsement, and eventually, my administrative certificate."

"Did he mentor others?" he inquired, narrowing his eyes.

"Yes, Bill treated all his employees with a great deal of respect and pushed them to develop their full potential. Sometimes he succeeded and sometimes he didn't."

"What happened when an individual did not meet his expectations?"

"He felt that individual was challenging his authority," I disclosed, measuring my words carefully.

"And if you did challenge him?"

"He never forgot the betrayal."

"What was your betrayal?" the sheriff asked, looking straight at me.

My lips parted slightly, stunned with his directness. "After teaching several years, I spoke out candidly on educational issues and the rights of public school employees."

"Are you still a member of the teachers association?" he asked as I nodded yes. "Please elaborate your involvement."

"I have served on the association's board of directors, as well as being a member of the contract negotiating team twice. During the last negotiations, I became their spokesperson."

"What were Dr. Austin's issues with you?"

"He and I had a philosophical difference."

"How so?" he insisted quietly, observing my body language.

"Our differences were about labor versus management."

"Were those differences well-known?"

"Oh, yes," I smiled, seeing his quizzical look. "Everyone in the educational community knew."

"How?" he sighed.

"For the first time in the district's history, we conducted our negotiations in public. The sessions were televised on the public access channel. At times, our exchanges became rather heated."

"Over what?" he pressed.

"For one thing, I believe that all administrators should be in the classroom teaching at least an hour a day. He didn't. He felt it undermined their authority."

"I don't get it. If you had such differences, why would he recommend your appointment to the school board?"

"Dr. Austin was politically astute. Both Thomas Ryan and Henry Samuels, my father-in-law, lobbied him and the school board on my behalf," I admitted, knowing that they were really afraid that I had fallen into a deep depression since Maxie's death. "The Samuels and the Ryans are powerful forces in this community."

"Okay, but why this school?" he asked, scanning the lab again.

"Why not? Madison is not an easy school to run. It has the worst reputation in our district and is located in a high-crime and drug-infested area. Besides, he had everything to gain if I succeeded and nothing to lose if I didn't."

"But why put an inexperienced principal in such an impossible situation?"

"He wanted to teach me a lesson in reality, or maybe a lesson in humility."

"Still, would you have been a major thorn in his side?"

"Probably," I uttered truthfully.

"How—specifically?"

"He and most of the other principals viewed me as a maverick, because I planned to implement the new program I designed during my administrative internship."

"What kind of program?"

"Basically, I would be putting my core beliefs into action," I asserted. "In other words, I would be teaching every day in different classrooms as part of my administrative duties."

"How did your program work?"

"It went very well! My supervising principal was very enthusiastic about the results and is planning to continue the program at the middle school."

"Why?" he demanded, surprised at my answer.

"Test scores were up significantly and discipline behavior was notably lower."

"I see," he commented.

I stopped for a moment to consider how dilapidated Madison School had become over the years. It was the victim of declining enrollment and too many unfunded repair orders. The exterior of the building summed up its plight. It looked like a sunbaked snake starting to shed its skin in large patches of peeling stucco and peach paint. The surrounding grass was mostly dead and the old trees were withering, suffering dehydration from 110-degree temperatures and insufficient irrigation.

"Sheriff, it's a sign of the times that inner-city schools named after the first five presidents are not in good locations. On good days, parents are anti-establishment, and on bad days . . . well, you know that better than me. There are language barriers to contend with. And, if that's not bad enough, the teachers' morale is in the toilet. They don't trust the school district or the state's Department of Education. Dr. Austin needed someone here with some credibility with the teaching staff and the community."

"But why you?" he pressed again.

"I taught here for three years and know the community well and most of the staff. I still have the ear of the president of the teachers association. I think he felt I would be very busy implementing the cultural changes he wanted."

"In other words, he was setting you up for failure."

"No, I don't think so. Dr. Austin knew something had to be done here. Even though we've had our differences, we were both . . . committed to quality education. He made it clear that he would support me and the changes necessary to turn Madison around. If we succeeded, Madison would become a model for the other elementary schools in the district."

"And if you failed?"

"Well, then his stature would rise among the district's administrators who viewed me as a threat," I conceded.

While the sheriff wrote down my comments, I stared out the window, trying not to panic. The parking lot was filling up with an odd collection of older, well-used cars; some looked so old it was amazing that they still ran. Some teachers carried instructional materials and others lugged boxes, but they all paused at the sight of the sheriff's vehicles parked in front of the school.

A blue Lincoln sailed into the school lot and parked illegally next to the sheriff's black Tahoe. Ruth Beaker, president of the school board, was the driver. She had been Peter's first girlfriend and, I had always believed, the love of his life.

I was stunned to see her. Had someone called her about Dr. Austin, or had he invited her without telling me? I knew he had been distressed about something going on in the district, but I didn't have a clue what it was. Could her visit possibly have something to do with the dilemma or, worse, his murder?

The sheriff twisted around to see what I was staring at and then faced me.

I could feel his eyes boring into me. It was as if he was evaluating everything I said and, probably, wondering if I'd told him the truth.

Finally, he glanced down at my stained fingertips, still blackened from the fingerprint ink that a deputy had applied earlier. He added to his notes: "Fingerprint all school staff for elimination comparisons."

A deputy knocked on the opened door. Sheriff Peterson gestured for him to enter. Once inside, he informed us that Mrs. Beaker and the teachers were waiting for me in the lounge.

I glanced at my watch and, to my horror, it read nine-fifteen. "Sheriff Peterson, I know you have a job to do, but so do I. Could we continue our discussion later?" I suggested. "I really do need to meet with the staff."

"That sounds fine," he declared, getting up from his seat. "Just so you know the crime scene investigation will take about seven or eight more hours. I may have more questions to ask you later on. So how about meeting at three-thirty this afternoon?"

"That will work," I agreed, realizing how tense I was when I stood.

17

"I have one more question right now."

"Yes?" I asked, looking up at the tall man.

"What was your personal relationship with Dr. Austin?"

"There was none. As I said before, we were colleagues. He encouraged me to continue with my education, which I did. And that was it."

"Thank you for your candor this morning, Ms. Samuels," he stated.

"You're welcome," I replied and walked away.

The sheriff spoke with Deputy Allen about what he needed done as I called out for Mrs. Campbell, my fifty-ish secretary, to bring her notepad.

Blanche rose from her temporary desk in the lab's office, glanced in the mirror to make sure her blonde hair was still in a French twist, and then straightened her light blue shirtdress. Always the professional, she handed me a mug filled with fresh coffee, which I accepted gratefully. She began relaying the morning messages as we left the room and walked down the long, drab hallway to our meeting.

Monday: 9:20 A.M. at Madison Elementary School

Just steps away from the doorway of the teachers' lounge, we heard the staff conversing in hushed tones. Everyone stopped talking in mid-sentence as we entered, closely followed by the sheriff. Their silence was deafening.

I hesitated, unsure how to begin.

Blanche leaned forward. "You've worked hard for this, Sam. If anyone can turn this school around, it's you. Now, show them."

I looked back into her dark eyes, still feeling ill-at-ease. "I don't know . . . so much has happened this morning."

"You can do this, Sam. You're a teacher at heart. Go on; everyone's waiting for you," she prodded, and then ambling to the nearest table to take her seat.

Holding my head up high, I walked to the front of the dingy lounge and turned to face the anxious group. I took a deep breath, surveyed the audience, and began my first official meeting as the acting principal of Madison Elementary School.

"Good morning, ladies and gentlemen. Thank you for your patience. I am very sorry to inform you that Dr. Austin has died. His body was found here earlier this morning. Sheriff Peterson is investigating the circumstances surrounding his death. I have assured him that we will cooperate fully in his investigation. If you know of something, no matter how insignificant you think this piece of information may seem, or if you have heard or seen anything, please inform the sheriff or one of his deputies."

I paused for a quick glance around the room only to see brittle faces, reeling from the news. The first day of school was generally chaotic, but Bill Austin's death really made matters worse, and I made a mental note to call the district's crisis team. I waited anxiously for a response but, instead, everyone just sat there, staring at me, quietly sipping coffee, or playing with their pens. Their anxiety continued to build as I met Ray Lopez's worried eyes. He was a short, burly man and my oldest association buddy.

When no one volunteered, I didn't know what to think, so I took a sip of coffee and hoped that no one noticed my hand shaking. Putting the mug down on the table, I plunged forward. "Mrs. Beaker, our school board president, is here," I stated, taking note of the very attractive, wealthy woman in her late thirties. Ruth sat stone-faced, looking like a Barbie doll, with perfectly bleached, ash-blonde hair and make-up.

I'd met her causally through my husband, Peter. Whenever I bumped into Ruth and RJ, her husband, their shallowness was unbelievable. She had nothing in common with anyone in the room and only dabbled in politically correct social projects. And here she was, out of her element. In fact, she was slumming in this neighborhood. School board members never visited run-down schools like Madison . . . so why was she here?

"I want to welcome you to our school and thank you for coming today, Mrs. Beaker," I said, keeping my contempt in check.

Everyone turned in her direction, waiting for her to comment. She nodded slightly in acknowledgement. Tears were now apparent in her light brown eyes, but she remained reticent.

So I went on. "School will open next week as scheduled, and we have a lot of work ahead of us. Students will be arriving at eight-thirty Monday morning. For any other information about schedules or the school and district policies, please consult your handbook, which is located in the front of your notebooks. If you have any questions or concerns about these policies, please bring them to our next meeting."

Taking another sip of coffee, I deliberately dropped the formality and spoke freely. "Look, Bill Austin sent me here to prove a point—that public education can still work. Our goal at Madison is to help each child achieve his or her full potential." Surveying the room, I realized I had everyone's attention, including the sheriff's.

"The truth is that this school is in trouble and has been for some time. It is our job to turn this learning environment around. Unfortunately, change has already occurred—not slowly and steadily as we might have hoped, but abruptly. I know what I am asking you is difficult under these circumstances, but I also know that you will rise to the occasion." I stopped for a moment to allow my message to resonate.

"How?" Ray demanded, drumming a pen on the table.

"With your intelligence, grace, and humor," I answered. Gazing at this dejected crowd, I pressed on, knowing this was a battle of wills. "Let us begin. Blanche, please pass out the construction paper and Ray, please hand out the markers to each table."

21

As Blanche and Ray completed their tasks, some teachers whispered within their social groups, while others looked around the room at one another, seeking the comfort of familiarity.

This group had always known me as a younger colleague and now I hoped they would accept me as their administrator. "Since we already have five groups of seven, please select a recorder for your group." I stopped for a moment to allow them to select their secretaries.

When everyone was ready, I started our mission. "Title each sheet as follows: one, Problems; two, Solutions; three, Goals; four, People; and finally, Setting. Now, for the next fifteen minutes, each table will define the problems at this school, and the recorder will log your comments. Don't worry about the time; just do your best. Now, get ready, get set—begin."

As the groups chattered among themselves, I wandered over to the sheriff, who was standing by the doorway with one ear to his cell phone. I explained that we would probably be here until noon. He nodded his head, returning his attention to his call, and left the room, barking orders to someone at the other end.

I moved from one table to another, listening to everyone sharing their ideas. I missed being one of them. After glancing at the time, I announced, "Stop."

They were all so absorbed in their discussions that they were surprised.

I asked, "Which are your most important concerns?"

As they answered, Blanche recorded their ideas on the sheets attached to the blackboard.

Ray voiced loudly, "Not enough books and supplies."

A fourth-grade teacher was next. "Lack of discipline."

"Lack of parental support," piped up a fifth-grade teacher.

And the rest of the staff joined in. Once we had defined the school's problems, our next task was to search for solutions.

At first they were hesitant but, then, Ray declared, "Holding the principal accountable!"

The teachers snickered as I smiled in agreement. Over the next ninety minutes, we continued the process until each topic was met. At the end of the session, I announced a break.

The tension in the room appeared to be finally dissipating, and I felt the first moment of normalcy since I'd found Dr. Austin's body. It was as if I was in front of a rowdy classroom on the first day of school.

The staff started talking all at once, first softly, then in normal tones. Some individuals went to the bathrooms, while others refilled their coffee cups and munched on pastries. A few stood and stretched as Blanche left to compile the data.

Ten minutes later, it was time to return to work. "I want to thank you for your candor, your expertise, and your insight this morning," I told them. "You have done a wonderful job, and you have also just experienced how I want you to teach in your classrooms."

Everyone froze. It seemed as if the room temperature instantly dropped twenty degrees, even though the thermometer still read seventy-five degrees Fahrenheit. Frowns gathered on most faces, with looks of confusion and anxiety on others. No one seemed happy with my statement.

"Take reading, for example. Before the children read a story, have them predict what the story is about, who the characters are, where the story is taking place, what problems might the characters encounter, how the characters resolve their problems, and the themes of the story."

Some teachers made annotations while others folded their arms across their chests with clenched teeth.

"Once you have recorded their opinions, read the story to them in order to confirm or deny their predictions and then briefly discuss the tale by asking probing questions. On the second day, have the children read the story with a buddy. Afterwards, brainstorm each element of the story and record their observations. On the third day, have your students retell the story as you take their dictation. Then, have them practice reading their narrative, as well as copying the story in their reading journals."

The group could no longer contain itself. There was outright rebellion.

"Sam, we'll lose control. They won't learn anything, and talk about discipline problems!" stormed a fifth-grade teacher.

"Let me ask you something. Did you learn anything this morning?"

"Yes, but . . ." she protested in a defensive tone.

"Did you enjoy this process?"

"Yes.

"Then the children will too," I assured her. "They will feel valued and take responsibility for their learning. In addition to this, their language skills will improve dramatically."

"But, Sam . . ." she complained, still angry.

"Be firm, expect the best, and you will get the best from them in return. We need to shake the kids up a bit. Let them know we value their ideas. Get them thinking about problems and solutions. And, yes, maybe we do run the risk of getting them excited about learning, but isn't that our job?"

"But, Sam, be reasonable! You just don't know what you're talking about," griped another fourth-grade teacher.

"We're going to lose control with this nonsense. And where will you be?" Ray smirked, with a twinkle in his eye. He was giving me my opening. Having seen me in action in his classroom when I was his student-teacher, he knew what was coming.

"I'll be working with you and your students," I asserted, smiling as a few individuals sneered at the thought of a principal toiling in their classrooms. "We'll start slowly with the reading program. I want you to relax and enjoy the process like you did this morning, and the kids will enjoy it too. And if there are behavioral and learning problems, I want to know about it immediately."

Looking around the room before anyone else could object, I stood up straighter and announced firmly, "This is not a choice, ladies and gentlemen. The kids come first, and failure is not an option. Intermediate teachers, I want to meet with you today at one-thirty to discuss how I want this program implemented. Tomorrow I'll meet with the primary grade teachers at eight o'clock in the morning."

Everyone wrote down their times. I was no longer a colleague in their eyes but an administrator. I felt empowered that I'd taken control, and they knew it.

"Also, before I forget, my temporary office will be in the computer room until further notice. There will be an all-staff meeting Wednesday at one-thirty here in the lounge. We will be discussing peer mediation techniques. If time permits, we will continue to prioritize our main problems and develop a strategy to implement our solutions. If you think of anything to add to this, bring it up at the meeting." I stopped to meet their gaze.

"I want to thank you again for your patience and understanding today. If you have any questions or concerns, please see me. And if you have any information about Dr. Austin's death, please speak to the sheriff or a member of his staff as soon as possible. I'll see you after lunch."

A deputy entered the lounge and announced that the fingerprint technician was ready to fingerprint the faculty in the cafeteria. Now they were really unhappy. Quietly, they gathered their belongings while they watched the deputy seal my shoes in a clear plastic bag.

I slipped into a pair of black heels that he had retrieved from my car. As the staff followed him out the door, I walked over to the table where Ruth Beaker was still sitting. Her expression seemed somehow fragile and, at the same time, dazed. She had observed the entire meeting without offering a single suggestion.

"Oh, damn," I thought, noticing the fresh tears. The last thing I needed was for the president of the school board to fall apart in my teachers' lounge. "Ruth?"

I placed my hand on her shoulder. "Ruth, are you okay?"

She glanced up, as if finally noticing my presence. "Well, Samantha, I'm impressed. You handled yourself very well under such stressful circumstances. I'm beginning to understand why Bill—I mean, Dr. Austin—insisted on sending you here."

"Thank you."

Glancing at her watch, she regained her composure, rose from her seat, and walked out of the lounge toward the front door. As protocol dictated, I followed.

At the door, she stopped. "I wish you and your staff a successful year. If there is anything that the board can do to help, please let us know. In any case, it seems as if you have everything under control."

"Thank you again for coming and for . . . ."

"Peter would've been pleased with your performance today," she blurted out curtly, cutting me off. "For your information, there is an emergency school board meeting scheduled at three this afternoon."

I was dumbfounded by both the compliment and the fact that the board had already scheduled a meeting. Before I could utter a word, she pushed open the door.

"Have a nice day." She turned and left the building.

Stunned for a moment, I just stared at her in disbelief. I walked back to the computer lab, thinking about what I needed to do next.

Blanche was on the phone with a parent when I sat down.

"How are you doing, Blanche?" I solicited when she finished the call. The rims of her dark eyes were red.

"I'm doing okay, Sam; keeping busy," she replied, biting down on her lower lip. "I just can't believe Dr. Austin was murdered."

"Neither can I!" I volunteered, visualizing the murder scene again. My chest tightened, not wanting to dwell on the subject for fear I would start hyperventilating again. "Anything else I need to know about?"

"No; not really. The medical examiner and his assistant removed his body thirty minutes ago," she informed me.

"Any phone calls?" I asked.

"Just the usual calls asking about what time school will begin and end. How much does the school lunch cost? What about the free lunch program? What about the after-school program? Do we have a nurse this year?"

"I get the idea. Nothing out of the ordinary," I concluded.

Blanche nodded in agreement.

I took a moment to center myself. "Have we had any calls concerning Dr. Austin's death?"

"No," she said, her eyes beginning to water.

"That's surprising. I guess the news isn't out yet," I declared, sighing. "What are your thoughts about the meeting?"

"Sam, I think it went better than well. Some of the teachers were discussing the reading program favorably on their way out to lunch."

"I'm glad, but we still have a long way to go."

The phone rang and Blanche reached to answer it, but I interceded and told her to go to lunch. Reaching across the desk, I grabbed the receiver on the third ring. "Good afternoon, Madison Elementary School. This is Ms. Samuels speaking; how may I help you?"

"Thomas Ryan here, Ms. Samuels," his warm voice replied.

"I guess the sheriff told you about Bill," I said.

"Yes. Jack called me first thing this morning. How are you doing?"

"Okay," I uttered softly.

"Are you sure?" he explored further.

"Yes. In a strange way, I feel pretty detached about what happened to Bill."

"What do you mean?" he solicited.

"The simple answer is I didn't have to watch him die. And I'm busy dealing with the aftermath."

After a moment of silence, Thomas asked, "Have you spoken to his wife?"

"No, I really haven't had the time. I'm still trying to take it all in."

"Do you need me to come over?" he asked, having heard a sad tone in my voice.

"For Pete's sake, Thomas, no!" I snapped sharply. I knew he was worried because I'd pulled inward after Maxie's death, not allowing anyone in. But this was no time to show weakness, and we both knew it. "Remember, I'm the new principal."

"Yes, I do remember," he said softly. "I'm the one who talked you into taking this job. Now, I'm not so sure that it was a good idea."

I knew he felt like he was treading on a bed of quicksand. "Thomas, I'm sorry for being so short with you. I guess I'm still upset at finding Bill's body."

"Oh, honey . . ." he began.

"And as much as I hate to admit this to you, you and Henry were right," I confessed, softening my tone. "I needed to get back to work. Thomas, I needed a distraction—a cause. Maybe not to this extreme, but I can deal with it."

"Sam, I . . . ."

"Please hold, Thomas. The other line is ringing."

"Good afternoon. Madison School," I declared in an authoritative tone.

"Hello, Sam. We need to talk."

"Just a minute, Patty. I'm on the other line." I put her on hold and pressed Line One. "Honey, I've got Patty Steward on the other line. Is there anything else?"

"Yes. I'll be there at three-thirty this afternoon with Jack."

"Thomas, am I the main suspect in Bill's murder?" I demanded a bit testily, shocked at the possibility.

"Sam, everyone is a suspect right now," he barked, which was unusual. Then, taking a deep breath, he went on gently to explain, "A violent crime has been committed. I'm the chief deputy of the county

29

attorney's office, and it's my job to gather all the facts on high-profile cases, regardless of who is involved."

"Do I need an attorney?" I inquired with a catch to my voice. The silence that followed seemed to last forever but, in reality, it was only a nanosecond.

"No."

"Okay, Thomas, I'll see you later," I said. I knew all he wanted to do was protect me, but I was still scared. I stared at the blinking red light for a moment longer. Mustering my courage to speak with Patty Steward, the president of the teachers association, I pressed the flashing button. "Yes, Patty, how is your day going?"

"Awful!"

"I'm sorry to hear that," I said, detecting her heated tone. I was in for it since I had joined the dark forces of administration.

Patty broke in. "Sam, it is only noon on the first day of school. What the hell is going on over there?"

"Patty, the sheriff is personally investigating the circumstances into Bill Austin's death. His task force is collecting evidence and questioning witnesses."

"Well, I've had over twenty calls from your staff. Everyone is scared to death about this investigation. They want to know if they need to hire an attorney."

"At this point, all the sheriff wants is information, and I expect the staff to cooperate fully," I stated, hearing her high-pitched voice. I knew she was under a great deal of pressure.

"Another thing," she asserted. "A couple of the teachers are concerned about you teaching in their classrooms. They don't like it!"

"I'm firm on that, and I expect them to be professional and work with me."

"Now, Sam, you know the contract."

"I know the contract intimately. Remember, I was the association's spokesperson on the bargaining team. So don't preach to this choir."

"Touchy, aren't we?"

"Look, Patty, I found Bill's body. He was a friend, even if he was a bastard at times. He sent me here to make some changes, and I intend to do just that. Now, if there isn't anything else, I really need to get back to work."

"Whoa, Sam, we're old friends. I know you don't want this piece of advice, but here it goes anyway. This is your first day on the job and you're moving too quickly for everyone. All I'm saying is go with the flow until this mess is cleared up."

"Patty, the fact is that no one likes change, but it has already occurred. Bill died here, and we have to move on. The faculty needs to focus on their teaching, for their own good, as well as for the kids. I can't have everyone paralyzed with fear or grief," I stated, stopping suddenly as I realized that was exactly what I had been doing—wallowing in my own grief. No wonder Thomas and Henry had been pushing me to go back to work.

"I need your help with this. Can I count on you?" I pressed her. Patty had been there as I'd picked up the pieces of my life after Peter was killed, and she had seen me go through hell when Maxie was battling leukemia.

She hesitated, taking in a deep breath and then letting it out slowly. "I see your point," she conceded quietly. "If there is anything I can do, holler."

"Well, I'm hollering now. I need your support," I stated. "How about meeting tomorrow afternoon at four so we can continue this conversation?"

"Okay, four it is. Sam, are you all right?" she asked anxiously.

"I'm fine."

"I'm worried you may have bitten off more than you can chew."

"That may be true, but we'll deal with it. I'll see you at four tomorrow. Bye."

Blanche entered the room just as I hung up the phone. "You're back early."

"Yes, I have a lot of work to do," she declared, heading to her desk.

"Blanche, I need you to initiate a robocall to the parents and also the community leaders," I directed, handing her a list of names I'd written down while speaking to Patty. "Invite them to our school meeting tomorrow evening at seven. Tell them that we will be discussing our plans for Madison and the investigation into Dr. Austin's death. Make sure they know that we will serve refreshments and that I'm looking forward to working with them again."

I started to go to my office but stopped abruptly at the sight of the crime-scene tape draped across the main office door. For a moment, I felt nauseated at the sight of the yellow plastic tape emblazoned with the words "Police Barrier—Do Not Enter," repeated over and over again in three-inch-high black letters.

The phone rang as I walked back into the computer room.

"You need to take this call," Blanche stated, disgusted. "It's the head of maintenance. He says he can't fix the leak in the boys' bathroom before school begins."

I walked over to the desk and took the receiver from her hand. "Mr. Brown, this is Samantha Samuels speaking. What is the problem?"

"Well, the part we need to fix is out of stock," he snapped in a raspy, sixty-year-old voice with a condescending manner. "Besides, your school is already over budget on your maintenance line, so I can't go purchase the item. Additionally, you'll have to pay overtime if you want it fixed today."

"Let me see if I understand this correctly. The part necessary to fix the bathroom is not in the district's inventory, but you can purchase the item at a hardware store."

"Yeah, that's right," he grunted.

"How expensive is this item?"

"Around fifteen dollars, more or less," he sneered.

"Mr. Brown, I want you to purchase the necessary items to fix the bathroom and have them installed today. This is a health-and-safety issue," I stated in a straightforward tone. I could almost feel him sitting up straighter in his chair, realizing that the rules had changed. "I will personally reimburse you when you hand me the receipt for your purchases. As for overtime, you and your crew are district employees. There will be no overtime, and this job will be completed by four today. If you are unable to do this, please let me know now so that I can make other arrangements."

"All right, Ms. Samuels, the job will be completed per your instructions."

"Thank you, Mr. Brown, for your prompt attention in this matter. I look forward to seeing you this afternoon and inspecting your work. Until then, goodbye."

I stood there, wondering what was going on with the district's finances. How in the world could we be over budget when the school year hadn't even started? My stomach growled again, so I grabbed my purse and keys and left the building.

Walking into the parking lot, I felt the sun's scorching rays searing through my blouse. I glanced over at the playground. Trash was strewn everywhere, and there were deep red ruts in the clay under the swing sets. The soccer field needed chalking, and the basketball court looked a mess. Cracks took up more space than the pavement did, and the whole court needed to be resurfaced and lined. This represented nothing but neglect.

Maintenance was just going to love me. I would submit my emergency repair requests to the department this afternoon. In the meantime, I would purchase ten large trash cans and several removable basketball hoops. With that thought, I walked to the silver Jeep.

As I drove toward McDonald's, I started wondering why Bill was murdered. For the most part, everyone liked him. If pushed, he could be a tyrant but, on the whole, he was a nice man who cared about kids. Who had he pissed off recently? Ruth Beaker—she and Bill had had some major disagreements lately, but nothing out of the ordinary. Who else? Patty Steward? I knew that they had spoken bitterly about teachers being transferred and about several grievances. But that was crazy; Patty wouldn't hurt a fly.

None of this made any sense. Why had he been so adamant about me coming to Madison? And why was he slain in my office? Was he just an innocent bystander in the wrong place at the wrong time, or was he the intended victim? Was it meant to scare me off, or was I the next target? That was a depressing thought and also a frightening one; after all, it wasn't every day you find your boss as a murder victim sprawled across your own desk.

I drove into the parking lot and slid the Jeep between two Plymouth Voyagers. Two moms were simultaneously emptying herds of tiny toddlers from their vehicles.

Hurrying inside, I ordered a Big Mac, fries, and a chocolate shake—my comfort food for the day. While waiting for my order, I watched two little girls running around in the play area just like Maxie had. She loved tumbling down the slide and laughing without a care in the world. I smiled, grateful for those memories, fingering my heart-shaped locket that Thomas had given me with Maxie's picture.

The server called out my number. I quickly picked up my order and sat down at the first available booth. With each bite, I reviewed the day's events. After arriving at school, I found Bill's body; underwent an interrogation by the sheriff; held a faculty meeting, which generated more than twenty complaint calls to the association; and antagonized the district's head of maintenance. To make matters worse, I had been short with Thomas. I had accomplished all of this before 12:31 in the afternoon!

This clearly had been the most dramatic beginning of any school year to date. Honestly, I'd have to say that just like Alexander in the Judith Viorst book, *Alexander and the Horrible No Good Very Bad Day*, I was having a horrible, no-good, very bad day. Maybe he was right about moving to Australia. Instead of running away like Alexander wanted to, I stood my ground and began to jot down the title of Viorst's book and what I needed to do.

*(*Alexander and the Horrible No Good Very Bad Day*, by Judith Viorst, ©1972, Simon & Schuster)

Monday: 1:05 P.M. at Madison Elementary School

checked in with Blanche, gave her my "to-do" list, and then proceeded around the building. I stopped in every classroom to verify that the teachers had received their textbooks and supplies. Some asked a few questions while others voiced their concerns. Finally, I inspected the boys' bathroom and was relieved to find Mr. Brown's crew working.

The building as a whole was in need of major repairs, ranging from a leaky roof to an obsolete, air-conditioning system. Cracked windows demanded replacement, and after thirty years, the dingy, green walls shouted for a fresh coat of paint. I'd often thought that someone must have made a mint selling this putrid paint color to the district.

The air in the building was hot, humid, and sticky—a situation certainly not conducive to a learning environment. Something had to be done immediately. Glancing at my watch, I wondered what was wrong with the coolers. I needed maintenance to check them. In the meantime, I would purchase fans for every classroom.

I entered the lounge with just enough time to call Lois Cameron, the finance director's secretary. I needed another copy of Madison's budget since all of my papers were now part of the crime scene. The phone quickly clicked through to Twenty-Twenty. The nickname was a play on the district's Administration Building address at 2020 Blueflower Street. I asked to speak to Lois and waited for the call to be transferred.

"Good afternoon; Mrs. Cameron, speaking."

"Hi Lois," I stated and went on to explain my dilemma.

"I'll have it ready for you tomorrow morning." Then she told me how upset she was about Dr. Austin's sudden death. She had worked with him for many years.

Ending the call, I said, "Thank you for your help, Lois."

I placed my next call to the local hardware store to order fans and trash cans. The manager promised that the items would be delivered in the morning.

At one thirty, the intermediate teachers traipsed into the lounge one-by-one. They sat at the large tables near the blackboard. Their anxiety level was still high, but they realized I meant business. For the next ninety minutes, we worked together developing and refining strategies for how to teach reading as a thinking skill. By the end of the session, their apprehension was beginning to thaw.

"Sam," Ray spoke up. "Have you heard anything new about the investigation?"

"No, and I don't expect to for some time," I stated, seeing how upset they all were. "Look, I know this is one hell of a way to start the school year, but we need to put the kids first. Life goes on—at least, that's what my family keeps telling me."

This statement was met with silence and then with nods of acknowledgement. As the teachers left the room, I overheard a few of them exchanging ideas on how to implement the strategies in the different content areas. I let out a sigh of relief as I headed for the computer lab. "Blanche, I'm back. Are the maintenance forms ready for my signature?"

"Yes," she declared, handing me a stack of papers to sign.

"Is Thomas here yet?" I wished.

"Not yet, Sam," Blanche grinned, hearing my voice soften upon saying his name. "But I did arrange the neighborhood meeting. I also called Security and asked if they could send out several people. They said they would do what they could."

"That's typical," I said, handing her the signed maintenance forms. "Anyway, here's a list of the textbooks we still need. Please call the district's warehouse and ask them to deliver the books by Friday."

"Will do, boss," she teased.

"As for the supplies, I'll make a run to Jo's this weekend and see what I can get."

"That sounds great," she commented, clicking "Save" on her computer screen.

"Do you know if Mrs. Austin is accepting any phone calls?"

"She's not, according to her daughter."

"Okay. Any calls about Dr. Austin?" I asked, biting my lower lip.

"We've had several sympathy calls. People want to know when the funeral service is. When I find out, I'll post it by the counter."

"Thank you," I said, grateful for her help. Blanche had worked for the district for more than twenty-five years and I was lucky to have her as my secretary. "I don't think I could've survived this day without your help."

Blanche started to respond, but stopped.

A tall, dark-haired Irishman with a beguiling smile appeared in the doorway. Thomas Ryan greeted Blanche cordially. Then, he strolled over and gave me a kiss on the top of my head.

My heartbeat accelerated at his touch confirming what I already knew: he took my breath away. And I couldn't help looking up at him as I met his gray-green eyes. Smiling, I noticed he wore a dark suit with the hand-painted silk tie that Maxie had given him for his birthday.

Sheriff Peterson entered a few minutes later.

I ushered both men to the teachers' lounge. Closing the door, I offered them bottled water. They refused, saying they would prefer coffee. Each one filled a Styrofoam cup to the brim. They soon discovered a crucial secret: that the coffee was from the same batch I'd made very early this morning. After a few sips, they eyed my bottle of water greedily.

Thomas gagged. "Did you import this coffee from the Student Union?"

"No, the coffee is strictly brewed here, especially for you!"

The sheriff was quiet at first and then started laughing.

The tension I'd noticed on his face this morning had disappeared, revealing a glimmer of trust, which I hoped meant that I'd passed his credibility test.

"Ms. Samuels, your alibi checks out. You were at the San Diego airport at the time of Dr. Austin's death. Everything else you told me checks out as well."

"Gee, thanks," I jested lightly. "I'm glad to know that I'm not the main suspect."

"Sam, that's not fair," Thomas countered, noting a change in my demeanor. "Jack had to check you out; otherwise, he'd be negligent."

"I know," I uttered softly, looking at him. "I've scheduled a neighborhood meeting in the cafeteria tomorrow night at seven. Community leaders and concerned parents will be here. We will be discussing the changes that I will be implementing at Madison and Dr. Austin's death. You're both welcome to attend." I stopped and looked at both men. "On second thought, your presence is mandatory."

Blanche entered before I could object. "Sam, Darrell Jefferson wants to see you right now," she stated, trying to keep her anger in check. "Is this a convenient time?"

"No. Ask him to wait; I'll be out in a few minutes," I said as a large, African-American man barged into the room, shoving past Blanche.

"There's no need for that, Blanche. Sam and I go way back," he stated with scorn in his voice. Then, turning toward me, he added, "Now, don't we, Sam?"

"Hello, Darrell. Is there something I can do for you?" I posed, taking note of how his clothes now sagged over his formerly obese body.

"Not really," he blurted out, louder than he intended. "I heard about Bill and thought I could help. Now, before you say anything, I want you to think of what's best for this school and everyone else."

"Really?" I commented, smiling.

He looked at Thomas and Jack for moral support. "I know you're a smart girl but murder—on your first day on the job? You don't have the experience to handle this situation! After all, you're just a teacher—a damn good one at that—but you're not an administrator. I tried to tell Austin that last spring, but he wouldn't listen."

I met his icy stare with one of my own. As I glanced at Thomas, he leaned back in his chair, waiting for the fireworks to begin. The sheriff sat on the edge of his seat. And Blanche stood at the entrance with her hands on her hips, fuming.

"Why thank you for your vote of confidence, Mr. Jefferson. I appreciate your offer of help," I acknowledged, smiling. "If the occasion ever arises that I should need it, I will call you. Now, if you will excuse us, I'm in a meeting with the sheriff and the chief deputy county attorney. Unless you have information about Dr. Austin's death . . . ."

"If I had any information, I would've spoken with the sheriff already," he suddenly ranted in a loud, fiery voice. The veins in his neck were pulsing rapidly as he glared at me. "GO TO HELL! I came here out of the goodness of my heart to help you. Well, sink or swim on your own, lady!" He stormed out of the room, yelling obscenities as he forced Blanche aside.

I watched her follow him out of the door.

"Who was that?" Sheriff Peterson inquired, writing the volatile man's name down.

"That was the former principal of Madison Elementary School. Bill forced him into accepting an early retirement package."

"How long had he been the principal here?"

"Twelve years."

"Has he always been this explosive?" Thomas probed.

"No. Mr. Jefferson was the first African-American principal in the district. For most of his tenure, he was an effective administrator, but he lost it when his wife died of breast cancer last fall, and he has never been the same."

"How so?" the sheriff pressed.

"Madison began slipping academically. Parents were up in arms and teachers were furious because he was never around. He had a ton of grievances filed against him last year. And believe me—that's unheard of."

I felt awful revealing this information. Then, thinking of Maxie, I felt a flash of sympathy for Darrell. I knew all too well that surviving death was by no means easy. The devastation he must have felt could almost justify his administrative neglect.

There was a knock on the door. I motioned for Mr. Brown to come in.

"Ms. Samuels, excuse me," Mr. Brown mumbled, glancing around the room rather nervously. "We finished the bathroom and everything is in good working order. I thought you might want to check."

"Yes, I do, Mr. Brown. Gentlemen, please excuse me for a few minutes."

~~~~~

We went on our inspection tour. I was pleased with the work that had been done and also by the fact that they had discovered some other problems and simply had fixed them. Much to my surprise, Mr. Brown was turning out to be a nice man. I handed him a personal check.

He seemed surprised and reluctantly took it. "You don't have to do this, Ms. Samuels."

"Oh yes, I do. I really appreciate your willingness to work with me."

He gave me the receipt. Afterwards, he stared at the name that appeared on the check. "Are you related to Henry Samuels?"

"Yes, he's my father-in-law." From Mr. Brown's expression, I knew they had crossed paths. And Henry could be difficult at times.

"I don't get it. With all the money your family has, why are you working here?"

"Money doesn't buy happiness."

He stood there staring at me as if needing further explanation.

"Mr. Brown, it makes me happy to work with children."

A slight smile spread across his face. There was nothing else to say. So we reviewed my stack of emergency request forms, as well as the air-conditioning system. Afterwards, he handed me a list of other plumbing problems that needed to be brought up to code. His crew would start on all the repairs tomorrow morning.

I thanked him again and strolled back to the lounge in a much better mood.

~~~~~

Thomas was on the phone discussing another homicide case when I entered the room. The sheriff was rereading his notes and took a sip of his bitter brew. Looking up from his notebook, he gave me a funny look. "You remind me of a young model."

"Thanks," I said, feeling uncomfortable. What an odd thing to say, I thought. Was he testing my commitment to Thomas? Then, looking over at Thomas, I wondered if they'd been discussing me. And, if so, why?

He read my reaction instantly, reverting back to the inquisitor. "Do you have any thoughts as to why someone would kill Dr. Austin?"

I took a sip of water. "No, but if I think of anything, I'll let you know."

"Dr. Austin's wife seems to think that you were involved with her husband," he stated in a matter-of-fact tone, gauging my reaction.

"What?" I gasped, taken aback. I met his intense stare. "We were involved professionally, but not personally. Mr. and Mrs. Austin always kept their private life private."

"What about socializing?"

"We met at professional functions."

"Someone reported that you were more than good friends and implied that was the reason you got the job," he suggested, still scrutinizing me.

"Sheriff, for the past three years, my world revolved around my daughter. I had a small circle of friends that included Thomas, Henry and Marge Samuels, Judge and Mrs. Ryan, Patty Steward, and Maxie's doctors. I went to work every day to support my daughter and myself. I didn't have the luxury of time to socialize with co-workers," I asserted a bit testily.

"Okay, but . . . ." he stated.

"There was never anything between us, except our work. Bill knew my record and thought I could make a difference at Madison, and that's why I got the job."

"Who arrived at school first this morning?" he interjected, sitting back in his chair.

"The night custodian arrived first. Then I got here and, a minute later the day custodian showed up. Basically, we all arrived at about the same time."

"Are you sure?"

Thinking back, I added, "Yes, I'm sure. But if you're wondering, none of us had blood splattered all over our clothes."

"But both men have keys to the building," he asserted. "They could have changed their clothes before coming to work."

"True." I could see him considering something sinister but dropped it.

"Did you see anything unusual when you drove into the school parking lot?"

"Come to think of it, I did. There was an old yellow Ford Mustang leaving the parking lot as I turned in."

"Could you identify the year?"

"Yes, it was a sixty-seven."

"Are you sure?" he demanded, surprised.

"Yes, my late husband rebuilt one just like it."

"Did you see the driver?"

"No, I wasn't paying attention. And I don't know if the driver had just been turning around or if he'd been at the school. Maybe the night custodian can give you more information."

"Do you know who Dr. Austin's confidantes were?"

"No, he was a private person," I said. "I know he spoke to the president of the teachers association and, probably, the president of the administrators association. He kept in close contact with the school board and his department heads, as well as all the principals in the district."

"Anyone else specifically?" he pressed.

Stopping a moment to consider who Bill might entrust with his secrets, I realized how little I knew about this man. "Other than his wife," I thought, "maybe Paul Mendoza. Dr. Mendoza is now our acting superintendent."

"Did Dr. Austin have any major concerns other than the usual day-to-day problems of running a school district?"

"I knew he was upset about something; maybe it had to do with the budget."

"Why the budget?" he insisted.

"I heard him say that the numbers just didn't add up."

"When did he say that?" he pressed, noting the information in his notepad.

"Last week, he was on the phone with someone," I explained, watching his eyes narrow. "I overheard part of their conversation. When he realized I was in the room, he ended the call abruptly."

"Do you know who he was speaking to?"

"No," I remarked, recalling how upset Bill was. "I asked him about it but he said it wasn't any of my business."

"Is Madison having plumbing trouble?" he inquired, switching topics.

"Yes. I don't know what transpired before, but the head of maintenance seemed surprised when I demanded the boys' bathroom be fixed today."

"What do you mean?"

"Well, Mr. Brown informed me that the part necessary to fix the bathroom was out of stock and that Madison's maintenance line was already over its budget limit."

"That is strange," he commented, tapping the pen on his notepad. "How were you able to get him to fix the problem?"

"I wouldn't take no for an answer so, ultimately, he fixed it."

"Isn't it a bit early to be over budget?" the sheriff asserted, underlining the words "over budget" in his notepad.

"I think so. Unfortunately, my copy of the school budget is now part of your crime scene. I've requested a new copy, and I guarantee you that I will go over it."

"Are you familiar enough with the school's budget to find a discrepancy?"

"Possibly. I've served on two bargaining teams, so I am familiar with most staffing costs that the district incurs. As for the maintenance lines, I don't know enough to say anything without the budget in front of me. I might have Henry take a look and see if he can find any irregularities."

"Who's Henry?"

"My father-in-law, Henry Samuels," I said. "He's semi-retired but a whiz at accounting and detecting irregularities in financial reports."

"Do you think Mr. Brown was pulling a fast one?"

"I just don't know. He seemed genuinely surprised when I reimbursed him for the cost of the part. His crew did a good job, and he was concerned enough to tell me about some other plumbing problems. They're coming back tomorrow morning."

The sheriff took a sip of coffee as Thomas joined us at the table. Jack looked at Thomas and then at me. It was as if he was assessing the implications of his next question. His eyes hardened. "Your appointment to Madison is only for one year. Why?"

"That's typical for an acting administrator in most school districts. I'm on probation for my first year as an administrator. But, in general, all administrators serve at the pleasure of the school board. Their contracts are usually just for one year."

"Why is that?"

"I think it's a way of avoiding power struggles within the school districts. Supposedly, it keeps everyone on their toes."

"Isn't it typical for acting principals to serve their apprenticeship at a middle school or a junior high before they're assigned to their own elementary school?"

Jack Peterson obviously knew more about school districts than he was letting on. "That's true. And that's why I believe there was so much opposition to my appointment as acting principal of Madison. The consensus is I haven't paid my dues."

Thomas stated, "And that explains why Mr. Jefferson is so pissed at you."

"Partly, but he was forced out before I was offered the position."

"Was the position offered to anyone else?" the sheriff asked.

"I have no idea," I stated. "I was preoccupied with Maxie at the time those discussions were going on."

Blanche knocked on the door again, entering cautiously. After glancing at the three of us at the table, she gave me a look that only concerned mothers give their wayward children. "I'm sorry about disturbing you; it's after four-thirty, Sam. I wanted to let you know I was leaving."

I walked out the door to thank her but noticed how drained she looked. She'd been running on adrenaline all day. "Blanche, are you okay?"

"Oh, yes, I'm fine; just a little tired," she muttered, brushing a loose strand of blonde hair away from her face. "This is nothing unusual for the first day of school, except for the stress of finding out that Dr. Austin was murdered."

"I'm sorry, Blanche. I should have been there for you today."

"You did, but I've been waiting to talk to you. I wanted to check on you and make sure you knew that James Hill called."

"Thank you for your concern, and I'm fine. What did James want?" I inquired, remembering him with a smile. James was one of my all-time favorite students. When I first met the athletic, black eleven-year-old, he was standing in the doorway, looking into my classroom with dark, soulful eyes. He had lost his father when he was two years old. His mother was mentally ill and tried to take care of him, but was unable to deal with the stress of losing her husband and raising their child alone. To make matters worse, she had refused to take her psychiatric medication after a bad reaction to a new drug. No one else had the time to care for him, so he had to fend for himself.

"He wanted to know if you're really the principal."

"Why?" I asked.

"Because he wants to come to the meeting tomorrow night."

"That's interesting," I volunteered, "I'll call him back and invite him. Did he leave a number where I could reach him?"

"No, he didn't. He said he would call back tomorrow morning. Are you sure you want him here?" Blanche questioned, frowning. "He was a major-league troublemaker."

"You're right," I declared, recalling how hostile he was toward most of the adults and to his classmates. "He was a pistol back then and now I'm told he's a member of a set of the Bloods. But if we're going to turn this school around, we're going to need everyone's help."

Blanche stood there with her mouth slightly ajar.

"I know you won't believe this, Blanche, but he really does have a good heart," I confided, giving her a big smile. "James brought an injured bird to class one day and spent weeks nursing it back to health. It was the first time that he let his guard down long enough for me to teach him how to read. I would love to see him and, yes, I want him here."

"I'll extend your invitation if he calls back," she conceded, looking down at her watch and hesitating. She looked through the door at the sheriff.

"Blanche, everything is going to be okay. We're off to a great start with the faculty and maintenance. I really can't thank you enough for all your help," I reassured her, looking directly into her eyes.

"You're welcome," she uttered, blushing. She started to smile, and then, as if she suddenly remembered the horrific crime, her eyes watered. "Dr. Austin . . . ."

"The sheriff is doing everything in his power to find out who the killer is," I assured her gently as we started walking down the dimly lit hallway to the front door of the building.

She stopped midway. "Are you in trouble with the sheriff? Because, if you are, I'll set him straight right now!"

Seeing the concern in her eyes, I replied softly, "No. I'm just answering questions and providing background information on how the district is run."

"Why is he still asking you questions?" she insisted as her body became rigid.

"I don't know if you realize this, but anyone who discovers a body is always a potential suspect. But the sheriff knows I was in San Diego last night."

She seemed to relax, but there was still something else on her mind. She stood there, fidgeting with a loose strand of hair again, and then lowering her hand. "Sam, are you going to quit?"

"No, Blanche, I'm not, especially after what has happened today. I'm going to take each day as it comes and move forward. I don't want you to worry. Now, you better go home and get some rest before your husband has my head."

"For what it's worth, Sam, I really think you're going to make a difference here."

"Thank you," I beamed. I gave her a hug and sent her home.

Walking back to the teachers' lounge, I thought again about how lucky I was to have Blanche as my secretary. Truth be told, she actually ran Madison. She knew all the ins and outs of the entire operation. If I wanted answers about the plumbing, the budget, or anything else, I'd better ask her.

I could hear Thomas and Jack discussing the case through the partially open door. When I entered the lounge, they both stopped talking hastily. Thomas' rigid posture appeared unyielding.

Worried, I wondered if he was okay or if something else had happened. Could the sheriff have told him that I was possibly having an affair with Bill? Fear ran through me as I ran my hands through my hair. I hated being under suspicion, because it made me feel guilty.

Sensing my nervous mood, Thomas charged in. "My God, Samantha, you look as if you have been through World War III," he stated with a wide grin.

I realized then that my hair was literally standing straight on end. Patting it down, I uttered, "Gee, thanks for the compliment, Thomas."

The sheriff stood up. "We're basically done for today. We've seized the crucial evidence and have begun to process it. I'm leaving the crime scene tape up overnight because there may still be a few things I'll want to revisit in the morning. A deputy will be checking on the school tonight."

"Thank you, sheriff," I declared.

Then, looking directly at me, he advised, "Ms. Samuels, I'd suggest that you go home and get some rest. Something tells me you're going to need it." With that statement, he briskly walked out of the lounge, leaving us both staring at the door.

"I like your tousled look," Thomas confessed, breaking the silence with a sheepish grin.

Smiling, I responded warmly, "Thank you, sir."

"Are you ready, Sam?" Thomas asked.

"Oh, yes, I am!" I declared dramatically, in a feeble attempt to inject humor into our conversation.

Thomas waited for me to gather my things and then we went to locate the custodians who were locking up the building. I informed them about the sheriff's plans. Then I reminded them to call me if there were any problems and wished them a quiet evening.

As we walked toward the parking lot, I realized that Thomas' tan Trailblazer was missing. I was really upset now. First, the murder, and now Thomas' car was stolen! What was next? Just as I was about to say something, I remembered that his car was in the shop for repairs. I guess I really wasn't handling Bill's death very well after all. I was clearly still shaken.

After handing Thomas the keys, I climbed into the Jeep's passenger seat and fastened the seat belt. He drove out of the parking lot and headed to Lou's Service Station.

"Hey, you do know that you are my Sir Galahad." I whispered softly, looking over at him. "Thank you for being there for me. I don't know what I would do without you."

"Well, it's the very least I can do for my lady." He smiled his best smile.

I couldn't contain myself. I had to laugh at his faux British accent, which reminded me of his English mum. This gentle caring man always made me laugh and, more importantly, feel safe. I adored him and leaning over the console, I kissed him tenderly on the cheek, wondering why it had taken me so long to realize I was in love with him.

After drying my tears of laughter, I solicited coyly, "So I'm your lady?"

"That you are, Sam," he boasted, smiling.

"Then I'm truly blessed, my lord," I admitted, genuinely happy. "When we get to the house, I want to take Bear for a walk."

"That sounds like fun," he commented, glancing in my direction.

I could tell from his relaxed posture that he took this as a good sign. It had been months since we'd walked Bear together.

Thomas fell silent as he drove, preoccupied with the case.

With that thought, my eyelids grew heavier and heavier . . . .

Monday: 5:15 P.M. on the Road Home

Thomas parked in front of Lou's Service Station as I opened my eyes. I was happy until I remembered the day's horror. Still in shock, I sat up in my seat, wondering how in the world I'd been able to sleep. Exhaustion was the only answer.

He waited for me to walk around the Jeep and then helped me into the driver's seat. After he shut the door, I rolled the window down as I fastened the seatbelt. "I'll see you at the house."

"I'll be there in a while. I need to go home and change my clothes," he replied. Mischievously, he held my gaze, knowing that cooking was not my forté. "Do you want to go out to dinner or stay home?" He waited for an answer, grinning from ear to ear.

As I thought about the dinner choices, I recalled our history together. We'd met by chance at the University of Arizona. He was on campus to give a criminal procedure lecture, and I accidently bumped into him in the Student Union. We had instant chemistry that was hard to miss and we still did.

When Maxie became ill, Thomas was by my side through the countless hospitalizations and visits to the doctors. He relentlessly searched the Web for new medical information to save her life and made sure she received the best care possible. I will never know where he found the time to spend with her. He read stories to her and even made up adventures about a brave little girl named Maxie who conquered the universe with love. Thomas encouraged her to compose her own stories, which I recorded.

During the hospital stays, they both tried to top one another with their own versions of their favorite fairy tales. Our loud giggles brought in children from the pediatric cancer unit to hear the stories and, eventually, they told their adaptations too.

Thomas and I constructed a makeshift stage for the hospital's playroom. The children acted out *The Three Little Pigs*, *The Three Bears*, and many other fairy tales. Now, in retrospect, these recordings held some of the most blissful moments of Maxie's life.

One Saturday morning shrieks of laughter floated out of her hospital room when Thomas, wearing a clown costume, tried to teach Maxie how to finger-paint. The mess those two created was unbelievable, but the laughter coming from the room enticed the other patients and nurses to join in the fun. Soon everyone was covered with splotches of paint.

When I looked around the room at the end of the day, there was not a clean spot to be found. I still wondered why we weren't asked to leave. I think it had something to do with the fact that Thomas and I stepped in as the clean-up crew.

That day Maxie had painted a remarkable masterpiece. She and Winnie the Pooh were having a tea party with Grandpa Henry, Thomas, Bear, and me. Despite the bright colors and blurry lines,

I loved it. I framed and hung it so that it's the first thing I see when I wake up.

Knowing I was a teacher, the hospital administrator asked me to create a fun learning environment for the patients and their families. I enlisted Maxie, Henry, and Thomas to help with the project. Maxie and Dakota—a bald, brown-eyed leukemia patient—wanted a larger puppet stage and a painting area.

Henry and Thomas constructed a portable stage, large enough for three puppeteers, and then built five wooden easels. I bought an assortment of all kinds of material to make puppets and painting supplies. Henry donated books, games, CDs, DVDs, and players, as well as two computers with printers and educational software. Once our mission was completed, the kids reveled in the center.

On the first day of spring this year, we had an adventurous fishing trip. Maxie caught her very first fish. She was so excited that it was all she could talk about. Later that evening, Thomas and I put her to bed and stayed until she fell asleep. Then we left the room.

I tapped Thomas' arm gently before we entered the kitchen.

He turned and saw that I was anxious about something. "Sam, are you okay?"

"Yes, I'm fine," I murmured.

"You're scaring me. Is something wrong with Maxie that you're not telling me?" he pressed, wondering what the doctors had told me about the blood test.

"No, she's fine; really, she's fine," I reassured him quickly, thinking at that time she was out of the woods. "It's just that I need to tell you something."

"Honey, you can tell me anything," he said quietly, his eyes lingering.

"Okay, here it goes," I began. "Thomas, I love you. And I want you . . . ."

"Are you sure, Sam?" he interrupted, relief shining in his eyes.

"Yes," I answered, smiling.

Months later, Thomas was with me at Maxie's bedside. He held her in his arms and passed her to me just moments before she died. Through all the ups and downs, we'd become a family. Now, Maxie only existed in our hearts and memories. The unshed tears I'd been holding back stung my eyes as I thought about my five-year-old baby leaving us softly that night.

Turning my thoughts away from the past, I pulled myself together, wondering if I would survive the crisis at school. "Thomas, please spend the night."

"I was already planning to. But, my lady, you still haven't answered my question about dinner," he insisted, seeing the tears.

"Let's just go to Frankie's after our walk."

His grin widened and then suddenly disappeared, leaving behind a weary look. "Sam, Henry called. He's very upset about Bill's murder and wants you to quit."

"Oh, my God!" I exclaimed with a hint of laughter. I knew I was in for it when I saw my father-in-law. Henry loved to project an image of being a gruff, stern dictator but, in reality, he really was a gentle man who cared about his family and had worked diligently to turn the family business into a financial empire.

In the beginning, Henry and I did not get along but forged an uneasy truce for the family's sake. But when Maxie was born, everything changed. She became the apple of his eye and the center of our lives. We developed a deep affection for one another. And, in many ways, Henry filled the parental void in my life.

Once Maxie became ill, Henry devoted most of his time to be with her because I had to work to maintain our health insurance. His schedule included making her favorite sandwich for lunch: peanut butter, pickles, and bananas, with just a touch of mustard. He took her horseback riding at his ranch or for a walk and then brought her home so she could rest. During that quiet time, he read or told her stories about her daddy and when Grandpa was a little boy growing up in the Old West.

At precisely two o'clock every afternoon, he would take her in his strong arms and rock her to sleep so she would be rested when I got home. Henry would do anything within his power to make her happy. He even bought her a golden retriever puppy. Bear turned out to be a gift from heaven. He made Maxie laugh and, when she would cry, he would lick her tears away. Bear was always by her side and ready to join into any mischief she could invent. They were quite a team.

As Maxie's illness progressed, I thought Henry might crumble but he didn't. He stood by us. We spent many sleepless nights together, pacing the floor and praying. In many ways, I felt like the luckiest person in the world because of Henry and Thomas. My life was filled with wonderful memories of my baby, thanks to them. We were a team; regardless of win, lose, or draw, we remained there for each other.

Thomas tapped my arm, bringing me back to the present. "Sam, Henry really is worried about your safety. And so am I."

"I know, but I'm okay," I admitted, looking up at him tenderly.

"I'll see you an hour," he said, gently squeezing my shoulder. He then trudged toward Lou's office to pay the bill for his ailing Trailblazer.

~~~~~

I pulled out of Lou's station, listening to my mom's old Tony Bennett CD. I made my way onto the freeway and headed out of the Old Pueblo's city's limits. Fifteen minutes later, I exited the freeway onto a frontage road, feeling relaxed, and definitely ready for a long walk.

I gazed out into a stark desert landscape. The surrounding mountain ranges reminded me of the stoic people who had roamed this area for centuries. Although they had vanished hundreds of years ago, they'd left behind the saguaros as witnesses to their existence. And now, the mighty giants stood erect, still flanking this desolate tract of land and guarding their secrets.

Slowing down, I drove across a rusty cattle guard at the entrance of my driveway as a long-eared jackrabbit suddenly darted across the dirt road and disappeared into the brush. The house sat on an unpretentious hill overlooking the valley. The front yard had natural vegetation with large mesquite and palo verde trees scattered about. Yellow and purple lantana plants were nestled at the front of the house.

Henry had parked his white Avalanche at an odd angle in the driveway. Bear barked as I approached the adobe ranch-style house that Marge and Henry had given Peter and me on our wedding day. The tall robust man looked up for an instant and then continued pacing back and forth on the terrace with an unlit Porto Fino cigar. He was slowly rolling it between his fingers, trying to keep the promise that he'd made to Maxie to quit smoking.

Even before I came to a complete stop, Henry bounded off the porch. Bear was at his heels when he opened my door. "Sam, thank God you're okay! When I heard the news about Bill Austin, I called Thomas. I think you should quit!"

"I'm not doing that, Henry," I replied, smiling. I saw concern in his brown eyes. Stepping out of the Jeep, I gave Henry a hug and a kiss on the cheek as Bear jumped up, wanting my attention too. So I gave him a big hug and a kiss on the nose.

"I can't believe how calm you are," he blustered, scrutinizing my every move.

"Well, I'm a full-fledged administrator now," I confided, taking his arm.

"Really?" he sputtered.

"Everything is under control," I stated as he opened the front door. "And the sheriff is doing everything possible to find Bill's killer."

We went directly to the kitchen and sat at the table. Then I briefly told Henry the highlights of the day. When I finished speaking, he was barely able to contain himself. The debate about my job took off as Bear hid under the table next to me.

As Henry spoke, I listened to all of his concerns.

"Henry, I'm not quitting. You and Thomas were right. I need to move on with my life, and working at Madison is a start."

He raised his hands up in the air as a sign of surrender. "Sam, I'm going to be monitoring the situation, but . . . ."

"I know, Henry," I commented, getting up and massaging his tense shoulders.

"Thank you," he whispered, relaxing a bit.

Afterwards, I'd gathered a variety of healthy snacks and a pitcher of lemonade. He carried the tray out to our usual spot under the ramada by the pool. Smelling food, Bear followed along. He was no fool, and he loved carrots. After eating his second, he sauntered out into the yard to retrieve a tennis ball from under the old mesquite tree. Returning with his prized possession, he snuggled under the table and began gnawing the green cover off the ball.

I had seen the fear still looming in Henry's eyes. He turned away, pretending to watch the clouds in the sky. He hadn't gone back to work since Maxie's death. Just as I needed a cause to move on, so did he. "Henry, I need your help with a budget problem at school."

"What kind of a problem?" he pressed, with a hint of curiosity in his voice.

"Somehow Madison's maintenance line is overdrawn. And, before you ask, I'll have a new copy of the financial statement tomorrow morning."

"Why don't you have a copy now?" he demanded, perplexed.

"The copy and everything else in my office are part of a crime scene," I explained, continuing on to tell him about the rest of my day.

Henry's eyes ignited with intrigue. He asked a few questions for clarification as Bear barked occasionally, joining the conversation. He glanced down at Bear, who was wagging his tail and noticed that my heels didn't match my outfit. "What happened to your shoes?"

"They're part of the crime scene too," I disclosed, picking up a carrot.

Bear began barking wildly, announcing Thomas' arrival. But when he saw him in jeans, a white shirt with his sleeves rolled up, and tennis shoes, he ran to the kitchen door to get his leash and rushed back to the table.

"Heel, Bear. We're not going just yet," I commanded as Thomas sat down in an empty chair next to me. I handed him a glass of lemonade.

Bear dropped his leash and picked up his ball, only to drop it in Thomas' lap. Undaunted by his look, Bear sat next to him, waiting patiently. Finally, his head brushed against Thomas' leg to remind him it was time to play. When Thomas picked up the ball and threw it, Bear eagerly chased after it. Their game had begun.

"How's the Trailblazer running?" I asked.

"A little hot, so I guess I'm going to have to take it back in the morning. If I'm lucky, it will only need a new thermostat," he groaned, frustrated.

"After coping with my 'gently used car,' I would recommend buying a new vehicle," I teased, avoiding their stare as I took a sip of lemonade.

Both men exchanged stunned glances across the table and then faced me with a look of awe. It had taken them months to convince me to buy a new Jeep.

I added with a straight face, "It's just easier to have a dependable car."

They burst out laughing, hearing their repeated advice thrown back at them.

"Now, gentlemen, if you will excuse me," I said, flashing a smile.

Monday: 6:05 P.M. at Home

I needed to bathe the day's stress away. As I stepped into the shower, I heard the phone ringing on my nightstand and let it go to voice mail. By the time I'd returned to the kitchen, I was feeling better. Thomas and Henry were eating a combination of healthy snacks and chips with salsa. Bear remained at their feet, feigning sleep, hoping that someone would drop another carrot or two.

Thomas gave me an admiring look when he saw me dressed in dark jeans and a midnight-blue tank top. "I love your hair that way."

"You mean the tousled, gypsy look." I teased.

"Absolutely."

"How long have you been inside?"

"Only about five minutes," Thomas said. "Why?"

"I thought you might have heard the phone call," I said lightly. Then, walking over to retrieve the message, I pushed the button. Much to my surprise, I heard a gritty voice mutter, "Bitch, get out of Madison or you'll regret it."

Henry stopped eating. Fury appeared instantly on his face.

I looked at Thomas for his reaction. With an unyielding poker face, he quietly ordered, "Play it again, Sam."

Frightened, and for some unknown reason, I thought about the old movie, *Casablanca*. I replied in a bad Bogart imitation, "Anything you say, sweetheart."

I played the message again, listening to the low, guttural voice drone over the speaker. Hearing it for a second time, I told Thomas that the voice sounded familiar, but I wasn't sure who it was. After transferring the message onto a CD, I handed it to Thomas.

He checked the phone's caller ID screen, which displayed "anonymous." He punched star-six-seven, hoping to identify the caller's number. Unfortunately, nothing appeared. Finally, he used his cell phone to call the sheriff. "Jack, I think you'd better come to Sam's house as soon as possible."

"Has something else happened?" the sheriff asked, hearing tension in his voice.

"Yes, but I don't want to discuss it over the phone."

"I'm on my way." They spoke for a moment longer about directions.

"Before you say anything, I'm telling you both that I am not resigning as principal of Madison. And I will not allow some unknown thug to dictate my life."

Henry and I exchanged gazes; we had come to a mutual understanding. We both turned to Thomas, who sat there quietly.

Looking directly at him, Henry said, "Sam wasn't born a Samuels but she is one now, and Samuels don't run from a fight. So we'd better figure out who is behind this. Sam, do you still have the big blackboard that we used with Maxie?"

"Yes."

"Go get it," Henry asserted, taking charge. "We need to assemble the facts."

I jumped up and retrieved the blackboard from the storage room. After placing it by the table, I went to find some chalk from a cabinet labeled "useful junk."

Henry and Thomas were arguing about the likelihood that I would stay out of this investigation. Henry knew I wouldn't, and Thomas knew he was right. And during the heated discussion, Henry made it clear he would follow my lead.

Thomas was not pleased. It was a rare occasion to see him upset with both of us. And, to top it off, Henry assigned him to record the information on the blackboard.

I said nothing as I took my seat across the table from Henry.

"Sam, who did you see at school today?" my father-in-law asked.

Thomas started to say something but thought better of it.

"Well, I saw the sheriff and a few deputies, Thomas, the custodians, Mr. Brown and his crew, Darrell Jefferson, all the teachers and Blanche. That's all I can think of." I silently reviewed the list on the blackboard. "Oh, yes, and Ruth Beaker."

"Did you speak to anyone outside the building?"

"I spoke to Patty Steward and Lois Cameron. I also had Blanche initiate a robocall to the community regarding tomorrow night's meeting."

"Who did she call specifically?" asked Thomas, sounding more like himself.

"She called the parish priest, the Baptist minister, as well as the PTA committee."

"Did anyone call the school that surprised you?"

"Yes, James Hill called. He wanted to know if I was the principal and if he could come to the meeting tomorrow night."

Thomas stopped writing at the mention of the name. "How does he know you?"

"Relax, Thomas; he's a former student of mine."

"Why are you so concerned?" Henry questioned, shifting his attention to Thomas.

Without missing a beat, Thomas answered in a firm voice, "James Hill is a member of the Broadway Gangsters—a street gang, which is a set of the Bloods. He's also been in and out of juvenile court for years."

"I think you're overreacting, Thomas," I countered, trying to keep my voice even. "I've known him since he was eleven years old."

"He's a suspect in the Hernandez murder."

"If you had any hard evidence, you would have charged . . . ."

"Sam, I'm not debating this with you," he asserted, cutting me off in mid-sentence. "Why does he want to come to the meeting?"

"I don't know, but I've extended him an invitation. Who knows; maybe he has some information concerning Bill's murder."

Henry coughed loudly. "Sam, did you see or talk to anyone else?"

I looked over the list and shook my head.

"Did you have any run-ins with anyone on the list?" Henry persisted.

"Yes—Mr. Brown, Mr. Jefferson—and Thomas," I interjected mischievously.

He turned to face me with a scowl, gripping the chalk. "Samantha!"

"Okay, Henry," I said sheepishly, catching a gleam in his eye. I glanced at Thomas and gave him an affectionate look. "Just Mr. Brown and Mr. Jefferson."

Henry's posture relaxed a little, pretending to ignore our exchange. He asked, "Did anything happen today, besides the murder, that concerned you?"

"Yes, the budget problem," I mentioned again, noticing a slight smile on his face. "I just don't understand how we're over budget in the maintenance line, especially since the district only adopted its financial plan on July first."

Henry asked Thomas to start a second column labeled "Questions." "Please write down 'District's Financial Problems' under that heading. Sam, I also need copies of the district's financial statements for the past year, as well as the corresponding bank statements."

"I don't know if I can get access to the banking records."

"Do the best you can. By the way, do you know which bank the district uses?"

"Well, my paycheck is drawn on a Mission Bank account. Why?"

"If there's a problem, it will give Thomas and the sheriff a place to start. On second thought, forget about the bank statements. It might make someone nervous."

"Henry, what are you looking for?" Thomas asked, sitting down at the table.

"I'm looking for patterns of irregularity in the budget. Unfortunately, I won't know anything for sure until I check the district's records. Sam, do you still have the records from the contract negotiations?"

"Yes, I do." I left to get the files from the office. It seemed like a century ago that I'd been living with those budget numbers. The world had been different then. Maxie was in remission and seemed to be growing stronger by the day.

Every evening, after doing battle with the district's chief negotiator, I rushed home to have dinner with my daughter and then we'd play her favorite games as we talked and laughed. But midway, when I noticed that she was beginning to tire more easily, I wanted to resign from the bargaining team. She'd had a fit and wouldn't hear of it. She liked seeing her mommy on television and knew that what I was doing was important. On the day we reached a tentative agreement with the district, Maxie reentered the hospital. She died two weeks later on May 15.

Walking back into the kitchen, I handed Henry the bargaining documents. "Patty Steward has copies of the district's current financials. She should also have records for the prior years. Would that information be useful?"

"Honestly, I don't know, but the more information I have the better," Henry noted, beginning to peruse the records. "Let me know when you get your copy of Madison's budget."

"Will do," I answered, happy to see a light in Henry's eyes. "I'll call Patty tonight."

Thomas finished taking notes for the murder file. "I'll circle the individuals Sam had run-ins with," he said, getting up. When he was finished, he turned to face me. "Sam, was there anything from the crime scene that struck you as odd?"

Silence filled the kitchen as I recreated the horrible scene. "You know, something did strike me as odd. It was the knife in Bill's back."

"What do you mean?" Thomas questioned, coming over to sit down.

"There was dried blood on the desk and all over the floor, but there was no blood around the knife wound. It looked like someone stabbed him as an afterthought."

"Anything else?" he pressed.

"Bill might have been calling someone for help."

Henry stopped scouring the district's financial records. "Why do you think that?"

"The phone was at an odd angle, partially trapped underneath his body. The receiver was hanging over the edge of the desk as if Bill had been holding on to it."

Both men remained quiet for a long time.

Thomas thumbed through his previous notes. "You told Jack that Bill was concerned about numbers not adding up, and you thought there might be a budget problem."

"That's true."

"How did you come to that conclusion?" Thomas pressed.

"When Mr. Brown mentioned that Madison's maintenance's line was over budget, I recalled Bill's conversation that the numbers didn't add up."

"Is that why you assumed that there was an issue?"

"Yes," I stated.

"Could Bill have been searching for evidence of fraud at Madison?" asked Thomas.

"I don't know," I admitted, stunned at what he was suggesting.

"What about during negotiations? You . . . ."

"Thomas, my responsibility was to serve as the spokesperson. Patty crunched all the numbers and gave me general information. If I needed specifics at the table, I deferred to her. I'm afraid I wasn't as focused as I could have been." That was an understatement. Most of the time, I'd sat there like a zombie, going through the motions of answering questions while I worried about my little girl.

Had I been so insulated in my grief that I didn't realize that Bill told me something important and, if so, what was it? All these questions kept popping into my mind without answers. Glancing over at both men, I could see that Thomas looked concerned and Henry was beside himself with worry.

"Would Bill have told you about Madison's budget problems?" Henry probed.

"I think he would have after he investigated the situation."

"So why was Bill at Madison?" Henry pressed.

"I think he was looking for evidence of something, but that doesn't even make sense."

"He was either looking for proof, or planting something," Thomas interjected, meeting my gaze. "Would you be able to tell if something was missing from the office, or added?"

"No," I stated immediately. "I've been on the job for almost two weeks and spent most of that time at the district's Administration Building. When I was at Madison, my focus was on getting ready for the school year."

"And Madison's budget . . ." Henry began.

"The budget was a limiting factor, so I ignored it. Besides, Bill said that when I got back from San Diego, we would go over it line by line."

"Is it usual for the superintendent to go through the budget with a new principal?" Thomas questioned, handing Bear a carrot.

"I don't know," I asserted. "Bill led me to believe that he was going to be hands-on for most of the year to avoid any problems."

Thomas picked up another carrot, mulling things over. "Did he specifically mention that Madison was having budget problems?"

"No."

The doorbell rang, and Thomas went to get Jack.

In the meantime, I called Patty. She agreed to bring me copies of the district's financials tomorrow afternoon. As I hung up, Thomas introduced the sheriff to Henry.

Henry stood up and they shook hands.

"Just call me Jack," the sheriff declared.

Henry pointed to the empty chair next to Thomas.

As he sat down, Jack glanced at the blackboard. "What's this about?"

"Before I explain the blackboard," Thomas said, "I want you to listen to a message Sam received around 6:10 this evening. Sam, please play the voice mail for Jack."

I pulled up the audio file to replay it. Once again, we heard that menacing, gritty voice. "Bitch, get out of Madison or you'll regret it."

The sheriff said, "Play it again, Sam."

Over and over the message spewed out the muted threat. My bright warm kitchen began to feel like a cold, dark tomb. A shiver ran down my back. I was sure I knew the caller, but I just couldn't put a face to the voice.

"Is your phone number listed, Sam?" asked Jack.

"Yes and no, Jack," I said, realizing I'd started thinking of him as a friend rather than an inquisitor. Somehow, Thomas had made this happen. I continued, "The district has a directory with everyone's phone number, but my number is not listed in the phone book or through Directory Assistance."

"Do you recognize the voice?"

"Sort of. I just can't place who it is."

Jack sat there staring at the blackboard, taking in all the names and information. "Thomas, go ahead and explain the board."

As Thomas began, I couldn't sit still any longer. I got up, made a fresh pot of coffee, and started preparing a vegetarian pizza for dinner. By the time I popped it into the oven, Thomas and Henry had gone over the chart with Jack.

Jack had taken possession of the CD. "Did Dr. Austin ever mention that Madison was having a budget problem?"

"No, he never indicated that but, if Madison really does have a problem, it has an effect on the entire school budget. And that's not good," I stated. "I wonder if other schools are having problems too."

Frowning, the sheriff flipped through his notes again and started adding details. Henry searched through the budget documents again. And I assumed both were looking for the missing clue in this tragedy.

Thomas sat quietly, reviewing the information on the blackboard. Finally, he asked, "Sam, did anything else seem strange to you today?"

"Ruth Beaker sat through my first staff meeting."

"Why is that odd?"

"I wasn't aware that she was coming to Madison. And I certainly didn't inform her of Bill's death before the meeting. So why was she there?"

"Don't school board members usually go to schools?"

"No, Thomas. They usually show up for photo opportunities but never to welcome the staff back, especially not at a school like Madison."

"Well, how the hell do they govern the district?" demanded Henry, frustrated.

"They rely on the superintendent and his staff for information. And, occasionally, they speak with the association."

"Do they really know what's going on?" Jack asserted, looking up from his notes.

"To some extent they do, but they don't understand the day-to-day realities of teaching in the barrios. Just to mention a few of the teachers' concerns, there's a language barrier, a lack of educational skills, a lack of parental concern, and not enough textbooks or supplies to meet the needs of our students."

"What do the teachers do for supplies then?" Henry asked, knowing from my experience that teachers were not well-paid.

"Usually, they buy their own materials and supplies for their classrooms."

"Are they reimbursed?" Henry pressed as his lips thinned into a straight line.

"No."

"Well, how much money are we talking about?" inquired Jack.

"Five or six hundred dollars a year, sometimes more," I mused, recalling how much money I'd spent annually. Jack's look told me he'd lost interest in that topic.

"Well, that's a lot of money for some teachers!" Henry blurted out, perturbed. "What role does the school administrator play in this scenario?"

"We're limited by the budget's constraints. Our job is to make sure the school runs smoothly," I declared. "Principals are nothing more than gofers between the superintendent and the school."

"You don't like the board's system?" Jack asserted, catching a hint of contempt in my voice.

"That is true. They rely on a 'good-old-boy' network to hire administrators. Some principals were incompetent in the classroom and should have been fired. Others have never taught in a regular classroom."

"What about you?" Jack posed.

"Political pressure," I reported, meeting his gaze head-on.

"And that's better?" he questioned, gauging Henry's and Thomas' expressions.

"No. It isn't."

"What role do administrators actually serve on a day-to-day basis?" he persisted.

"From what I've experienced, they attend numerous meetings and do tons and tons of paperwork to cover their collective asses in order to keep their schools in compliance with the district, state, and federal mandates."

"You seem bitter," Jack commented.

"I am, because it is a waste of resources. Principals are the educational leaders in their schools and should be teaching, but instead they shuffle paperwork."

"I heard you tell your staff that you'll be teaching in their classrooms. Is this true?" asked Jack, arching a bushy eyebrow.

"Yes, it is."

"Aren't you setting yourself up for failure?" Henry inquired, concerned.

"I don't think so. I believe . . ." I started.

Jack interrupted, "Did anything else strike you as odd today?"

"No," I sighed, hearing my stomach growl. I was tired and getting cranky. I needed to eat something and, thankfully, I heard the oven buzzer announcing that dinner was ready.

"Gentlemen, shall we eat?"

I placed the pizza on the counter and we fixed our own plates. At first everyone was silent, either deep in thought or maybe just hungry.

Henry broke the silence. "What are the Cardinals' chances of making it to the Super Bowl again?"

The debate was on. Thomas, Jack, and Henry discussed the odds, along with the fates of the rest of the NFL teams.

As I ate my slice of pizza, I thought about how other principals felt at the end of their first day of the school year. I wondered what the school board's reaction would be if I petitioned for a raise. Why I thought that was funny, I will never know, as I pictured them in a singing chorus, collectively repeating, "No, No, No!"

The sheriff's cell phone went off, and he left the room.

Minutes later my phone rang.

We all froze.

Monday: 7:38 P.M. in the Kitchen

By the time I was able to move, the answering machine started recording the call. I stopped in mid-stride, hearing the rage in the caller's voice.

"Ms. Samuels, this is Ned Tomer, head of the school district security. I'm calling to let you know that there's been another break-in at Madison School. The principal's office has been vandalized. Rob Stone, one of my security guards, was shot around seven-fifteen."

I picked up the phone. "Mr. Tomer, how serious is Mr. Stone's injury?"

"I don't know," Mr. Tomer replied anxiously. "The paramedics are working on him right now. Once he's checked out, they're taking him to University Hospital."

"Was anyone else hurt?" I asked.

"No. But your office is a mess."

"Mr. Tomer, make sure no one enters the office until a sheriff's deputy arrives. I'll be there as soon as I can."

"The scene is already secured."

"How?" I demanded, wondering how this happened so quickly.

"A deputy was checking the grounds when he heard shots fired. He called for backup. Once they arrived, they entered the building and found Rob inside your office. The responding officer called the paramedics and me."

"Did you call Dr. Mendoza?"

"No."

"I'll call him and explain the situation. I'll need Mr. Stone's personnel file in order to notify his family," I stated. "I also need a written statement regarding this incident as soon as possible for Dr. Mendoza."

"You don't need the file, Mrs. Samuels. Stone is my son-in-law. After the medics take him, I'll let my daughter know what happened and then take her to the hospital," he said with raw emotion. "Dr. Mendoza will have the report and Rob's file tomorrow morning."

"Thank you. Mr. Tomer, please let your daughter know that they are in my prayers."

"Anything else you need?" he asked.

"Yes. I need a list of security measures for Madison."

"I'll have it ready for you, but what about the school board? You know when it comes to money, they're really tightfisted," he countered with a hint of sarcasm.

"With a murder and now a shooting at the school, I don't think they have a choice. Anyway, that's my problem. I'll be at the hospital later tonight. Please let me know if Mrs. Stone needs anything," I stated, hoping he hadn't heard my voice quavering. "We'll talk about your suggestions in the morning."

"I'll be prepared. Thank you for your concern, Mrs. Samuels," he stammered. "I know this has been a tough day for you, finding Dr. Austin's body and all. And now this . . . I just don't understand any of it."

"Neither do I," I pointed out, bewildered. "Mr. Tomer, right now your priority is your family. Thank you for informing me so quickly."

I placed a conference call to Paul Mendoza and Ruth Beaker. After explaining the latest crime scene at Madison, Ruth decided to convene another emergency board meeting and made it clear that my presence was mandatory.

I called Blanche to let her know about the latest incident. Then I told her about the board's meeting at eight o'clock in the morning and that I needed to reschedule the primary teachers meeting to the afternoon. By the time I ended the call, Jack had left with both CDs—a copy of the threatening call and Ned Tomer's phone call. Henry and Thomas had reached an agreement about something. This was not good.

"Thomas. Henry. Don't start; I'm the principal, and I have to go," I stated, before they could object.

"Sam, we want you out of the house for a couple of days," Thomas declared.

"Why?" I demanded, stunned at the suggestion.

"You're not safe here, honey," Henry replied. "These thugs know where you live, so I'm calling Pepé to come keep an eye on things here."

"Henry," I sighed, knowing that I would not win this argument. I appreciated his point of view but wondered if he would request his alarm system. "Is Pepé bringing the geese?" Then, thinking better of it, I really didn't want to know. "Don't answer that, Henry. I'll go get my clothes."

As I started out of the room, I stopped and then turned around. "Henry, I don't want anyone taking any chances. Believe me; it's not worth having any of you hurt. Promise me that, whatever you and Pepé do, it will be safe."

"Sam," Henry responded deliberately, "We are not fools, nor are we stupid. We are not taking any chances, especially since we don't know what's going on."

"Henry," I pleaded, "please take Bear with you. I need to know he's safe."

"I was planning to," he said, smiling. He already had Bear's leash in his hand.

When I left the room, Henry made a call to Pepé Martinez, his trusted friend and employee of forty years, and explained the situation. This pint-sized man had been there for Henry when Peter died and during Maxie's illness. Every morning, he had brought her a beautiful pink rose from his garden.

His wife, Maria, had watched over Maxie since her birth, treating her more like a beloved granddaughter than the daughter of a family friend or employer. And, when she died, they had both grieved as grandparents.

It took me five minutes to pack. After changing my appearance slightly, I applied a bit of makeup and fixed my hair. Then I added silver earrings, a black belt over the tank top, and slipped on a black shrug. When I returned to the kitchen, I also had a jean jacket. I watched Thomas download another audio file from the answering machine as he discussed the new crime scene with Jack on his cell phone. He ended the call and then picked up his dark leather jacket and my bags.

Henry had Bear leashed and was ready to go. Together we walked out the door. Then I closed it, wondering when I could come home.

Monday: 8:08 P.M. at Home

Pepé Martinez stood outside the house waiting for us to leave so he could unleash the screeching geese he'd brought over from the Samuels' ranch.

As we stepped off the terrace, I thought about Henry's alarm system. He became an avid reader of military history when he'd served in the Marines. He had never forgotten the story about the geese. According to legends from the fourth century, these noisy birds saved the city of Rome by alerting the Roman soldiers of an impending Gaul attack when the dogs had failed to sound the alarm. After the battle, the geese were highly revered, but what history did not record was how vicious these birds became when they were startled.

I turned to Pepé to thank him for his help. He lowered his brown eyes while his dark, sunburned face reddened. I still had to warn the sturdy man. "Pepé, the geese are your first line of defense. At the first sign of trouble, I want you to leave immediately and then call the sheriff. Keep your cell phone with you. Whoever this is, he's already killed one person and injured someone else. He won't hesitate to hurt you. Promise me that you will play it safe."

Pepé looked uncomfortable, but agreed after getting a nod from my father-in-law.

Henry knew I was worried. So, he acquiesced, "I'll be careful, but I want you safe too."

"Oh, I will be, Henry," I declared, giving him a hug as Thomas watched, smiling. Bear barked, looking up at me. I knew he wanted a hug, too. So I gave him one and a kiss.

Then wordlessly, Thomas and I watched Henry walk Bear to his Avalanche. When he opened his truck's door, Bear jumped into the backseat, wagging his tail. Once he buckled the golden retriever in, Henry climbed into the driver's seat and drove home.

I knew that my mother-in-law hated dogs and only tolerated Bear because he'd belonged to Maxie. Strangely enough, though, Marge never seemed to mind taking care of him when I couldn't. I was beginning to think that she secretly found him as irresistible as I did.

Once we'd crossed the cattle guard in the Jeep, Pepé unleashed the loud screeching geese.

"Thomas, did the deputy arrest the intruder?" I asked as he turned onto the frontage road.

"No, he didn't. By the time they entered the building, the intruder was gone. Sam, do you have any ideas as to what's going on?"

"No. I wish I did. I just keep thinking that I'm asleep having a nightmare from hell. When I wake up, Bill will be alive and everything will be fine."

"I hate to burst that bubble of yours, but that's not happening."

"Why the second break-in?" I considered, wondering if it might be a warning.

"I don't know," Thomas conceded as we drove down the deserted highway under twinkling stars, partially hidden by the mounting cloud cover. "I do know that the crime scene investigators removed all of the evidence from your office today."

"Do you think tonight's break-in has something to do with damage control?" I suggested, as I felt my locket.

"I don't know," he repeated again. "Would you be able to tell if something is missing from your files?"

"I doubt it," I asserted. "I haven't even inventoried them, and I certainly don't know what was left in the office after the crime-scene investigators left. If tonight's break-in was related to Bill's murder, then obviously the murderer didn't find what he was looking for the first time. Or worse, we have two separate crimes."

"That's not good," Thomas asserted gravely. "I want you to watch your back."

"No kidding, Thomas. And I want you to watch your back too," I said softly, thinking of what was at stake. "Blanche might know what's missing from the office. If anyone knows, she would. After all, she's been at the school for over twenty years."

He handed me his cell phone.

When Blanche answered the phone, I explained that I needed an itemized list of what was in the office, including the files. After I assured her that there was nothing she could do at school, she agreed to stay home and compile a list of what was in the principal's office and the filing cabinet.

I returned the cell to Thomas. "Do you think drugs are involved?"

"I don't know, Sam. Why?" he asked, stunned.

"A drug operation might be far more lucrative than skimming money from Madison's budget. The school is in a great location to run a drug distribution center. It has immediate access to the freeway. And, with the economy right now, the neighborhood is struggling," I declared.

"If this is a drug operation, your little friend, James Hill, is involved."

"I know that you don't like James because he's a gang member but, underneath that bravado, I really believe he's a good kid."

He sighed, taking a quick glance in my direction.

"Don't look at me like that, Thomas. I'm not that naive," I asserted, seeing disbelief in his eyes. "I'm just as baffled as you are. But, I am scared."

"Honey, I'm not going to let anyone harm you," he said, putting an arm around me as I placed my head on his broad shoulder.

The more I thought about it, the day's events just didn't add up. "Thomas, someone is upset that I'm the principal at Madison. They must have a lot to lose."

"Why do you feel that way?"

"It's just a gut feeling. Whoever is behind this must know that business as usual has ceased. This break-in feels like a desperate attempt to maintain control."

"That may be true, Sam. That's why I want you to be careful."

"You have no argument from me on that point," I declared, worried. "I have no intention of getting myself killed."

"Who do you think is behind this?" probed Thomas.

"It has to be someone who knows how the school is run and who also knows me."

"Blanche is in that position," he ventured, assessing my reaction out of the corner of his eye. "Furthermore, she has the flexibility to move about the building without calling any attention to herself. And, more importantly, she has phone access."

83

"Thomas, I've known Blanche for years. She wouldn't do that," I stated.

"Sam, don't be naive. Everyone connected with the school is a suspect until we know what's going on. Just keep that in mind."

"All right, then, what about Ned Tomer?" I countered in a huff, wondering how he was able to arrive at Madison so quickly, unless he was the one who pulled the trigger.

"What do you mean?"

"Well, he too is in a position to know what's going on at Madison. After all, he's head of the district's security operations."

Thomas clearly did not like that suggestion, and we rode the rest of the way in silence.

I glanced down at my watch and saw it was only 8:16 and still the first day of school. No wonder why my head was throbbing! I opened my bag and began a desperate search for aspirin. Incredibly, my luck was still holding: no aspirin. As a last resort, I ran my right hand through my hair, looking for calming points to stop the headache cycle. Then I closed my eyes, hoping to relax, but instead I kept reviewing the day's events over and over.

Thomas entered the school's driveway and parked behind Jack's unmarked Tahoe. Our focus went directly to the new crime-scene tape strung across the front of the building, blocking the entrance. Then, without a word, we got out of the car and gained access to the building through the back door. He stopped to speak with Deputy Allen while I proceeded on the brown butcher paper taped to the floor to the principal's office.

Once I was at the entrance, I surveyed the chaos in the room.

A photographer in a mask and blue booties stepped gingerly over the scattered wreckage. My computer looked like it had been run over by a MACK truck. The filing cabinet had been overturned with the contents strewn everywhere. The intruder had destroyed the desk, slashed the framed paintings, and shards of glass littered the entire office. Nothing was left untouched by the intruder's fury. How Rob Stone had survived remained a mystery!

Thomas now stood next to me, gazing at the debris in disbelief.

The foul odor finally hit me. Oh damn, it was shit! Someone had taken a dump in the middle of this mess and smeared it on walls, documents, and what was left of the ripped furniture. No wonder everyone was wearing masks. I pinched my nose, trying to block the disgusting smell. I looked up at Thomas. "Whatever you do, don't say 'shit happens.'"

No one could keep from laughing.

I took a sweeping glance of what was left in my office. "Jack, where did that briefcase come from?"

"What briefcase?" he asked, scanning the chaos.

"The one under the chair next to the potted plant in the corner," I stated, pointing to it. "It's not mine."

Everyone stopped and stared at the briefcase. They had seen it, but assumed that it belonged to me.

Jack directed the CSI tech to the briefcase. Wearing gloves, she photographed the attaché case in its resting place. Next, she secured the briefcase to take to the crime lab. As I watched her, I knew that later that night she would photograph each item, look for prints, and bag each article inside the briefcase and then log the bag's number into a data system.

I was in the way, so I went to the computer lab. I didn't have a clue as to Madison's crime wave. The only thing that made any sense was that Bill's murder and tonight's break-in were connected. Obviously, the computer in my office was a focal point of the invasion. Why else would the intruder destroy it? I'd backed up all of the PC's files Friday afternoon on a flash drive. So I retrieved it from my purse.

I booted up the computer at the teacher's desk and inserted the flash drive. I copied the files to the hard drive, and burned three CDs for Thomas, Jack, and Henry. For the next forty-five minutes, I reviewed the files, looking for evidence, but nothing seemed out of the ordinary.

While the computer printed a couple of files that I found interesting, I began outlining my presentation to the board. Absorbed in my work, I didn't hear Thomas enter the lab until his cell phone went off. I was barely able to stifle a scream.

He looked at me apologetically as he answered the call. "Thomas Ryan from the county attorney's office; how may I help you?" He paused, listening. "Oh, no," he voiced quietly.

I stopped what I was doing and listened to his end of the conversation.

"Ben, how serious is it?" he asked.

I came to his side and held his hand. When he ended the call, he turned to face me, and his eyes were moist. "Thomas?"

"Dad's having heart problems again."

"Oh, I'm so sorry," I said, saying a silent prayer. I adored his dad just like he did. "Ben will make sure your dad is okay."

"I know."

"We need to go," I declared, worried. I quickly gathered the printouts and the CDs, and put them in a tote bag I found in a desk drawer. I jammed the flash drive in a pocket and grabbed my outline, purse, and jacket.

I walked into the hallway, only to hear Thomas and Jack speaking in muffled tones. As I approached them, Thomas said, "Sam, Jack needs you to stay here."

I started to protest, but I knew he was right.

"I'm going to the hospital, and Jack will bring you later."

"Honey, tell your dad that I love him and give your mum my love also." Standing on my tiptoes, I kissed him gently as he held me tightly. Then I whispered in his ear, "I love you too."

Jack and I stood in the hallway and watched him leave the building.

I was afraid to think what was next, except we needed to solve the mystery surrounding Madison School sooner rather than later. Caught up in my own thoughts, I was startled when Jack took the tote bag. We walked to the teacher's lounge where he set the bag on the table.

"Sam . . . ."

"How about a lousy cup of coffee, Jack?" I suggested.

When he didn't answer, I prepared two cups of instant. He sat down at a table, watching me. After he accepted the mug, he took a sip.

"Judge Ryan had a heart attack about a year ago. He's been in and out of the hospital ever since," I said, answering his unasked questions. I joined him at the table.

"You seem almost resigned to the possibility that he won't survive."

"It's not that. I've learned that if it's your time, it's your time. It comes no matter what you do. Death is the great equalizer. It doesn't care if you're young or old, rich or poor, black, white, or covered with pink polka-dots. It's a constant in life—just a mere fact, so to speak. Unfortunately, the turmoil it leaves behind is immeasurable." I took another sip. "The real challenge is learning to live in its shadow."

"Sam, I . . . ."

"Look, Jack, I'm tired. Today has not been a picnic. That's not to say it hasn't been productive in some ways, but it has . . . ." Unable to finish my thoughts, I stood up, knocking my outline off the table.

"I'll pick the papers up," Jack said.

I walked over to the sink and splashed water on my face to wash away the evidence of the tears running down my cheeks. After toweling off, I returned to my seat.

Jack was scanning my notes. So I peered at his open notepad. He had written "Briefcase?" And "Dung DNA?" He appeared upset with the situation. "Can you make any sense of what's going on?"

"No. All I have are some facts, questions, and suppositions."

"And they are?" he asked.

"Bill knew that there was a financial problem in the district. Maybe he thought the evidence was hidden here. Why he thought that, I don't know," I stopped. "And, unfortunately, someone discovered him snooping around."

He noted my observations and then looked up from his pad. "What about Stone?"

"He has to be a suspect."

"Why?"

"He's a district employee and has access to the building. The district's incident policy clearly states that the employee must call the Sheriff's Department first, then the principal. The employee is required to remain outside until the building is secured. Rob clearly did not do that."

"So what do you think he was doing here?" he pressed.

"Just like Bill, I think he got caught in the middle of something. He either interrupted someone who is involved in Bill's murder, or something went terribly wrong when Rob tried to cover up his involvement. Either way, my office has been the scene of two violent crimes: Bill's murder and Rob's shooting. And I bet money is at the root of all of this." I took another sip, hoping the caffeine would kick in soon as I stifled a yawn.

"Interesting suppositions," he admitted, adding notes to his pad. "Anything else?"

"The only things that weren't destroyed were the computer files that I backed up on my flash drive Friday afternoon I just downloaded the files onto the teacher's computer in the lab, burned several CDs, and printed a few interesting documents for you and Thomas. They're in the tote bag," I stated, pointing to the bulging sack on the table.

"What about the other computer files?"

"From what I was able to pull up, they seem to deal with the school's day-to-day operations, or school forms dealing with parent conferences and standard letters to parents. If you want, I'll check the rest of the files after I finish my coffee."

"Please do. The answers to our questions may be in there."

"I don't think so, but you never know," I admitted, stifling another yawn.

"Mrs. Austin seems pretty adamant that you were having an affair with her husband."

"Absolutely not," I asserted firmly. I knew Jack was on a fishing expedition. "Bill was my boss. I will admit that, for the past week, we were working together on what needed to be done at Madison. And, for your information, Bill always kept his office door open. If you're still concerned, ask Thomas about our relationship."

"I have," he admitted, watching me closely.

"Oh," I sputtered, stunned. "Then why do you keep asking me about this?"

"I know how Thomas feels about you, but . . ." he began.

"But what?" I challenged, upset.

"You're still wearing your wedding ring," he said. "And that says a lot about you."

"Then this is about Thomas, and not Bill," I stated, meeting his icy blue eyes.

"How well do you know Mrs. Austin?" he asked, ignoring my last comment and moving forward with his interrogation.

"Not well. She was my university professor. I've rarely spoken to her outside of school functions. The last time I saw her was at Maxie's memorial service in May."

"Why would she accuse you?" he pushed.

"I don't know," I stated, beginning to wonder if she had gone berserk. Maybe she had killed her husband in a fit of jealousy, or maybe she had a lover. Grasping for straws, I added, "Maybe she and Bill were having marital problems. I just can't believe Bill was having an affair—he wasn't the type."

"But you don't know that for sure?"

"Look, Jack, if Bill had a zipper problem, I was unaware of it. My impression was that he appeared to be a very private person and did not allow anyone to cross that line."

"What if someone did?"

"I don't know what would happen," I replied evenly, feeling pressured. "To be perfectly honest, the thought had never even occurred to me."

A deputy knocked on the open door, holding a scruffy ball of fur. It was a shivering puppy. "Looks like we've got another victim, sheriff," he reported, speaking softly so as not to frighten the puppy. "We found her outside scratching the front door."

Jack spoke to the deputy while I walked over and took her out of his arms. Cuddling the small puppy, she cried out in pain when I touched her ears. I sniffed the ear canal and the smell was horrible. This poor baby had an ear infection.

"Well, I know how to solve this problem," I commented as both men looked at me.

It was 9:20 p.m., but I dialed Doc Simpson's number anyway. Not only was he the best veterinarian around, but he was also Henry's cousin. And when it came to me, Doc had always felt that he was Henry's backup, and I knew I could call him anytime with an emergency.

After he answered on the second ring, I told him about the puppy. Being a sweetheart, as always, he agreed to make a school visit.

I placed the little one on the floor, found a blue bowl under the sink, and filled it with water. The puppy drank greedily.

Monday: 9:36 P.M. at Madison

Doc Simpson was on his way and that gave me time to switch gears. I went back to the computer lab and began pulling up files with the puppy sleeping on my lap.

A deputy knocked at the door.

The loud noise woke the puppy. As I comforted the whimpering little one, I accidently pressed a key on the keyboard. Suddenly, a new folder appeared on the screen. "What in the world is this?" Looking up at the deputy with a baffled expression, I uttered softly, "Yes?"

"Ms. Samuels, are you okay?" he asked, surprised at my reaction.

"I'm fine; you just startled me," I replied, with a nervous laugh. *Damn it, I could just kick myself for being so transparent.*

"Dr. Simpson is here. He said you'd called him about the puppy."

"I did. Please show him in."

Waiting for Doc to arrive at the lab, I quickly backed up the new file on the flash drive, burned the CDs, and began printing this odd folder, which consisted of a list of names, figures, and dates—none of which had anything to do with Madison. Could this be what Bill and the intruders were looking for?

"Samantha, what the hell is going on here?" bellowed the bald, seventy-two-year-old, carrying a vet's satchel. Doc was dressed as usual in jeans, a white shirt, and old comfortable boots. At six feet, he was a shorter version of his younger cousin, Henry.

His crass hello only made me smile as I met his troubled gaze. Doc always spoke his mind, whether you wanted to hear it or not. But before I could answer his question, he walked over and gave me a crushing hug, then pushed away when he heard the puppy whimper.

Doc took the puppy out of my arms and gave it a perfunctory examination. He decided I was right about the ear infection and gave the puppy back to me. Then he purposely complained in a loud, gruff tone, wanting to observe the puppy's reaction. "Sam, you haven't answered my question."

"What can I say? There's always a little stress involved on the first day back to school," I declared as the puppy whimpered at our loud voices. I gave Doc a kiss on the cheek and we sat down at the desk.

"Where's Thomas?" he demanded, expecting to see him appear at any moment.

"He's at the hospital with his dad."

"What happened?" inquired Doc, concerned.

"The judge is having heart issues again."

"I'm sorry to hear that, Sam. The judge is a good man, like his son. Please tell Thomas that he's in our prayers," Doc said solemnly.

"I will," I stated, cuddling the small mass of fur.

"Sam, pardon my French, but dammit, you should be at home. This is a dangerous situation," the man boomed, discharging another salvo.

"Gee, Doc, you sure know how to make a girl feel safe."

"Well, I'm worried about you," he declared. Doc's voice escalated an octave. "Any fool can see you're scared stiff, or should be."

The puppy began squirming at the sound of his booming voice. Stroking the quivering Shih Tzu-poodle mix in my lap, I looked him straight in the eye. "Of course, I'm scared. Anyone in his or her right mind would be."

"Maybe," he hesitated a moment, which was unusual. "I think you should quit."

"I'm not quitting, Doc."

"What does Thomas think about that?"

"He wants me to be careful," I admitted, measuring my words carefully.

"Bullshit!" he exclaimed, leaning forward. "He wants you safe. And, speaking of Thomas, you need to give that young man a break, Sam."

"What do you mean?" I asked, wondering where this was going.

"You heard me; give that man a break! He's been mad about you from the beginning, even after you married Peter. And it's time you got on with your life."

"What?" I choked out, staring at him.

"At the very least, I hope you're sleeping with him," he declared.

My mouth fell open, and I remained silent for a moment. His salvo had definitely hit a nerve. I loved Thomas and always had. Looking down at my wedding ring, I wondered why I was still holding on to Peter. Was it out of loyalty or guilt? Upset, I exclaimed, "That is none of your business, Doc!"

"I think you and Thomas should get married," he pushed, meeting my eyes. "You're crazy about him and always have been.

The whole family has known about it for years. Don't waste any more time, Sam."

"For one thing, he hasn't asked me," I asserted, lowering my gaze to the puppy.

Once he had my attention again, he began pounding the table with his index finger. "You need to let the professionals handle this murder business. And, as far as Thomas is concerned, why don't you ask him?"

"To do what?" I asked.

"To marry you," he came back, exasperated. "I bet he'd say yes in a heartbeat, Sam." Then, leaning back into the chair, he closely studied my reaction.

For once in my life, I was totally speechless. Taking in a deep breath, I met his unflinching gaze without hesitation. "Thomas and I will decide what is in our best interest."

This conversation was over. He'd said his piece and so had I.

Doc pushed his chair back and stood up with some difficulty due to his arthritis. He slowly walked around the desk and took the puppy. As he did, he began speaking softly to his trembling patient. Then he performed a more meticulous examination.

I slipped Henry's CDs into Doc's satchel and snapped the side pocket shut.

A few minutes later, Doc announced that his patient had an ear infection and a slight respiratory problem. "Sam, I need your help," he stated. He handed me the puppy to hold as he squeezed fluid into one ear, cleaned it, dried it thoroughly, and then repeated the process with the other ear before applying medication. Carefully, he massaged ointment into each ear canal. Then he took the puppy from my arms.

"Thanks for coming, Doc. I really appreciate it."

"No problem, honey. Just think about what I said," he ordered.

"I have, Doc," I said quietly.

"Yes?" he asked, expecting something he wasn't going to get.

"I put something in your satchel for Henry," I whispered in his ear, then gave him a kiss on the cheek.

As he picked up the battered bag, he replied softly, "I'll see that he gets it tonight."

He left the room, cradling the puppy in the nook of his arm and humming an Irish lullaby. I could swear that I heard the puppy humming along.

Jack stood in the doorway, assessing my mood. He probably heard a good bit of Doc's and my banter. "Sam, are you all right?"

"I found a file on this computer, which had nothing to do with Madison. I printed the data from the file and then burned CDs for the investigation," I said, ignoring his question. I hoped he hadn't seen me slip the CDs into Doc's satchel as I stashed the printed file into the tote bag and then dropped the flash drive into my purse. Finally, I faced Jack. "I'm ready anytime you are."

He walked over and picked up the heavy bag. "Shall we?"

I grabbed my jacket and made sure that all the computers were turned off. The last thing I needed was to set the building on fire.

As we walked down the hallway, Jack informed me that he had made arrangements to secure the premises for the next several days. Hopefully, by the time classes started on Monday, the perpetrators would be caught.

~~~~~~

Outside, humid air rested on us like a warm blanket. Storm clouds were gathering overhead, waiting for the right moment to release their stash of rain. In some strange way, the weather and the heat radiating from the pavement reassured me.

We climbed into Jack's Tahoe, buckled our seatbelts, and began our journey northward to the hospital. I told Jack about what I'd found on the new file. Once he was sure I'd told him all I knew, he began probing in a different direction. "Why don't the Beakers like you?"

"I guess it would have something to do with their son, DeMorgan," I answered, fixating on the moving traffic ahead.

"I don't understand."

"After DeMorgan transferred to Madison from a private school, I was his fifth-grade teacher. He had some behavioral problems that his parents were unwilling to acknowledge."

Never taking his eyes off the road, he inquired, "What kind of problems?"

"Well, let me think . . ." I mused, turning slightly toward Jack, and then looking back at the lights that illuminated the neighborhood. "For one thing, DeMorgan thought he was above everyone else and believed he didn't have to follow any rules."

"How did the other kids react to him?"

"They hated him. They called him an 'arrogant bastard.'"

"Who said that?"

"Mario Lopez. Why?"

"Just curious, I guess. Pretty good vocabulary for a fifth-grader," he commented. "So it's your assessment that DeMorgan was not well-liked by his fellow students?"

"That is an understatement."

"What sort of problems did he have other than his elitist attitude?"

"He was a bully. And, if the kids responded to his abuse, he blamed them. And, by that, I mean he intimidated his classmates by using put-downs, threatened them if they didn't do what he wanted, and if all else failed, he physically attacked them."

"Anything else?"

"He disrupted the classroom in any way he could imagine. Once he smeared BM all over the bathroom walls because he was mad at a custodian."

Taking his eyes off the road for a split second, he looked at me. "The BM spread all over your office; do you think there is any connection here?"

"God, I hope not. But I just don't know."

"What other trouble did DeMorgan get into?"

"He was suspended from riding the school bus for spitting and swearing at the driver. He was arrested several times for shoplifting."

"Was that all?"

"No, he exposed himself to a kindergartener."

"How did his parents react to all these incidents?"

"Quite simply, they blamed the school and, to be more precise, me—for all of his problems."

"Well, were they right?"

"No. He had a long-documented history of acting out, starting in pre-school and continuing through the fifth grade and beyond."

"How did the parents explain his behavior?"

"They felt he was normal and that these incidences were just boyhood pranks. In other words, 'boys will be boys,'" I recalled, thinking back to several contentious parent conferences with the Beakers.

"When I spoke to the Beakers, they seemed to be well-meaning people. What happened?"

"DeMorgan is their only son. When he was born, there were medical problems and he almost died. I think his parents were overprotective from the start, which is understandable, but over time they developed a laissez-faire attitude concerning his behavior."

I stopped, observing the first lightning strike streak across the darkened sky. Then I added, "It's funny that their daughter was the complete opposite of her brother. Where Lisa was constructive, DeMorgan was destructive. She was caring, and he was hateful. His parents knew something was wrong, even when I taught him in the fifth grade, but they refused all kinds of intervention, ranging from counseling to testing to see if he had a learning disability. I think they still believe that his failure to thrive was our fault."

"Why would they ignore their son's abnormal behavior?"

"The Beakers couldn't accept the fact that they were part of the problem," I commented.

"You sound like you don't like them very much," he posed, raising his eyebrow.

"I guess I don't."

"Because of the trouble they caused you?"

"No. It's because they allowed DeMorgan to fail. They could've listened to what we were saying and made things better for him."

"You sound like you care."

"Well, call me crazy, but I do."

"What happened to DeMorgan?"

"He ended up in an alternative high school for kids who have emotional problems. Eventually, he dropped out due to substance abuse. His mother sent him to a detox center this last January, and I haven't heard anything about him since."

"How old is DeMorgan now?"

"He should be about seventeen."

"Do you think her son's problems influenced Mrs. Beaker to run for the school board?"

"Probably," I conceded.

"Was DeMorgan ever involved with tagging or gangs?"

"I don't think either one. From what I observed, he didn't have the interest or motivation to stick to anything in or out of the classroom, even though he did have some artistic talent."

Jack's cell rang. He automatically reached down, unclipped the phone from his belt, and read the small illuminated numbers. It was a call from a detective. They began discussing another case.

I tuned out, watching the flow of traffic, wondering where everyone was going.

After ending the call, Jack posed, "What about the father?"

"He was the major obstacle in getting DeMorgan help."

"What do you know about DeMorgan's father?" Jack inquired.

"Ronald Jasper Beaker III, better known as RJ, is a real-estate developer who got caught short in the real-estate crash a couple of years ago. I know that the Justice Department investigated him for some of his financial dealings."

"Anything else?"

"Personally, I know very little about RJ, except that he is an egotistical elitist. His kids were conflicted about him."

"What did DeMorgan think of his father?"

"Sometimes he idolized him but, at other times, he was disgusted with him. I remember DeMorgan telling me a strange story about his father at Disneyland. He said his dad always rented a wheelchair when they went there."

"A wheelchair—what for?" asked the sheriff.

"Well, Disneyland has a policy to assist disabled individuals and their families. So RJ pushed DeMorgan around Disneyland in the wheelchair and that way they were ushered to the front of every line."

"So they cheated?"

"I don't think that they viewed it that way. It was more of a statement that they were entitled. Rules in general just don't apply to them."

"Did you ever socialize with the Beakers?"

"No," I replied swiftly. "Peter and Ruth Beaker dated before I came onto the scene. But Peter's parents are still friendly with RJ's parents. They're all active in politics."

"How well do you know Bill Austin?" pondered Jack, continuing his interrogation.

"Not well at all, period. This is the third time you have insinuated that I've had a personal relationship with Bill," I asserted abruptly, wondering if I should ask Thomas about his friend's obsession.

"Isn't it true that you singlehandedly averted a district-wide teacher's strike after Dr. Austin asked you for help?"

"No."

"The newspapers reported you did," he challenged, surprised at my answer.

"Bill asked us to rethink the district's new proposal. Patty Steward and I crunched the numbers several different ways, including the effect the strike would have on the financial package. The bargaining team agreed that a strike would not be beneficial.

Together, we reasoned with the members of the association about how we could resolve our differences. They listened. Bill listened. Both sides compromised. The strike action was averted."

"Didn't you threaten to resign if they went out on strike?"

"Yes."

"Did you mean it?"

"At that time, I did. I don't make idle threats." Taking my eyes off the road, I turned to face Jack and asked, "Have you ever been involved in a strike action?"

"No."

"Well, I have, and it's not fun. A strike causes hurt feelings that last for years and, in a school district, this means that it hurts children and everyone else involved."

"Would you have crossed the picket line?"

"That's the $64,000 question, isn't it?"

Jack stopped at a red light and turned his head. "You didn't answer my question."

"I know."

"If you crossed the picket line, you would lose credibility with the association members."

"That is true, Sheriff Peterson," I confessed. I turned to face him. "William Shakespeare wrote, 'Above all, to thine own self be true.' And I ascribe to his philosophy. If I had believed that children's and teachers' rights were violated, I would walk the picket line. But, since that wasn't the case, I would have crossed the line."

The sheriff glanced at me and smiled. When the light turned green, he drove through the intersection and changed the subject. "Were you aware of any gambling problems that Bill Austin had?"

"I knew that he had a problem about fifteen years ago and still went to Gamblers Anonymous meetings religiously."

"What about anything currently?"

"I don't know."

"Do you think it's possible that he was having an affair with someone at school or had money problems?" the sheriff persisted, combining two loaded questions into one.

"If he was having an affair, I don't know anything about it. And, regarding money matters, Mrs. Austin would be the best person to judge," I declared.

"One more thing, Sam," he emphasized in a serious tone. "I know you had significant financial resources at your disposal from the Samuels' family and your grandparents, the Cabots. So why did you continue working after your daughter became ill?"

"Maxie was my child, not theirs. She was my responsibility, and I had to work to support us and keep our medical insurance in place," I answered, surprised that he knew about my grandparents' financial status. I had learned two things about Jack Peterson today: that he was thorough and completely loyal to Thomas.

"You obviously have money of your own. You dress well and carry Gucci bags," he remarked as he looked over at me.

"Jack, I'm very frugal with my money," I maintained, smiling, "I've had to work hard for it. As for the Gucci bags, either they belonged to my mother or my gram purchased them as birthday gifts. A week before my daughter died, I inherited my parents' estate, much to my surprise. I thought they had left everything to charity, except for my college expenses."

"Weren't you angry when you only inherited your school expenses?"

"No. My parents had told me that I had to make my own way in life, and I am, so I wasn't expecting anything else from them."

"What about Peter Samuels' life insurance?"

"I never collected it."

"But your daughter's medical bills must have been enormous."

"Yes, they were, and the insurance paid some, but not all of them. Toward the end of her life, I was desperate and borrowed money from Henry and Marge Samuels on the condition that it was a loan, which I have since repaid."

"I see," he conceded, giving me a quick glance again as he glided the Tahoe into a designated law-enforcement spot next to the entrance of the emergency room.

After he locked the vehicle, we headed into the hospital.

Monday: 10:23 P.M. at University Hospital

The doors opened automatically, blasting arctic air out into the desert sauna as Jack and I entered the impersonal lobby. Uncomfortable green chairs lined the white walls. A table sat in the center of the small room, with old magazines strewn about. Although the ER staff worked tirelessly around the clock, the waiting line never seemed to end.

Scanning the room, I shivered even though I was wearing a jacket. I saw two adults at the registration desk—a woman entering triage and a room filled with patients waiting their turn. Then I heard a baby giggling in the corner as his mother played with him. And that made me smile, thinking of Maxie as a toddler.

Jack and I left the lobby and entered the ER, looking for the head of that department. I immediately spotted the tall, dark, handsome man in his late thirties at the hub of the trauma center. Ben Machado certainly did not dress like a doctor but, instead, wore jeans, a plaid shirt, and a Mickey Mouse tie under his long, white lab coat. His stethoscope hung loosely around his neck, waiting to be used at any moment.

Ben was speaking with distressed family members about their loved one's condition. When he finished, Ben motioned for us to join him. "Sam, what brings you here at this hour?"

"We're here to check on Rob Stone and Judge Ryan," I said as he put his arm around my shoulders. I saw Jack's uneasy reaction and wondered if he was going to accuse me of having an affair with the head of the ER department too.

Ben saw his forbidding glare as well and cocked his head in Jack's direction. This was my cue to introduce the sheriff to this wannabe comic.

After the introductions, Jack asked, "What's Stone's condition?"

Ben removed his arm from my shoulders as he began his report. "The bullet passed through the muscle tissue of the right arm, causing relatively minor damage. My main concern is blood loss, which was fairly significant. But he is stable right now and, if he continues to remain so throughout the night, he will be released in the morning."

Jack asked a few more questions for his report. After we agreed to meet Thomas in thirty minutes, he departed to find his deputy.

"Friendly guy!" opined Ben, facing me.

"He's had a rough day, and so have I."

"So I've heard. But what can you expect when you join the enemy's camp?" Ben mocked. His jab was light, but he obviously disapproved of my new job.

"Are you so sure? Maybe I'm just a spy sent in on a reconnaissance mission to dig out the deep dark secrets of the administration," I joked, watching his silly grin grow. "Either way, it may be a moot point now."

"Why?" he asked, frowning.

"Well, the board now has an excuse to close Madison and exile me to some other position within the district for the remainder of my contract."

"That would be a big mistake, Sam," he declared.

"Ben, that's sweet of you to say, but . . . ."

"No, I mean it. It would be a colossal error of judgment on their part," he argued adamantly. "Sam, I watched you work with Maxie and the other kids in the educational center you set up in the pediatric cancer unit. You made a difference in their lives. I know that you can make a difference with the kids at Madison."

As Ben continued speaking, I turned away, unable to hear anything except the gut-wrenching screams of a hysterical child two cubicles away. My heart stopped as I recalled when Ben told me Maxie had leukemia.

"Sam, you made learning fun for everyone," Ben asserted, unaware of my grief.

"What?" I asked, turning to face him.

"Come with me," Ben coaxed gently, seeing how upset I was. He led me inside the small lounge behind the center's hub.

My thoughts remained focused back on the nightmare of Maxie's life-threatening visits to the ER. During her insidious battle, he guided me through her ups and downs. He always made my little girl laugh and, for that, I would always be grateful.

I sat at the table and watched him gather some comfort food. Smiling, I thought he knew me far too well. He placed a water bottle on the table and handed me a bag of potato chips. Grinning

lightheartedly, he watched me rip open the bag to take a handful.
"I see you're still drinking sodas," I teased, trying to suppress a
smile. We both knew it wasn't a healthy choice.

"What can I say . . . I'm addicted," he confessed. "And you're
still munching on potato chips, I see."

"Chips are my comfort food!"

"Really," he replied, taking one out of the bag. "In my
professional opinion, I think you're addicted to them."

"Oh, no!" Relishing another chip, I watched him roll his eyes
upward. "Potato chips are on the top of my healthy food chart, along
with dark chocolate."

He roared at my outrageous statement. Afterwards, in a sober
tone, he said, "I know you haven't been back to the hospital since
Maxie's death, and I understand that, but the kids miss you. They
have learned how to use the Internet; some have become artists; and
they all love to read stories. Somehow you taught them that learning
can be fun."

"Thank you for saying that, but . . ." I stopped, unable to finish.

Ben took a handful of chips and consumed them one at a time.
After finishing the third, he pushed, "I hope you'll come back to visit
the kids. But I also hope that you'll fight for the kids at Madison just
like Judge Ryan did for me."

"I don't understand," I declared.

"Don't you know that you're working in my old neighborhood?"

"You're kidding, right?" I asked, seeing the gleam in his eyes.

"I'm not, Sam," he admitted, eating another chip. "I'm a graduate
of Madison Elementary School. And at one point, I was a delinquent
high school drop-out, besides being a major pain in the ass."

"You?" I questioned, stunned at his description.

"Yes," he confessed.

Knowing he was a prankster, I jokingly added, "You neglected to add 'criminal.'"

"Smartass!" he retorted with a smirk and then added softly, "See, you're so smart; you've just figured out how I met Judge Ryan."

"All kidding aside, I can't believe this, Ben," I stated.

"Believe it! I was on my way to prison," he declared.

"You're joking," I insisted, seeing his coloring redden.

"Nope, I was a regular comedian back then. I'm only telling you this so you'll fight to keep Madison open," he asserted adamantly. "Judge Ryan made a difference in my life, like you did with the kids here. The judge took the time to make sure I understood that I mattered, and that I could make something of myself. Sam, I think you can do the same thing for the kids at Madison."

"How did Judge Ryan get involved?" I asked, now knowing Ben had a history outside the hospital that I hadn't ever imagined.

"At that time, he was a Superior Court judge serving on the Juvenile bench. It was just my luck to be assigned to him when I was arrested for shoplifting a bunch of graphic novels."

"How did the judge handle your case?"

"Judge Ryan told me that life was tough enough without an education and that I was going to get one. I had two choices: one, straighten up on my own, or two, he would help me. Either way, I was going to comply with the court's wishes."

"And which option did you choose?"

"My way, of course," he revealed. "Fortunately for me, the judge meant what he said. If I ditched school, he'd have Mr. Joe, a truant officer, pick me up and bring me to his judicial chambers where I would write an essay on education. And believe me, Mr. Joe was psychic. He knew where I was all the time."

"You're kidding?"

"No. And, if that wasn't bad enough, Judge Ryan would have the school fax over my homework assignments. While he focused on his under-advisement cases, I did my homework. Then he would go over each assignment and make suggestions. And, heaven forbid, if it wasn't neat!" he exclaimed with a smile. "I would have to redo the whole thing."

"How long did this last?" I inquired.

"For most of my probation," he revealed, meeting my puzzled gaze. "This went on until I discovered it was just easier to go to the judge's chambers."

"What happened after your probation ended?"

"I continued to go and do my homework under his supervision."

"Really?"

"Yes, between the judge and Mr. Joe, those two men changed my life," he said. "And then there was Mrs. Ryan."

"So, are you the teenager who lived with the Ryans during the summers?" I asked, vaguely recalling bits and pieces I'd heard but never once connecting them to Ben.

"Sure was," he stated.

"So how did you come to meet Mrs. Ryan?"

"I was upset about something and told the judge that he was abusing my constitutional rights. Then I insinuated that he wouldn't treat his own son this way."

My jaw dropped, visualizing the scene in his chambers. "What did he do?"

"He laughed and laughed until tears ran down his face. He told me his wife was a drill sergeant in the Marines before they were married. Then he invited me to his home, where I met Thomas and the real boss of the family, Mrs. Ryan."

"Don't tell me you actually thought she was a Marine!" I declared.

"Okay, I won't," he admitted, as his eyes softened when he spoke of Thomas' mum. "It was her warm smile and English accent that gave her away. And, I have to tell you, she made sure we had fun, but we had to work."

"I bet you did," I teased, knowing her passion for helping others. "Do you know how they met?"

"No."

"Judge Ryan traveled to London for a human rights symposium. At one of the lectures, he became captivated with this young English beauty advocating children's rights. She had a warm smile so he asked her out to dinner and, shortly afterwards, they were married."

"I can picture that. They are a great couple."

Burning with curiosity, I prodded, "So how did they treat you that summer?"

"They treated me just like their own son. And Mrs. Ryan made the judge look like a pussycat when she wanted something done. My God, she was tough when she had to be."

"From the stories I've heard, Thomas and you gave Mrs. Ryan a run for her money."

"I don't know about that."

"Well, were you glad the judge invited you into his home?"

"Yes," he declared wistfully. "They were great parents. They cared enough to set down rules and mean it. Thomas got the better end of the bargain, and I had to go home at the end of each summer."

"Have you told the Ryans how you feel?"

"Oh yeah, all the time," he disclosed fondly. "Did you know that the Ryans not only helped me but other kids as well? The judge found mentors for his wards. If one of us showed an interest in school, he and Mrs. Ryan found the money for tuition and books, plus jobs, so we could go to school."

"No, I didn't know," I said thoughtfully. "They were very supportive during Maxie's illness. I've always known the Ryans were a special family."

"That's why I'm working here," Ben owned up. "It's my way of paying back the community that gave me the opportunity to meet Judge and Mrs. Ryan. All kidding aside, they taught me some very important values like responsibility, commitment, and integrity. I think that's why I was so shaken when they brought the judge into the ER this evening."

"What is his heart problem?" I asked, expecting to hear the worst.

"Atrial fibrillation," he said, seeing my puzzled look. "The heart's electrical system is causing it to beat abnormally. The upper chamber is beating faster than the lower one."

"Oh," I gulped.

"The cardiologist will implant a pacemaker to regulate the judge's heartbeat," he stated, seeing the color drain from my face. "The procedure will be done in a couple of days."

Concerned, I knew that surgery was always risky. "Is he going to be okay?"

"I hope so; the indications are that he will be fine. He will probably be in the hospital for a day or two after the procedure in order to monitor his condition. I'm more concerned about the judge's mental status and Mrs. Ryan's."

"How so?"

"The way you feel has a lot to do with your physical recovery," he said. "Mrs. Ryan told me that the judge doesn't seem to have the same zest. It's as if he's given up on life since leaving the bench six months ago."

"Is this your assessment or Mrs. Ryan's?"

"Both, I think. Why?"

"Just wondering," I pondered, picking up his uneasiness when he said her name. "What about Mrs. Ryan?"

"I've spoken with Thomas about getting her to come in for a checkup."

"What's wrong?"

"Her coloring is off. Granted, she's worried about the judge's condition, but she also seems very fatigued. Sam, do you think you can convince her to come in for an exam?"

"Yes," I declared without hesitation, now alarmed about her.

"It's odd, though; you're kind of like her," he stated.

"Me?" I mused, unsure if I'd heard him correctly.

"You're both very civic-minded women who care about people, but you're also both shy." Seeing bewilderment in my eyes, he said, "You're both very private people."

"Except when we have a cause," I pointed out, realizing he was right.

"Exactly," he said, grinning. "During those summers, Mrs. Ryan had us cleaning up neighborhoods, painting houses, delivering food to needy families, visiting nursing homes—you name it, we did it."

"Who is the 'us?'" I asked, picturing the tall, agile, dark-haired woman directing her work crew.

"Thomas and me, mostly, and sometimes Peter came along. At the end of the first summer, I knew I wanted to be a doctor."

"How?"

"There was a huge accident on the Gilbert Expressway. Mrs. Ryan heard a woman yelling that she was in labor and immediately went to help her," he confided as his eyes glistened. "She sent us to find a clean blanket or an unused newspaper to wrap the baby. After a man gave Thomas a newspaper, he ran back and gave it to his mum. Moments later Mrs. Ryan delivered a baby girl. She carefully wrapped the infant in the paper and handed me the baby so she could help the mother sit up," he boasted. "She was incredible!"

"Wow, that's a great story."

"I'll never forget the thrill I had holding that baby in my arms and then giving her to her mother."

The head nurse interrupted us. "Dr. Machado, there's been a serious accident on the freeway. The paramedics just radioed in that they are transporting three victims to the ER."

Our conversation had come to an end. It was time for him to go to work and for me to check on Rob Stone and the judge. We began cleaning up our mess.

"Who is Mrs. Ryan's doctor?" I asked, wiping down the table.

"I am, at the moment. She refuses to see anyone else."

"Don't worry; she'll be in to see you," I promised as we left the lounge.

"Sam, if there's anything I can do to help keep Madison open, let me know."

"Come to the school meeting tomorrow night."

"What time?" he asked, hearing his name.

"Seven o'clock, in the cafeteria," I replied.

Monday: 10:45 P.M. at University Hospital

Once I arrived on the fourth floor, I went to the nurses' station and was told that the district's head of security was in the family waiting area.

"Mr. Tomer," I said, looking down at the disheveled man with bloodshot eyes and reeking of caffeine and alcohol. He gripped the coffee cup, staring mindlessly at a television set.

"Yes," he slurred, looking up at me. He seemed puzzled for a moment until he realized who I was.

"How's Mr. Stone doing?" I asked, sitting down next to him. I watched him pull a flask from a jacket pocket and pour a substantial amount into his coffee and then return the container to its hiding place.

"He's fine for someone who's been shot," he sneered, waving someone away.

I turned to see who it was and thought it might be his daughter coming toward us. Instead, the young woman turned around went back into the hospital room.

"It's a damn shame those bastards shot him!" he declared in a loud, gruff voice.

"Mr. Tomer, does Mr. Stone know who shot him?"

"No. But I bet it was one of those damn foreigners from that neighborhood!" he speculated in a disgusted tone, looking down his nose at me. His beady red eyes were filled with unrelenting hatred.

The sober professional I had spoken with hours ago was long gone. I cringed at his intolerable comments, knowing that the alcohol had loosened his tongue. I gave him the benefit of the doubt, but I needed to know the truth. "Do you have any proof to support that allegation?"

"Not yet, but I'll get it and then give it to Fred."

"You mean the sheriff, don't you?" I insisted.

"No, he's not one of us. I mean Fred, missy," he retorted under his breath.

"Who's Fred?"

"The county attorney," he spewed loudly. "You damn fool."

"Oh," I uttered, taken aback.

"He knows how to take care of his own people and what to do with troublemakers. He'll make the bastards pay for shooting Rob."

"Do you know when Mr. Stone is going to be released?" I asked, knowing the answer, but changing the subject.

"Probably in the morning," he disclosed.

"Mr. Tomer, if there's anything I can do for the family, please let me know," I stated, getting up. This man repelled me, and I wanted to get away from him as quickly as possible.

He grabbed my arm to stop me from leaving. He slurred his words in a dismissive tone, "I've got somethin' for you." He handed me a list of suggestions for Madison's security.

I quickly read it and thanked him.

"Let me know what the board's decision is."

"I will," I declared, leaving him in a stupor.

~~~~~

The elevator doors opened on the sixth floor. I spotted Thomas outside his father's room, thrashing something out with Jack. Considering Thomas' stance, I knew something else had happened. My pace quickened, fearing the worst.

When I joined them, Thomas quietly told me that his dad was stable and his mum was sitting by his side, holding his hand. He went on to say that the cardiologist would monitor his father's status throughout the night.

Jack checked his watch for the second time. It appeared as if he needed to be somewhere else. Then he announced that we had to go to the cafeteria. Thomas left to inform his mum and the nursing staff without saying a word to me. Their behavior seemed rather strange. And I began wondering if something else had happened at Madison, but said nothing.

Once we were in the elevator, Thomas told me about Jack's voice mail. "William Bennett and Mario Lopez want to talk to us. I've made arrangements to meet them in the cafeteria."

I couldn't imagine why two of my former students wanted to talk to us, unless they knew something about Bill's murder or tonight's break-in. After leaving the elevator, we walked down a short corridor and entered the cafeteria.

Jack stopped at the dessert counter and placed our order.

We walked away from the palm trees and lush plants in the atrium. Somehow, this area always reminded me of the old movie, *Jurassic Park*. It was supposed to be a soothing zone but, for me, it wasn't. I had spent a lot of time there, just thinking how to save my little girl.

Thomas and I continued walking to a small table away from other customers. As we sat down, I told Thomas about my meeting with Ned Tomer.

"That's really weird," he stated.

"No kidding!" I added, reaching for his hand. Thomas had a harried look about him that made me uneasy. He reviewed his father's medical condition and how it was affecting his mum. It was so hard to picture Judge Ryan, a tall robust man, with a heart condition. Thomas looked so much like him, except his father had blue eyes and gray hair.

As we chatted, I told him about my conversation with Ben.

Thomas smiled, recalling their teenage days. He suggested that his parents should form a platoon of senior volunteers to help at-risk kids.

"Do you think they'd do it?" I asked, surprised at his suggestion.

"Yes, he'd love it and so would my mum," he asserted, watching Jack put the tray down and handing each of us a cup of coffee and a dessert.

I sipped the scorching coffee and burned my mouth, wondering why I had ordered this swill. It was worse than mine but, fortunately, it had a kick to it. This coffee would definitely keep me awake. So I started eating my frozen yogurt.

Thomas and Jack discussed the case as we waited for Mario and William to arrive.

"Apparently, someone from Madison called for help at seven-thirty Sunday evening," Jack reported, shoveling a bite of pie onto a fork. "Deputy Allen found the 911 recording. Unfortunately, the dispatcher heard the sounds of a struggle in the background and was unable to make out what the caller said. A split-second later, the call was disconnected. She called the school back, but no answer."

Stunned, I asked the sheriff if anyone was sent to check out the call.

"Nobody was dispatched," he replied, clearly upset. "I'm looking into that." Jack wrote down: "Get copy of the 911 file from night of murder, listen to entire call, and talk to night shift commander re: no dispatch."

"Sam, what's your take on the break-ins at Madison?" Thomas remarked.

"The first scene was quite neat—impersonal. It felt orderly, in a way. Nothing was thrown around like tonight's eruption. The second break-in was disorganized and personal. There was shit smeared around the room. Whoever broke in was livid about something or someone."

"That's interesting," Thomas noted, sipping his coffee. "So you feel that two different people committed these crimes?"

"Yes," I responded.

"Well, our lab technicians are almost done processing the first crime scene but they're also starting to process the impounded evidence from tonight. We should have some answers soon," Jack informed us.

"What happens during the processing?" I asked.

"After the crime-scene technicians collect all of the evidence at the scene, they return to the lab and begin the process of drying all the samples to avoid contamination and bacterial growth. Once everything is dried out, they repackage each item individually and label it. Then the items are impounded either in dry storage or in the freezers."

"Then what happens?"

"The case agent submits a lab request for DNA testing. The medical examiner draws blood from the victim—in this case, Dr. Austin. Then he sends a sample of Dr. Austin's blood over to our lab, which becomes our known DNA profile. The lab techs take all the blood samples from the impounded evidence and compare them with the known sample. If they find a different DNA profile, they enter it into a computer database called CODIS. This is a nationwide data system of DNA profiles collected from convicted felons. If we have a hit, then we know who we're looking for."

"How is this done exactly?" I queried.

"In essence, imagine that we're looking at an individual's DNA bar code like items scanned at the supermarket," Jack explained.

"It's that simple?" I questioned, surprised.

"Yes," Thomas chimed in. "Right now we know that at least two other individuals contributed blood splatter at the first crime scene."

Jack added, "We still don't know the cause of Dr. Austin's death. It's possible that he may have had a heart attack and just died."

"What about all the blood I saw?" I asked, troubled.

"The whole room may have been staged," Sheriff Peterson stated, watching me.

"Why would someone do that?" I wondered.

"To throw us off," Jack said simply, finishing his pie.

"The autopsy is taking place tomorrow morning and that will give us more information," declared Thomas, who had been quietly listening to Jack.

"We found Austin's car in the Old Pueblo Mall this afternoon, but no sign of the car keys or the district's master keys to all the buildings," the sheriff disclosed, worried. "I contacted the district's security office and informed them that the keys were still missing and assigned a deputy to protect Mrs. Austin."

"Jack," I began, remembering a conversation, "The custodians told me that Madison's security system was disconnected in May. But, interestingly enough, the system shows the school as being on-line at the district's security office. So I will bet that they don't know who's been in and out of the building."

"When did you find this out?" Thomas demanded.

"Tonight at school. I called the custodians to tell them about the break-in. I asked them if they knew of any security problems in the building. That's when they told me."

"Is the system malfunctioning or has it been deliberately tampered with?" Thomas posed thoughtfully. "Either way, the security guards could still be watching a video loop."

Thomas and Jack swapped glances.

Jack added "sabotage" to his list. Then, looking up from his notepad, he asked, "If the custodians knew there was a problem, did they report it?"

I replied, "Yes, they did. They reported it to Darrell Jefferson, who submitted a work order to the district's main office, but nothing was done. The custodians mentioned the problem again to Dr. Austin last Thursday afternoon. Bill was furious and immediately called the security department. The supervisor told him that he was unaware of the issue."

"Why was Dr. Austin at Madison?" Jack asked.

"According to the custodians, he didn't say," I replied, seeing their quizzical expressions. "Blanche left early that day for a doctor's appointment."

"Where were you, Sam?" the sheriff asked.

"I was at a reading workshop sponsored by the University of Arizona."

"So you didn't know any of this?"

"No."

Monday: 11:05 P.M. at University Hospital

The conversation ground to a halt when two rock-solid young men—William Bennett, an African-American, and Mario Lopez, whose heritage was a mixture of Native American and Mexican descent—entered the cafeteria. These boys had known each other since the age of two and were more than just friends; they were like brothers.

They slowly swaggered up to the table, dressed alike in baggy jeans. Chains hung from their side belt loops connected to wallets in their back pockets. Their white T-shirts and Nikes did little to complement their outfits.

I introduced Sheriff Peterson to the seventeen-year-old boys. Thomas and Jack extended their hands, which the boys reluctantly shook, and everyone sat down.

Mario and William had tough images to protect. They both sat back in their seats with their arms folded across their chests and heads slightly cocked as if in defiance. Their downcast eyes were skimming the tabletop, surveying everything around them.

It appeared to be a Mexican stand-off. No one said anything until Thomas offered to get everyone drinks.

William gave a quick nod as Mario leaned forward. "Cokes would be okay."

The boys traded glances after Thomas left.

Mario sat up with his hands folded. "Hey, man, we've had our differences," he spewed, not quite meeting Jack's gaze, "but we don't trash our own neighborhood. We ain't like the Bloods and Crips. We're civilized."

William nodded in agreement, and then pointed his index finger at me. "The only reason we're here is 'cuz of Miz Samuels. Lady, you be tough, but you be fair."

Mario continued in his modified English. "If she says there be changes, then there be changes. We wanna help."

I sat there, amused with their language usage. They had been among the most articulate in my class. "Gentlemen, thank you for the compliment," I responded, watching them smile. "Now, I would like to hear you speak proper English."

Mario joked, "See, I told you she would say something."

"You were right," William croaked, chuckling.

"Ms. Samuels, you haven't changed a bit," Mario stated, sitting up in his chair a little straighter. "Is this better?"

"Yes, it is." I didn't want them to put their guards back up. "I need you both to tell Sheriff Peterson what you know about Dr. Austin's murder."

"That's the point; we don't know anything about the murder."

"What about tonight's break-in?"

"Same thing, miss," responded William this time.

"Okay, then tell us what you do know."

They stared at the table, avoiding my gaze. I could see that they were both having second thoughts. I lowered my voice, causing them to look me in the eye. "Have you seen cars coming into the neighborhood that don't belong?"

Jack saw William flinch. So he began asking a series of questions, "Can you describe the cars? Where were the cars parked? Did you recognize anyone? Can you describe them?"

The boys had reverted back to their tough image. Their faces had closed, and their arms were once again folded across their chests in defiance. They remained silent.

I knew drug dealers were ruthless, not only to snitches, but to their families as well. "Mario, you and William know what's going on in your neighborhood. We need information. Please help us stop the violence before it spreads any further."

Jack pressed for information using a different tactic. "There is an anonymous hotline number that people can call and report criminal activity. When we get a tip about drug activity at a certain location, we send a surveillance team to gather information."

"How does this work?" William demanded.

"Undercover officers keep records on individuals, car descriptions, and license plates, plus when and how often the cars are there. It is with this information that we build our case, not from the unidentified individual who gave us a tip," Jack explained, seeing a flicker in Mario's eye. He removed two business cards from his wallet and wrote his direct number, as well as the hotline number on the back. He then handed each boy a card, hoping one of them would call.

I was glad Jack had given them another course of action to take. I knew the boys were conflicted . . . their code of honor was on the line, and yet, they still wanted to help. They had something to tell us that they thought was important.

Then we sat in silence until Mario leaned forward. "The only thing goin' on is this one guy and the weirdo."

Jack persisted, "Did you recognize either of them?"

William said, "Yeah, it's that weirdo DeMorgan driving around and showing off."

"He showed up at Marta's party a couple of weeks ago," Mario contributed.

"What happened?" I asked.

"A bunch of us homeys told the motherfucker to get out."

"What did he do?"

"He got mad—the way he used to in class."

"He dissed them," I informed Jack. "Did he leave before a fight broke out?"

"Yes, he did because there were too many of us!" The boys laughed, remembering how DeMorgan always retreated when he was outnumbered.

"So he left without making a major fuss. That's different," I remarked, surprised.

"Not exactly. When he drove off, he capped off a few rounds into the air," William reported nervously.

I shuddered, wondering why DeMorgan had a firearm. "What kind of gun did he have?"

"It looked like a nine- or maybe a forty-caliber, silver piece of shit. Not as nice as mine."

I was horrified at the thought that the boys were carrying guns . . . but that was their way of life.

Jack ignored this piece of information. "Was this on July first?"

"Yeah, how did you know that?" William asked, surprised.

"A 911 call came in that night about a drive-by shooting," he stated. "Tell me about the car. Color? Make?"

"A black Chevy."

"Who was he with?" the sheriff fired off.

Mario spoke now. "Some older guy in his late forties or fifties, you know, out in the sun too long. He acted like he . . . ." Neither boy finished the statement; instead they traded anxious glances.

Fortunately, Thomas returned and handed them their drinks along with some chips. Then he asked, "Have you ever seen this guy before or since?"

"No," Mario answered, surprised at his question.

"I heard part of the discussion," Thomas said.

"Could it have been DeMorgan's father?" I speculated, thinking how badly RJ was aging. He had been muscular when I first met him but now, in his early forties, he had a distended abdomen and his face was splotchy and covered with deep lines. Then I gave the boys a simple visual. "He's tall with a pot belly and blond hair that is thinning on top."

"No, this guy had dark hair," Mario divulged, leaning forward so no one else could hear what he said.

"But DeMorgan still comes around," William expanded in a lower voice.

"Where does he go?"

"He drives around the neighborhood mostly. Except the other day, he picked up a man in a three-piece suit at the school. They both sped away laughing."

"Did you witness this?"

"No. Two five-year-old kids did."

"Do you know who the kids are and when this occurred?" I persisted, alarmed.

"Pancho Sanchez and Miguel Gonzales," Mario revealed. "They were practicing soccer kicks on the playground Sunday morning."

"Do you think they saw them?"

"Probably."

"Has there been anyone else in the neighborhood that doesn't belong there?"

"No," William replied as Mario made an involuntary move.

Jack turned and asked, "Mario, anyone else?"

"There was a lady who was asking for directions to the school."

"When?"

"Last fall sometime."

"Can you describe her?"

"No, because I wasn't the one who spoke to her," Mario admitted.

"Who spoke with her?"

"Old man Gomez. He was sitting by the water fountain in the park," he disclosed, then folded his arms across his chest.

William followed suit.

Our discussion had concluded, so I asked Mario how his GED classes were going.

He sat quietly for a while. "I quit because it was too far away."

Then William volunteered that he'd also quit.

I watched Jack back away from the conversation to add their information to his notes. I saw "Int / Pancho / Miguel / Gomez" appear on his pad.

Thomas sat back in his chair, trying to keep a straight face as he listened to our exchange. He knew what I was up to.

I looked at each boy. "You both want to be part of the change, don't you?"

"Yeah," they replied apprehensively, looking at each other and then at me.

"If GED classes are offered at Madison, will you come?"

"Maybe . . . but," Mario volunteered, hesitating.

"We need jobs more than school," asserted William.

"Can you get other kids to come to the classes?"

"Oh, miss!" they said together as their dark eyes widened.

"Just think about it; that's all I am asking for now."

"We need jobs, Ms. Samuels," Mario pleaded their case.

"If I find you both part-time jobs, can I count on you to attend the GED classes?" I countered, watching them wince.

"But miss!" they exclaimed together.

"Come on, you guys. If I'm going to succeed at making the changes necessary at school, I'll need your help. Can I count on you?"

Dead silence was my answer. The boys squirmed, looking for a graceful way to escape. They looked at Thomas and Jack for support, but none came.

"You came here tonight because you wanted to help. Isn't that true?"

They sat there with a look of dread on their faces. Their coloring waned; their dark pupils widened; and they both rolled their eyes upwards toward the ceiling.

I knew I was winning. "The kids around the neighborhood look up to you two."

"Yeah, but miss . . ." objected William, raising his hands in protest, trying to avoid looking at me.

"You could work in our after-school program as sports monitors and help the kids with their homework."

"You can't make enough money to support a family playing with little kids," Mario protested.

"Look, I'll find a way to get you both jobs," I said. "What if I can get you college credit for community service or on-the-job training too?"

"But, miss . . . ." Both boys now sat in their seats with their arms folded across their chests, leaning back so far that they were almost tipping the chairs backwards.

"Just think about it." I knew they wanted to leave, so I leaned forward. "Remember our motto?"

Wincing, they smiled, breaking the tension. The boys brought their chairs upright and met my gaze as they rested their hands on the table. Both boys voiced the class motto with me: "I can make a difference."

"She's a steamroller, guys," Thomas asserted, watching them nod in agreement. "Believe me; she really does care about both of you. If you give her half a chance, she'll make all of this happen. Even if it kills us."

"Mr. Ryan, if you think she's demanding now, you should've seen her in class," Mario remarked with a big grin.

I started to protest as the group began laughing.

"It's okay, Mario. I know what you're up against," Thomas said, winking at me.

"Just promise me you'll think about the GED classes and get the others to come too," I pressed one final time, giving them one of my serious looks.

Both boys exchanged ambiguous glances. Then they asserted, "We surrender!"

"Well, man . . ." Mario began, looking straight at Sheriff Peterson. "We just wanted you to know that shit is happening in the neighborhood." His demeanor had changed. He'd suddenly gone back to being a tough guy.

"It may not be much to look at, but it's our home," William asserted. "We're no angels. But nobody from the barrio killed Dr. Austin or was involved with tonight's break-in."

They stood up and held out their hands. Jack and Thomas shook their hands and thanked them for coming forward. I waited my turn and gave each one a hug. I was surprised that Mario and William were both about three-to-four inches taller than me.

Their faces reddened, embarrassed by my display of affection.

"Please come to the community meeting tomorrow night."

They quickly agreed and then left.

Jack declared, "That was interesting."

And Thomas mused, "What kind of hold do you have over those kids?"

"None, really. I was just their fifth- and sixth-grade teacher at Madison."

"If you hadn't been here, Sam, all we would have heard was 'yep, nope, and motherfucker,'" Jack observed.

"Probably, but I have an advantage. I know their mothers and I've kept in touch with them throughout the years."

"They know you care about them and they seem to really care about you, Sam," declared Jack, meeting my gaze. "When they called wanting to meet, I read their juvenile files."

"They've had their rough patches, but I think they're good kids who've just had some problems growing up," I stated, smiling.

"You've had a definite impact on them," Jack asserted, still stunned that the boys had given them some useful information. "I'm glad that you were here because I have a newfound respect for these young men."

"Well, they certainly made an impact on me too. They were part of Maxie's fan club."

"When Maxie was in the hospital, they came and played with her," Thomas revealed, taking my hand.

"I will never forget the day when Henry and Marge came into her hospital room and found William standing on his head. Maxie was laughing so hard that she was crying," I added, wiping the tears away. "William left five minutes later, leaving Henry and Marge speechless. The next day Mario came in and taught Maxie how to weave an Indian basket."

"I remember that day," Thomas stated wistfully. "Henry and I stood in the hallway and watched him patiently show her how to weave a simple design into her basket."

"I didn't know that you were there."

"You'd fallen asleep in a chair, Sam. But when Mario noticed that we were watching him, he felt uncomfortable and said he had to go. Maxie gave him a big hug and he left."

"I think that's why they came," I said, grabbing my notebook from my bag. I jotted down: "Earn college credit for life experience;

offer GED classes at Madison," and "call Henry about part-time jobs for the boys and others."

Jack interrupted my train of thought. "Sam, this DeMorgan—is he the same kid we talked about earlier?"

"Yes."

Thomas questioned, "How did the other kids treat him?"

"Basically, they barely tolerated him," Jack stated, going on to explain. "Sam told me he was an out-of-control kid with a very strong sense of self-importance."

Jack's cell rang.

Thomas appeared startled and immediately checked his own phone. I could see the tension in his face as he tried to relax but couldn't. He was worried about his father.

Jack left the table to return the call from a pay phone in the hallway.

"Thomas, why is Jack using a pay phone?"

"He's uses land lines for security reasons. Cell phones can be overheard by almost anybody who can afford a good scanner."

I was surprised at this revelation and wondered about some of my own conversations in the past. I'd have to be more careful in the future.

On his return, Jack informed Thomas that his SAU detectives had Campbell, Tomer, and Jefferson under surveillance.

"Who is Campbell?" I recognized the other names and wondered what "SAU" meant.

"Blanche," Thomas answered.

"But why Blanche!" I exclaimed, stunned that she was considered a suspect.

"Two reasons: One, we're still looking for suspects; and two, some individuals might be targets. Blanche might turn out to be a suspect, but she may also need protection," Thomas declared, taking my hand.

The sheriff looked me straight in the eye. "Sam, what you've heard tonight is confidential. Blanche can't know about this."

Taking this new information in, I shuddered. Surely she wasn't involved, but Thomas was right—she could definitely know something that might put her in danger. "What does 'SAU' stand for?" I asked.

"It stands for 'Special Assignment Unit,'" he elucidated, as we all stood to leave. "It's a group of detectives with rotating responsibilities. They don't have a permanent assignment. Primarily, they serve as the Sheriff's Department SWAT team, but they also do undercover surveillance as well."

After quickly checking on his dad and mum, Thomas and I drove to the West Valley Resort to catch whatever sleep we could before the new dawn arrived. As I closed my eyes, I wondered if Jack had me under surveillance too.

Tuesday

August 16

Tuesday: 7:25 A.M. at the District Office

Since the crack of dawn, I'd been dreading the emergency board meeting, Peter had always laughingly mocked, "Dress the part, and the power will follow." So I dressed carefully, wearing a beige silk shell and a black tailored suit. I hoped that he was right, because today I had a feeling I would need to be influential.

At 7:25 a.m., I walked across the parking lot into the sandy-colored, two-story building that had housed the school district's offices for more than thirty years. Like many of the district's buildings, it looked well-cared for.

The meeting was scheduled in the conference room on the second floor, across from the superintendent's office. I climbed the circular staircase, one step at a time, until I reached the landing. Walking down the corridor, I stopped in front of Bill's office, half expecting him to walk out the door, and when he didn't, I felt a profound sense of loss.

I entered the posh conference room. It perfectly illustrated how the board evidently cared more for its own comfort than the educational needs of the students. With papers scattered in front of them, the board members sat in exquisite wine-colored leather chairs around a large glossy oak table. It was then that I caught a glimpse of their callous expressions.

Gingerly, I sat across from Ruth Beaker. "Good morning, ladies and gentlemen."

"Good morning," the board members mumbled in unison, trying to avoid my gaze. They turned to Paul Mendoza as their spokesman.

"Mrs. Samuels, the board has voted to close Madison Elementary School."

"Dr. Mendoza," I asserted pleasantly, smiling at the pompous ass. "I would like to know the reasons behind their decision."

He began reciting their grounds, alluding to the recent violence at the school, safety issues, declining enrollment, and the budget problems. "The board and I feel that there are better ways to allocate the district's resources."

"Really, Dr. Mendoza, I find this turn of events very interesting," I remarked, hiding my anger behind a smile.

"What do you mean?" he asked, confused.

I decided to play their game and hit them where it hurt—their tenuous political status in the community. "Dr. Austin appeared only last Wednesday on 'The Arizona Talk Show,' in which he spoke about our plans to make Madison a model school."

"So what?" he challenged angrily.

"The public's response was overwhelmingly positive. They expressed their views on the radio, on television, and even, wrote letters of support to the local newspapers," I said, handing him copies of several newspapers' letters to the editor.

"Get to the point, Sam," Paul declared.

"The board is making a terrible mistake by closing Madison," I asserted, watching the members cringe.

"Why do you think that?" Mrs. Beaker demanded. Her smile had disappeared as she glared at me.

"The public is upset because of Dr. Austin's death," I pointed out, observing the glum faces around the table. "The community wants to see his recommendations implemented. They will view Madison's closure as a direct slap in the face to Dr. Austin—a man who they admired and trusted."

"It is our decision to close Madison—not Dr. Austin's or the community's," Mrs. Beaker asserted, infuriated.

"That is correct, but this is an election year, Mrs. Beaker," I stated, meeting her anxious gaze. "The voters of this community expect the board to educate all of the children in this district."

"That's what we're doing!" she declared.

"That may be true but, at the polls, in November, they will remember the board's failure to implement Dr. Austin's recommendations and your hasty closure of Madison. They could also begin to wonder what might happen to their own children's schools." I met the board's hostile stare. "The voters will decide your fate."

"How dare you threaten the board!" shouted Mendoza.

"I'm just stating the reality of the situation, Paul," I affirmed, smiling politely. "But, as Mrs. Beaker has already pointed out this morning, the decision to close Madison School rests with the board. So I respectfully ask the board to rescind its decision and keep Madison open."

Faces grew red as I met their worried gaze. Moments later, the board members erupted into a loud debate. Some puffed out their chests, jockeying for the upper hand. One pounded the table with a fist as others "back-pedaled" their positions, while Ruth tried to maintain order.

It was truly amazing to watch how a hint of bad publicity could bring out their collective sensibility. Finally, after a lengthy debate, the board rescinded its closure decision and, reluctantly, agreed to keep Madison open. They even agreed to attend the meeting tonight.

Paul Mendoza was not a happy camper.

I'd won the first scrimmage, but I had made an enemy. I knew that this was not going to be the end of our discussion.

On the way out of the building, I stopped by the main office to see Jane Fuller, the new district finance director. She was a Yale-educated blonde with powerful friends—Ruth's husband and the county attorney. When her predecessor retired last October, they were instrumental in helping her win her new position.

I entered the office and saw the receptionist dealing with a persistent reporter. I immediately retreated to a corner by the window. Waiting for the reporter to leave, I recalled my first encounter with Jane outside the scope of school business. We had just finished a contentious negotiation session on class size as we stood in line to use the restroom.

She turned toward me. "Did you hear the joke about the doctor, the lawyer, a used-car salesman, and the priest?"

Before I could reply, she started telling her version of this old joke. So I listened.

"You see, these guys were old poker buddies, and they'd been playing cards for years. The used-car dealer had just visited the doctor because he wasn't feeling well. At the next poker game, he said, 'Boys, you know I won't be here too much longer. So I want each of you to do me a big favor. I just don't believe in the old expression that 'you can't take it with you.' But I'm going to need your help," Jane continued in a whisper, winking at me.

"And with that, he gave each of them a briefcase filled with $100,000 in cash. He instructed them that, after his death, they were to put the money into his coffin so he could take it with him. Each of them gave him their solemn promise that they would do so. Sadly, they never had the chance to play poker again because, a few days later, the car dealer passed away.

"After the funeral, his poker buddies spoke privately. The priest was deeply saddened at his friend's death and quickly confessed, 'I feel so guilty, but it has been a really bad winter, and we had to replace St. Katherine's roof. I'm sorry to say, but I only put $60,000 into the coffin.'"

"The doctor seemed relieved, because he blurted out that the IRS had just nailed him and he too had used some of the cash to pay them off. He'd only tossed in $40,000."

"The lawyer looked at each of his friends, saying, 'I am really disappointed with both of you.' He told them he had tossed in a check for the whole amount."

When she concluded the joke, Jane giggled and then leaned over, "I'm wondering who I'm dealing with concerning the school district's budget: the priest, the doctor, or the lawyer!"

I started to ask her what she meant by that odd comment. But, Jane cut me off. Her demeanor had suddenly changed when she saw her assistant, Cindy Cameron, charge toward her with a stack of papers. It was obvious that the Amazonian redhead was furious with her boss.

Stunned, I'd wondered what was going on with both of these women but said nothing. Throughout the negotiation process, emotions had been contentious on both sides of the table. The main problem was the fluid budget. Jane Fuller and Cindy Cameron seemed incapable of producing the district's spreadsheets accurately. Their numbers conflicted, and no one seemed to know which ones were correct.

Cindy kept chalking it up to a computer glitch. Jane blamed her for everything but offered no help. I'd often wondered if their incompetence had cost us our raises. Even now, rumors still persisted that Cindy had only landed her job—despite a business degree from Harvard—because of her mother, Lois Cameron.

Considering the past few days, I needed to clarify the budget lines with Jane. After the reporter left, the receptionist informed me, "The computers are down, and we weren't able to print a copy of the budget for you."

"Oh," I uttered, surprised. "Is Miss Fuller in?"

"She is out of the building and won't be back until tomorrow."

I made an appointment to meet with her next week.

Lois Cameron entered with an arthritic gait. "Sam, come with me." She slowly walked to her private office. At sixty, she was quite plump, with short brown hair and dark sad eyes. She gingerly sat down at her desk and apologized because the document was unavailable. "Is there anything else I can help you with?"

"Can you make a copy from the hard file?"

"Sam, I looked for the file this morning when I saw you entering the building, but I don't know what's happened to it . . . it's not in the file drawer."

"It's missing?" I exclaimed.

She sat for a moment, cautiously folding her hands on top of the desk as she considered her answer. The knuckles on both hands were red and swollen, and the fingers on the right hand were beginning to show signs of arthritic deformity. "Oh, no, I don't think so," she finally announced in a quiet voice. "Ms. Fuller may have taken it home."

"Why would she do that?" I asked, flabbergasted.

"She's the director, so you would have to ask her that question, Sam. You know, Friday was the last time I saw Dr. Austin alive," she stated, turning the conversation away from the budget as she wiped tears from her eyes. She had worked closely with Dr. Austin throughout the years and now she was the only one left who knew the district's history.

"Had anything happened recently to upset Dr. Austin?" I asked, hoping to get some clues on why he was killed.

"I don't know for sure," she said loudly. Then, dropping her voice to a whisper, she added, "He was swearing at the top of his lungs at Ms. Fuller on Friday."

"Swearing?" I choked out, stunned. Dr. Austin had a temper, but I'd never heard him swear at anyone, especially if he was reprimanding an employee. "Why was he so upset with her?"

"I think it had to do with budgetary problems he'd discovered online," she remarked vaguely, looking down at her manicured pink nails and then up at me. "After Jane left Friday afternoon, he had me pull the hard copy of the budget so he could have a closer look. When he was done, I filed it in its proper place."

"Did anyone hear the argument?"

Lois nodded as she answered the district's ringing phone. I waited until she finished the call before asking her if Jane had been in yesterday.

"Oh, yes!" she exclaimed. "When she heard the news about Dr. Austin, she cried. Then she left for the day and hasn't been back since."

"That's a bit strange, don't you think?" I stated. Why did Jane leave? Could she be involved with Bill's murder, or was she his lover?

"Especially since she took several folders with her . . . one of which might have been the hard copy of the budget," Lois divulged, breaking my train of thought.

The phone rang again. She apologized once more and said she would send the budget report over as soon as the computer system was working.

~~~~~~

Once in the car, I called Henry to tell him the latest news.

"Henry, I can't get a copy of the budget today," I revealed on speaker mode. "The computers are down."

"What the hell is going on over there?"

"I wish I knew. By the way, Lois Cameron insinuated that Jane Fuller may have taken the hard file home with her yesterday after she found out about Bill's murder."

"Why would she do that?"

"I don't know," I commented, entering the freeway. "And, apparently, Bill reprimanded her on Friday."

"Now that's interesting," he mused. "Do they know how long it will take to get the bloody system back up?"

"I don't know, nor do I care at the moment, because the board wants to close Madison," I stated calmly as I told him about the emergency board meeting.

"What are those damn fools thinking of?" he blurted out, exasperated.

"Covering their collective asses," I said, picturing Henry smiling at my comment.

"How do you feel about this?" he pressed.

"I'm pissed! I've got some ideas on how to keep Madison open, but I'm going to need your help," I confided in my father-in-law.

"I can be at your office in about thirty minutes, Sam."

"No, Henry; I can't meet with you then. I've scheduled a meeting with the primary teachers, so I'll be tied up for most of the afternoon."

"Okay, Sam, then tell me what you have in mind."

I began listing my ideas on how to keep the school open. They ranged from extending the school year to applying for drop-out prevention funds and establishing GED classes, after-school programs, parenting classes, and . . . .

"Henry, I need you to see if the Samuels Foundation can help with some of these programs," I probed. After I gained control of my parents' estate, I established two foundations to help individuals in need: one was for education and the other for medical. Thomas and Henry were in-charge.

"Sam, of course it can."

"Thanks, Henry," I said, slowing down for a stoplight.

"You know, Sam, I think I'll call in some favors, and I'll also talk to Marge about this. If someone can do something about this situation, she can," he stated confidently.

"Henry . . ." I uttered, thinking of his very politically astute wife. Marge Samuels had served as a state legislator and chaired several task forces for various Arizona governors. By profession, she was a corporate lawyer who knew how to work the system and win controversial cases.

"I'll take care of this, honey. I'll see you at the community meeting tonight. Bye." Henry ended the call abruptly.

"Henry!" I shouted into the dead cell as the light turned green. I knew Marge would make mincemeat out of the school board, but he had other resources. I tried to call him back, but he'd turned off his cell so I couldn't reach him. "Oh, God, please help him listen to Marge."

Closing the cell phone, I drove straight to school, wondering what I had actually accomplished this morning. I came to the conclusion quickly: very little.

Tuesday: 1:00 P.M. at Madison in the Teachers' Lounge

Primary teachers walked into the lounge quietly. I took a moment to review my notes for the meeting. I wanted to make sure I covered all the bases with this group because I wouldn't get another chance. They were realists and, if the program worked, all would be fine but, if not, there would be hell to pay.

When they were all seated, I began with an overview of how I wanted reading taught throughout the school year. Children needed help to define the elements of a story, which I identified as character development, the setting, the author's themes, and finally, the plot of the story divided into problems and solutions.

When I finished the outline, skeptical faces glared at me. So I chose the classic fairy tale, *Little Red Riding Hood*, as an example. We brainstormed each element and discussed the pros and cons of each character's decision. During the process, teachers were able to see how students could develop their language skills as they worked together exploring each building block of the story. At the end, there were still some looks of defiance.

But I didn't let that intimidate me. "As a matter of fact, I want you to use this story as your first reading lesson and take it a step further into how choices are made," I asserted. "Ask your students to evaluate how the characters resolved their problems. Could they have solved them differently? Make a list of the pros and cons of the characters' choices. Then ask your students what they would do in the same circumstance and why they chose that approach."

"I get it, Sam. You want us to discuss which choices would've been better and why," asserted a third-grade teacher. She had been nodding for most of the meeting.

"That's the idea," I said. "I want the kids to look at their choices and, hopefully, this will influence them to make better decisions in their own lives."

"Sam, we'll have these kids bouncing off the walls," bellowed Gina Spinelli, the most conservative member of the group. "My question is: What about discipline?"

"Gina, I think that once the kids become involved in their own education, they will want to learn, and discipline won't be an issue. I'm sure there will be some rough moments, but I am convinced that we will succeed in the long run."

"I think you've lost it!" she spat in a huff.

"Well, everyone is entitled to his or her own opinion. But, as long as I'm principal of Madison, we are going to proceed with this reading program."

"How are you going to handle disruptive children?" demanded a third-grade teacher.

"I want to know immediately if there is a problem," I asserted, realizing that several teachers had experienced trouble with unruly students last year. "Believe me, I'm not forgetting about discipline. I'll take each child on a case-by-case basis, and I'll get the parents involved and do whatever is necessary to resolve the behavioral problem."

The third-grade teacher rolled his eyes upwards in response.

Gina spoke again, this time pounding her index finger on the table to emphasize each and every word. "Let me make this perfectly clear. I won't tolerate any individual disrupting the learning process in my classroom."

"I'm not asking you to compromise your standards. I am asking you to implement a new reading program—one of which, I may add, I have used in my classrooms with success."

"What about the other subjects? Do you expect us to use this method, as well?" Gina challenged, realizing I wasn't going to back down.

"The answer to your question is yes. I expect you to do whatever is necessary to teach your students how to think. And, by that, I mean the ability to define a problem, look for different solutions, and evaluate the pros, the cons, and the consequences of their choices. It seems to me that it would be a natural way to go in science, in social studies, and in math."

Their eyes narrowed in disgust as everyone just sat there. So I asked, "Any questions?"

"We heard a rumor that Madison might close. Is that true?" Gina pressed, watching me while she took a sip of coffee.

"Whoa, the rumor mill is alive and well, I see. I'll admit that there is a real possibility that Madison could be closed, but no final decision has been made. As a matter of fact, the school board has agreed to attend our community meeting tonight."

"Can we attend?"

"Absolutely! Your input is very important."

A voice creaked over the intercom, "Sam."

"Yes, Blanche."

"The sheriff is on Line Two."

"Tell him I'll be with him in a minute."

"Okay, Sam."

"Does anyone have any further questions at this time?"

Since no one spoke up, I barreled forward. "Listen, we're in this together and, once we get into the full swing of things, you'll see that teaching this way can be fun." Hearing my stomach rumble, I turned around to check the clock. It was three. "This meeting is adjourned. I'll see you tonight."

As the teachers left the room, I picked up my notes and walked over to the phone. "Hi, Jack. What can I do for you?"

"Did Bill Austin play the stock market?"

"I know he had money in the stock market."

"Do you know how he traded?" he pressed.

"He used an E-STOK-TRADE account."

"How do you know this?" he asked abruptly.

"He told me during one of our meetings."

"When?"

"At the beginning of August."

"Was he a day trader?"

"I don't know."

"That's kind of like gambling."

"I guess, in a way," I speculated, puzzled with his line of questioning. "Are you suggesting that Bill was gambling again, only this time online?"

"Yes. So what do you think?"

"I don't know. I think he was still going to Gamblers Anonymous meetings," I said, a little testily. "But here again, I think Mrs. Austin would know better than me."

"By the way," the sheriff declared, changing tactics, "I gave your computer printouts and the CDs to our computer expert. He sent copies to the money laundering division."

"What did they think?" I asked, turning the tables on him.

"Unknown at this time. But I have a subpoena for your flash drive and the lab's computer you were using last night."

"Why?"

"Our expert wants to review all the files as well as retrieve any deleted ones."

"Okay," I said, wondering what he found. "I thought I downloaded everything."

"You may have. But, just to be on the safe side, I want to make sure."

"Are you sending someone over?"

"I already have. He should be there soon," the sheriff said, cutting me off.

"I'll give Blanche the flash drive."

"Thanks. Anything else?"

"Yes. The district's main computer is down, and I can't get a copy of the budget. The strange part is that Jane Fuller may have taken the district's hard file home after she heard about Bill's death."

"That is odd," he stated with hesitancy. "Are you sure about this?"

"That's what Lois Cameron told me when she couldn't locate the file this morning."

"Who is she?"

"She's the finance director's secretary. She also said that Jane and Dr. Austin had a very loud discussion about a budgetary problem Friday."

"That's interesting," he commented. "Was Jane Fuller at work today?"

"No."

"Thanks for the info. I'll check it out."

"How did the autopsy go?"

"It raised more questions than it answered. I've got to go; I'll see you tonight."

"Bye," I added, ending the phone call.

~~~~~

It was three-fifteen in the afternoon when I entered the main office as teachers were checking out to leave for the day.

The crime scene tape from last night's explosion was gone. The district's hazard crew had thoroughly cleaned my office, scrubbing the walls and floors with industrial disinfectants. A maintenance crew redecorated the office with a mirror on a dilapidated desk, a swivel seat, and two shabby chairs. They really shouldn't have bothered.

I gagged as I entered my closed office. The room reeked of bleach and something else. Pinching my nose, I opened all the windows, hoping to circulate some fresh air and then lowered the air conditioner's thermostat five degrees. As I took a deep breath in, I heard Blanche knocking on the open door.

"Phew! This smells awful!" she exclaimed, surveying the toxic room. She shook her head in disgust.

"I agree!"

Blanche announced that Patty Steward was on Line One.

I looked at the new phone on my desk. Then, considering the stench, I followed her into the main office to answer the call. "Hi, Patty. Are you still coming?"

"Yes. I'll be there, but I'm running late as usual." At this point, we both laughed. It was her standard answer for almost everything. When the laughter died down, Patty asked, "Do you need anything else besides the budget records?"

"No . . . but, if you pass a McDonald's, I could really use a break today!"

"Very funny. What do you want?"

"Big Mac, fries, strawberry milkshake, and your support for a year-round school program."

"You're a regular comedian today. Are you serious?"

"Yes. Think about what we'll need to do regarding contracts, salaries, benefits, etc."

"Sam, are you sure?"

"Believe me, I'm sure. Please hurry; I'm starving."

"Okay, I'm on my way," she declared. "Are you thinking about the year-round school concept that we discussed at the bargaining table?"

"Basically, yes, with some modifications to fit Madison."

"Do you think the board will go along with you?"

"Probably not. In fact, they're already thinking about closing Madison."

"How are you going to . . . ?"

"If I can get the teachers, the parents, the community, and you . . . ."

"Plus Henry and Marge Samuels behind you," she charged confidently. "You're planning to sandbag the board tonight, aren't you?"

"Patty, how can you say that?" I teased innocently. "Nothing is set in stone. The meeting will be the determining factor whether Madison remains open."

"Are you going to tell the teachers about the board wanting to close the school?"

"They already know via the rumor mill. As for the parents and the rest of the community, I think they have a right to know."

"Well, you've given me some food for thought," she stated. "Okay, kiddo, I'm on my way and I won't forget your food."

"Thanks, Patty. We'll talk when you get here."

Blanche had been listening to my side of the conversation. Once I hung up, she pointed to the principal's office. "Nice digs, Sam."

"Do you think I can requisition a new office?"

"No." Then, looking at the clock on the wall, she added, "I'm definitely coming tonight."

"Thanks, I'll need your support," I said, sitting down on the stool next to her desk.

"Sam, as I was going through the office files this afternoon, I found this envelope stapled on the outside of a student activity file. It's a list of names and numbers that I've never seen before.

"Did you tell the sheriff?"

"No. I don't work for him; I work for you," she insisted, giving me a concerned look. "If you think he should see this, then I'll give it to him. That's your decision."

"Okay, Blanche, I get the hint. Let me see it." She handed me the envelope that had neatly written names and numbers on the back side. This information meant nothing to me. "Where's the file that this was attached to?"

She reached into her desk drawer, pulled out the blue folder and handed it to me.

I reviewed the contents, which contained the business records from Madison's spring fund-raiser. There were copies of bank deposit receipts, purchase orders for athletic equipment, and canceled checks stamped "paid in full."

"Who kept these records?" I asked, noticing that the handwriting in the file differed from the one on the envelope.

"Darrell did."

"Are all the files this complete?"

"Yes."

"When Darrell gave you the school activity file, was this envelope attached?"

"No. And I know it wasn't there at the end of May, because I checked all the files."

"Blanche, do you have any idea where this envelope came from?"

"No, Sam; I don't even recognize any of the names."

"Do you recognize the handwriting?"

"It looks a little like Jane Fuller's, but I'm not sure."

"Why would Jane attach this envelope to one of our school files?" I wondered, stunned that the finance director might have been going through Madison's files.

"I don't know, Sam."

My head began pounding as I tried to make sense of this information. I got up and made two copies of the file's contents and the list of names. I gave Blanche a copy for our files, placed another set of copies in my shoulder bag with a note to call Darrell Jefferson, and placed the originals into a large envelope to give to Jack. This was his area of expertise, not mine. I put the envelope next to my purse under the counter.

"How do you think everything will go tonight?" Blanche asked, looking uneasy as I sat down again on the stool.

"Blanche, your guess is as good as mine," I stated, pondering why she changed the subject. "You've heard the phrase 'defining moments.' Well, tonight is going to be one of those."

"Are you prepared for what's coming?"

"I hope so."

"The board isn't going to like the fact that you're setting them up," Blanche declared with concern. "And the teachers already feel threatened about the possibility of the school's closure and the changes you want to implement."

"That's true," I noted.

"I'll tell you something else; the entire neighborhood has an uneasy feel to it."

"I know," I said softly. "I'll give it my best shot tonight."

Tuesday: 4:15 P.M. at Madison in My Office

f I'd thought yesterday was busy, today was turning out to be a real whopper. I felt shaky since my blood-sugar levels had plummeted and my stomach grumbled loudly. I hadn't eaten since breakfast. So I hoped Patty would arrive soon.

I looked up and smiled when the president of the teachers association knocked on the door. Patty sauntered in wearing a wine-colored sleeveless dress, dripping in sweat.

"Can I get you something to drink—coffee or a soda?" I offered, getting up. I smiled, relieved when she dropped her jacket on the chair, exposing two bags filled with food.

Patty dumped the bags onto the desk and then placed her purse and briefcase next to her jacket. Grabbing several tissues from the Kleenex box, she systematically mopped the sweat off her face. "Coffee is just fine."

"Are you sure?"

"Yes," she asserted in a sharp tone, discarding the used tissues into the wastebasket next to the desk. She sat down in the ugly, green vinyl chair. A moment later, she looked up with a funny expression on her face. Her nose was scrunched up, sniffing the air. "Unique room deodorizer!"

"Really funny," I teased, thinking this is the reality of teaching in a barrio school. As I handed her a cup of coffee, I realized how frazzled Patty was. Her black, cropped hair was in disarray. The red glasses had slid halfway down her nose, exposing her alert, brown eyes.

She took a sip of coffee, savoring the strong brew, and placed the cup on the desk.

I went on to say, "Thankfully, the real stench has dissipated, leaving us with only a slight scent of industrial cleaners. It could be worse—the maintenance crew could've painted the room the putrid color green to match the hallways."

"That's true," she agreed, smiling at last.

"And, just so you know, the crew added the mirror," I declared, smiling.

"Who is your decorator?"

"I'm beginning to think it is Paul Mendoza," I remarked offhandedly, grinning at this athletic woman as she fumbled through her bulging briefcase filled with folders.

"Don't mention that bastard's name; that's why I'm late!" Patty cautioned, placing the files on the desk. Furiously, she ran her hands through her hair, leaving some strands standing straight up.

"And I thought I looked bad," I teased, sitting down on the rickety brown swivel chair behind my desk. "What the hell happened to you?"

"You wouldn't believe me if I told you," she snapped.

"I'm here to listen if you need me," I volunteered, watching her fix her hair.

"Thanks, but . . . ."

"But what?" I probed.

"Don't you think that you have enough to worry about?"

"Who knows; maybe a distraction would help," I stated as I grabbed my bag of food.

"Well . . . ."

"Well, what, Patty?"

"Well, what was Bill doing here Sunday night?"

"To be honest, I haven't the foggiest idea. Do you know something?" I nudged, before taking a bite of my cheeseburger.

"Well," she began with a conspiratorial tone, "did you hear about the row between Jane and Cindy Cameron on Thursday afternoon?"

"No, what happened?" I sighed, sitting back waiting to hear.

"Jane finally called Cindy on the carpet for her ineptitude," she reported. "That idiot doesn't have the ability to input data or anything else."

"Whatever do you mean?" I teased, knowing exactly what she meant.

"Everything she's touched for the last nine months has been riddled with mistakes. Her data entries, her spreadsheets, and the financial reports she's prepared have all had to be redone by Jane, including the one for the upcoming board meeting."

"You're kidding!" I teased.

"Jane was so irate that she told Cindy to clean up her act, or else. And, if she continued to run to Mama for help, her mother would be fired for insubordination as well."

"Wow! Where did this confrontation take place?"

"Outside of Bill's office." She beamed with delight.

"Was he there?"

"Oh, yes, and he supported Jane. You can imagine how Cindy took that," Patty stated smugly. "In front of everyone, Cindy thanked Bill for the opportunity and that he would have her letter of resignation effective immediately. Then she turned around, walked into her office, and slammed the door shut."

"How did Lois respond to Cindy's resignation?" I asked, recalling her gloating comments about Bill reprimanding Jane.

"She ran into Bill's office and began making excuses for her daughter. As Jane escorted Lois out the door, she told her that this wasn't her concern and ordered her to bring the latest computer printout of the district's budget, the hard copy, as well as the financial statements for the fiscal year."

"What was Lois' reaction?"

"She was furious, but she didn't say a thing. When Lois returned with the items, Jane thanked her and shut the door in her face," Patty smirked with a big smile stamped across her face. "Jane and Bill spent hours going over the budget."

"Wow! I was there on Friday morning for a quick meeting with Bill. I can't believe I didn't hear anything about it."

"I can't believe you didn't either. Tongues have been wagging ever since," Patty declared in a catty voice.

"Bill wouldn't have said anything to me."

"True—but someone else would have."

"I don't think so. Everyone was on edge," I said.

"Well, that's weird."

"That's what I thought. As a matter of fact, the atmosphere was similar this morning, but I thought it was because everyone was upset about Bill's murder."

"I would say it is worse," Patty asserted. "Everyone liked and respected Bill. But Paul Mendoza is another story."

"What did Cindy do after she went to her office?" I asked, going back to the awkward confrontation.

"She packed her stuff. Then, she handed Bill her letter of resignation and walked out. Lois tried to stop her and that's when she screamed that she didn't need 'this lousy fucking job.' She told her mother that she was going to marry Carlo and, if Lois didn't like it—tough!"

"Who is Carlo?"

"Carlo Santini. Why?"

"Just curious," I said, puzzled. I knew the Santini name but couldn't place Carlo. That was strange. Usually, I was great with names, but . . . maybe it was the stress of the job. "Who heard Lois' argument with her daughter?"

"You should be asking who didn't."

I sat there, comparing what she had just told me with Lois' earlier comments. Patty blamed Cindy for everything, but then she and Jane had become pretty good friends of late. It was only natural that she believed Jane's version and that Lois wanted to protect her daughter. So who was reprimanded—Jane or Cindy, or both at different times? What a mess!

"Let's get down to business." Patty interrupted my thoughts, brushing crumbs off her dress. She pulled a notebook out of her briefcase.

Patty was a dear friend but, as the president of the teachers association, she had a one-track mind. We'd always been on the same side of the bargaining table, but now things were different. I was an administrator, cleaning up a school that was in desperate need of help. Hopefully, we could remain friends in the process.

"The faculty is upset and some are ready to walk out," she began. "First, Bill was found dead in your office, and then you started making quite a few demanding changes." She went on to list the teachers' grievances.

"Patty, we've already been through this. Think of it this way. If Madison closes, how many teachers and students will be displaced?"

"All of them!" she declared, visibly upset.

"And how happy will they be?" I asked, observing her. "I have one year to turn this school around. One year. And I'm going to do whatever it takes to keep this school open. Let's face it: Change is always difficult and traumatic."

"Even at the best of times," she added, looking over her glasses, assessing my posture for any signs of weakness, which weren't forthcoming.

"That's true," I declared, meeting her gaze.

"So what are you planning?"

I sat still for a moment. "I plan to work in all of the classrooms and also help children at-risk develop their reading comprehension, vocabulary, and math skills."

"Are you nuts? When are you going to have time to attend all those infernal district meetings and do the mountains of paperwork necessary to document your job?"

"Well, I guess I'll have to work overtime. As for those meetings, I'll send a digital recorder so I won't miss a thing. Come on, Patty; you know how I feel about principals. They belong in classrooms working with kids, not just shuffling papers and ass-kissing the powers that be."

"That's part of the problem, Sam. Not everyone feels comfortable with you changing the status quo, especially with Bill's murder."

"I'm sorry about that, but that's our life for the next year. I expect the best from the teachers, the students, and the parents."

"You're taking on too much!" she lamented. "Besides, Paul won't give you the support you need to make this work."

"That may be true," I declared. "But, if everyone takes on their responsibility, the load will be manageable."

"On top of that, gossip has it that the board plans to close Madison before the end of the year," she affirmed with a scowl.

"The school may close, but it won't be without a fight."

"Even if the school doesn't close, rumors are flying that you're going to take advantage of the situation and ask for waivers above what we discussed in the past."

"Patty, I'll discuss each proposed waiver with you. If we can figure out a better solution, I won't ask for one. As far as the teachers are concerned, you can go a long way to reassure them. We taught together, remember? And, yes, I have high standards, but I like to have fun in the classroom, too," I reminded her.

"Well, you don't ask for much, do you?"

"Just what I can get away with," I declared, beginning to laugh. "Seriously, it would help if you support me. How about it?"

"Okay, Sam; count me in," yielded Patty quietly. "We need to meet every week to keep our lines of communication open. Now, I remember why I recommended you to be on the bargaining team as our spokesperson."

"Whatever do you mean?" I stated with a straight face.

"You know exactly what I mean. You and that Cheshire-cat grin of yours."

"So you think I'm tenacious," I retorted, smiling. The next thing I knew, we were both laughing, and it felt good. The tension seemed to melt away.

"Exactly," Patty chuckled. She met my eye with a mischievous expression as she changed the subject. "You know what we need?"

"What?"

"A body wrap."

"What's that?"

"They wrap you all over with mud. It's supposed to detoxify your body and help you relax." And then she asked the question that I had been thinking about ever since my conversation with Doc Simpson. "How are you really doing since . . .?"

"I'm fine. Really, I am. I'm living one moment at a time."

"Sam?"

"I've spent so much time mourning for what could have been and should have been but will never be," I said, playing with the locket.

"Sam?" she pressed, seeing my eyes water.

I focused directly at her as I thought about my baby girl. "What's that old cliché—'Live for the moment'? They should have added 'because that's all you have.' And that's what I'm trying to do."

Patty understood. "So, how about going for a body wrap?"

"That sounds great. If I survive my first week on the job, we'll go on Saturday," I suggested, laughing as I visualized the two of us coated with mud and wrapped in plastic for forty minutes . . . or at least that is what I remembered from watching the Travel Channel's visits to health spas.

"That works for me. I'll make the appointment for ten o'clock in the morning."

"Enough talk about me, Patty. How is the rest of the district holding up?"

"That's an interesting question. White Middle School is short on supplies, and there's no money left in its budget to buy anything."

"Are you kidding? How can White be out of money?"

"That's what the teachers want to know. Besides, most of the classes in the district are out of compliance with the consensus agreement. And, with Bill's death, the chain of command is almost nonexistent."

"Do you think that the district is up to its old games?"

"No, Sam, I don't. First, Jane wouldn't have yelled at Cindy in public. And, second, she and Bill worked together on the budget for most of the day on Friday."

"Oh." Steepling my fingertips, I tried to figure out how this puzzle fit together. "Was Lois able to talk Cindy into returning to work?"

"Samantha, no. Just remember that curiosity killed the cat."

"I know," I agreed seriously, wondering about Patty's new friend. "You've gotten pretty close to Jane these past few months."

"Yes, I have. Who would've ever thought that the president of the teachers association and the district's finance director would get to be friends? Jane did confide in me a while back that something was fishy with the budget."

"Like the numbers never really adding up during negotiation," I surmised, probing gently to find out what else she had told Patty.

"Right on. Remember, Bill asked Paul to work with Cindy to project the district's budgetary responsibilities for the next five years."

"Wasn't that before Jane was hired?"

"No, it was afterwards."

"Didn't the confusion start when Jane arrived?"

"I think that's the way Cindy and Paul planned it," she asserted angrily. "You know Paul was opposed to Jane's appointment."

"I didn't know that," I said, leaning back in the uncomfortable swivel chair. "Did Jane ever bring her budget concerns to Bill, or her suspicion that Paul and Cindy were setting her up?"

"I think she did after we signed off on the agreement."

"Do you know if Bill ever confronted Paul or Cindy?"

"No. But Bill did tell Jane that he needed proof before he could confront them. So she started going over the books but was constantly stymied by Cindy's mistakes and Paul's interference."

"That's strange," I stated softly, wondering who was really telling the truth. "Did Paul continue to monitor the budget?"

"Good question, and, yes, he did. Rumor has it that Paul and Cindy were having a real hot affair during negotiations. Then Cindy broke it off and Paul couldn't accept it."

"Does Paul's wife know?" I asked.

"I would assume so, because she just filed for divorce two weeks ago."

"Or, could the divorce petition be a result of a sexual harassment complaint against Paul, which was just filed in July?"

"That wasn't supposed to be public knowledge." she marveled, stunned that I'd heard about the ultra-secret complaint. "How did you hear about that?"

"It was easy. Right place; wrong time. I was waiting in the lobby to see Bill about this job when all hell suddenly broke loose. The doors opened, and there was Paul yelling at Bill, telling him that the complaint was bogus and that woman was just a troublemaker looking for a fast buck. Bill had heard enough and told him to clean up his act and get back to work."

"Interesting. Well, did you hear about the fight that Bill and Jane had on Friday over the budget?" Patty revealed, pouring herself another cup of hot java.

"I heard something about a disagreement," I volunteered, burning with curiosity to hear her version. "Tell me what happened."

"During the negotiations, Jane kept saying that they didn't have any money. Remember, she was working with Paul and Cindy's figures. Just recently, Cindy found an extra two million dollars in the district's bank account through some form of divine intervention. Bill was furious and felt that he had been played for a fool," Patty declared. "Just think of the raises and the smaller class sizes that we could have negotiated."

"What happened to the money?"

"That's the question everybody's asking and no one seems to know. It just disappeared, and I think that's the main reason why Bill and Jane were scrutinizing the budget," she revealed.

"Lois didn't mention a thing about this when I tried to pick up a copy of the budget. She apologized that the computers were down and implied Jane had taken the hard copy home."

"That's Lois for you—the ever-faithful district employee," Patty asserted in a sarcastic voice. She'd never been a fan of Lois since the older woman regarded the association as a nuisance.

"So what has Paul been up to?"

"Being a total jackass," she said, looking down at her dark red fingernails. "Paul Mendoza has been busy play-acting as the new superintendent."

"Gee, Patty, don't suppress your hostile feelings about him."

"I'll try not to."

"So just let it out, Patty," I said, watching her tense posture.

"I'm sorry to unload on you about Paul. But he has been such a prick and today of all days! He won't make any decisions; he won't talk to anyone; and he's been an absolute idiot from the word 'go!'"

"No wonder Blanche got the runaround this afternoon. I hate to say this, but I think he's in trouble."

"You think? I know!" she declared adamantly. "Sam, did you hear the latest rumor about the school board president, our dear righteous Mrs. Beaker?"

I shook my head.

Patty revealed, with a hint of pleasure ringing in her voice, "She's having an affair with Fred Monti."

"The county attorney?"

"The one and only."

"When did this come out?" I asked, skeptical of these facts.

"Three or four weeks ago. See what I mean, Sammy? You've been isolated for so long. It's time you came out and smelled the air, if not the flowers."

"Cute, Patty, cute. Why on earth would Ruth Beaker be seeing Fred Monti unless it has something to do with her son?"

"What's that kid's name?"

"DeMorgan Beaker."

"Wasn't he one of your pistols?"

"That's one way of putting it," I stated, then meeting her gaze. "Who is spreading this rumor around?"

"I can't say."

"Well, I saw RJ and Jane . . ." I began, hinting at whom I suspected as the culprit.

"So what?" she exclaimed angrily.

"They were embracing," I disclosed, watching her jaw drop.

"That means nothing," she huffed, biting her lower lip.

"No, but RJ did recommend her to the board," I said as she played with her glasses.

"When did you see them . . .?" she asked hesitantly, in a wary tone.

"The word is 'embracing.' I saw them at the airport as I was rushing to board my flight Friday afternoon."

"Embracing in the 'get a room' sense?" she asked, disgusted.

I nodded yes. "You got it."

"Is that why you suspect Jane?" she pressed, upset.

"Patty, she's a district employee and everyone who has had contact with Bill is a suspect," I acknowledged, "including you and me."

"Shit!" she exclaimed, furious. "You just added the cherry to top off my day."

"Patty, calm down . . . ."

"There's no way anyone is going to pin Bill's murder on you—or me, for that matter," she declared, placing her glasses back on top of her head.

"So why was Jane with RJ?"

"She's been helping him out with his bookkeeping since his dad's accountant quit several months ago," Patty reported, defending her chum.

"Why is she working for RJ?" I raised. "Does she need the money?"

"No, she just wanted to help a friend out. After all, RJ was instrumental in getting her the position," she huffed, feeling pressured to explain.

"So 'someone' starts spreading rumors about his wife having an affair with the county attorney; I don't think so, Patty. Come on; you're angry with Ruth Beaker for her stand on teachers' salaries and for pushing Paul's appointment through as the acting superintendent."

"Shit! You know me too damn well," she retorted as she began fidgeting with her French fry container. "Maybe you're right, Sam. She's not the type to be having an affair. Besides, several weeks ago, Ruth was in court testifying on DeMorgan's behalf. And after the hearing, she spoke to Fred Monti in the hallway of the court building."

"Oh," I murmured, observing my friend. Worry-lines appeared on Patty's face as she watched me gather the empty food wrappers from the top of the desk and toss them into the wastebasket. Leaning forward across the desk, I insisted, "Now, who told you about the affair?"

"Why do you need to know?"

"Because it might be important to what is going on here!" I asserted, exasperated.

"Ned Tomer swore me to secrecy when he told me three weeks ago," she said, dejected.

I saw her lower her head and knew that the guilt would eat at her for months.

"Do you think this has something to do with Bill's murder?" she inquired timidly.

"I don't know," I confided, thinking of my hospital visit with the intoxicated man. "Can you think of anything else that might explain why Bill was murdered?"

"Bill and his wife were having problems. Kind of makes you wonder."

"I'm not touching that with a ten-foot pole," I countered, leaning back in my chair. "Was anyone holding a grudge against him?"

"Norman Orson hated Bill," Patty stated, mopping her brow again.

"The former principal at Davis Middle School!" I snapped, recalling how angry Norman was when his assistant principal filed the sexual harassment allegation against him.

"Yes," Patty replied. "He blamed Bill for his ouster, especially since Bill had the same problem with a university intern two years ago. Gossip has it that Bill was seeing someone else."

"You're kidding!" I exclaimed, wondering if the Austins' marital problems had anything to do with his murder.

"No, I'm not. Bill was quite a ladies man and came on to anyone wearing a skirt."

"Not everyone. He never came on to me."

"You've never been interested in anyone other than your family. Besides, after Peter's death, that would've been political suicide, considering who your father-in-law is. And let's not forget to mention your relationship with Thomas Ryan."

"Getting back to Norman, did the grievance go to arbitration this summer?" I asked.

"It did," Patty answered, "and the judge ruled against him. Norman went ballistic and blamed Bill for his firing."

"Why?" I asked, puzzled. "Bill was only enforcing the arbitrator's decision."

"He felt that Bill didn't support him," Patty stated.

"So how bitter was he?"

"Very bitter," Patty revealed, taking two aspirin from her purse and choking them down with coffee. "He bad-mouthed Bill even after he heard about his death."

"That's not good."

"At the time, I thought Bill was using a double standard, since he wasn't fired for sexually harassing that intern," Patty asserted. "I still think that he should've given Norman a second chance, especially since the board gave him one."

"Are you saying Bill should have been fired for his inappropriate conduct?"

"Yes. But, on second thought, I don't think so, because that would have meant Paul Mendoza would be the superintendent, instead of just the acting one."

"Why would Paul have been appointed to the job then?" I asked, confused.

"Because he has most of the school board in his pocket," she declared with a knowing look as she met my gaze. "He can be very charming when he wants to be."

"Okay, I see that," I considered, recalling how Paul could mesmerize a crowd but could also be a real jerk. "But what exactly did Norman do after Bill fired him?"

"Norman spread stories about Bill gambling again."

"Any truth to the stories?" I asked.

"Some. Bill's wife was constantly calling the office to check on him. I heard that he was going to file bankruptcy because he'd dropped a bundle at the table."

Shaking my head in disbelief, I inquired, "Where would he go?"

"I imagine to the Indian casinos."

"Any proof?"

"None that I know of personally," she confided, leaning forward. "But he was seen at the Durango Casino on Wednesday evening."

"By whom?"

"Jane, for one, and I think others as well."

"That's really strange," I stated, changing gears as I rubbed my head. "Why would a man who lectured on the ills of gambling start up again?"

"Your guess is as good as mine. Bill probably had a relapse—maybe pressure-induced."

"Do you think it had to do with the budget problems?" I asked.

"Maybe, but here, again, that's pure speculation," she purported.

"Seriously, going back to Norman—do you think he was angry enough to kill Bill?"

"No, he's all talk and no action. That's why his assistant principal filed the harassment claim against him. She wanted to marry the bum and, when he didn't ask, she threatened to destroy him and the rest is history."

"I would think that Norman would want to kill her!"

"Maybe, but I think they have this love-hate relationship."

"Is there anyone else who was upset with Bill?"

"Sam, I can't think of anyone. Bill was pretty even-handed on most issues. Now, if they find Paul Mendoza's body, I will be the Number One suspect. He is such a prick."

Feigning surprise, I chided, "I've never heard you speak that way."

Patty groaned. "I can't even talk about him. He's always made my life miserable."

"Now, are you saying that because you find him alluring?" I hinted teasingly.

"No!" protested Patty, but her eyes sparkled. "When I worked for him at Cotton Middle School, he was such a condescending asshole!"

"Have you given this poor man a complex?" I pressed, wondering if she really did have feelings for this man.

"Are you kidding? He is an absolute jerk!" exclaimed Patty, spewing so much venom that it was almost comical. "He's a wannabe human!"

A teacher knocked on the open door. "Patty, we need to talk with you before the meeting tonight."

"Hey, that sounds great. Why don't we go to Fernando's for nachos?" Patty asserted.

"Works for me; I'll tell the others in the lounge," said the teacher.

"See what I mean? There's no rest for the weary!"

"Patty, thanks for your support."

"Don't mention it. I'll see what I can do, but I can't make you any promises."

"I know," I said, as she left.

Where were all these rumors coming from? Mrs. Austin? Jane Fuller? Ned Tomer? Fred Monti? Lois Cameron or her daughter, Cindy? RJ Beaker? Norman Orson? But, why? Did the rumors have any grains of truth to them? If so, what were they? Somehow, there had to be a connection.

Why was Bill's wife so insistent that I had an affair with him? Did Bill really have a zipper problem? Who had he been seeing? Was it the university intern? Had he started gambling again? I didn't think so, but maybe I was wrong.

Where had I been, for the past three years, that all of this had eluded me? Glancing at my baby's picture on my desk, I knew the answer.

Tuesday: 5:35 P.M. at Madison in My Office

Sitting behind the desk, I realized how angry I was about Bill's murder. Nothing seemed right and, what was worse, I now had the beginnings of a throbbing migraine. As I turned on the local news station, I saw an ambitious reporter standing in front of Bill's house. She shoved a microphone into his daughter's face.

"How do you feel about your father's murder?" the perky blonde asked. Then she panned to the camera, her crimson-shellacked smile filling the screen.

This was just too much! My blood pressure soared with each heartbeat, leaving my head feeling like it was about to explode. "How do you think she feels, you fool?!"

I had little respect for the press. After Peter's death, I had been a victim of a few seedy reporters. They hid behind the "public's right to know," spreading their version of the facts, regardless of whom they hurt in the process. I wondered how the reporter would feel if she was ever under the horrific spotlight. Would she appreciate the media's intrusion?

Turning off the television, I reached into my purse for a bottle of aspirin but, instead, found my serenity coin. It was funny. Whenever I felt emotionally drained, the coin seemed to appear out of nowhere. But, in reality, I never went anywhere without it.

God, grant me the serenity to accept the things I cannot change,
The courage to change the things I can,
And the wisdom to know the difference.

After reading the inscription, I placed it back into my handbag. My parents had given me the coin on my tenth birthday. It had become my connection to God and to them. Over the years, I held onto it during the best of times and the worst of times.

I went back to work and simplified my outline. I wanted to be concise, as well as prepared for tonight's drama. Twenty minutes later, my headache had faded to a dull throb. Putting my notes aside, I caught a glimpse of my reflection in mirror. I looked awful. My face was devoid of color, except for the mascara that had smeared.

Picking up the clothing bag that Marge had dropped off, I went to the bathroom to revitalize my appearance. I slipped into a pair of sheer hose, black pumps, and a soft, charcoal-colored knit sheath. After fixing my makeup and hair, I centered the locket over my dress.

The clock read 6:20 when I entered the cafeteria to set up the refreshments. I hadn't asked anyone to help because I needed some downtime alone. The empty room was quiet as I made fresh coffee, set out deli trays, and arranged condiments, plates, silverware, and cups on a long table in the back of the room. By the time I finished, parents and community members began arriving for the meeting.

I greeted more than 350 guests and took note of the parents' anxiety as Dr. Mendoza and the board members clustered together in the front of the room, ignoring everyone else. Mrs. Austin's presence added a sobering effect as she sat by them. Teachers huddled in the back with an uneasy air. No one smiled.

At seven, I walked to the podium at the front of the room. The school's fate rested on my performance this evening. I scanned the troubled audience as I silently said the Serenity Prayer. Then I introduced the school board members and Dr. Mendoza.

"Welcome, ladies and gentlemen, to Madison Elementary School. I want to thank you for coming, and I also want to express our deepest sympathy to Mrs. Austin who is here with us tonight. Dr. Austin was a man of integrity who believed in quality education for all children. His wisdom and guidance will truly be missed."

Stopping for a moment, I chose my words carefully, "Dr. Austin's death and the subsequent break-in have created an atmosphere of fear. The Sheriff's Department is investigating the circumstances of his death and the break-in. If you have any information, please speak to the sheriff or one of his deputies," I said, watching their collective trepidation.

"And now to the subject of Madison Elementary School. It is my sincere desire that Madison becomes the model school for this district. In order to accomplish this goal, we will need to work together.

"Education begins at home. It continues in the schools and is reinforced in the community. The fate of Madison is in your hands tonight, ladies and gentlemen," I stated directly. "I will briefly outline everyone's concerns.

"The school board wants to close Madison for two main reasons. They feel that the children would receive a better education at another school and that the money would be better allocated elsewhere."

The crowd gasped. Some were whispering furiously to their neighbors while others stared at the board.

"But, after a lengthy discussion this morning, the board agreed to keep Madison open for the time being." I paused, letting the audience assimilate the information.

"The teachers are worried about the changes that I have mandated in their classrooms this year. I have asked them to modify their teaching styles and have informed them that I will be working with them in their classrooms."

The parents nodded in approval as the teachers glared at me. The board members smiled, delighted to see dissension in the room.

"Parents have the hardest job of all—they raise their children. In order to do a good job, they need to become involved in their children's education. Dads and moms need to work with their children at home and alongside their children's teachers."

Everyone nodded in agreement to some extent.

"Failure is not an option. We need to set the example for our children."

The parents and teachers applauded.

"Students will have new learning standards. I firmly believe that learning can be fun, but it takes commitment . . . a can-do spirit, a willingness to accept responsibility for one's own learning, and the ability to cooperate with others. In other words, it's hard work."

The tension in the room had mounted as parents, community leaders, teachers, and the board sat on the edge of their seats. Dr. Mendoza leaned forward, glaring at me.

The defining moment had arrived. "Ladies and gentlemen, should Madison Elementary School remain open?"

The crowd gasped. Quietly, I asked for a show of hands. Parents and teachers raised their hands as a vote of confidence.

"The decision to keep Madison open belongs to the board," I said, turning to face them. The governing board looked grim. Dr. Mendoza was fuming.

"How can we keep the school open?" asked a fourth-grader's mother.

"That's a great question," I said, smiling at the audience. "We'll begin by working together in small groups to define the problems at Madison and then the solutions. When you entered this evening, Blanche placed a colored dot on your name tag. The colored dots represent your group. The different-colored banners designate each group's location.

"We'll take a five-minute break so you can find your banner. Once you place your chairs in a circle, please get some refreshments."

I watched the attendees find their site and introduce themselves to their fellow group members. After scanning the room, I met Paul Mendoza's stern look. He was beyond seething. If looks could kill, I would be dead.

I avoided his glare and thanked Blanche. She had done an excellent job of mixing the groups. Each group was composed of parents, teachers, school board members, community leaders, and my former students.

When everyone was seated, I began my pitch. "Ladies and gentlemen, let's be honest. Madison has some problems that need to be addressed. What I would like you to do right now is to think of all the problems that exist here."

Mario raised his hand as Blanche began passing out paper to each group.

"Yes, Mario."

"Isn't this how we used to do reading?"

"Yes. My former students are experts in the brainstorming process. Each group will select someone to write down your ideas. You will have fifteen minutes to list the problems. If you have a question, raise your hand and I'll come to you. Otherwise, I'll walk around the room. You may begin."

Slowly, they began working together. As I walked around to each group, I was pleased that everyone was contributing ideas, with the notable exceptions of Ruth Beaker and Paul Mendoza.

Jack and Thomas were standing at the back of the room, watching everyone and no one in particular. Walking over to them, I told them about the list of names attached to the school's student activity file.

Fifteen minutes later, I announced loudly, "Time to stop."

Everyone looked up, surprised at how quickly time had passed.

"I want to compile your ideas so we can work together to solve the problems," I explained.

"Sam, would you like me to record the suggestions?" Blanche volunteered, suddenly beside me.

"Yes, that would be great," I stated, which left me free to interact with the audience. I handed her the black marker.

Mario started and everyone else just chimed in.

Blanche wrote:

> Violence
>
> Gangs
>
> Homework / lack thereof / no support from parents

Building run down / not clean

No equipment / balls, books, computers

Lack of music programs

Lack of cultural awareness classes

Drugs

Acting out TV violence

Lack of in-service time

Playground supervision

Boring lessons

Length of the school year / school day

Bilingual classes? ESL classes

Drop-outs hanging around the school

Parents unable to help with homework

Attitudes

Self-esteem

Education not valued

Tardiness

Absences

Low test scores

Kids below grade level

Discipline

"This is a great start," I acknowledged, smiling when everyone had his or her say. "Now, I need you to brainstorm solutions to the problems we have just listed. You will have twenty minutes. You may begin."

Again, at the end of the time period, we compiled a list of suggestions:

Discipline policy

Parental support

Conflict resolution – pride/respect

Year-round school

Parental classes

GED classes

After-school programs

Smaller classes

Volunteers

Redefine our mission statement

When we had finished listing the solutions, Paul Mendoza stood up and introduced himself to the crowd again. "Ms. Samuels, this has been very educational but, as you well know, the funding for the school year is set. And this is not to mention that there are major safety and liability issues here."

"Thank you for stating the facts so succinctly, Dr. Mendoza," Mrs. Beaker agreed tersely. As she walked to the podium in a showy amber dress, she seemed to almost glow. She was the image of affluence and she knew it. "The district simply does not have the funds available to finance such extravagant programs, no matter how many volunteers you can recruit, Mrs. Samuels."

"Mrs. Beaker, the only way the children in this community will flourish is if we allow everyone to do what they can. By keeping Madison open, we give the children control over their future," I stated, playing to my audience. "As to extending the school year, it can be phased in over time."

"That is all well and good, Mrs. Samuels, but the district has responsibilities beyond this school, and the resources are limited. We cannot allow sentimentality to rule," she retorted.

"I realize that the district is financially strapped. What I am asking for is the opportunity to accomplish Dr. Austin's goals for this school without additional expense to the district. It is my understanding that Madison has been funded for this school year."

"It has, but not for a year-round program. How are you planning to pay the teachers and the support staff, let alone furnish the supplies and the liability insurance necessary to carry out some of your outlandish solutions?" Mrs. Beaker challenged boorishly. "You certainly can't expect people to work for free. They're not as fortunate as you are."

"I know. And, for the record, I work for my living, Mrs. Beaker . . . unlike you."

A hushed gasp swept across the room.

"Ms. Samuels, that was uncalled for," Dr. Mendoza declared in a condescending tone. "You are too young and inexperienced for the position you find yourself in tonight." He stopped for an instant, glancing back at Ruth Beaker, before going on. "Maybe the board should reconsider closing the school and busing the students elsewhere. We are not the cold-hearted public servants that you make us out to be. The transfer to other schools could take place in January, allowing you and your staff time to help in the transition process."

"Dr. Mendoza, my age is not the issue here," I corrected, watching Thomas walk over to his mum, who was seated in the back of the cafeteria. He knew I was furious but that I would never surrender the cause.

"It certainly is," Dr. Mendoza declared.

"The issue is the board's commitment to quality education for all children in this district," I asserted. "If the board is now taking a different position from this morning, I'm here to tell you that is deplorable!"

Parents and teachers applauded, finding themselves on common ground. It was the first time they'd seen anyone stand up to a school superintendent and the board.

"Ms. Samuels, we are aware of the loss you suffered this summer. I believe your grief is clouding your judgment," Dr. Mendoza asserted, interrupting the applause.

"Try as you may to exploit my personal life, Dr. Mendoza, the issue on the table is quality education for these children. The funding is in place to keep this school open, and I expect the board to honor its commitments."

The audience was growing more agitated by the second. They started shouting out, "That's right!" A moment later, I requested for them to quiet down so individuals could speak on the subject.

"Mrs. Beaker, members of the board, and Dr. Mendoza," Henry addressed as he rose to his feet in a dark suit. "The M. E. Samuels Foundation is prepared to fund a pilot program for a year-round school, which would include an after-school program. The funding would be based on the process that we started tonight with Mrs. Samuels. We are also prepared to help drop-outs."

"How, Mr. Samuels?" Mrs. Beaker demanded. Her lips pressed together.

"The students would receive a stipend for attending GED classes and volunteering in the after-school program, or working in the community. We are . . . ."

"Mr. Samuels," Dr. Mendoza interrupted, trying to recapture control of the meeting.

"Furthermore," Henry went on, ignoring the blustering man at the podium, "if Madison's kids need help, tutors will be provided."

"That is correct, Dr. Mendoza," Mrs. Ryan voiced in her English accent as she stood at the back of the room. She was an activist at heart, especially where children were concerned. Normally, she was shy in public, but tonight she was livid. The tall, elegant woman glared at the newly appointed acting superintendent. "My husband and I have a core of volunteers ready to help the children in this community."

The audience seemed pleased with Henry's and Mrs. Ryan's suggestions.

"Mr. Samuels and Mrs. Ryan, I want to thank you for your generous offers. But what you are proposing requires time, which we simply do not have," Dr. Mendoza stated in a patronizing manner, meeting their fierce looks.

Upset, the crowd grumbled as they glared at the superintendent.

I smiled inwardly when I saw my mother-in-law's stern look. She was prepared to do battle with the district officials and would bring them to their knees. Slowly, the petite, sixty-three-year-old woman with short, dark, red hair stood up next to her husband. Marge was furious, but smiled pleasantly as she met the board's anxious eyes.

Everyone took note of her presence.

She spoke in a clear, firm voice as she addressed not only the president of the school board but also the members of the community. "Mrs. Beaker, one of the many things I have learned during my tenure in the state legislature and on various governors' task forces is that if there is a will, there is a way."

Marge Samuels knew she had taken charge as the audience fixated on the diminutive woman in a dark suit. "I am sure that this can be worked out to everyone's satisfaction," she declared, using her courtroom voice. She paused a moment and met each board member's gaze.

"The foundation lawyers are prepared to meet with the board and your counsel to work out any legal problems. I have spoken with the governor and members of the legislature and they have pledged their support for the pilot-program that Mrs. Samuels has proposed."

Ruth Beaker stood there scowling at Marge. "Is the foundation prepared to pay the teachers their per diem to make up the difference between the standard and a year-round school contract?"

"I believe that an agreement with the foundation, the teachers association, and the board can be worked out by Friday afternoon," Marge proposed, pressing the issue.

"Mrs. Samuels . . . ." Ruth Beaker hesitated as she faced the stiff opposition from the audience. Somehow, she and her golden outfit had dimmed in the presence of Marge Samuels. "We are unable . . . ."

At first, one school board member and then all of the others walked over to her. They huddled on the platform, whispering. Ruth Beaker and Paul Mendoza exchanged infuriated looks as they listened to the other board members.

The audience sat still, watching this high-stakes drama unfold. I stepped away from the podium while we waited for the outcome.

Finally, Ruth Beaker faced the crowd. "The board will accept the Samuels' gracious offer. Dr. Mendoza and the district's counsel will meet with your attorneys in the morning, Mrs. Samuels. That is, if that is acceptable to you."

Glancing at me, Marge smiled and then established her set of ground rules. "That will be fine as long as Samantha Samuels is involved in the discussion and the final outcome."

"Agreed," Ruth Beaker finally uttered, glowering at me.

I replied with a smile. Before the tension could spike one degree higher, I thanked everyone for coming. Then I asked, "Does anyone have any announcements to make?"

Several individuals formed a line at the mic and took turns making their statements.

To my surprise, the PTA president suggested that we should continue this dialog. The group agreed and decided to meet again next week. Henry informed everyone that staff from the foundation would arrive at Madison at eight in the morning. They would start taking applications for part-time jobs and scholarships immediately. This offer would be open to both drop-outs and adults. Mrs. Ryan continued by addressing the teachers. She would meet with them in the morning to set up a schedule for cross-generational tutoring and also would have volunteers here to help. Dr. Machado offered to organize a health screening but needed community volunteers. Patty Steward announced that she wanted to meet with the teachers in the lounge.

Taking the mic again, I spoke from the heart. "I want to thank you again for all of your help. I know we can make a difference here." I stopped for a second, observing a sea of mostly satisfied expressions, except for the board's glum appearance. "This meeting is adjourned."

The energy in the room was unbelievable as parents and teachers started mingling.

After leaving the podium, I went to the kitchen with the head of the cafeteria staff. She began to explain the procedure for the Health Department's annual inspection slated for the morning.

Suddenly, someone tapped me on the shoulder. To my surprise, it was Paul Mendoza.

The head of the cafeteria took one look at the angry superintendent and quickly assured me that everything was fine and left the kitchen.

I was left alone with Dr. Mendoza. As I started to leave, he grabbed my upper arm with such force that I thought he was going to break it. With my teeth clenched, I demanded, "Let go of my arm!"

He released his grip immediately, leaving finger marks. "I want to talk to you, Ms. Samuels," Paul hissed in a belligerent voice. "You were insubordinate this evening!"

"How?"

"You set the board up," he stormed, pulling himself up to his full height.

"Where are you going with this, Paul?"

"Let me make this perfectly clear. Just because you are associated with the Samuels family doesn't mean you can manipulate me or the school board."

"I see."

"You'll have to live within your budget, or maybe even a little under because of your frivolous programs. Madison is falling apart because of Bill's inability to manage the district," he spewed in a denigrating tone.

"Are you saying that you are not going to follow the board's directive to cooperate with the Samuels Foundation?"

"Don't try this mumbo-jumbo on me! I'm not Bill!" he snapped.

"That's for damn sure, Paul. And I expect Madison to receive the amount of money that has already been allocated," I countered firmly.

"You'll get whatever you have coming to you but nothing more!"

"Thank you."

"Don't forget; you serve at my pleasure and that of the board."

"And you serve at the pleasure of the citizens of this district. One more thing, Paul," I disclosed evenly. "Don't ever threaten me again!"

"I'm not threatening you. I'm just clarifying your position as an employee of this district. There are a lot of other schools that deserve the board's attention and funding. Madison is a dump and should've been closed years ago. Your incompetent staff is the worst in the system," he asserted aggressively. "They're nothing but the scrapings from the bottom of a tainted barrel."

"Wait a minute, Paul! The teachers here are dedicated professionals who have been shafted by you."

"What do you mean?" he bellowed.

"As the assistant superintendent for this region, you failed to support them."

"They all should have been fired years ago!" he charged furiously.

"You're way off base, Paul. They've done their jobs brilliantly! They are good teachers who care about the kids in this community!"

"Really!" he huffed angrily. "The only reason the school is still open is because of your connections to the Samuels and the Ryans."

"Well, thank goodness for that!" I voiced louder than intended, thinking what a bastard he was. "The truth is that money should not matter in doing the right thing. You and the board should be ashamed for not valuing these kids and Madison's staff."

His angry eyes widened for a split-second before he sneered, "You're out of your league, Sam. I can't imagine why Bill ever considered you for a principal's position. He must have been going senile."

"I am sorry you feel that way because you're wrong. Bill was an honorable man who believed in public education."

"Your appointment was a joke and you're too stupid to know it!" he mocked. "You're nothing but an inexperienced, glossy-eyed idiot who doesn't even have the qualifications to be a principal."

"You're right," I acknowledged, stunned at how much Paul's aggressive behavior reminded me of Peter. "I'm inexperienced, but I'm a quick study."

"Spare me your inadequate platitudes."

"I get it, Paul. You're afraid I'll succeed and that terrifies you."

At that moment, Mrs. Ryan knocked on the door. "Sam, I don't mean to interrupt, but I wanted to thank you for the note you sent the judge. It had him in stitches."

"You're very welcome," I said, turning my attention to Thomas' mum as she entered the kitchen. Annie Ryan stood in front of me, smiling. Tonight, her gray-green eyes, which usually sparkled with joy, were dark. Apparently, she'd overheard my exchange with Dr. Mendoza and was incensed with his rudeness. There was no mistaking her animosity toward him.

"The meeting was very informative," she stated warmly. But her icy gaze was still fixed on Paul, watching him squirm as he started fidgeting with his car keys.

"Thank you," I said sincerely, ignoring the prickly man standing next to me while I met her gaze. "How's the judge doing?"

"He is doing much, much better, Sam; thank you for asking. The doctors are implanting a pacemaker Thursday afternoon."

"Thomas didn't mention that," I murmured, stunned at this turn of events.

"That's what the surgeon recommended late this afternoon."

"Oh," I uttered. She and the judge had welcomed me into their lives and had treated Maxie as their granddaughter. And now I would be there for them.

"He's going to be fine," she promised, seeing my coloring diminish. "They think this will solve his problem, Sam."

Paul coughed, interrupting our discussion as we both turned, glowering at him.

"Thomas is taking me back to the hospital and said that he'll see you there."

"Thank you for your help and support, Mrs. Ryan," I acknowledged, smiling. "Give my love to the judge."

"Good night, Sam. Dr. Mendoza," she asserted, giving him a stern look and then leaving.

"Sam, remember my warning!" blustered the incensed acting superintendent. He stormed out the door, shoving an unsuspecting Mrs. Austin out of his way.

"Are you okay?" I asked Mrs. Austin, feeling responsible for his actions. Paul was such a jackass!

"I'm fine," she said, shaking a bit.

She and I spoke for a few minutes and then she left. I hoped she had not heard much of our argument. But from the look in her eyes, I could tell that she had.

As I double-checked everything in the kitchen, I was still stunned at how much Paul Mendoza's confrontational temperament reminded me of Peter. And then I thought about Jack's remark about the wedding ring. It was time to let go of the past. Outside of Maxie, my marriage to Peter had been a sham and I had become tired of pretending it wasn't. So, without a second thought, I took off his ring and tossed it into the trash can as I reentered the cafeteria. I instantly felt lighter. Then I thought that maybe I should follow Doc's sage advice.

"Sam!" Patty shouted, walking toward me.

"Yes, Patty." I quickly scanned the room to make sure everything was in order for the morning. Thankfully, it was.

"What in the world happened in the kitchen?" she asked.

"Not much. Why?"

"Well, Gina Spinelli was standing in the doorway waiting to speak with you. The next thing I knew, she was back in the group ranting about Paul being a total bastard. And that we needed to support you."

"You're kidding."

"No, I'm not. Just think, this morning she was your strongest critic. Now, she's your staunchest supporter. As for the others, they were impressed with your performance tonight."

"Interesting. Why do you think they changed their minds?" I asked.

"I think that they're beginning to realize the situation is not what they originally thought. Gina told them that you stood up for them when Paul made disparaging remarks."

"True enough. But Patty, please caution them that this is not over. We may have won the first battle tonight but the war rages on. And I'm sure that my sudden popularity will be in the toilet before this is over. Weird, isn't it?"

"Sure is, but don't knock it."

"Believe me, I'm not. I'm just trying not to let it go to my head," I teased, grinning.

"Sam, I spoke with Henry and Marge about my concerns with the potential agreement between the district and the Samuels

Foundation. Afterwards, he introduced me to the foundation lawyers and we're planning to meet at eight-thirty tomorrow morning."

"Great!" I exclaimed, relieved that the work had started. "They will follow Henry's instructions to the letter, or else they will have to deal with Marge. If there is a problem, don't hesitate to call them."

"Believe me, I won't," Patty assured, taking off her red glasses and placing them in her bag. "I never realized how persuasive Marge could be."

"She is amazing in court," I commented, proud of my mother-in-law's acumen. "I took Maxie to watch her in a trial. And we were both mesmerized by her knowledge and demeanor."

"After tonight, I'm glad she's on our side. But I still can't get over Gina," Patty expressed gleefully, still astonished at the older woman's change of heart. "When I informed the group about tomorrow's meeting, she was still fuming. She told everyone that she didn't care what they get paid as long as we can ram our success up Paul's ass."

"Wow! She's really angry at him."

"That she is and, by the way, she likes Annie Ryan," Patty revealed.

"Really!" I exclaimed.

"Apparently, she saw Mrs. Ryan make Paul squirm and, in her book, that makes her okay."

"So does that mean she's going to let volunteers in her classroom?" I hoped.

"Probably," Patty surmised, pleased with how the evening had turned out. "Anyway, it's time to get outta here, Sammy. Do you want to join us for a drink at Rosita's?"

"I'd love to, Patty, but I can't. I'm meeting Thomas at the hospital," I said, seeing her disappointment. "Can I take a rain check?"

"Anytime, Sammy," she teased. "Everyone is waiting for an update and they're probably there by now, so I'd better get going."

"Patty, thanks again for everything. I can't tell you how much I appreciate your support."

"You're welcome. Sam, one more thing: Be careful," Patty advised as we walked out of the cafeteria. "Being a Samuels can only take you so far, and it would be a big mistake to underestimate Paul. Remember, he's backed into a corner now and will come out swinging."

"I will, and thanks again."

After she left, I ran into a sober Ned Tomer, who was systematically locking up the building with the custodians. "Mrs. Samuels, a deputy is waiting for you at the front hallway."

"Thank you." I quickly made my way to the foyer.

"Mrs. Samuels, the sheriff said you had something for him."

I handed the deputy the large envelope and he left. Ten minutes later, I walked out of Madison.

Tuesday: 9:35 P.M. at Madison

Entering the dimly lit parking lot, I saw Ned Tomer's and the custodians' cars parked next to my Jeep. There were no other vehicles in the parking lot, but then I spotted a car idling by the back fence.

The driver flashed blinding headlights directly at me as he revved his engine. Slowly, he drove his vehicle over the gravel, keeping me in view, and then stopped.

I heard him rev the engine again. The hair on the back of my neck stood on end. Hastening my pace, I climbed into the Jeep and locked the doors. My heart pounded as I left the school grounds, thinking about Patty's warning to be careful.

Who was in that car? I knew I had pissed off Paul Mendoza. He was an ass at times but he wouldn't harm me, at least not physically. Who else had I pissed off—the board, or was it someone else? I needed to stop being so paranoid and just concentrate on driving to the hospital.

As I turned onto Mission Road, the car followed me out of the parking lot. Two blocks later, the driver was still behind me but keeping his distance. Now that made me nervous.

Taking a fleeting glance in the rearview mirror, I saw the car abruptly turn off onto a side street just as I passed an idling pickup truck on the side of the road. The truck driver turned on his headlights and merged into the flow of traffic.

My cell rang, startling me as I glanced at the screen. It was Thomas calling. Relieved, I thumbed the speaker button. "Hello," I greeted warmly.

"I'm so proud of you, Sam. You did a great job tonight!" he exclaimed.

"Thank you, honey. How's your dad?"

"He's fine," Thomas said with laughter in his voice. "But Mum is beyond livid at Paul Mendoza."

"I know she made him squirm." I smiled, visualizing Paul fidgeting with his keys.

Thomas went on to tell me about his day in court.

When I looked in the mirror again, the pickup suddenly changed lanes as I drove up the ramp to enter the freeway. Now that wasn't good at all. "How is your mum getting home?"

"Marge and Henry are taking her home as we speak," Thomas said.

Once the pickup was on the freeway, the driver advanced at an alarming speed.

"So, Sam, do you have any suggestions for dinner?"

Thomas seemed so calm, but my heart was racing. I could hear his voice but couldn't comprehend a word. I swallowed involuntarily as a cold shiver passed through my body, leaving nothing but goose bumps behind. I accelerated to seventy-five miles per hour and merged into the fast lane, trying to get away from the pickup.

At that precise moment, a semi pulled in between us, blocking his view. The pickup driver swerved erratically into the middle lane in order to keep me in sight.

Frightened, I gripped the steering wheel with enough force to turn my knuckles white. I had already accelerated way over the speed limit but the semi kept inching up to my bumper, pressing me to move faster than I wanted to go. With no exits nearby and traffic sparse, I was now traveling at eighty-five miles per hour.

"Sam, what's wrong?" Thomas asked when I didn't respond.

"Someone is following me," I said, trying to keep the fear out of my voice. Nervously, I glanced in the rearview mirror again. The truck, still in the middle lane, kept its distance.

"Why do you think that?" he asked, measuring his words carefully.

"A car beamed its headlights directly at me when I came out of Madison, and the driver followed me out of the parking lot. But then, when I passed a pickup idling on Mission Road, the car veered off onto a side street . . . ."

"Were the lights off when you passed the truck?" he asked calmly, cutting me off.

"Yes, but they're on now."

"Where is the truck now?"

"He is in the middle lane . . ." I observed anxiously, glancing in the mirror again. "He's about four car lengths behind me."

"Sam, can you tell what kind of truck it is?" he inquired, alarmed.

"It's a dark Chevy pickup. I'm sorry, Thomas, that's all I can tell you."

"Hold on; I'm calling Jack."

It seemed like hours before he came back on the line but, in reality, it was only a matter of a few seconds.

"Sam, Jack is on his way. Which lane are you in?"

"I'm in the fast lane."

"Move over into the slow lane and get your speed down to sixty-five," he ordered, knowing I had a lead foot.

"Okay, I'm moving over," I gulped, noticing that the semi was now pulling away.

"Are there any other cars around?" he asked, picking up on my fear.

"No, Thomas . . ." I admitted, moving into the slow lane. Suddenly, something pinged loudly off the Jeep's rear bumper. I was now officially terrified.

"Sam! What was that sound?"

"I think someone just took a shot at the Jeep!" I exclaimed, breaking out into a cold sweat and yet, somehow, feeling strangely calm.

"Where's the truck now?" he pressed.

"It's pulling up next to me right now."

"Okay, Sam, let him pass you," Thomas said calmly, trying to keep me focused.

I slowed down and caught a glimpse of the truck's passenger aiming a gun directly at me. Terrified, my heart was beating erratically. As I clutched the steering wheel, I held onto it for dear life, thinking mine was about to come to a sudden end. I went into survival mode by hitting the brakes and ducking down as I covered my head with my hands. I stopped breathing, petrified for what was coming next. In that instant, the bastard fired.

Rounds pierced the front windshield but, for the most part, it remained intact.

Over the cell phone, Thomas heard the shots popping. He yelled frantically, "Sam!"

The driver nudged the front end of the Jeep with his bumper. The Jeep shuddered as I bit my lip praying.

Hearing the truck speed away, I sat up to take control but it was too late. The Jeep veered off to the right and, suddenly, I heard the awful sound of metal warping while the seatbelt held me in place. As the Jeep hit a concrete barrier and came to an abrupt stop, the airbag exploded in my face.

"Sam!" Thomas shouted desperately. He'd heard the sudden impact and then nothing but silence. "Sam, are you okay?! Sam!" Then he heard sirens in the distance. "Sam! Please answer me! Sam!"

Pinned back into my seat, I couldn't move and my heart was pounding. There was smoke everywhere and I couldn't breathe. I was terrified that I would be incinerated just like Peter. Oh God, please help me! "Thomas. . ." I moaned. Then I lapsed into a state of total darkness.

"Sam, answer me! Are you okay?!" Thomas yelled frantically again. "Sam! Please answer me!"

Tuesday: 10:20 P.M. at University Hospital

Ben Machado had seen me as soon as I entered the emergency room. Now, resting in a hospital bed, I was shivering. The room temperature read sixty-eight degrees, but it felt much colder. A male nurse entered and took my vitals for the third time in the last fifteen minutes.

When I saw his worried expression, I looked over at the screen. My blood pressure was elevated from the last reading. I knew then that this could explain my throbbing headache. Slowly, I returned my gaze to the white curtains that separated the treatment cubicles.

The room did little to create a sense of privacy and left me feeling exposed. I overheard Ben rattling off a series of tests he wanted run stat in the next cubicle. His tone indicated that this accident victim had sustained extensive injuries. Then I heard someone moving the patient down the hallway. I hoped that he would be all right.

Thomas pulled the curtain aside and entered the cramped cubicle. His face looked pale as he stood silently at the foot of my bed, holding a steamy cup of coffee. He took a sip and then stared intently at the evidence bag that contained my blood-stained clothes.

The nurse finished the assessment and left.

We heard a monitor's alarm dinging, and Thomas ran a hand through his dark curls, leaving a strand over his brow. His eyes narrowed as he watched the changing numbers until my vital signs returned to the normal range.

Anxiously, I reached for the locket, but it was gone. "Where's my locket?"

"I have it, Sam," he stated, watching me closely. He glanced at my hand and noticed that the wedding ring was gone but made no comment.

"I'm okay, Thomas. Really! I just bumped my head," I insisted, sitting up to prove my point. The throbbing came back immediately with a vengeance. I grimaced helplessly as the monitors began dinging again.

The crow's feet flanking his eyes deepened, watching the monitors record the changes in my condition. He took my hand as we waited for numbers to stabilize. Once they did, he placed the cup on the stand next to the bed. "I spoke with Ben. He says you're going to live."

"Thank goodness!" I laughed, trying to be humorous—more for his benefit than mine. "I can't believe this evening . . . it certainly has been eventful."

Letting go of his hand, I ran both hands through my hair, searching desperately for pressure points to alleviate the throbbing pain. Tears oozed down my face as I clutched my head, unable to maintain my composure.

He handed me a tissue and looked away. Taking time to wipe my tears and runny nose, I laid back down. Crying had never been easy for me; it was private. I felt angry—not depressed or defeated—but the tears kept on coming. There was nothing I could do about it.

"Do you think I have a concussion?" I sniffled, my voice creaking with anguish. I felt so powerless seeing Thomas' worried expression.

"A slight one to be sure," he answered simply. "And, before you ask, you can't have anything for it."

Having learned a painful lesson the last time, I sat up slowly. "Figures," I said, feeling the tension radiating throughout my body. My shoulders were tightly drawn upwards, almost touching my earlobes. It felt as if the pain was protecting me from some unknown horror. I added, "It's typical of the week I'm having."

Thomas moved behind me and started gently massaging my shoulders, trying to relax the tense muscles. Thankfully, his fingers worked their magic. My blood pressure dropped slightly and the tears had slowly subsided.

"So, kiddo, what happened?"

"Well, I had nothing better to do than run off the road," I snapped.

"Testy, aren't we?" he quipped.

I gave him a look and then smiled as his lips brushed the top of my head. Thomas always remained professional, even under stress. I'd come to believe that this was his coping mechanism.

"Seriously, we need to know what you remember," he prodded gently as Jack entered the small enclosure.

"Feeling any better, Sam?" asked Jack. Apparently, he had been waiting outside until Thomas gave his okay to enter.

I nodded and then immediately closed my eyes. I felt a stab of pain echoing back through the walls of my skull . . . when would I learn not to move my head? Soon, I hoped.

They waited for me to open my eyes.

Instead of answering the question, I wondered about the contents of Jack's black book. Where that came from, I didn't know, and why would I care when someone had just tried to kill me? I realized I was in the Twilight Zone. Strangely enough, I'd never circumvented a problem, but I wasn't ready to answer any questions. I needed a moment longer for the pain to subside. When it became a dull roar, I opened my eyes.

"Tell me what happen," Jack demanded.

"After I left Madison, I drove toward the hospital. Thomas called and we began discussing how mad his mum was at Paul Mendoza. Then I noticed a truck following me."

Jack noted my response in his black notebook. "Had you seen the truck before?"

Concentrating on my reply, I spoke softly. "Yes, I saw the truck on Mission Road near the school. It was parked by the side of the road with its lights off."

"When did you realize someone was following you?"

After hesitating a moment, I replied, "I think when the driver changed lanes abruptly. He followed me onto the freeway."

"When was the first shot fired?" Thomas pressed, still seething.

"After I started moving into the slow lane, I guess," I said, trying to remember accurately. "I was in the middle lane because the truck was behind me."

"What happened then?"

"I moved into the slow lane. Thomas told me to slow down and let the driver pass," I said, looking into his worried eyes. "The next thing I knew the driver pulled alongside the Jeep, and I saw someone pointing a gun at me."

"Were you able to recognize the person who fired the gun?" Jack pressed.

"No. The only thing I remember thinking was that he was odd looking."

"Why would you think that?" Thomas asked, surprised.

"I think it was because he was wearing dark sunglasses and a cap."

"Can you think of anything else?" Jack inquired, meeting Thomas' gaze and then jotting down the almost total lack of description.

"No."

"What about the truck driver?"

"I caught a glimpse of him in the mirror, but he was also wearing a dark ball cap."

"What did you do when you saw the gun pointing at you?"

"I slammed on the brakes and ducked. A split-second later, I heard bullets shatter the windshield as the truck bumped the front end of the Jeep."

"What happened next?" Jack pressed.

"The Jeep swerved to the right and hit the barrier," I reported, tensing up. I took a moment to try to control my breathing. Then I added, looking at Thomas, "It was over in a matter of seconds."

"Is that all you remember?" he asked.

"No. The airbag exploded," I said, recalling how scared I was.

"Did you lose consciousness?"

I was quiet for what seemed to be a long time. "I don't know for sure. The last thing I do remember is the massive amount of smoke in the car."

"Do you remember anything else?" Thomas asked.

"Someone was yelling at me to wake up." I bit my lip, realizing I had been unconscious.

"Can you describe the scene when you came to?" Thomas asked softly. His sweaty palm gripped my hand.

"There was a lot of smoke. And I was gasping for air, but I couldn't move because of the airbag. I remember feeling something sticky," I disclosed, bringing a hand to my nose as I looked at the evidence bag. "I must have had a bloody nose. The blood dripped onto the airbag and then I guess onto my dress."

"Were you able to see who fired the gun?" Jack pressed directly.

"No, nothing other than what I've already told you," I reasserted, closing my eyes, trying to recall what else had happened.

Jack had arrived within moments of the impact. Luckily, the damage to the Jeep occurred on the passenger's side, so he was able to open my door, assess my injuries, and immediately carry me to his vehicle. After buckling me into the passenger's seat, he had continued barking orders to the deputies.

Once he climbed into the Tahoe, we raced to the hospital. Jack had pinched my nose in order to stop the blood flow while I covered my ears, trying to deaden the shrieking siren sounds that surrounded the moving vehicle.

"Describe how you felt at the time of impact," Dr. Machado directed, entering the cramped cubicle with my chart.

"My head was throbbing," I said.

"Did you see stars?"

"Yes, and I felt the blood dripping from my nose."

"I'm going to give you a list of five things and, at the end of your examination, I'm going to ask you to repeat the five objects in order," he stated, watching me.

"Okay," I uttered as I bit my lower lip, afraid that I wouldn't recall his list.

"Ladder, apple, kite, ring, and boat," he said, in a deliberate manner.

I repeated the list twice, feeling like a total idiot.

Then Ben went on with the examination. "Did you have a headache before the accident?"

"A slight one," I conveyed, defiantly sitting up straighter in the bed. "I was tired."

"Did you feel any paralysis in your extremities?"

"No, but I couldn't move."

Alarmed, Ben softened his voice. "What do you mean that you couldn't move?"

"The airbag had me pinned in, and I couldn't get out of the car," I added anxiously as I saw him arch his left eyebrow.

"Sam, I want you to walk for me," Ben requested, pulling the sheets and blanket off me. He helped me out of bed and led me through a series of different activities.

I walked a short distance outside the cubicle and back inside the small enclosure. Next, I stood on one foot and then the other. I raised my arms in different directions while standing on each foot and then on both feet together.

Finally, he helped me back into the bed. "Sam, raise your right arm and hold it in the air."

I did as he asked.

"Good. Now, raise the left arm and wriggle your toes," he ordered, watching my movements carefully. "Slowly lower your right arm; now the left arm."

After lowering both arms, I snapped, "Ben, what type of game are we playing?"

"This is no game, Sam," he stated seriously. "What day is it?"

"Today is Tuesday, the second day of school."

"What time is it?"

"Almost eleven at night, I think."

"Where are you?"

"I'm in the hospital's emergency room."

"What is your full name?"

"For someone who has known me for a long time, that's an idiotic question, Ben."

"Sam, sometimes silly questions help diagnose serious problems," he asserted patiently.

"My name is Samantha Cabot Samuels."

"What's four times four?" he peppered.

"Sixteen."

Then Ben inquired, "Sam, along with this headache, did you feel any dizziness or nausea at any time?"

"I was never nauseated, but I did have some dizziness."

"What about double vision?"

"No, Ben."

"I believe you may have a simple concussion, but I want you to have a CAT scan to make sure you're okay."

"Is this really necessary?"

"Yes!" responded my trio of inquisitors.

"Look, Sam, you suffered a head injury tonight when you hit the guardrail," Ben stressed seriously. "Even if there was no direct impact to the head, the sudden stop could have led to a blood vessel rupture."

"I'm fine, and I'm able to answer your questions," I pointed out, seeing Ben's stern look and Thomas' worried eyes.

"I know, Sam, and your blood pressure is still elevated. What makes this so dangerous is the fact that there is only a brief window of time to diagnose an epidural hematoma, which occurs between the brain's dura matter and the skull. A person who suffers a head trauma may act and feel fine but remains totally unaware of the damage caused by a ruptured blood vessel. Unfortunately, the bleeding continues until it creates enough pressure, which leads to irreversible brain damage or sudden death."

"That serious, huh?" I gulped, clearly understanding the life-and-death situation. As my eyes left Ben's face, I looked directly at Thomas. No wonder he was tense.

"The CAT scan is a standard procedure," Ben assured as he met my eye. "I want to make sure you don't have a skull fracture or an epidural hematoma. And also, I want to check for internal injuries."

"What if I have an epidural hematoma?"

"Then we operate immediately to reduce the pressure on the brain," Ben advised, noting my vitals. "But, if your results are what I expect, you may leave this evening. Of course, I'll want to see you sometime tomorrow to make sure you're okay."

"Thomas, if I promise to behave during the CAT scan, I want a hot fudge sundae with lots of pecans and whipped cream. Do we have a deal?" I asked sheepishly, trying to inject some humor into this dismal situation.

"It's a definite maybe," Thomas teased, breaking into a smile for the first time since I'd arrived at the hospital. I knew he would wait for Ben's nod of approval.

"Okay, Ben, let's get this show on the road." He handed me release forms to sign. Once I had signed the documents, he placed them in my chart.

"Sam, I need you to repeat the list of objects I gave you earlier," Ben demanded.

"Ladder, apple, kite, ring, and boat," I recited, relieved that I remembered the list.

Wednesday

August 17

Wednesday: 1:05 A.M. at University Hospital

The doctors discharged me from the emergency room wearing hospital greens. Thomas had been issued instructions in case my condition changed in any way. He drove us to the Arizona Resort—now my temporary home—nestled at the base of the Old Pueblo Mountains. And Jack followed us.

My headache had now diminished to a dull ache. Even though I just wanted to go to sleep, that was not going to be an option for the next hour or so. Once in the room, Thomas called room service and ordered food and coffee. With all of the night's excitement, both men were starving.

Leaving them to discuss the case, I went into the bathroom. The nurse had washed the blood from my face and hands in the hospital, but I still felt disheveled. Stripping off the green scrubs, I became irritated . . . my clothes were now part of another crime scene. At this rate, I was going to need a whole new wardrobe. Carefully, I stepped into the shower, letting the hot water wash away the grime. By the time I put on a pair of gray sweats, I felt a great deal better.

I reentered the room and heard Jack and Thomas discussing the evidence.

Thomas came to my side and helped me onto the bed. He placed several pillows behind my back and then covered me with a blanket. Afterwards, he brought me cream of wheat.

As I ate, I considered the mystery surrounding Bill's murder and Madison School. Taking my last spoonful, I turned to Jack. "What did you find out about Jane?"

"Ms. Fuller is at a loss to explain why Dr. Austin was at Madison Sunday evening."

"Why did she leave work Monday?" I persisted.

"She claimed to be upset about his death and indicated that she feared that she would be blamed for the district's financial problems."

"That's beyond strange! She's the district's financial director and should know what is going on," I declared emphatically, stating the obvious. "Where did she go?"

"She went to an independent accountant to help her audit the district's books," Jack reported, seeing my look of disgust.

"What exactly did she take to the accountant?" Thomas asked, meeting my gaze.

"She took her laptop and the hard copy of the budget," Jack reported.

"Why seek outside help now?" I declared, exasperated with the situation. "There has been a budget problem for months!"

"She thought her assistant was embezzling money from the district," Jack reported, reviewing his notes.

"You mean Cindy Cameron."

"Yes."

"So Jane sat on this information!" I snapped.

"Jack, were you able to find anything on the CDs that Sam gave you?" Thomas interceded, seeing how agitated I was becoming.

"Kevin Braun, one of my computer crime detectives, discovered that some of the district's money was electronically transferred to a New York bank. From there, the money was routed to a bank in Lima, Peru. After that, they're not sure where the money went because of the firewalls put in place by the perpetrators. Oddly, at the same time, money was transferred back into the district's accounts."

"Cindy found two million dollars in the district's bank account and, shortly afterwards, the money disappeared from the account," I said, watching both men sit up.

"Did she report this to Bill?" Thomas asked.

"Yes, she did. Sam, who told you about this?" probed Jack, worried.

"Patty Steward," I divulged, watching them assimilate this bit of information. "Can Kevin trace where that money came from?"

"He's already working on it," Jack said. "Kevin was able to find one source transferring money back into the district's accounts. The others are still unknown because of the firewalls."

"What about that one source?" I pressed, seeing him frown.

"That account belonged to a holding company based internationally with Dr. Austin's name on the corporation's documents."

"Obviously, there are global implications," Thomas asserted, turning to Jack. "Have you contacted the FBI?"

"Yes, they're providing us with technical support to track the money coming and going from the district's accounts. They are also running background checks on Jane Fuller and Cindy Cameron. In the meantime, I have both women under surveillance."

"Is that the reason you asked me about Bill playing the stock market?"

"Yes," he stated, without giving away his hand.

"So you do suspect that Bill was involved in this scam?" I asked incredulously.

"Possibly," replied Jack thoughtfully.

"How?" I demanded.

"He had two E-STOK accounts at the time of his death. One was under his name. The other one is in the name of a holding company," Jack revealed, looking straight at me. "He was clutching a scrap of paper with a partial E-STOK account number in his hand when he was killed."

"So you think he's part of this scheme?"

"I'm beginning to think so."

"But why would he do this?" I pressed.

"To launder illegal money," stated Thomas.

"I just don't believe it. Is there actually money missing from the district's accounts other than the two million dollars?" I asked, still stunned. I knew in my heart that Bill would never jeopardize the district. There had to be another explanation.

"Yes, about $100,000," Jack stated matter-of-factly. He looked exhausted, stifling a yawn. "The bank alerted Dr. Austin on Friday about the shortage."

"How do you know this?" Thomas demanded.

"The branch manager called me and reported his conversation with the superintendent. Apparently, the manager had been trying to get ahold of Ms. Fuller for several days but couldn't make contact with her. So he spoke to Dr. Austin, who was furious about the missing money. He ordered copies of bank statements for the past eight months."

"Wow, I wonder if the bank manager reported this to you in order to cover his ass, or someone else's," I offered, also wondering why Jane hadn't taken the manager's call. Still upset, I asked, "How are these raiders manipulating the district's accounts?"

"Once they hack in, I'm told that it's just a matter of programming instructions," Jack informed me.

"No one in the district caught this?" I declared, wondering how Jane and Cindy missed it . . . or had they? Was this the reason for their constant bickering?

"Ms. Cameron may have," Jack reported, reviewing his notes. "She told Ms. Fuller months ago that something was wrong but her boss told her to leave it alone. Instead, she started documenting her suspicions."

"Did Cindy take this information to Bill?" I asked.

"Yes, she did, but nothing came of it."

"That's interesting," Thomas commented, looking up from his note taking.

"Jack, who do you believe: Jane Fuller or Cindy Cameron?" I pressed, wanting to know what he thought.

"I don't know which one is telling the truth. They could both be working together on this scam, or not. But one thing is certain—they successfully created enough chaos so that no one knew what was really going on until after Dr. Austin's murder. Once we analyzed that odd file you found on the computer, we started investigating the district's finances," Jack asserted, looking directly at me. "Someone from the administration is definitely involved."

"Like the acting superintendent, Paul Mendoza," I suggested. Then I watched Jack press his lips together when I added, "Bill had him helping Cindy with the budget."

"Shit," he muttered under his breath as he included this little detail into his notes.

Thomas waited for his friend to finish writing. "Jack, has there been anything else that struck you as odd?"

Jack took his time rereading his notes. "Ms. Cameron found a payment voucher to Santini Construction Company for repair work completed at Madison in the middle of May. When she questioned her fiancé, Carlo Santini—the owner's son—about the work, he stated that he knew nothing about it and thought it was odd that his father's company would have been involved."

"He's right, Jack. The Santini Construction Company doesn't do small jobs. I would have known if a contract had been awarded to them."

"How would you know, Sam?"

"Because Henry would have told me, but I also read the board's minutes," I replied, thinking that this was around the time Maxie died.

Thomas took a sip of his water. "Why are you so sure, Sam?"

"The building is dilapidated. There has not been any construction or repair work done at Madison for a long time. Besides, Henry's construction company would've submitted a bid to the district."

Jack went on to tell us about what he had gleaned from Carlo Santini's interview. "When Santini spoke to his father about the construction job, the father denied any knowledge about the work. He was worried enough to have his son go through the business records and bank statements. And when Santini did, he found that the district had electronically deposited money into their business account in July."

"That is odd," Thomas commented.

"Yes, it is," Jack agreed. "He called the bank and was told that the money was only in the account for three days."

"How did that happen?" Thomas pressed.

"Apparently, a district official called the bank and claimed that the payment was made in error, and had the funds transferred to a bank in New York."

"Was the money sent to the same New York bank account in the past?" Thomas asked.

"Yes," Jack asserted.

"Do you know who requested the transfer of funds?" I inquired.

"No."

"How could they do this without Santini's approval?" I asked.

"We're checking on that," Jack revealed.

"I'll get a subpoena for the district's financial records relating to the transfers," Thomas stated, writing down specific information he needed for the warrants. "And I'll also get subpoenas for Jane's and Cindy's computers, cells and land phones, and all their bank statements, as well as the bank manager's."

"I'm curious if Henry has experienced any unsolicited deposits into the Samuels' accounts," I said, growing more wary of the money's movement.

"That's a good question, Sam," stated Thomas, adding a question mark next to Henry's name.

"I'll call Henry and have him check his bank records for any electronic money transfers."

"And while you're at it, Sam, you need to have your accounts checked also," suggested Thomas.

"And so should you, Thomas," I directed, meeting his intense gaze.

I called Henry and woke him up. I told him about the accident and explained what I needed him to do, while Jack and Thomas continued to discuss the banking implications quietly.

"Jack, could this have happened to Bill without his knowledge?" I suggested, ending the call. I was still stunned at how easy it was to transfer money from one account to another.

"Possibly," he said, beginning to tap his notebook.

"Sam, what are you thinking?" posed Thomas.

"None of this makes any sense. Bill wouldn't be involved in a scam to ruin the school district he worked so hard to improve."

"What are you getting at, Sam?" questioned Jack, turning to face me.

"We know that someone is moving money around electronically, right?" I addressed, looking at both men.

"Yes," Jack replied, sipping his coffee.

"Could someone open a financial account without the individual's knowledge—in other words, steal his identity?"

"Yes, they can, Sam, if they have the individual's social security number, address, phone number, and maybe a credit card number or two," Thomas stated.

"Well, both Jane and Cindy had access to Bill's personal information. One of them could have easily set up an E-STOK account in Bill's name without his knowledge," I asserted.

"If he didn't set this up, where did he get the account number from?" Jack replied.

"Perhaps he came across it in one of the district's financial files after he spoke to the bank manager," I assumed.

"That sounds plausible," Jack considered, looking at me.

I walked over to the table and poured coffee into Jack's empty cup and water into Thomas' glass and then mine. I stood there sipping ice water, trying to assimilate all the information we had been discussing.

After Jack doctored his cup with sugar and cream, he took a swallow. "Any other thoughts, Sam?"

"Why transfer money electronically all over the world for a lousy $100,000? That's nuts. Thomas, you're right about someone laundering money through the district's bank accounts," I stated. "But I still think that there's a drug component involved and somehow Madison is in the middle of all this."

"Sam, I hope not," Thomas stated softly, giving Jack a wary look.

Jack picked up on Thomas' uneasiness. He stood up to leave. "It's late. We all need some rest."

"Good night," I said.

Thomas walked Jack out as they discussed their strategy.

Wednesday: 2:30 A.M. at the Arizona Resort

Thomas was setting the alarm clock as I climbed back into bed.

"How are you feeling, Sam?"

"Okay. I think I'm gonna live," I teased, smiling.

"I'm glad to hear that. Do you have any bruising yet?"

"A little; it's mostly where the seatbelt was. I'm just happy that I don't have a broken nose and two black eyes."

"So am I!" he exclaimed, relieved.

"You know, when that airbag exploded, I thought a bomb had gone off."

"You must've been panic-stricken!" Thomas sympathized, knowing I was claustrophobic.

"I was. I thought the car was about to ignite."

"I swear, Sam, I aged twenty years when I heard the impact and you didn't answer," he declared as he sat next to me on the edge of the bed.

"Thank God Jack arrived when he did. What I don't understand is how he got there so fast!"

"Mario called 911 and reported that you might be in danger. The dispatcher relayed the message to Jack right before I called him."

"What did Mario see?"

"He saw a dark-colored sedan follow you out of the parking lot. He thought the driver was the same guy spotted with DeMorgan in July."

"Really?"

"Yes, I have to admit these kids really do care about you. Personally, I'll do whatever I can for them."

"That's a promise I won't let you forget," I stated, caressing his face. "They're really good kids and just need a chance to be winners—just like Ben Machado."

Thomas brought my left hand to his lips and then lowered it, looking a little nervous. "Sam, I can't imagine my life without you. When I heard the shots ring out and then the Jeep crashing into the barrier, I thought those bastards had killed you."

"But they didn't," I said, seeing the fear in his eyes.

"I just can't bear to be without you."

"The answer is yes," I declared softly, looking up at him.

"I still would like to ask you, if you don't mind," he snapped, slightly aggravated. He went down on one knee.

"Sorry," I whispered, beaming.

"I want you to know that I fell in love with you the first day I met you. And I have loved you ever since, Sam," he said tenderly, scrutinizing my face. "Will you marry me?"

"Can I say yes now?" I solicited as I met his loving gaze.

"Yes, please," he requested, smiling back.

"Yes, I will marry you."

"Are you sure?" he fretted, remembering Ben's admonition not to make any life-altering decisions for the next twenty-four hours.

"Thomas, I want you to know that I've always been in love with you—and not Peter. And, before you ask, this is not the concussion talking. I love you and want to spend the rest of my life with you."

"I love you so much," he said, taking me into his arms.

Wednesday: 5:30 A.M. at the Arizona Resort

"**S**am, it's time to get up," Thomas whispered softly, nudging me awake.

I don't know why but I felt energized, despite what had happened last night. Not that I'd had much sleep, since he woke me up every hour on the hour per Ben's orders.

"Good morning, Thomas," I managed to say with a smile as I sat up in bed. I noted that he had never looked more dashing in a charcoal-gray suit with a red tie loosely knotted around his neck.

After he handed me a steamy cup of green tea, I took several small sips, wishing it were coffee. I watched the weather report on television for a few minutes. "The morning temperature is sixty-six degrees, which is unusually cool for this time of year," the weatherman remarked in a folksy way. "But don't worry, folks; the day will heat up quite nicely to around ninety-five degrees by mid-afternoon. And tonight there is a high chance for thunderstorm activity."

"You need to get going," Thomas announced.

Beaming, I set the cup down on the nightstand.

He helped me out of bed, murmuring that he had ordered breakfast.

Once I was on my feet, he kissed me. I pretended that it had no effect, but it had. I was on fire, wanting so much more than a kiss. I looked up at the strong man standing in front of me and blushed. His lips brushed against my cheek and then he directed me toward the closet.

Now, it was my turn to dress. I opened the mirrored closet doors and selected dark trousers that were an easy fit and a chili-red blouse with cap sleeves. Picking up my trusty pumps and dark bomber jacket, I took the clothes into the bathroom.

~~~~~

I returned to the bedroom with a mischievous smile and the jacket draped over my shoulder.

Thomas ended his call as he turned to face me. "My, my, don't we look chic today," he mocked, pretending to shield his eyes.

"My clothes only reflect how I feel," I said, setting the jacket on the bed next to my purse. I was so relieved that I didn't have two black eyes to contend with this morning. Besides saving my life, God had granted me some small favors last night.

"You're radiant," Thomas grinned.

"No, just happy," I declared, touching his shoulder before I joined him at the table to wait for our six o'clock breakfast.

It was now 5:50. Thomas was preoccupied going over his notes on the case.

I sipped my tea as I watched my future husband relish drinking his. He looked up and smiled at me. I felt a warmth I'd never experienced with anyone else. Thomas was not only the man I loved, but he was also my best friend. He'd started drinking green tea when Maxie became ill and raved about its immunity-building properties, as well as its ability to stop some cancer cells from growing. Unfortunately, leukemia wasn't one of them. Our hope was that it would help boost her immune system, at the very least.

Maxie hosted a tea party almost every afternoon, and Thomas was her guest of honor. Together, they would drink green tea and talk about their day. For months, they'd tried to get me to switch from coffee to green tea. Even though I remained loyal to a coffee régime for the most part, I'd finally relented to one cup of green tea per day. But today I definitely needed coffee!

The porter delivered our breakfast and the local newspaper precisely at six.

After pouring our first cup of java, Thomas and I scanned the morning paper looking for stories about my accident. We were relieved that Jack had been true to his word and kept it out of the news. Then we began to eat our breakfast.

"Sam, you do realize that everyone will know that something is up if you keep smiling like that," he teased.

"I know," I grinned softly, fingering the locket. "I won't tell them anything. I'll just be very mysterious."

Laughing, he then checked his watch and announced that it was time to go. I quickly grabbed my things from the bed, and we left the room. Walking into the coffee shop, he ordered two large coffees to go. Thomas was a health nut but, fortunately, not a purist. Afterwards, we crossed the parking lot to the rental car and he drove me to Madison.

As I sipped a rich mocha coffee, I thought about the day ahead.

Wednesday: 7:10 A.M. at Madison

Thomas dropped me off at Madison and then headed to court. Today he was covering Judge Ditka's morning calendar. As chief deputy for the county attorney's office, he felt it was important to participate in this process, even though he didn't have to. It was boring rote work but it helped keep morale up in the office. It also enabled him to solve day-to-day problems in the court's proceedings as they developed, rather than have them fester into major dilemmas. After all, it was his job to keep the office running smoothly and, more importantly, to make sure that the current county attorney looked good in the press.

Once inside the building, I found the county health inspector and his aides waiting for me in the hallway. I escorted them to the cafeteria, where they went to work immediately. They inspected every nook and cranny in the kitchen and systematically checked all of the canned goods in the pantry for expiration dates and against their recall list.

The inspector and his aides quizzed the cafeteria staff about how the food was prepared and served. They wanted to know what was done with leftovers, how the cafeteria was cleaned between serving sessions, what was used to clean spills when the children were still eating, and how the kitchen was cleaned every day. By the end of the kitchen's inspection, I was impressed with the knowledge and thoroughness of the county health workers, as well as our kitchen staff.

Then we walked to the bathrooms. As the inspector's team scrutinized each restroom, I was relieved that the district's maintenance crew had brought everything up to code yesterday. Finally, the inspection crew had completed their job, and the inspector gave Madison a clean bill. I thanked them for their work and they left the building.

I needed to establish a normal routine. The phone rang as I entered the main office. "I'll get it, Blanche," I shouted, walking over to the phone. A parent wanted to know about the after-school program. I briefly outlined the curriculum, which consisted of tutoring, learning centers, and recreational sports activities. She seemed pleased with what she heard, since she promptly enrolled her daughter and son.

Meanwhile, Blanche had registered two new students.

During a lull between phone calls and parents registering their children, my curiosity got the better of me. "How are things going?"

Blanche succinctly briefed me. Molly Carpenter, the dean of students at the local community college, was advising our students about GED classes and educational degree programs. Henry's staff had streamlined the processes of enrolling students and helping them apply for scholarships, as well as filling out job applications. Mrs. Ryan had sent volunteers to greet the parents and help with registration.

Interestingly enough, Ben Machado had convinced Henry to fund a doctor's office on wheels. The doctors would donate their time and services to the project, while the Samuels family would help fund medical costs.

"How are the negotiations going?" I asked, concerned that Paul would attempt to sabotage the agreement.

"Marge is sitting in for Henry and they're still working out some details," she said, seeing my surprised reaction.

"Now, that's thought-provoking," I commented. I knew Marge would exact a fair compromise to keep Madison open. But, I wondered what Henry was up to . . . oh well, I would know soon enough. So I took a stack of messages back to my office and began working through the pile. As I finished returning my last call, Blanche entered and handed me a message from Paul Mendoza to call him back.

"What's this about?"

"He didn't say."

"Is this something urgent, or can it wait?"

"He just said to have you call him back sometime today."

My headache from last night had almost disappeared, leaving only a hint of pain, but the thought of speaking to Paul Mendoza was enough to bring the throbbing back. "I'll deal with this later. Do you need me for anything else?"

"No."

"Good," I declared, pleased that I didn't have to address any other issues.

~~~~~

I left the building and proceeded down the walkway to the library. Stopping midway, I surveyed the playground. A landscaper was mowing Madison's almost nonexistent lawn. Dirt swirled into the air, creating miniature twisters behind the mower. When the landscaper finished, he stopped for a moment. He wiped his forehead and then drove around to the back. A large dump truck meandered slowly toward the playground equipment. Once in position, the driver unloaded his cargo of sand. Then he began shoveling sand underneath the swing set and monkey bars. Somehow watching these two men work gave me hope that life at Madison was not only returning to normal, but improving.

When I entered the library, I remained near the doorway because I'd forgotten to wear my sunglasses. Once my vision adjusted to the change of light, it was amazing to see the number of people standing in line to sign up for classes or job interviews. Ben and the parish priest were engaged in an animated discussion about the community involvement. The lawyers and Patty were listening intently to Marge's proposal. Mario and William were helping out as gofers. I felt so grateful for all of their support.

I greeted everyone as I moved from one person to another, making my way over to Mrs. Ryan. Once I arrived at her table, I could see that she was brimming with excitement and looked much younger than her sixty-three years. "How are things going?"

"Fine," Mrs. Ryan declared, smiling.

"Have you been able to speak with the teachers?"

"Yes, I have. I've already assigned two volunteers to each classroom. They are working with their designated teachers as we speak."

"Wow! That is amazing," I declared. "Anything else?"

"I have volunteers helping Molly at the career placement table, as well as several seniors helping Blanche," she said with enthusiasm. "Thank you for thinking of us, Sam."

"I really can't take the credit. It was Thomas' suggestion," I revealed, smiling as I thought of her son.

"Do you think he's trying to . . . ?"

"Hi, Ben," I said, seeing him approach us with a big smile.

"You're just the person I need to see," he declared, addressing Mrs. Ryan. "I've booked an examination room by the ICU for your physical tomorrow afternoon. Since the judge will still be in recovery, you won't have to worry about him."

"Is this really necessary?" Mrs. Ryan demanded, looking somewhat put off.

"Yes!" we exclaimed together.

"You're both sure, then?" she questioned in an accusatory tone, pretending to be upset with our collusion, despite the spark of humor in her eyes.

"Yes, we are, Mrs. Ryan," I asserted, looking directly at her. "Besides, Ben said he would treat us to a huge hot fudge sundae in the hospital's cafeteria if you cooperate. Now, how can you possibly resist a bribe like that?"

"Well, since you put it that way, I can't," she remarked cheerfully. "And I think it's time that both of you start calling me Annie—not Mrs. Ryan."

Ben and I were both stunned at her suggestion. Looking at her rather suspiciously, I wondered if Thomas had told his mum. "Okay, Annie," I conceded with a smile.

Ben stood there, watching her carefully. "You'll always be Mrs. Ryan to me, but I'll call you Annie, if that's what you really want."

"Ben, for heaven's sake—you're my doctor! We are all adults. And friends call one another by their first name," she suddenly declared in a more pronounced English accent.

"Yes ma'am," Ben obeyed, properly chastised.

"Sam, you look wonderful today. No one would ever know you've been . . ." she hesitated, looking around to see if anyone was nearby. Then she lowered her voice to a whisper, "in an accident."

"Thank you for the compliment, Annie," I acknowledged, flashing a Cheshire cat grin. "How did you know?"

"I was in the hospital cafeteria very early this morning when I heard several nurses talking about the mishap," she reported, giving me a knowing look.

"Oh," I uttered, wondering what that look meant. Just at that precise moment, I heard Mario call my name. "I'll see you both later then. I need to speak with a student." Smiling, I'd kept my promise to Thomas and didn't say a word as I walked away.

Annie and Ben both exchanged puzzled looks.

As Mario approached, I noticed that he was dressed conservatively. He wore jeans, a white T-shirt, and athletic shoes instead of the usual baggy clothes.

"I'm glad you're okay," Mario said, a bit anxiously. "I thought you might be in trouble when I recognized the driver, so I called the sheriff."

"Mario, thank you for calling when you did," I stated gratefully. "You saved my life. If you hadn't acted so quickly, who knows what would have happened?"

"Sorry you got hurt," he said apologetically. "Still, if I'd called the sheriff when William and I first saw the car, then . . . ."

"It's only a bump on the head," I assured him, "And Dr. Machado says I'm going to be fine." I changed the subject when I noticed how uncomfortable he was. "I'm glad you're here."

"Yeah, well, it means something to my mom that I get my GED. I've got responsibilities now that my mom is so sick."

"I'm sorry, Mario. I didn't know your mother was ill," I said, concerned. "What's wrong?"

"She's got the big 'C' . . . breast cancer," he announced quietly.

Now, I recognized the fear in his eyes. "Mario, is there anything I can do?"

He stood there quietly, shaking his head. When he was ready, he told me what the doctors had said.

"You know, there are new treatments, and cancer doesn't mean you're going to die. The doctors now consider it a chronic illness."

"I know. She's gonna have surgery . . ." he admitted quietly. He turned away to wipe the tears from his eyes.

"Is she scheduled to undergo chemo or radiation treatments afterwards?"

"Chemo," he cleared his throat. "She's supposed to start her first treatment at the Indian hospital when she heals from the operation."

"How is the family surviving financially?" I inquired, seeing him flinch.

"We're struggling since . . ." he began, avoiding my gaze.

"Mario, there's a foundation that helps families experiencing a medical crisis. I would like to recommend your family to the organization. What do you think?" I solicited, watching him go through an internal debate.

"Do you think they would accept us?"

"Yes, I do. Your family meets the foundation's criteria."

"Did they help you?" he questioned, meeting my eye.

"No," I stated, returning his gaze. "The foundation didn't exist until just recently."

"This is one of your foundations, isn't it?" he guessed, watching me smile.

"Yes, it is, Mario," I admitted. "I know how difficult living with cancer can be and, if I can help anyone going through this nightmare, then my daughter's battle wasn't in vain."

"I'm sorry about Maxie. I really liked her," he acknowledged. Then he lowered his eyes to the floor. "Okay, Ms. Samuels, submit our name."

"So how are you doing?" I coaxed, watching him shove his hands into his front pockets. I knew Mario was the eldest of the family's five children. His mother had always been his Rock of Gibraltar and now he had stepped in as the rock for the family.

"I gotta be strong now— *por que soy el hombre de la casa.*"

"And?"

"Dr. Machado says she's doing okay. He says I'm doing the right thing getting my GED cuz it makes her happy."

"He's right. This gives her hope and that's important." I put my arm around his shoulders and lowered my voice. "When Maxie became ill, I read everything I could get my hands on. I needed to know what to expect, what questions needed to be asked, and how to ask them."

"Dr. Machado says knowledge is power."

"It's true, Mario."

"Did it help?" he probed, pulling away to look me in the eyes.

"Sometimes, but not always," I replied, clutching my locket. "There were times when I wanted to bury my head in the sand. But

I couldn't. I had to know everything regarding leukemia in order to make the right decisions about her medical care. I always had hope. And I still do, except now it's for others."

Embarrassed by his vulnerability and mine, Mario looked quietly out the window. Upon hearing footsteps approach, he turned and saw William coming toward us.

William punched him slightly on the arm. "Hey, man, did you ask her?"

"No, I haven't," Mario said. "Ms. Samuels, we heard the teachers talking about a peer mediation workshop this afternoon. We were wondering if we could come . . . ."

"Of course, you can." Thinking for a moment, I asked him, "Do you think the parents would be interested in coming too?"

"Maybe," William answered.

"Mario, would you design a flyer for the workshop?"

"Sure," he said.

"The more people we have involved, the better off we are." I turned to William. "Would you pass out the leaflets?"

"Sure, no problem," he declared, turning around and scanning the room. "But I'd better go check with Mr. Samuels."

Both Mario and I stared at him.

As if to answer our unspoken question, William informed us, "You're not going to believe this, but Mr. Samuels made me his assistant for the day."

"That's great news, William." I smiled, amused. "How do you like the job so far?"

"Well, for a *viejito*—sorry about that—Mr. Samuels sure has a lot of energy for an old guy," he reported in a serious tone. "I think we've walked five miles this morning."

"Be grateful that's all you've done," I stated, laughing.

"Why?"

"Oh, nothing," I said, burning with curiosity. "What's he been up to this morning?"

"Well, I couldn't believe the way Mr. Samuels talked to the lawyers and the district guys."

"What do you mean?" I gulped, glad I wasn't there.

"He just told them to get down to business and stop all the damn bickering."

"He didn't!" I exclaimed, feigning surprise.

"He sure did. Then he had Mrs. Samuels come and deal with them. The district guys weren't happy when she told them what she wanted. Everyone got real quiet and got to work. I think they're afraid of her!"

"They should be," I replied.

"Well, I'd better get going," William said. "By now, Mr. Samuels has probably thought of something else for me to do. You know, he's really not so bad. But please don't tell him I said that."

Mario and I laughed as we watched William walk away whistling. I wondered if they were on their way to becoming the dynamic duo of this project. And, if they were, heaven help us. I said a grateful prayer: *Gracias a Dios.*

The two of us exchanged ideas for the flyer as we walked to the teachers' workroom. As we entered the small room, several teachers were busy working. I handed him some paper and he began to sketch several designs for the leaflet. Gina Spinelli came over and made a few helpful suggestions. Once we selected a sketch, he finished the design and then we printed copies.

Mario took the leaflets and went to find William. They would distribute the flyers to the parents, who were at school, and then around the neighborhood.

"I'm surprised at Mario's artistic talent," Mrs. Spinelli stated, still wary of him. "He seems like a nice kid."

"He is, Gina."

"I've always been afraid of him and the others," she declared offhandedly.

I was stunned by her admission. "They're good kids." Then I smiled, thinking that they had a lot in common.

Wednesday: 10:10 A.M. at Madison

The empty bulletin boards in the hallways needed attention. I gathered materials from the supply closet and had the custodians cover all of the boards with butcher-block paper of different colors. This created a more welcoming environment.

On the main bulletin board, I fashioned a tree with multi-colored tissue paper. Both the children and adults, including parents as well as teachers, were drawn to my work space as they entered the building.

I wanted the community to pull together so the children would feel valued. I asked everyone to draw a self-portrait for the bulletin boards. The children were eager to comply but most of the adults simply preferred to observe.

While the artists concentrated on their images, we shared stories about our summer experiences and our dreams for the future. Once they finished, with scissors in hand, they carefully cut out their drawings. Together with their parents, we figured out where they wanted their pictures located in the hallway.

The parents then helped them place their portraits on the different bulletin boards. Afterwards, the children were chatting enthusiastically with their parents about the experience as they walked down the hallway to meet their new teachers. Others came over and took their places at the table and began drawing their self-images.

My biggest laugh came when Henry stopped by and drew himself as a slender young cowboy with a large-brimmed hat. The kids went wild giggling when they saw his caricature placed in the center of the main bulletin board. He asked if anyone was interested in listening to a story. Of course, the younger children agreed and the older ones followed along, not wanting to be left out. Henry went off like a Pied Piper, leading them to the family center room.

Before I knew it, the bulletin boards were done and everyone had contributed either an idea or a self-portrait. The undertaking had not only been successful but fun. As I cleaned up the mess, Patty Steward came by to report that they had reached a tentative agreement. The teachers would review the contract and vote on the proposal at noon. If they approved the tentative agreement, it would then go to the governing board for its approval.

I listened closely to her narrative and asked a few clarifying questions.

"Those flyers that William and Mario are passing out are generating a lot of interest among the parents," Patty informed me, pulling out a chair.

"That's great," I declared, piling the leftover construction paper on the cart and then joining her at the table. She looked tired, and the gray suit only accentuated her flat demeanor.

"It was a good idea to ask the parents to attend the workshop."

"Well, I'll mention it to the boys," I asserted, smiling.

"What boys?" Patty asked, distracted.

"Mario and William. They gave me the idea."

"Oh," she said with a look of surprise. "Mrs. Ryan and her friends volunteered to watch the children so their parents could participate in the workshop."

"I wish I had their energy," I replied, grinning.

"Me too!" she grunted, stifling a yawn. "I spoke to Jane last night and told her about the community meeting."

"What was her reaction?' I asked with interest.

"She seemed impressed," Patty declared and then frowned. "Funny thing, though; she seemed rather on edge."

"Why?"

"Well, I really don't know for sure," she said hesitantly. "It was more like . . . ."

"Like what?"

"A feeling of . . . terror, but she wouldn't tell me what was bothering her."

"Do you think that she may know something about Bill's murder?"

"No. If she did, I'm sure she would have spoken with the sheriff," Patty declared with an uneasy tone.

"Does she think her life is in danger?"

"No, why would it be?"

"Well, she was working on the budget with Bill most of Friday."

"True, but they weren't working here," Patty snapped.

"Do you have any idea where Jane was on Sunday?" I persisted.

"Sam, I don't like what you're insinuating."

"Look, Patty, I'm not suggesting anything."

"It sure sounds like it," she retorted irritably.

"I'm concerned. Everyone connected to Bill or Madison may be a target until we know what's going on," I said, growing more concerned about the depth of their relationship.

"Sorry. I guess I'm a little jumpy today," she admitted.

"Why?"

"Oh, hell, I got this call last night," she confessed, seeing my determined look.

"Okay . . . so?" I pressed.

"It was late and I'd just fallen asleep when the phone rang."

"Who was it?" I asked.

"I don't know, and I don't want to discuss this anymore," she declared, suddenly looking frightened.

"Patty, why would anyone threaten you?"

"I didn't say that."

"But your body language did. So answer my question," I demanded, facing this dynamic woman. As I watched her fidgeting with her ring, I became alarmed. This behavior was so unlike her! "Patty," I gently prodded, "what's really going on?"

She sat there, looking down into her lap.

"Are you scared, or . . . ."

"Hell, no! I'm just mad as a wet hen!" Taking in a deep breath and letting it out slowly, she chose her words carefully. "I think I know who the bastard is."

"Who?" I demanded, worried.

"Do you remember that punk kid I had in my class six or seven years ago?"

"Which one?"

"The one who vandalized my new car by keying the driver's side," she revealed, lowering her voice.

"James Hill," I gasped, surprised at her bitterness.

"Yes, that's the snot-nosed punk," she asserted angrily. "And, according to the newspaper, he's a suspect in a murder."

"I don't get it. Why would James call you after all this time?"

"I don't know why the bastard called," she declared.

"What would be his purpose?" I pressed.

"That's the point . . . he has none. And that's what scares me."

"You're not sure it's James," I declared, watching her nod in agreement. "Then who else could it be?"

"I just don't know."

"In order for someone to implicate James, he or she would have to know your past history with him," I surmised.

"Well, that's the entire school district."

"Tell the police your suspicions and let them investigate," I suggested, trying to figure out if she was hiding something else.

"Sam," Patty asserted. "That's the problem. If he's not the one, then who is—a disgruntled member of the association, or someone else in the district? I can't make wild accusations. Everyone will think I'm losing it."

"Okay, then." I looked directly at her. "Why did you think it was James?"

"It was the bastard's voice and language pattern. The caller had a pitch in his voice that reminded me of that kid."

"What did he say?"

"Stay out of Madison, bitch."

"That's strange," I mumbled, recalling my phone call from the other evening.

"You bet, Sherlock."

"You have nothing to do with Madison."

"Except for negotiating this new contract," she stated solemnly.

"James has nothing to do with this school and it would be impossible for him to get your phone number," I remarked, wondering if I could be wrong.

"I know, because it's an unlisted number," Patty voiced, drumming her fingers. "That's why this doesn't make any sense."

"What did you do after the meeting last night?"

"I met the teachers for a drink and then I went home. Jane had left a message on my answering machine, so I returned her call. After that, I took a shower and went to bed. I must have fallen asleep watching the news, because it was ending when the phone rang. Why?" she pressed.

"I was run off the road last night."

"Omigosh! Are you okay?" she demanded.

"I'm fine," I murmured. "Patty, there's a lot going on here, and I certainly don't want to add fuel to a bonfire. So please keep this information to yourself."

"Okay, you have my word," she said, unnerved. "Sam, what's going on?"

"That, my dear, is precisely what I'm going to find out."

"Be careful," she pleaded, reaching for the cell phone clipped to her belt.

"Will do," I promised.

"I've got to go—I have a 911 message. And the worst part is that I still have to deal with Paul Mendoza this afternoon. That bastard drives me nuts."

"Good luck," I said, seeing her frustration.

After listening to a message, Patty left.

I returned the unused material to the supply closet. As I started walking toward to the office, I heard Ben yell out. "Wait up, Sam."

I waited patiently for him to catch up. He was probably functioning on less sleep than I was but he sure looked good. Maybe we had discovered the secret to looking fabulous: trauma, no sleep, and spending the night with someone you love. I didn't know about his love life, but we both certainly had the first two down to an art.

Startled by his determined look, I inquired, "Hey, Ben, what's up?"

"Have you forgotten already? Not a good sign for a trauma victim," he stated, shaking his head. He was carrying his medical satchel and a large paper bag. "I need to check you out."

We walked into my office and shut the door. He placed his things on the desk. After he opened his medical satchel, he seemed puzzled. "You look different today."

"Thanks, Ben," I beamed, trying not to blush. "I feel fine and, thankfully, the black eyes didn't develop. Is this really necessary?"

"Yes."

I sat on top of my desk as he repeated some of the same neurological tests from the previous night and a few new ones.

"You're okay, but take it easy for the next couple of days," he ordered. "And, if you develop any of the symptoms we discussed last night, call me immediately."

"I will," I conceded, jumping off the desk and walking around to my creaky chair.

He pulled out two turkey sandwich halves and our comfort food from the huge paper bag and set them on the desk. Then he took a seat. As we ate, we began shooting the breeze, discussing everything from his morning meeting with Henry to the football season. Before we knew it, twenty minutes had passed.

Blanche came to the door. "Sam, people are arriving for the workshop."

Sadly, our conversation had to end. "I guess it wouldn't look good if I'm late," I said.

Ben agreed. We cleaned up our mess and then walked out of the office together. He strolled out of the building, whistling the university's fight song.

As I headed to the cafeteria, I stopped along the way to greet parents, former students, and teachers. Mario and William had done an excellent job of distributing the flyers for this workshop, and I was grateful. But also, I saw everyone's apprehensive faces.

Wednesday: 1:00 P.M. in Madison's Cafeteria

As I surveyed the uneasy room, I stood at the front of the crowd. "Ladies and gentlemen, welcome. Conflict resolution offers a safe and effective way for children and adults to resolve their differences. The process allows individuals to state their feelings, air their grievances, and have a hand in resolving the disagreements. We choose how we respond to conflict. The choice is between a peaceful resolution and a possible escalation to a violent confrontation. My desire is for all of us to learn to deal with conflict in a peaceful manner.

"Molly Carpenter, the dean of students at the community college, will conduct the workshop," I stated, relinquishing the microphone to her.

The large brunette took the podium. She quickly launched into defining the process and how to construct the non-combative statement. She went on to clarify the importance of "I" messages as the mediator collaborates with the parties to resolve the dispute.

Looking around the room, Molly saw the parents' stoic expressions as most of them sat with their arms folded across their chests. She stopped lecturing and asked for three volunteers from the audience.

To my surprise, Mario and Gina Spinelli volunteered. Everyone else sat still, hoping someone else would get called. I was no different as I shifted in my seat, trying to make myself invisible. The next thing I knew, Henry nominated me for the job. So up I went to meet my fellow thespians onstage.

Molly gave us the scenario that we were to perform. Mario would be the mediator; Gina would be the "child" who had a grievance; and I would be the offender. As we went over the skit amongst ourselves, Molly continued her lecture.

Five minutes later, all eyes were on the stage.

"Mrs. Spinelli, please give Ms. Samuels an 'I' message on how you feel," stated Mario, standing up straighter.

"I feel sad when you call me names because it hurts my feelings," Gina whined, panning to the audience by wiping a pretend tear from her eye.

Mario turned to me in a stern voice, "What did you hear Mrs. Spinelli say?"

The audience snickered. Mario raised his brow as he turned and glared at the spectators. They immediately quieted down.

I wanted to laugh but didn't.

He prodded me again. "What did you hear Mrs. Spinelli say?"

"That I hurt her feelings when I called her a crybaby," I asserted snidely, thinking that Mario was doing a terrific job.

"Thank you for listening to Mrs. Spinelli," he declared.

"But that's what she is!" I declared defiantly. Turning toward the audience, I blew a huge bubble. When I popped the bubblegum, it made a loud smacking noise.

The audience laughed nervously, watching me imitate children's obnoxious behavior, and then quickly quieted down when Mario glared at them again. The skit continued back and forth as Mario skillfully resolved the conflict in a win-win situation for both parties. Then we took our bows while the audience applauded.

As I walked off the stage with Gina and Mario, Mrs. Martinez raised her hand. She wanted to ask me a question. I looked over at Molly as she motioned me back.

"Yes, Mrs. Martinez," I addressed.

"Ms. Samuels, this was all good fun. But, how is this going to help our kids?"

"It gives them tools to use in difficult situations. Eighty-one percent of students throughout the country have been confronted or, worse, bullied by fellow classmates."

"You mean teased?" countered a parent from the back of the room.

"Yes and no."

"It's no big deal; bullying has been going on since the beginning of time. A little teasing helps kids grow up," the father insisted, seeing others nod in agreement.

"That may be true in some cases. But the majority of students who experience bullying internalize the rage and shame they feel," I stated.

"So what?" chimed in the father, exasperated. "Kids are kids . . . everyone gets bullied. It's part of life."

"Well, I don't like it. It's just purely mean," shouted a mother."

"Life's not easy. The kids gotta toughen up," Juan Espinoza countered defiantly.

"Mr. Espinoza," I asserted, looking at the audience. From their expressions, I knew the only reason they were here was because of last night's meeting. "Life is tough, but sometimes this type of harassment can change a child's self-worth and who he or she becomes as an adult."

Parents squirmed in their seats. Some were frowning, while others stared at the floor.

"Ladies and gentlemen, if we don't address conflict and bullying at an early age, your children will experience a rough life. Some of them will grow up frustrated and angry and will not have the skills necessary to deal with difficult situations."

"You're just speculating," Mr. Espinoza asserted angrily.

"Yes, I am—to a certain extent. As children become teenagers and then adults, sometimes they may act out their grievances in a violent manner, which could lead to someone being injured, killed, or sentenced to life in prison. I don't believe that is what you want for your children."

"It is what it is . . . the kids have to toughen up to survive," Mr. Espinoza declared.

"*Dejala*, Juan. She's right. I've already lost one son to gang violence. I don't want to lose another," Mrs. Gomez admitted through the tears rolling down her face. She stood up with the priest's assistance.

"The kids need to learn how to defend themselves," Juan retorted, standing up to face the large woman. "This isn't going to protect them if the son-of-a-bitch has a gun."

"It might if we stop them from bullying each other," Mrs. Gomez yelled back, going toe-to-toe with Mr. Espinoza. "My son might be here today if we had done something about the violence in our neighborhood."

"So you're saying Gabriel's murder was our fault?" the infuriated man roared.

"Yes, because we did nothing to help Luis Castro," she shouted, glaring at Juan.

"It wasn't our job!"

"Ramón is a drunken bastard. He beat his kid every day and look what happened," Mrs. Gomez snapped. "Luis grew up to be an angry adolescent."

"So what?!"

"He bullied all of our kids, including your own son, Juan. If Luis had known how to deal with his rage, maybe Gabriel would be alive today," she asserted. Then, looking around the room, she said, "We can't ignore this kind of violence anymore."

"Look, ladies and gentlemen, all I want is what is best for your children," I stated in a deliberate tone as I watched the two battling parents sit down. "I too have lost a child, not to violence but to cancer. It was the most painful experience of my life, and I do not wish that on anyone.

"What I know is that children need to learn how to deal with conflict. Conflict resolution shows them how to express their feelings and grievances and work out a solution to a problem. Bullying, on the other hand, is an aggressive form of victimization. Bullies intentionally abuse their victims in a subtle or vicious manner. This destructive behavior can cause their victims to feel worthless and, potentially, drive them into isolation, alcohol, and drug addictions or, worse, have a psychotic episode or commit suicide."

Stopping for a moment to assess the faces in the crowd, I met their uneasy gaze.

"We need civility in our lives. Peer mediation is a beginning step to help your children develop respect and confidence in dealing with conflict on a daily basis. I'm asking you to give them this opportunity to work together to resolve their issues." Then I handed the mic to Molly and returned to my seat.

Somehow, this exchange had softened the room's reluctance. During the next sixty minutes, everyone had a chance to formulate "I" messages in a small group and act out scenarios similar to the one we had demonstrated. Molly and her staff walked around the room helping each group.

At the end of the session, parents and teachers looked gratified and, more importantly, they had become acquainted. I explained how we would implement the conflict resolution process at school. Then I asked the parents if they were interested in learning how to help their children with their studies and how to stop bullying. A multitude of hands rose in the air, including the two battling parents.

"You can sign up in the office. Thank you, Molly, and everyone else for coming."

It was now three-fifteen, according to the clock on the wall. Everyone was free to leave for the day. Parents stopped to tell me that they had really enjoyed the workshop and were looking forward to other get-togethers.

After they left, I stayed behind to clean up the cafeteria. Although everyone had been snacking, the mess wasn't too bad.

Gina had stayed behind to help me. "I was surprised at how well Mario handled the skit."

"Why?" I asserted, meeting her eye.

"I guess I'd never taken the time to see him as a real person," she admitted.

"Gina, Mario is a special kid. When Maxie was sick in the hospital, he came and played with her every chance he got."

"William, too?"

"Yes. And, before you ask, so did a lot of my other students. These kids may not have the advantages you and I had growing up, but they have heart."

"Aren't you ever scared of them?"

"Sometimes," I admitted, picking up some trash from the floor. "It's a matter of respect. If you respect them, they will respect you."

"I just don't know."

"Just be yourself, Gina. Nothing more—nothing less," I suggested, smiling.

"Do you think Mario would help out in my classroom?" she asked hesitantly.

"It depends. What do you want him to do?"

"I'd like him to teach the kids how to draw," she said. "I was impressed with the flyer he created."

"Just ask him," I suggested. "I'm sure he would love to work with the kids."

"I think I will. I'll ask him tomorrow morning when he comes in to help Ray with his bulletin boards."

"Gina, thank you for your help today," I remarked appreciatively. "Let me know how it goes with Mario."

"I certainly will," she smiled.

Things were looking up for Madison School—maybe this just might all work out.

Wednesday: 3:35 P.M. at Madison

"Hi, Blanche; I'm back." As I heard the sound of music in the background, I smiled.

"Hi, yourself," Blanche said, putting away the last of the office supplies in the lower cabinet. She stood up from a squatting position behind the counter. "Mr. Samuels called and said he would pick you up at four-thirty. If that's not okay, call him."

"Actually, that's great. It gives me an opportunity to catch my breath. Let's grab a fresh cup of coffee," I suggested, feeling tired. I was relieved that the day had gone by quickly and that there had been no new surprises, except for the monsoon clouds rolling in earlier than usual. "This way I'll be awake when you update me on the registration numbers and everything else."

"Are you sure that you want coffee?" Blanche asserted with a knowing smile as we entered my office. "It's been on the burner for hours."

"It'll be okay," I said, desperately needing a pick-me-up. Ignoring Blanche's warning, I poured a cup of coffee and took a swallow. "That's awful!" I sputtered, choking down the murky brew, now clearly understanding her hesitance. "What would you like to drink?"

"A soda would be all right," she said, perspiring. She twisted her long grayish-blonde hair into a knot and secured it with a clip.

I grabbed the cans out of the small refrigerator. Sitting down in the swivel chair, I handed her a soda and opened mine. I took a sip.

Blanche updated me on the student registration numbers, the after-school enrollment, and some of the parents' concerns about the changes. At the end of the briefing, she told me about a strange call from Loretta Burton, the lead secretary for the school district.

"Blanche, did Loretta say what this district meeting was about?"

"No. She just said that it was mandatory for all principals to attend."

"It's probably about the changes that are going to occur now that Paul is in charge."

"Maybe," she hesitated, before going on, "but she sure was pissed about having to make the call."

"Why?"

"Well, it was like you were singled out for a special invitation."

"I probably was. I haven't returned Paul's call. There's no need to worry."

"He sure doesn't like you," she declared, concerned.

"Well, he doesn't have to like me. We just need to work together."

"I heard through the grapevine about your confrontation with Paul last night."

"The grapevine, huh?" I feigned, surprised. "So does everyone know about our exchange?" I watched her nod yes. I sighed, "Wonders never cease."

"Not only does everyone know, but anyone with common sense sides with you."

"You mean, except for the politically challenged," I mused, raising a hand to my mouth in an exaggerated motion. "Oops, excuse me; I mean the politically correct."

Blanche laughed until tears trickled down her face. For the most part, she was conservative, but she did have a funny side.

It felt good to hear laughter in the almost odorless office. Much to my chagrin, the district had decided to repaint the room to cover up its recent violent history. I could hardly wait for the painters to arrive with their putrid color.

"Loretta is having a horrible time," she volunteered, distracting me from my painting hallucination. I noticed she had become quite somber. "She'd worked for Dr. Austin for over ten years. So not only is she grieving his loss, but she has to contend with . . . ."

"A jerk," I inserted, finishing her sentence in a flat tone. Picking up the soda, I took another sip. "Dr. Mendoza will calm down once he establishes his footing as Bill's successor."

"Do you really think he'll be appointed?"

"Probably. He has the board president and two other board members in his back pocket. Anyone with that kind of help is usually a shoo-in."

"God help us all."

"He's a good administrator. Come to think of it, he really isn't a bad choice. Everyone knows him. There will be no new surprises. And that's important right now," I stated. "We've already had enough chaos."

"Maybe you're right. But I sure don't like or trust the bastard."

"Blanche, no one is asking you to."

"I just don't know. I've worked a long time for this district, and I hate the thought of working for someone . . . ."

"Look, our job is to give the kids in this community the best possible education. How we accomplish this feat is our challenge," I insisted.

"But, Sam . . ." she countered.

"We have choices. I'm choosing to change the school's culture—not only by changing how we teach, but by involving everyone in this endeavor, whether they like it or not."

"You're certainly doing that," she commented, taking a drink of her soda. Then, placing the can on the edge of the desk, she asked, "Do you think we can succeed?"

"Realistically, I don't know, but I hope so. Hillary Rodham Clinton was right. Love her or hate her, it does take a village to raise a child." I knew Blanche detested the Clintons and their politics, but I used the adage anyway. I went on with eyes wide open: "Our village is this community."

"I guess you're right," she conceded grudgingly.

"Blanche, why was Dr. Austin here Sunday?"

"I don't know what he would be looking for and, for the life of me, I can't figure it out," she declared, raising an eyebrow. "Since you were out of town, why didn't he call me or Jane Fuller for that matter?"

"Why would he call Jane?" I asked, flabbergasted.

"Well, Jane's been out here reorganizing some of our files."

"That's not her job," I stated simply, growing wary. "The district's financial records are her primary responsibility, not our files. And there is no reason for Jane to be working at Madison instead of working in her office."

255

"Well, if you put it that way, I guess you're right, Sam," she admitted, hearing the cautionary tone in my voice.

"How did this come about, Blanche?"

"When Jane first arrived in the district, she came to every school and met the principal and the staff. I'll tell you—everyone was very impressed with her."

"After your initial meeting," I paused for a moment, choosing my words carefully, "when did she indicate that Madison needed her personal expertise?"

"Let me think . . . it was about two weeks later."

"Are you sure?"

"Pretty sure," she insisted, playing with a loose strand of hair. "I know that the bargaining sessions were still going on."

"Didn't you think it was odd that she was offering to help?"

"Kind of, but I thought maybe we'd be getting more office help. Darrell was always out of the building, attending district meetings, or golfing," she emphasized, making a face.

"What did Darrell think about Jane coming to help?"

"He wasn't very happy about the situation and confronted Dr. Austin when he found out. I thought it was nice of her to lend a hand," she stated.

Knowing Darrell's temper, I could only imagine his discussion with Bill. "Do you know how their meeting went?"

"Darrell said that Dr. Austin would take care of it. The next thing I knew, Darrell announced his retirement."

"When was this?"

"In the middle of May," she declared.

Sitting back in my chair, I mulled over this new information. Jane Fuller was up to something—but what? It was either an act of kindness, or something more sinister. "Have you been able to determine if anything is missing?"

"Yes. And that's the funny part. Nothing of real consequence is missing."

"What do you mean?"

"The only things that I know are missing are Jane's files from the cabinet."

"Jane's files?" I repeated, stunned.

"Yes, the ones she needed to do her financial reports."

"Do you know when those files were taken?" I solicited.

"I think Friday afternoon."

"Does the sheriff know about this?"

"Yes, and he wants me to continue looking for anything else that strikes me as being odd," she answered apprehensively.

I could see she was uncomfortable, so I changed the direction of my questions. "Can you make any sense of the break-in Monday evening?"

"No," she replied firmly. "But why in heaven's name would anyone shoot Rob Stone? He's such a sweet boy. You know, he's married to Ned Tomer's daughter."

"Yes, I know," I said, thinking of the young woman I saw in the hospital.

"Rob was always stopping by and helping out."

"Why?" I inquired.

"He just wanted to help out, especially after Jane had a problem."

'What kind of a problem did she have?" I prompted, wondering what was going on.

"She couldn't get into the building one weekend. It was right after the district completed a security check on the alarm system.

After Rob fixed the problem, they got to be friends," she confided blithely, seemingly unaware of the possible criminal implications.

"Why was Jane here on a weekend?"

"She told me that she needed to get some work done on the budget."

"Was Darrell aware that Jane was working here on weekends too?"

"Not to my knowledge. But then Rob came out to check on everything again and assured Darrell that the security system was now working just fine."

"When was this?"

"May tenth."

"Did Jane tell you anything else that you thought was odd?"

"She told me that you were going to be the new principal," she volunteered, beginning to squirm in her seat. "But she asked me to keep quiet until it became public knowledge."

"That's weird," I asserted, focusing on the calendar. "When did she tell you this?"

"She told me at the end of April. And I thought that was strange because Darrell hadn't said anything about retiring at that point."

"You're right; that is strange," I confided, recalling that Thomas and Henry hadn't started lobbying Bill until the middle of June. So how did Jane know I would be selected as the principal of Madison? "Well, I wasn't offered the job until the end of July."

"Really?" she gasped.

My stomach was rumbling loudly. I got something to munch on from the cupboard and then handed the bag of potato chips to Blanche. She opened it and took a handful.

I sat down, wondering what else was going on. Why was Darrell forced to retire or, for that matter, why was Jane working here?

Did this have anything to do with the district's financial problems? Was she cooking the books or manipulating the reports? And if she was . . . was Bill part of the scheme or simply a pawn? Why would Jane tell Blanche that I was going to be the new principal? Better yet, was I the latest pawn in this bizarre mess?

I took a chip out of the bag and began munching absentmindedly. "Blanche, how often did Jane come out?"

"Weekly, at first, but then every couple of days," reported Blanche.

"Did she use the computers here or bring a laptop?"

"She usually worked on the computer in your office or the one you were using in the lab," she explained, fidgeting a bit.

"Did she log on to the district's mainframe?"

"No. She always brought CDs or a flash drive with her."

"Am I right in assuming that she created hard files too?" I prodded, in an attempt to understand the big picture.

"Yes, they're the files that are missing."

"Are there any of her other files missing?" I asked with an edge to my voice.

"As far as I know, I don't think so . . . but she did store a copy of her documents in the computer lab's filing cabinet," she stated apprehensively. Her coloring waned.

"Blanche, could you please get me those files?"

"Sure." Blanche walked out of the office as the phone rang.

"I'll get it," I yelled out. "Good afternoon, Madison School. How may I help you?"

"Sam, this is Lois Cameron," the speaker announced, recognizing my voice.

"Hi, Lois."

"Sam, we need to see you right away," she whispered adamantly.

"Lois, what's going on?"

"We'll tell you when you get here."

"Get where?"

"Oh, I'm sorry, Sam. I'm new at this cloak-and-dagger stuff. We're in the coffee shop at the Arizona Resort. Please don't tell anyone that we're meeting. It's a matter of life and death."

"Lois . . . ."

"I can't talk now. Please hurry!" she begged, hanging up.

Blanche returned in a panic. "Sam, those files are gone too! Jane's going to be so upset," she said, sitting down. "I never even thought to look for them. I'd better call Jane and tell her."

"Blanche, just call the sheriff."

"Why, Sam? They're her files," she remarked, visually upset.

"Because it's part of the criminal investigation," I stated curtly, putting down the receiver. Then, softening my voice, I added, "Patty told me that Jane's been having a hard time for the past few days and needs rest."

"Oh," Blanche uttered, surprised at my sudden change of demeanor. Then, changing topics, she asked, "Who called?"

"Someone from the district making sure that I would be at the meeting tomorrow," I lied.

"Those people are nuts!" she declared. "They sure have a lot of time on their hands to be making these idiotic phone calls."

"You're right. Either that, or they're afraid I'm not going to show up," I teased, smiling. "By the way, Blanche, did James Hill ever call back?"

"I don't think so. If he did, I didn't speak to him. Why?"

"No special reason . . . I was just curious, since you mentioned that he called on Monday."

Henry arrived to rescue me, wearing his traditional garb: jeans, starched white shirt, and boots. But this afternoon, he added a twist to his apparel—a white Stetson cowboy hat with a little yellow feather sticking out on the side.

I was about to tell him I liked his hat when the phone rang. It was Patty, so I took the call in my office as he took his hat off.

Blanche and Henry spoke while they waited for me to finish the call. Afterwards, I informed the custodians that we were ready to leave. Henry put his hat back on and the three of us walked out of Madison.

Wednesday: 4:30 P.M. at Madison

Henry drove out of the parking lot. The moment we were clear of the area, I called Darrell Jefferson about the odd list of names on the envelope attached to the school's fundraiser file and his thoughts about Jane Fuller.

After shouting profanities and telling me where to go, the former principal calmed down. He said that he didn't know anything about the envelope and suggested I should speak with Blanche. And, as for Jane, he couldn't imagine why she was working on the budget at Madison or checking on our files. He indicated that Bill Austin was furious when he found out what Jane was up to, but nothing came of it. He believed that she had been instrumental in his ouster.

Henry had been listening intently to my end of the conversation.

When the call concluded, I turned toward him and saw his wary expression.

He asked, "Why the call?"

"I needed to hear Darrell's side of the story," I declared. I told him about the strange envelope and then briefed him on Jane's odd behavior.

"Do you . . .?" he began as I interrupted his train of thought.

"Before I forget, were you able to find out if any money has been electronically transferred into any of the Samuels' accounts?"

"At this point, nothing has happened, but I've red-flagged all of our accounts. If anything comes in, we'll know about it immediately."

"Thank you, Henry," I said. "What about the CDs that I gave to Doc?"

"From what Doc and I can tell, it contains a list of clients and suppliers."

"For what?" I wondered if this really was a drug connection.

"I don't know," he stated, glaring straight ahead at the road. "But there are initials next to each date beside the amount that was either owed or paid."

"Anyone we might know?"

"Unfortunately, yes," he said. "Just so you know, from what we can tell, Bill was not involved in any of this mess. His initials never appeared on any of the files that we've opened. But, the initials 'RJ' appeared frequently."

"As in RJ Beaker?"

"We're not sure."

"You don't think that the Beakers are involved with this?"

"Well, Sam, there's a possibility," he sighed. "Since his father's stroke last year, RJ has been running the company. I know that a while ago they were in terrible financial shape. But, at this time, they appear to be swimming in blue chips."

"Now, that's interesting," I declared.

"The real kicker is that there was no reason for any money problems to begin with. Before Jasper's stroke, we discussed a possible real estate merger in Sonoita."

"Did you see his books?"

"Yes, I did. After our lunch meeting, we went back to his corporate offices, and I went through the books. We thrashed out several scenarios on how to finance the development."

"What did you decide?"

"I told him I needed to check it out with the boss and that I'd get back to him."

"Did Marge decide against the venture?"

"Well, no. That's the funny part. We were ready to set up a limited partnership with Jasper, but then he had a stroke. When I approached RJ about the partnership several weeks later, he said that he wanted to wait until his dad could participate in the negotiations."

"Did you have a problem with this?"

"No. In February, I approached RJ again. He said the company was near bankruptcy and so the deal was off the table."

"That's strange. Do you think that Jasper showed you doctored books?"

"No," he answered. "You know how I check and double-check everyone and everything involved in a deal."

I nodded, knowing his thoroughness.

"Jasper's company was sitting pretty. So was the family—except for RJ."

"What happened?"

"I expect RJ started siphoning company assets to pay off his debts," Henry implied.

"Were his debts so high that it crippled the family business?"

"I don't know, but he's become quite close to Fred Monti."

"What?" I gasped in disbelief. Just the mere mention of the county attorney's name gave me the creeps—I couldn't stand the man. Publicly, he professed the need for law and order in all matters but, in reality, Fred Monti was a sleazy dirtbag that couldn't be trusted. He'd been Peter's boss before he quit but now, ironically, Fred was Thomas' boss.

Glancing in my direction, Henry volunteered, "That was my reaction too."

"How do you know this?"

"Michael Beaker told me when he came to see me last week."

"When did he arrive in town?"

"Two weeks ago," he said. "He was concerned about RJ's sparse reporting to the board of directors."

"That's not good," I said.

"No, it isn't," Henry declared. "When Michael got here, he went directly to the office and started going through the books. He wasn't happy, especially when he found inconsistencies in the profit-and-loss statements. To make matters worse, RJ had taken a large personal loan without the board's approval."

"Did Michael confront him?"

"You bet! You know Michael," he declared, glancing in my direction. "He's a straight shooter. He went directly to their mother and told her what he found. She was devastated, but she wouldn't make a move against RJ."

"Is that when Michael came to you?" I asked.

"Not initially. But when he found out that Fred Monti was acting as RJ's advisor, he needed an objective listener to give him some advice."

"What did you tell him?"

"I told him he has a fiduciary responsibility to inform the other board members. And, believe me; this isn't going to be easy."

"I know, especially since the county attorney is involved in this mess," I stated. "Does Michael also think that RJ embezzled money from the company?"

"Yes, he does, and he has the supporting documentation. But, his mother wants to sweep everything under the rug."

"I would imagine that Michael found that solution unacceptable."

"You're right, Sam," Henry agreed. "The strange part is that the district's funds are somehow mixed up in this."

"How?"

"We don't know. Apparently, Michael approached Bill last Sunday afternoon. He showed him a slip of paper with his name. Bill told him that he didn't know what this was about, but he would get back to him later this week. Unfortunately . . . ."

"He was murdered in my office Sunday evening. Well, that may explain why Bill was at Madison."

"What do you mean?" Henry asked.

"Apparently, Jane Fuller has been working at Madison under the guise of helping Blanche reorganize the Madison's files. She was also keeping her financial records there."

"Why would a finance director do that?"

"Exactly—that's just my point. She wouldn't. But if you and Doc are reading the data correctly, then we may be in the middle of some type of drug operation."

"Sam, why would you say that?" he demanded.

"It is the fastest way of making easy money, especially if you don't have to worry about being prosecuted."

266

"Hence the friendship with Fred Monti," he stated matter-of-factly.

"You got it," I declared.

"What I don't get is—why involve the school district?"

"I think they're laundering money via the district's accounts while they setup their base of operation," I said, pondering all of the implications. "Then the real question becomes—who is behind this? And I certainly don't think RJ is the main culprit."

"I agree with you—he's an idiot!" exclaimed Henry, frustrated. "Look at all the attention he's drawn to himself!"

"RJ may be the front man, if we're correct in our assumptions," I asserted. My mind was racing now. "Henry, what is Michael going to do with his information?"

"I know he tried to talk to his mother again after Bill was murdered, but she refused to believe a word of it. She called him an ungrateful bastard and said that she had regretted the day he was conceived!"

"He must have been devastated."

"That's the least of it. I don't believe that he is going to sit around and watch his brother destroy the company their father worked so hard to build."

"Sad situation," I commented.

We drove for the next five minutes in silence.

I wondered how people found themselves in such convoluted situations. Were they just too trusting, or too greedy? Maybe the old sages were right: Money was the root of all evil. But, if Henry was correct about the information Michael gave him, the motive for Bill's murder might have been self-preservation. Whoever was responsible must have felt cornered. And that made this individual extremely dangerous.

"Here's something else I need you to tell you," I said, breaking his pensive look. "Before you arrived at school, Lois Cameron called and said 'we' want to meet with you as soon as possible at the Arizona Resort's coffee shop."

"So much for hiding you," he declared. "Are you going to meet with them?"

"Yes. Before you ask, I don't want you to be there. I want you to go to the room and wait for me. Call Thomas and tell him what we've discussed."

"Sam, I don't think it's a good idea."

"I agree," I said, seeing his worried look. "I need to know you're safe, Henry. And, if something happens, I can call you for help."

He drove into the resort's parking lot and found a space beneath a shade tree. Worried, Henry stood by the truck and watched me walk away.

Not knowing what to expect, I felt a bit nervous about my clandestine meeting.

Wednesday: 5:00 P.M. at the Arizona Resort

I stepped inside the resort's lobby and glanced toward the darkened dining area, which consisted of a five-star restaurant, an upscale bar, and a luxurious coffee shop. Then I heard a woman in stilettos approach the entrance of the lobby. To my surprise, it was Lois Cameron.

Although pain was etched across her face, somehow she held her arthritic body erect. She greeted me with a nervous smile. "Why, Sam, what a surprise to see you!"

"Hello, Lois. I think the surprise is all mine," I stated casually, bewildered why she was pretending that this was a chance encounter.

"Are you meeting someone here?" she asked, fiddling with a button so loose that it was barely attached to her beige suit jacket.

"No," I stated, looking into her pleading eyes. Something was wrong—but what was it? Lois was becoming more anxious with each passing second. So I added, loud enough for anyone else to hear, "I just wanted to get a quick bite to eat."

"Why don't you join us?" she insisted, taking a step toward the coffee shop.

For some reason, I didn't move. Instead, I scanned the bar area for a clue as to why Lois was so nervous. Two men were huddled together drinking at the bar. Fred Monti turned around. In that instant, I had my answer. Our eyes locked for a split second before he pivoted to his friend. A shiver ran through my body when I recognized his companion—Paul Mendoza!

"I'd love to, Lois," I said. "But first, I need to go say hello to someone." I left her standing there, much to her dismay, and I walked over to the two men.

"Hello, Paul; Mr. Monti," I greeted them, wondering what our acting superintendent and county attorney were discussing in a bar.

Startled to see me, Paul said, "Sam, what are you doing here?"

"I'm staying at the resort while my house is being painted."

"That's interesting. Thomas never mentioned a word about this," the large man scoffed, giving me a quick once over.

"I don't think he would, Mr. Monti."

"Wonders never cease!" he exclaimed in a mocking tone, needling me.

The bartender handed him a fresh drink and walked away.

Monti took a long sip. "I thought the two of you would be married by now. Thomas has always been . . . ."

"I am sure Thomas will be pleased to know how concerned you are about our relationship," I cut in, trying to keep the sarcasm out of my voice.

"Sam, did you get the message about the district meeting tomorrow morning?" Paul blurted out anxiously, attempting to diffuse the situation.

"Yes, I did. What time does it start?"

Before Paul could answer, Fred Monti spoke. "Sam, I've been meaning to send you a condolence card for your daughter's passing. It was such a shame."

"Yes, it was, Mr. Monti," I remarked, thinking this was a bit patronizing since he hadn't bothered to come to Peter's service and had spread disparaging comments about his former chief deputy.

"Can't we bury the hatchet over Peter's death?" he solicited, haughtily. He knew exactly how to push my buttons.

"I still don't have any answers as to what happened to my husband. All I've heard are the different rumors circulating for years."

"Really?" he sneered, "I haven't heard any gossip whatsoever."

I asserted, "Now, that's hard to believe, Mr. Monti. For example, you have deliberately kept me out of the loop in this investigation. Is it because you knew that Peter was set up and murdered?"

"Well, that's not true," he contested in a huff as the bartender handed him another gin and tonic. Fred took a long sip before dismissing me by showing me his back.

"It seems strange that after all of the time, money, and effort put into this investigation by the county and the FBI . . . nothing has ever come of it," I asserted.

Furious, he spun around to say something, sloshing the drink on his expensive suit, but then thought better of it. Instead, he blotted the alcohol stains as his hooded, cobra-like eyes glared at me. A moment later he responded loudly to my taunt. "Well, I am sorry you feel that way, especially since Thomas is the liaison with the FBI. We could always reassign someone else to the case if you're unhappy with Thomas' work."

Divide and conquer—that was this bastard's style. Peter had always been suspicious of this large man, and this conversation only reinforced those sentiments. I glared at him as my anger began to reach a boiling point, hoping that it would make him feel uncomfortable. It seemed to give him some kind of perverted pleasure. So I relaxed into a smile, staring at his increasing bald spot. Within seconds, I was rewarded when I saw him wince.

"Paul tells me that you're the acting principal at Madison," Fred commented, trying to shift the conversation with his oozing, ingratiating charm. "I just want you to know I wish you the best and that if you need anything at all, just let me know and it will be yours . . . of course, within reason."

Paul almost gagged on a sip of coffee.

"Always the consummate politician," I stated, smiling as he preened like a fat peacock, thinking this was a compliment. "Thank you for your interest in my career. And, speaking of careers, I'm assuming you're still planning to run for re-election?"

"Why, of course I'm running. I've got to keep Thomas and my staff employed," he boasted, chuckling to himself.

"I read that you released James Hill in the Hernandez case."

"Unfortunately, that's true. We just don't have the evidence to prosecute that disgusting thug," he gloated superciliously.

Then Fred suddenly changed his mind about discussing the case with me and his cold expression grew darker. "I get it now—why you're so angry about Peter's disappearance. You want to collect the insurance money."

"No, Mr. Monti; I just want closure," I stated, keeping my voice steady. I saw the maniacal smile on his face broaden.

Paul's mouth fell open and he stared at the man seated next to him. He obviously had never encountered this side of Fred Monti.

Suddenly, I felt the hair on my nape prickle. Why I had gone over to speak to them, I will never know. But now I needed to leave immediately, realizing that I never should have confronted Fred Monti. "I see that you have business to discuss."

"Yes, we do, Sam," Paul interjected quickly. He was clearly relieved that I was leaving. "I'll see you tomorrow morning at nine."

"It's been a pleasure, Ms. Samuels," Paul's malevolent companion scoffed, taking another sip of his gin and tonic.

"Gentlemen, the pleasure has been all mine," I stated. Then I left and walked into the coffee shop. Whatever they were up to certainly wouldn't be good for anyone, especially me.

I located Lois' table and sat down, wondering if the occupants had heard any part of the unnerving conversation.

"I'm sorry, Sam. I didn't know they were going to be here," Lois said nervously. "I tried to call, but you'd already left."

"It's all right, Lois," I asserted, watching her daughter clasp her hands on the table. "Hello, Cindy."

"Hi, Sam."

I paused before greeting the muscular bodybuilder seated next to her, realizing I knew this man. It was Carlos Santini, who had worked with Peter at the Justice Department. "It's been a long time since I've seen you, Carlos."

"Yes, it has, Sam. And I go by Carlo," he pointed out.

Now I understood why his name sounded so familiar. I took note of his rough outfit, which would have suited a day laborer—not a seasoned FBI agent. The last time I had seen "Carlo" was at Peter's memorial service.

"I was sorry to hear about your daughter," he admitted, meeting my gaze.

The waitress came and took our order. We waited silently for her to leave before continuing our discussion.

"Are you still with the FBI?" I inquired, still rattled by my encounter with the county attorney. I followed Carlo's gaze and saw Monti glaring at us.

"Yes," he replied, returning his gaze to me.

"Should I be seen with you?" I posed.

"Probably not, but it's too late now," he stated thoughtfully.

"Carlo, Mr. Monti still refuses to give me any information about Peter's death. There have been a lot of rumors about that plane crash . . . ."

"Yes, there have been," he admitted.

"So is it true that Peter was murdered?"

"I . . ." he hesitated, thinking of a way out of his predicament. Finally, he found one and advised me, "It's still classified."

"I have a right to know what happened to my husband. Was he killed in the line of duty, or was this just a freak accident? And why hasn't his body . . .?"

"Everyone on board that plane was burned beyond recognition," he stated, stalling for time.

"I want the truth, damn it!" My head was beginning to pound, so I reached into my purse for an aspirin, but then remembered Ben's warning about taking any medication without his approval.

"I promise you that, when this is over and I get clearance, I will tell you the truth."

I looked out the window. "Is the investigation still active?"

"Yes."

"Is Thomas involved?"

"No," Carlo asserted. "Contrary to what Mr. Monti just told you, Thomas is not our contact person in the county attorney's office."

"I assume it is Mr. Monti."

"But you're not sure. Correct?" he solicited.

"That's right," I agreed, getting a bad feeling. "Something is terribly wrong here. Somehow, Peter's death, Bill's murder, and the district's financial problems are connected . . . how this all works, I don't know."

"Why would you say that?" he demanded.

"Your involvement here, Lois' and Cindy's connection with the district, and seeing those two over there," I charged, gesturing toward Fred Monti and Paul Mendoza.

He leaned back in the seat, grimacing.

"Please stop evading my questions. I need information."

"As I said before, this is an ongoing investigation."

"I see," I commented, understanding that he was not going to reveal anything important. "Are you working undercover?"

"Yes and no."

"That's like being a little pregnant, isn't it?"

"I guess so," he admitted lightheartedly. "Peter always said you were relentless."

"So why are you here?" I pressed.

"I'm here as backup for Cindy and you."

"I don't get it; why do we need backup?"

"First of all, I was supposed to be on that flight. So I owe Peter. Secondly, things aren't what they appear to be," Carlo stated as the waitress arrived with our order.

I was stunned by his statement as I recalled my last conversation with my husband. He had called from the office to say he was flying to D.C. I was surprised, because we'd just finalized our camping plans at breakfast. I knew he had been working on a sensitive matter for the Justice Department, but I still wondered why he had to go to Washington. He could've called or, better yet, just faxed the documents to his handler.

After the waitress left, he cleared his throat. "Cindy decided to postpone her entrance into the FBI academy in order to help her family."

He stopped to look over at Cindy as he took her hand into his. "When she told me about the district's budget problems and that you were going to be the acting principal at Madison, my concern heightened. But the real clincher came when she told me about a voucher made out to the Santini Construction Company for work done at Madison. I knew that wasn't true."

"Okay, that makes sense," I said. "Cindy, when did you learn about my administrative appointment?"

"At the end of April," Cindy said in a soft, wispy voice. "I overheard Jane telling someone that your position was fixed. All they had to do was wait until the right moment."

"What's going on?" I demanded.

"I don't know where to start," Carlo admitted, glancing in the direction of the bar.

Fred Monti was still glaring at us.

"The beginning would be a nice starting point," I suggested, seeing their reluctance.

"I called Cindy," began Lois nervously, "and asked her to come home. She didn't want to because she was ready to enter the FBI academy as Carlo said. Fortunately, she was able to postpone her training for a year."

"Why did you need Cindy's help?"

"Patrick has always been a handful. He's been in and out of the juvenile court system since he was fourteen. No matter what we did, it just didn't seem to help." She paused for a moment, catching my puzzled look, and then added, trying to lighten the mood, "He was our surprise package."

"I'm sorry about Patrick's legal problems, Lois. But that still doesn't answer my question regarding why you asked Cindy to come home."

"Patrick was hanging around DeMorgan Beaker and they were experimenting with drugs and had become hardcore addicts. Patrick was stealing to support his drug habit. No matter what we did, it wasn't the right thing. We even confronted the Beakers, but they believed that it was all Patrick's fault and that their son was totally blameless. My husband and I were at our wits' end. Our only hope to save our son was Cindy. Since he was a baby, Patrick has been close to his sister, and we thought that she could talk to him."

"Did it work?"

"Not in the beginning," Cindy admitted, sitting up straighter. "We were unable to get him to go to a rehab center."

"Sam, Patrick was becoming more violent with each passing day. They couldn't control him," disclosed Carlo, much to the discomfort of both women.

"How so?"

"He began torturing animals and threatening the neighborhood kids. And you know what that means."

Unfortunately, I did know . . . Patrick was on his way to becoming a serial killer. If he didn't get help soon, he would become a danger not only to himself, but to others.

"Patrick stole my gun and threatened to kill Dad if we didn't give him money for his heroin fix. I signaled for my German shepherd to take him down. When he did, I snatched the gun away from Patrick," Cindy revealed softly. "We were lucky to survive that night, and I think maybe we saved his life."

"How?" I asserted.

"Carlo arrived the next day," Lois disclosed as her eyes darted nervously back and forth between her daughter and future son-in-law. "He convinced Patrick to enter rehab and he has been there ever since."

"How's he doing?"

"Better, but each day is still a struggle. It'll probably be that way for the rest of his life," commented Cindy, gingerly reaching out to hold her mother's hand.

"Okay, but why take a job at the district?"

"We needed money to pay the rehab bills, and Mom needed some help at work. She was having trouble with some of the financial records."

"At first, it was little stuff that didn't add up, and then it got a lot worse," Lois admitted.

"She asked me to look at the records and, even with my limited knowledge of accounting, I could tell something was amiss."

"Don't you have a degree in accounting?"

"No. I have a business degree in computer software design. I also have a degree in law enforcement."

"How did you get hired for your position in the district?"

"Well, Bill knew what my plans were, and he could see something weird was going on. So he thought I could use my computer skills to investigate."

"Wasn't that a bit naive on both your parts?"

"Yes, as it turned out. But, at the time, we all thought it was just a computer glitch in the new software. I'm a computer geek, so I thought I could locate the problem and fix it."

"Were you able to?"

"Sort of," she admitted. "After I reentered all of the budget data myself, the problem would be straightened out. Then I would print a hard copy for Bill to go over. He would make corrections and then I would input them and reprint another hard copy. By the time I needed to make copies for the board again, all the numbers were completely different."

"So you think someone hacked into the district's computer system?"

She nodded in agreement.

"Is that why you never came up with any of the 'right' answers during negotiations?" I solicited, becoming aware of Mr. Monti's unrelenting glare.

"You noticed."

"Everyone did," I confirmed.

"I was scared and needed help, so that's when I called Carlo and he came out."

"What was Bill's reaction?"

"He was furious. Only then did I realize that I was in over my head and something was terribly wrong. Luckily, when I started this project, I documented everything on CDs and printed hard copies. I have records of all the reports, the crazy numbers during negotiation, my corrections, Bill's corrections, Paul's revisions, and the screwed-up reports. I also constructed a timeline to determine if there was a pattern as to when the numbers were changed."

"Let me guess," I began. "It started to get crazy when Jane arrived."

"Yes. How did you know?"

"Lucky guess," I commented. "Did Jane spend a lot of time in the office?"

"No," Cindy declared. "That was part of the problem, especially during negotiations. That was her area of expertise. I was beside myself and didn't know what to do. So that's when Bill suggested that I start working with Paul Mendoza to see if we could make any sense of what was going on. He and I would go over the figures and do our best before each bargaining session. Then, in the middle of all the discussions at the table, Jane would walk in with new figures, making us look like idiots. We couldn't figure out why we were always so far off the mark."

"Did you ever tell Paul about your suspicions?"

"No, but I think he had some inklings."

"Did Bill tell him?"

"I don't think so, but I don't know for sure."

"What was Paul's reaction when your projections seemed so off target from Jane's?"

"He was embarrassed at first—then mad. He thought something was wrong with the new database. So we went over all the figures from the beginning. In the end, he seemed to think someone was setting him up because of his wife's gambling debts."

"Is that possible?"

"Sure, anything is possible. You learn in statistics that you can make numbers say anything you want them to say."

"Cindy, do you think Paul was responsible for the computer problems?"

"No!" she affirmed without hesitation.

"He had time, access, and motive."

"That's true, but he doesn't have the computer skills necessary to completely rewrite the program overrides."

"Does Jane have that knowledge?"

"Yes."

"Did you say anything to Jane about the inconsistencies in your numbers?"

"At first, I did. But, after a while, I began to feel as if she was setting me up. That's when I told her I was documenting some of the weird transactions that were taking place—like finding two million dollars on a banking statement one day and then having it disappear into cyberspace the next day. Jane was furious and demanded all my records."

"Did you give them to her?"

"Yes, but only a copy of the latest documents."

"What about Bill? Was he aware of what was going on?"

"Yes. I'd been reporting to him since the beginning. And, before you ask—yes, he had copies of my documentation."

"What was his reaction?"

"He said to sit tight. He wanted me to keep compiling the records."

"I'm confused. Didn't you start working before Jane came on board?"

"Yes, but she was hired two months before I was. I was the first one actually working in the building," she reported. "Jane had been telecommuting before she moved here. That's how she worked on the budget projections and reports."

"She used the Internet," I paused, wondering about the implications. "So she had access to all the monetary information, as well as the bank codes."

"Yes."

"Interesting," I commented. "What happened after negotiations ended?"

"Nothing, really. Jane continued to work out of the office. And, just recently, she became aware that I was still documenting the bank transactions. She blew a gasket!"

"Why?"

"She said that I was overstepping my authority and that, if I didn't stop nosing around, I would be fired."

"Is that what led to that public reprimand?"

"Probably."

"Before you informed her about your files, was she aware that you knew something was wrong?"

"I think so. She kept telling me that Paul had it in for me and was probably setting me up."

"Do you think any of this is true?" I asked, turning to the FBI agent.

"It might be," responded Carlo.

"Why?"

"I've been tailing him for some time, keeping an eye on his finances."

"Isn't that illegal?"

"No. You don't need a search warrant to follow someone or ask questions, and you'd be surprised how much financial data is available legally."

"Okay, how much money does Paul owe and to whom?" I asked, watching Paul Mendoza leave.

"I've heard that he owes $100,000 to a sweetheart named Louie 'Mad Dog' Pacano."

"How did you get that information?" I demanded, thinking that was the exact amount missing from the district's accounts.

"I have friends in some interesting places. Plus, when you factor in some of the information Peter and I were working on, I could see a pattern developing."

I fixated on this tidbit of information, quickly glancing into the bar area again. Fred Monti was exiting the building into the valet parking lot. I was relieved until I heard him yelling my name into his cell phone. He turned and glared at me. In that split second, my arms were covered with goose bumps.

"Sam?" Carlo asked, concerned.

"What kind of a pattern?" I asked, suddenly noticing a tall, bearded man seated in the back of the bar.

"Well . . ." Carlo began and then stopped when he followed my gaze.

"Before you answer that question, I need to do something," I said quietly.

I walked out of the coffee shop to a secluded corner. Then I called my hotel room. Henry answered on the second ring. I whispered, "May Day is a beautiful custom." Then I hung up. I was definitely in over my head, remembering Doc's words.

Two minutes later, Henry walked into the lobby with a briefcase full of documents he'd been working on. This former Marine knew exactly what the odd code meant. It meant "danger—proceed with caution."

As I approached Henry in the foyer, I remembered Thomas telling me to trust my intuition. I told him about my chance meeting with Fred Monti and Paul Mendoza and then with Carlo Santini. I needed him to get in touch with Thomas on a land line to alert him about what had transpired and that we needed to meet at my house in an hour.

Henry stood there listening with a grim expression.

Once I had finished speaking, he left the lobby to make his calls. I knew the first call would be to Marge, the second to Thomas, and the third to Pepé to be prepared for trouble. The next few calls would be to his unknown sources in Washington. What I'd just told him confirmed his suspicions that his beloved son had been murdered. Someone very powerful had covered up Peter's death for some unknown reason.

Returning to the coffee shop, I felt anger. I wanted all the facts that had been kept from me, but I knew that wasn't going to happen. So I sat back down at the table and just observed the situation.

Carlo took a sip of his drink, surveying the room. "Peter and I were working on a case in which money was being diverted electronically from federally mandated programs. We were convinced that someone in a position of power was behind it. This elected official had been embezzling funds from different programs for years. On the morning Peter left for Washington D.C., he got a lead to the identity of the man behind the operation. And, before you ask, I don't know who he is," he admitted, covering his mouth with a napkin. "That information died with Peter, along with the evidence that linked this individual to the crime."

I knew he wasn't telling me the truth. Peter was meticulous about keeping records up to date. I was sure that he would've sent the information to his handler before he boarded that plane. "Have you told Sheriff Peterson what you've told me?"

"I have an appointment to update him tomorrow," Carlo advised, looking at Cindy.

"I have told the sheriff what I know and given him all of my records," Cindy acknowledged.

"I don't get it; why are you telling me all of this?" I demanded.

"Sam, I think your life is in danger, and we can help each other by sharing our information."

"Thank you for your concern, but I don't know anything of value to share with you. If I think of something later, may I call you, Carlo?"

"Sure, want me to . . ." he began, handing me his card.

"Thank you," I addressed him hesitantly. "Carlo, I'm a little overwhelmed with what you have told me. And I won't lie to you . . . but I'm not sure if what you're telling me is the truth, or just your version of it. You've given me a lot to think about."

"Sam, I can assure you that we are telling you the truth," said Lois, looking rather surprised.

"Lois, I'm sure you all have. But, for the past three years, all I've worried about was my daughter's health, and now she's dead. The district was not a high priority. And now I find myself in an unbelievable position . . . trying to save Madison and being a target, as well as being involved in a murder investigation, which may or may not be connected to my dead husband."

"Sam, I know you're inundated right now, but you're wrong about Peter . . . ."

I was petrified when I caught a second glimpse of the bearded stranger at the bar staring at me again as he spoke on his cell phone.

"Thank you for the information," I stated. "I need to go now, but I promise to keep in touch." On that note, I rose from my seat, paid the bill, and left them speechless.

Wednesday: 5:45 P.M. at the Arizona Resort

Flushed with worry, Henry seized my elbow as soon as I exited the building. He guided me back through the lobby and out the resort's rear entrance to a weathered, green Ford Expedition waiting at the curb.

To my surprise, Doc Simpson was sitting behind the wheel, revving its earsplitting engine with the rear door open. Henry shoved me inside the vehicle and ordered me to get down on the floor. As soon as he slammed the door shut, he climbed into the passenger seat in front. Doc hit the gas and sped out of the parking lot and down Main Street.

"Can I sit up now?" I yelled at the top of my lungs, breathing in dog and cat dander. I felt like a total idiot.

"No," Doc shouted adamantly, placing his cigar in the ashtray. "We're being followed."

"By whom?" I wondered, worried. Could these be the thugs that ran me off the road?

"That's the problem, Sam—we don't know," Doc declared, glancing in his rearview mirror again. He recognized the Toyota Camry that had peeled out after them. "Henry . . ." Doc began, turning his attention back to the road.

"I'm on it, Doc. The Toyota is three car-lengths behind you, playing in traffic," Henry reported, watching the car's image on the passenger side mirror. The vehicle was weaving in and out of traffic, keeping Doc's Expedition in sight.

"Henry, were you able to contact anyone in D.C.?" I hollered, glancing at his hat.

"Yes, Sam, I was. They indicated that there was something funny going on," he shouted over the engine's deafening roar as he watched the Toyota slither behind the Suburban that was almost sitting on Doc's bumper.

This new bit of information scared me. "Did they say what it was?" I pressed.

"No," he admitted angrily, surveying the area as Doc sped down an uneven side street, leaving the Toyota stuck at a red light.

"Henry, did you speak to Thomas?" I yelled, feeling the floor's bumpy vibrations.

"Yes," he replied curtly, watching the Toyota reappear suddenly from a side road and then accelerate to catch up to us. "At this point, he knows everything we know but feels this is all circumstantial."

"Sam, did you learn anything new from Lois?" Doc coughed in his gruff voice, after taking another puff of his cigar.

Thank goodness he had rolled down the backseat window! I lifted my head to get a whiff of fresh air. "Apparently, Jane had the district's codes to work with via the Internet before she arrived in the valley."

"So she had access to their records," Henry stated, drumming his fingers on the door's arm rest.

"Yes," I shouted.

"Interesting," Doc noted, stopping at a red light. Then, looking in his rearview mirror, he tried to identify the driver and his companion but, unfortunately, the dark tinting on the Toyota's windows made it impossible. So he told us, "My source at the Sheriff's Department told me that they have a potential lead on the second blood sample."

"Did he tell you who it was, Doc?" I asked.

"The sheriff ordered this individual's DNA run through CODIS."

"Why," I blurted out, thinking Doc was being evasive.

"What is CODIS?" Henry demanded. He cringed as Doc picked up his cigar.

"It's an FBI computer system that stores criminals' DNA profiles," Doc answered, making a sudden sharp turn.

"How are they going to get this individual's DNA sample?" Henry persisted as he turned a funny shade of green, from inhaling Doc's cigar smoke.

Placing his cigar back in the astray, Doc replied, "The sheriff got a court order for a Buccal Swab late last night."

"What's a Buccal Swab?" Henry swore, frustrated that he didn't know the police jargon.

"A Buccal Swab is a sterilized Q-tip used to swab your mouth for epithelial cells. Afterwards, it is submitted to the police lab for testing. Once they have a DNA profile, the lab tech runs that sample through CODIS," I explained, sitting up onto the seat.

"Get down!" they shouted in unison. Then Doc picked up the cigar and took a drag as Henry rolled down his window for some fresh air.

"So who do they suspect?" Henry pressured, making sure I'd resumed my position on the floor.

"Rob Stone," Doc finally revealed, changing lanes rather abruptly when the Toyota almost nudged his bumper.

"Ned Tomer's son-in-law?!" Henry shouted in disbelief.

"Doc, if your source is suggesting that Rob Stone may be a suspect, there may be a problem with the dried blood sample that was found at Bill Austin's murder scene."

"Meaning what, Sam?" Doc asked, swerving to avoid hitting a car turning left.

"Rob's been at Madison for months helping Jane. Let's say that he cut his finger on one of his visits, or had a bloody nose three weeks ago," I theorized.

"Okay, so what's the problem?" Doc huffed.

"The problem is that the experts can't tell the age of a DNA sample—meaning that the DNA they collected might have been there for weeks and have nothing to do with Bill's murder," I explained.

"Oh shit!" he fumed.

"Do they at least have him under surveillance?" Henry uttered.

"Probably, until they get the DNA results," I replied. "Then they'll bring him in for questioning."

"Rob's a recovering addict and my guess is he's had a relapse," Henry injected into the conversation.

"How do you know this, Henry?" I shouted.

"Ned Tomer told me."

"Well, Ben Machado noticed that Rob had a nose problem the other night in the ER. When he confronted him, Rob stopped talking," Doc interjected, rescuing Henry. He could tell that Henry was bothered by his disclosure.

"Doc, how do you . . .?" I asked, amazed at his ability to gather sensitive information.

"My source works in the ER," he chuckled.

"If that is the case, I know Ben ordered a drug-screening test. And Thomas will be able to subpoena the results," I declared, recalling my conversation with Ned Tomer. "But all of this is only conjecture on our part."

"Why would Rob murder Bill?" Henry asked, still upset.

"Bill got in the way," asserted Doc, turning down a back alley as the Toyota came to a sudden halt in the middle of a traffic jam, unable to follow us.

"Let's assume that Rob did murder Bill. What was his motivation? Revenge for an injustice he felt—like being accused of using drugs or getting caught doing something illegal? For whatever the reason, I don't think he did this on his own. The question then becomes—who else is involved?" I posed, sitting up for a momentary gulp of fresh air.

"Now you're thinking, Sam!" declared Doc, exiting the alley and turning onto Power Road.

Henry remained conspicuously silent.

"Doc, how many different blood sources were there at the murder scene?" I wondered, thinking of RJ.

"At least three different blood types," Doc confirmed, bringing his speed down to make a sharp left turn.

"Have they identified anyone else?" I pressed.

"Just Austin's," he reported. "They're still working on the other profiles."

"Well, Jane could be one of the other blood sources and, here again, she may be innocent," I theorized, thinking about the age of the sample and how easily a lawyer could dismiss this allegation in court.

"That could be a possibility, Sam," Henry declared, turning around to check on me.

"How did Jane get the job in the first place?" Doc demanded. He was still driving evasively, even though he had shaken the tail.

Henry stated, "RJ and Fred Monti recommended her to the board."

"How do you know?" posed Doc.

"I have an unimpeachable source."

"Marge!" both Doc and I answered at the same time, laughing. We knew that she was the only unimpeachable source in this family.

Henry went on to tell us about the phone call with his wife. She told him that RJ and Fred had met Jane at an alumni party at Yale eighteen months ago. After he finished his narrative, we were all quiet, lost in our own thoughts.

Doc drove around for another fifteen minutes, taking back roads to our final destination.

I was beyond carsick, and my head was throbbing again. "Does Ned know about Rob's potential involvement?"

"I don't think so," Henry put forth, worried.

"Henry, do you think Ned may be involved in this too?" Doc pressed, taking his eyes off the road for a moment to look at his cousin.

"I hope not," Henry replied slowly.

"Well, if Rob and Jane are involved, they definitely are not in charge of the operation," I said. "So who's running it?"

"My money is on RJ Beaker," Doc declared. "He's on the hook for all the money he borrowed from the family's business, especially since his brother is pressuring him to repay the loans ASAP."

"He may be involved, but I don't think he has the brains to run an operation like this."

"Sam's right," Henry insisted, drumming his fingertips.

"Then who?" Doc speculated, turning into my driveway, only to be welcomed by a flock of screeching geese.

Henry and I remained silent, contemplating the answer to Doc's question as he parked close to the porch. I rose from the Expedition's floor, clutching my jacket and Gucci bag, completely covered in dog and cat hair. Henry helped me out of the pinging vehicle. Without warning, thirty geese broke away from the flock and charged in our direction. I was totally unnerved when I couldn't locate the house keys in my purse.

"Sam, I have mine," Henry yelled over the boisterous racket as he and Doc both dashed up the steps. They were running for their lives as I sprinted right behind them. I glanced over my shoulder and was stunned to see that the geese were advancing toward us at an alarming speed.

Henry fumbled with the key for a second but then opened the front door. Quickly, we ran inside and I slammed it shut, cutting off the aggressive fowls' pursuit. I leaned against the closed door, relieved that we made it inside safely.

Smiling, I saw Henry and Doc grinning from ear to ear, brimming with excitement as they tried to catch their breath. Then I took off my shoes, because my feet were killing me. "Gentlemen, make yourselves at home."

I left them to their own devices . . . .

Wednesday: 6:25 P.M. at My Home

Both men wanted snacks but, unfortunately, they were on special diets. As they entered the kitchen, they were each craving forbidden food. Henry chose chips and dip, but Doc preferred candy to satisfy his sweet tooth. By the time I had changed into jeans and a pink tank top, they were sitting at the table munching on their illicit snacks and discussing the case.

"Henry, did you tell Thomas about RJ's financial problems?" I asked, crossing the kitchen's threshold.

"Yes, I did," he uttered. "Funny thing, though, he wasn't surprised. I got the impression that RJ was also under the watchful eye of our new sheriff."

"That's interesting," I commented. "What puzzles me is I can't shake the feeling that Peter's death somehow triggered this whole mess."

"He's been dead for over three-and-a-half years, so that can't be true, Sam," Henry stated, looking distraught. "You're just upset because of your run-in with Fred Monti."

"Maybe." I shrugged, recalling the conversation with that condescending prick.

"Honey, do you still have Peter's old work files?" Doc asked cautiously.

"I think so" I volunteered, wondering if his hesitancy had something to do with what I said about Peter. "They may be in the office."

"Do you mind if I snoop around?"

"Of course not, Doc," I said. "What are you looking for?"

"Information," he declared.

I knew he was worried. "Maybe you can find the 'smoking gun' in this mess."

"Before you go, Doc—how's the puppy?" Henry asked, changing the subject.

"She's doing just fine. Miss Paws—that's her name, by the way— is responding well to the medication," Doc answered, getting up.

"Miss Paws, huh?" I said softly. "How did she come by that name?"

"Nora. She fell in love with that shivering little mass of fur the first time she cuddled her in her arms. This morning she took her to be groomed. Miss Paws came back looking like an Ewok from the old movie, *Star Wars*. Can you believe that?"

"So you're going to keep her?" I concluded.

"I don't think I have much choice in the matter. Remember, I'm just the husband." Seeing my wistful reaction, he inquired, "Do you mind?"

I knew he would be sleeping in his man cave in the garage if he forced Nora to give up the puppy. "No, Doc. I think Miss Paws will be very happy in her new home."

"She should be," he remarked, taking a handful of chips. "She's getting the royal treatment. Nora's been at a loss since Snowflake passed away. And the funniest damn thing is that Miss Paws likes to garden with her."

"Well, at least something good has come out of this nightmare," I grinned, picturing the pair gardening in their back yard.

"And, for another thing, she likes Country-Western music. Can you beat that?"

"No," I said as Doc left the room, gnawing on a chip.

Henry wanted to know what else I'd learned from Cindy and Carlo.

So I briefed him but didn't mention the uneasiness I felt about his son. Peter had withdrawn from the family weeks prior to his death. I knew he had been in constant contact with his handler but had refused to divulge that agent's identity or anything else about his work. Maybe Carlo could get Peter's handler to shed some light on this investigation.

"Sam, Bill was aware of Cindy's suspicions. Why did he go to Madison?" Henry posed, jarring me back to the present.

"After he spoke with Michael on Sunday, he probably became suspicious as to why Jane was working at the school. I guess he went to find the evidence to confront her."

"Okay, I buy that," Henry said. "But what I don't understand is how you ended up with the CDs in the first place."

"On Friday afternoon, I copied all of the office files onto a flash drive. After the break-in Monday night, I downloaded the files from the flash drive onto the teacher's computer in the lab and then created the first set of CDs. Later that night, in the process of going through other files, I accidentally hit something that caused the odd set of files to appear on the screen. I backed them up on the flash drive and then burned copies of those documents onto another set of CDs."

"Why did you backup your office files?"

"I needed to access various files to finish writing a report for the district."

"Oh," he uttered. Then he remained quiet for a long time. "Were there any CDs on your desk when you left for the airport?"

"No," I admitted, now puzzled. "What CDs are you talking about, Henry?"

"Blanche told me that Jane had been using your office computer."

"I know," I said, still not getting what Henry was implying.

He began, "Did you know that Jane showed up panic-stricken after you left Friday?"

"No," I uttered, stunned that Blanche had relayed this information to Henry but hadn't mentioned it to me.

"Apparently, Jane told Blanche that she'd misplaced her CDs. She thought that she'd left them on your desk or in the computer lab. When she couldn't find them anywhere, she tried burning duplicates."

"Was she successful?" I inquired.

"No. Your computer froze, and she thought she'd lost all the data," he stated.

"She must have been furious," I mused, picturing her tearing the desk apart.

"She was. She even called someone to help her fix the 'fucking computer.'"

"That's weird. Who did she call?" I questioned aloud.

"I asked Blanche that but she didn't know."

"Why were the CDs so important?"

"They contained the budget information for a special project she was working on. Then she asked Blanche not to tell anyone the real reason why she'd been working at Madison."

"Did Blanche mention this to the sheriff?" I wondered, trying to figure out where those CDs might be.

"Unknown," Henry disclosed, seeing the concern on my face.

"Why didn't Blanche tell me about this?" I retorted.

"Perhaps she didn't think about it until we were talking," Henry stated.

"Maybe so. When were the two of you talking?" I asked, knowing he was giving Blanche the benefit of the doubt but I still wondered what Jane was up to.

"When you were on the phone with Patty," Henry said, watching me carefully bite down on my lip. "By the way, Doc figured out how the Santini Construction Company ended up with an electronic bank deposit."

"What happened?" I asked.

"A couple of the banking numbers were transposed," he replied.

"That still doesn't jive, because Cindy has a payment voucher to the Santini Construction Company for the job."

"We'll look at it again," Henry promised, scratching his head. "We're dealing with professionals and not home-grown idiots."

"Maybe, but who is in charge?" I said, fixated on the answer to that question.

"Well, that's the big question. Sam, I need to get something to eat. Marge is going to kill me if she finds out I've been munching on potato chips instead of eating a healthy snack."

"Henry, I'm sorry; I don't know where my manners have gone. What would you and Doc like for dinner?"

"Sandwiches would be fine," he uttered.

As I started to enter the pantry, I heard a loud ruckus. The geese were on alert . . . whoever it was would have to be nuts to try to break in. Then I heard someone knock at the back door. I held my breath as Henry let the visitor in. It was Pepé. He was carrying a large picnic basket and placed it on the counter.

The unmistakable aroma of Maria's Mexican food made my stomach rumble. She had made my favorite chicken enchiladas with green sauce. They were carefully placed on top of refried beans, and corn and flour tortillas. For dessert, she had prepared flan. I gave him a hug and asked him to thank Maria for making dinner.

Henry and Pepé stepped outside to discuss a security matter with the other guards. I wondered how they could hear anything with that awful noise.

After I finished setting the table, I went to fetch Doc. He seemed unusually quiet but his coloring appeared—as if he'd seen a ghost. As we walked back into the kitchen, Doc went directly to the bar to find a bottle of whiskey.

Henry and I watched him pour a drink and down it in one gulp.

"Sam, when was the last time you went through Peter's desk?" Doc demanded, pouring himself another.

"About two weeks ago," I confirmed, wondering why he was so upset.

"Are you sure that Peter didn't leave you a letter in case he didn't return from Washington?"

"Yes," I asserted, giving him a quizzical look. "If he had, he would have placed it in the safe with all of our important papers."

"Sam, did you go through Peter's papers after his death?" Doc challenged.

"Yes, I gathered all of our personal documents from the safe and desk . . . and dealt with them shortly after he died," I acknowledged, feeling uneasy with Doc's strange behavior.

"Why didn't you go through his work files?" he pressed, taking a sip.

"I decided to deal with those papers in the summer, but I never did."

"Why?" Doc asked, pressing the issue.

"Maxie had just been diagnosed with leukemia and was fighting for her life," I stated as tears sprung to my eyes. "She became my top priority and Peter's files didn't matter."

"Are you aware that Peter left us each a letter?" he related gently.

"No!" I snapped, dumbfounded.

As if reading my mind, Doc answered the question: "They were hidden in his desk."

"Oh!" was the only word I could manage to utter. Suddenly, I needed to sit down. I'd emptied that desk less than two weeks ago and those damn letters hadn't been there. So, unless Doc had found a secret compartment, someone must have put them there. But who?

My stomach rumbled, but I'd already lost my appetite. I watched Henry collapse into a chair. He hadn't said a word but just sat there staring at the letters in Doc's hand.

"Sam, would you recognize Peter's handwriting?" Doc inquired, meeting my eye.

"Yes. Why?"

He handed me the letters. After all these years, the thought of receiving a letter from my dead husband left me feeling like I collided with a bombshell. I carefully inspected the handwritten envelopes and, to my horror, I recognized my husband's penmanship. "Yes, this is Peter's handwriting."

Henry just sat there in a daze, looking like he'd been struck by a bolt of lightning.

Doc poured him a shot of whiskey and told him to drink it. Henry obeyed without a whimper. Then, still at a loss for words, he held out his glass for another shot. Doc refilled the glass. Then, glancing in my direction, he held up the bottle.

I shook my head; I didn't need a drink. Tears streamed down my face. Damn the concussion! I hated feeling vulnerable. How could this be happening? Silently, I rose and gave Henry and Doc their letters.

Doc opened his letter first and handed it to me to verify the handwriting. There was no denying it: the writing definitely resembled Peter's. Then I focused on the date, gasping as the color drained from my face. It was dated a week ago!

"Sam, are you okay?" Henry demanded, watching me turn white.

When I didn't answer, he came to my side and glanced at the letter. He too saw the date. Henry cleared his throat, "How could this be? Peter . . . ."

"We don't know," Doc said just above a whisper, looking at the letter as Henry returned to his seat. "He could've postdated the letters, thinking Sam would find them at a later time. Or he may have left them as a kind of an insurance policy in case something went wrong."

"But why now?" Henry declared, watching me closely.

"I don't know."

"Doc, are you implying that Peter's alive?" Henry questioned close to tears.

"Maybe," he declared softly, unable to meet his gaze.

"I think I need that drink, gentlemen. Would either of you care to join me?"

"Yes, I think we would," responded Henry, still shaken.

I walked over to the bar—Peter's bar. I handed them the whiskey bottle and grabbed another container, poured tequila into a small glass, and downed it in one gulp. A burning sensation followed the amber liquid down my throat into the pit of my stomach. My face turned red, radiating heat from the alcohol. Then I felt ill. I ran to the bathroom and threw up, wondering—are you dead or alive, Peter? And if you did survive that plane crash, where the hell have you been all this time?

Doc picked up his letter, read it, and then handed it to Henry, who put on his reading glasses and scanned his son's epistle. Still in shock, he returned the letter to Doc. Both cousins were discussing the implications of Peter's letters as I returned.

I picked up my letter and held it for a long time. Its contents terrified me.

"Sam, do you want me to open the letter?" Doc prompted while I took my seat next to Henry, who put his arm around my shoulders. I froze, unable to answer his question. I stared first at the letter, then across the room at Peter's picture on the counter.

"Sam, we need to know what he wrote," Doc pressed. "It . . . ." He walked over, carefully removing the letter from my hand, and opened it.

Henry and I just sat there, holding our collective breaths.

"These are legal documents for you," Doc said gently.

"Those letters and documents weren't in the desk two weeks ago, and I don't know who put . . ." I stopped speaking abruptly. All of a sudden it hit me: The only person who could have put those damn letters in the desk was my dead husband! If Peter was really alive, he was playing one of his power games. And I wasn't going to let him win this time. Damn him, if he thought he could still control me, he was mistaken!

Both men remained quiet, watching my expressions move from shock to beyond furious.

"Are you okay, honey?" asked Henry. "Should I call Marge to come over?"

"No, I'm fine," I said. I retrieved Peter's letter and placed it with his photograph in a kitchen drawer. Then, I shifted back to the investigation. "Henry, let's review what we know about Bill's murder and the second break-in."

"Okay," he uttered, relieved to see that spark of self-assurance in my eye.

"Sam, get me some index cards," commanded Doc.

"Why Doc?" asked Henry.

"So I can write down each suspect's name on the front and the pertinent information on the back."

I smiled, opening a drawer and handing him the cards, thinking how much alike they were. Both used visual aids to organize complex information. Henry used a chalkboard, and Doc used index cards. I returned to my seat and spouted off names. "Rob Stone, RJ, and Jane."

Doc wrote each name in large block letters on individual index cards.

"What about Darrell Jefferson?" asked Henry.

"I really don't think he's involved, but we need to keep all possibilities open."

"Okay—write his name down," Henry approved.

"Henry, what about RJ's kid?" questioned Doc.

"DeMorgan?" I sputtered.

"Yes, Sam. How about James Hill? He's that kid in the Hernandez case?" Doc said.

"How do you know him?" I asked, amazed at his knowledge.

"His mother used to work for me as a vet assistant. Henry told me that he called the school Monday and wanted to attend the community meeting."

"That's true, Doc, but he never called back and didn't show up."

"Speaking of that meeting, what about Paul Mendoza?" Henry declared.

"Then add Cindy Cameron and Carlos . . . Carlo Santini to the list," I stated.

"You know, Sam, great minds think alike!"

"Thanks, Henry," I smiled as he took my hand and held it tightly.

"I've got a couple of more names," Doc added. "Fred Monti, our illustrious county attorney, and we also need to consider Mrs. Austin and Peter."

Just the mere mention of Peter's name sent shivers down my back. Grief was a funny sentiment. It held a wide range of strong emotions that came out at the oddest times and sent people reeling. Henry looked like he'd been slapped, and Doc looked slightly unnerved; I could only imagine how awful I looked.

"Doc's right, Henry," I reasoned, squeezing his hand. "If Carlo is involved, there is a connection with Peter. We just don't know what it is," I asserted quietly. I felt like such a fool as I wiped my angry tears.

"Let's start with a motive," Doc directed, clearly moving our investigation along.

"Money," I stated, croaking hoarsely. "It's the only thing that makes any sense."

"I agree with Sam," Henry added, taking a sip of coffee. "And drugs are one way of making money fast."

"Sam, any other thoughts?" Doc mentioned, looking up from writing.

"Only that Madison might be the staging area for a drug distribution center."

"Why do you think that?"

"Well, Doc, the fact that the school is in a barrio and the building is in terrible shape. Darrell Jefferson was removed unceremoniously as the principal, and I was placed in the position because I am inexperienced."

Both men began to defend my honor, but I stopped them with a flicker of an eye and continued to play the devil's advocate. "Bill Austin may have had a connection with the drug trade that cost him his life," I reflected, watching Doc write his name on a card. "Think about it: He wanted to be totally involved with the day-to-day operations at Madison. I took that to mean he wanted to help me succeed, but maybe he was setting me up to be the fall guy."

"That may be true, but do you believe it?" challenged Henry.

"I'm not sure what I believe anymore," I stated, hesitating. "But my gut is telling me that he was an innocent victim in this mess."

"Did Bill have any money problems?" Doc asserted.

"Doc, he had a gambling problem several years ago, but I know he attended Gamblers Anonymous meetings regularly. He also did a lot of community service work in that area."

"What about Mrs. Austin?"

"As far as I know, she was the last person to see her husband alive. She also seemed to think that Bill and I were having an affair."

Both men grimaced but let it go.

"Didn't she attend the community meeting the other night?" insisted Henry, clearly disturbed with the woman's allegation.

"Yes. Why do you ask, Henry?" I let go of his hand to take a sip of water.

"Mostly curious," admitted Henry, sitting back in his chair. "I just want a clear picture of who we're talking about. What was your impression of her that evening?"

"Well, she appeared to be a grieving widow," I described, thinking back. "I don't know why she came. Maybe she was curious about me and the school where her husband was murdered."

"True enough. Did she speak to you at all that night?"

"Yes, Doc, she did. It was strange though . . . she'd overheard my confrontation with Paul and seemed dismayed. But, then she volunteered to work with at-risk kids."

"Do you know anything else?"

"No, not really—just that she was my supervisor at the university."

"We'll have to find out more about her and her relationship with her husband," surmised Doc, writing himself a note.

"Paul Mendoza has zipper and alcohol problems," volunteered Henry, sipping more of his strong black coffee.

"Henry!" I uttered, surprised at his comment.

"I did some checking into his financial affairs. He's on the verge of bankruptcy. Not to mention that his soon-to-be ex-wife is out for blood."

"Where did you get this information?" I asked, concerned.

"From a source," he said mysteriously.

I knew that Paul's wife was a first-class bitch. No wonder he was acting like a jerk, with all these rumors flying around!

"What about Fred Monti?" Doc mused. "Peter didn't trust the man."

Henry went on, "I think that's why he quit his job and went to work for the Justice Department. It's weird that Fred's name keeps popping up."

"Especially if he's involved with RJ," I chimed in as both men met my gaze. "And, according to the district's gossip, Fred's linked romantically with Ruth Beaker. After seeing him in the bar with Paul Mendoza, it really makes me wonder what he's up to."

"It sure does, Sam," declared Doc. As we had been theorizing, Doc had written quite a lot of information about each suspect. Then, on a separate card, he created a list of questions that needed answers.

Somehow, during our discussion, we had managed to eat dinner.

The phone rang and I got up to answer the call. When I recognized Thomas' cell number, I looked over at Henry. He was just sitting there, staring into space as he turned Peter's letter over and over again in his hands. "Hi Thomas," I greeted, feeling a range of emotions. I needed to tell him about Doc's discovery.

"Hi Sam," he said. "Jack and I will be there soon."

"Okay, honey," I said a bit nervous.

"Did you crack and tell Henry about us?" he teased.

"No, I haven't, but I need to tell . . ." I began with a catch to my voice.

"I've got to go, something is breaking right now," he interrupted abruptly.

"Thomas, I need to tell . . ." I repeated as he disconnected.

Henry and Doc had been watching me. When they saw me hang up the phone, they quickly began reviewing the note cards.

I started cleaning the kitchen. While I worked, I thought about what I wanted in my life. The only thing I knew for sure was that I wanted to be with Thomas—whether Peter was alive or not. As I dumped the paper plates into the garbage can, I realized that Maxie and I had been nothing more than disposable trash to Peter. He walked out of our lives without giving us a second thought.

My thoughts ran wild. *Damn you, Peter. How could you do this to us? If you wanted out, we could have gotten a divorce. I knew we had our problems, but how could you turn your back on Maxie? I thought you loved our little girl.*

I shuddered; afraid that Thomas would step aside again believing it was in my best interest. I wasn't about to let that happen. I stood tearless in front of the sink for a long time, staring out into a dark sky.

Wednesday: 7:30 P.M. at My Home

Thomas waved at Pepé who stood on guard. As the pint-sized man returned the gesture, the sheriff crossed the cattle guard and proceeded at a snail's pace toward the house. He skillfully avoided the geese milling about the road.

Suddenly, the flock charged the vehicle when the sheriff parked behind Doc's Expedition. Thomas and Jack jumped out of the Tahoe and sprinted to the door as three wild determined geese flew directly at them. With dust swirling around them, Jack used his hat to propel the hostile birds back as both men ran inside. Thomas slammed the door shut when Jack entered, leaving the agitated geese outside.

"What the hell!" Jack declared, a bit stunned by the aggressive birds. "Who came up with this bright idea to have geese surrounding the house?"

"Henry," Thomas laughed. He brushed the dust off from his dark jeans and shirt. "Sam, where are you?"

"In the kitchen," I answered.

"Why the geese?" Jack demanded.

"It's Henry's way of protecting his family," Thomas said, seeing Jack's quizzical expression. "There's a legend that a gaggle of geese saved the city of Rome."

"I'm aware of that legend."

"Henry has never forgotten it," Thomas conveyed, seeing Jack's jaw drop.

"After tonight, I can certainly see why."

As they entered the kitchen, they heard us debating our take on the case.

Thomas kissed me on the forehead and then greeted Henry and Doc. When he sat down next to me, I heard his stomach rumbling. I knew that Thomas hadn't eaten much during the day because he was in trial. So I fixed both men a plate of Maria's remnants, as well as a dish of flan for dessert. While they ate, they listened to our competing theories.

"I still think this Hill kid is dangerous, Sam," Henry voiced, holding the card with the boy's name.

Thomas and Jack stopped eating and glanced at the older man.

"Why?" I asked.

"Primarily because he wanted to know if you were the new principal," Henry grumbled, taking a sip of lukewarm coffee.

"James has had a rough life, and I know he hasn't made the best choices. But, Henry," I stated, looking directly at him. "I don't think he would hurt me."

"Oh, to be both so young and naïve could be very dangerous, Sam," Jack asserted, savoring the last bite of flan.

"Do you think there's a connection between Fred and James?" I asked my future husband, who dropped his fork at the mere mention of his boss' name.

Instantly, he traded glances with Jack and then retrieved the fork from the floor.

Henry took note but said nothing.

Doc sat quietly, pretending to read the index cards on the table.

Thomas' stern expression made it clear that something had transpired, yet he said nothing. He took the empty dishes to the sink and stood there for what seemed to be an eternity, cooling down. He rinsed the dirty plates and placed them into the dishwasher. Afterwards, he grasped the coffee pot and poured everyone a refill.

Still, no one said anything until he sat down again.

"Sam," Thomas said calmly, masking his anger. "The reason James was let go was because Mr. Monti felt the evidence didn't warrant a prosecution."

"You felt it did," I asserted quietly.

"Yes. But he's the county attorney so he calls the shots," Thomas insisted.

Clearly, I had struck a nerve. Everyone was on edge. Shifting his weight in his seat, Henry accidently stomped on Jack's foot. The sheriff choked on his coffee, and a small stream of dark liquid dribbled out of his mouth. He turned and gave my father-in-law a dirty look. Embarrassed, Henry apologized.

"What about Carlo Santini? Is he for real or a renegade agent?" Doc posed, refocusing the discussion.

"Where's this coming from?" sputtered Jack, putting down his cup.

Doc argued, "Santini has computer knowledge as does his girlfriend, Cindy Cameron. They could've screwed up the district's programs without too much trouble."

"But they certainly weren't involved from the beginning," noted Thomas.

"That's true, but Lois Cameron was," I inserted. "She's definitely in the position to orchestrate a drug-smuggling operation from her desk."

"How?" Jack asked as Doc bumped his elbow, reaching for an index card.

"She has access to a phone and is under very little supervision," I countered, wondering what Doc and Henry were doing to Jack.

"I hadn't considered that scenario, Sam," Henry said quietly.

"Remember, Lois was instrumental in the purchase of the financial software. She controlled the data input and could've easily created an atmosphere of suspicion."

"Why would she do that?" Thomas quipped. "She's a valued employee of the district. There's no reason for her to ruin her reputation."

"Her son is in a drug treatment center," Henry disclosed.

"How do you know this?" Jack insisted, turning to the man next to him.

"That's what Lois told Sam this afternoon," Henry reported.

"Why would she tell you that?" Jack quizzed suspiciously, looking at me.

"Maybe she wanted to gain Sam's confidence," Henry asserted before I could respond. "Lois knows that Sam would pass the information on to you via Thomas."

Doc, who cherished playing the mediator role, buzzed in with his own scenario. "Could she be in charge of the money?"

311

"That's a damn good question," Jack declared. He looked over at Henry and then Doc. Cautiously, he took a sip of his coffee. "But why would she do that?"

"Maybe she needs money for her son's treatment," I countered.

"If that's true, why involve her daughter?" queried Jack.

"Her son became violent and she couldn't handle the situation," I stated.

"When did her son start taking drugs?" Thomas solicited.

"Lois implied that Patrick began taking drugs when he started hanging out with DeMorgan Beaker."

"Funny, isn't it? All roads seem to lead back to the Beakers one way or another," declared Henry, reaching over for RJ's card. "Well, if money laundering is the motive, then RJ is involved."

"But let's consider a different motive," mused Doc.

"Like what?" countered Henry, rubbing his chin.

"Revenge. Lois fits the bill because she blames DeMorgan for Patrick's addiction."

"She wouldn't have killed Bill," I said.

"Suppose he got in her way," uttered Doc, playing with Lois's index card.

"I still don't think so," I said, fingering my locket.

"Sam," Doc said gently. "Lois certainly had the opportunity to set everything up, since Jane was telecommuting the first two months."

"And, if she did, she certainly created chaos," Henry declared.

"Sam, that might explain why Jane was working at Madison," Thomas added.

"I don't think so, Thomas. Jane has her own agenda," I speculated.

"According to Cindy, Jane has the knowledge to reprogram the software," Doc stated.

"That might be true, but . . ." Thomas said.

"On Friday, Jane misplaced her CDs that she was using for a special project," Henry interjected, adding sugar to his coffee. "She was hysterical when she couldn't find them."

Thomas exchanged glances with Henry but said nothing.

"Jane also knew Sam was going to be Madison's new principal before Darrell retired."

"How do you know that, Henry?" Thomas pressed.

"She told Blanche at the end of April and Cindy overheard her telling someone."

"What do you make of this, Sam?" Thomas asked.

"I think someone is setting me up."

"Do you think Cindy's involved, Sam?" Henry sighed, looking at her card.

"Maybe, and if she is, she's protecting her mother. On the other hand, I don't see her jeopardizing her future with the FBI," I stated. "And that brings me back to the question Doc asked earlier about Carlo Santini. Jack, is he on the level?"

"He's on leave from the FBI but has an outstanding reputation."

"What's your interest in him?" Thomas demanded.

"He was supposed to be on Peter's flight but wasn't. Carlo said he was here to protect Cindy and me," I said, feeling guilty that I hadn't told him about the letters.

"So he feels responsible about what happened to Peter," Thomas stated thoughtfully, seeing an odd look cross my face. "Like Cindy, I don't see him throwing away his career for a small stake in a drug operation."

"Sam, you met him this afternoon. What's your take?" asked Jack.

"He's a smart FBI agent—and he's definitely working undercover. He knows something about Peter's death but isn't going to reveal anything until he gets clearance. Other than that, I'm frankly not sure," I said, thinking about Peter's letters. The timing was wrong and, yet, it seemed so surreal. I shifted my focus back to the investigation. "Jack, how did Bill die?"

"The official cause of death was a massive coronary, probably induced by a morphine injection."

"Oh my God!" I gasped.

"Did he have a history of heart problems?" asked Henry.

"Yes, as a matter of fact, he was having an angina attack when he received the fatal injection. According to the medical examiner, he had a partially dissolved nitroglycerine pill under his tongue," Jack reported. "A deputy found his nitro bottle under your desk."

"Was this a recent diagnosis?"

"No. Dr. Austin had heart problems for at least the last five years. He called his doctor last Friday to make an appointment because he wasn't feeling well. Funny thing was that the doctor told him to avoid all stress," Jack revealed.

"I guess he didn't take the doctor's advice," stated Doc simply.

"What about the blood in the office?

"He was shot in the abdominal region," Thomas revealed, catching my eye.

"Why shoot him if he was already dead?" I asked, confused.

"It was a diversionary tactic to make us pursue other leads," Jack reported.

"And the knife?" I inquired, still thinking that was odd.

"Just an afterthought, Sam," Thomas responded. "Austin was already dead when the knife penetrated his body. The medical examiner listed it as a post-mortem artifact."

I got up to get a drink of water, wondering how to tell the man I loved about those damn letters. Since Monday morning, I'd been dealing with one crisis after another: Bill's murder, being shot at and deliberately run off the road, and then, of course, the potential closure of Madison. These were only the latest calamities. The strife had actually started back when my mother's family disowned her. Honestly, I was still dealing with the aftermath of Maxie's death and, probably, my parents. As for Peter—I didn't know what to think!

Thomas picked up Doc's index cards and began thumbing through the notes. Jack glanced at his summaries. Henry exchanged seats with Doc so he could be next to Thomas. As I returned to the table, I heard Henry tell Thomas about Doc's discovery. My heart was pounding to the point that I was almost hyperventilating.

Everyone faded into the background, except for the two of us. Thomas' posture had stiffened as he turned toward me with a crushed look. His coloring had completely vanished. I met his worried eyes, and I swallowed hard, wondering what he was thinking.

"Are you okay?" he asked.

"Yes, nothing has changed between us," I said, gazing into his pain-filled eyes.

"Is this what you wanted to tell me earlier?" he asked, scrutinizing me.

"Yes," I stated, aching for him.

"Are you sure that nothing has changed?" Thomas posed cautiously.

"Definitely!" I exclaimed with a mischievous smile as his eyes softened. I retrieved the letter from the kitchen drawer.

He had noticed that I had taken Peter's picture down, but said nothing. As I walked back to him, I saw questions in his eyes.

"Sam?" he solicited gently from his seat as he looked up at me.

"Thomas, I haven't read the letter or the documents, but I want you to read them. Afterwards, we'll discuss everything." When I gave him the envelope, my lips brushed against his ear. "Thomas, I love you—and only you."

"But what if he's . . ." he asserted as he stood.

"It's a minor glitch," I insisted, looking up into his warm eyes. Then I wrapped my arms around his neck and kissed him passionately.

He pulled me closer and held me in his arms.

"Do you think Thomas finally plucked up his courage and asked her to marry him?" Doc speculated, nudging Henry.

"I think so," agreed Henry, watching us in a loving embrace. "Or maybe she asked him. Either way, I'm happy."

Even Jack appeared content.

But it would remain our secret for the moment.

Wednesday: 8:10 P.M. at My Home

When Thomas released me, I was still reeling from his passionate touch. He picked up Peter's letter and started reading the documents. I still didn't want to know what my husband had written, because I knew instinctively that it had to do with betrayal. So I picked up Peter's work files that Doc had been perusing and went to the family room. Slowly, I scanned the records, one file at a time, looking for clues.

I opened the third file and shuddered. I now knew the connection was Bill Austin's son. He'd been arrested seven years ago on drug charges, and Peter had been the prosecutor. I started to remember some of the facts in the case . . . .

The phone rang, breaking my train of thought. I answered the call. "Hello."

"Ms. Samuels, is that you?" a desperate voice probed.

I knew instantly that something was wrong when I heard the teenager's tone and then a loud, angry voice in the background. "Yes," I replied. "Is someone with you, Mario?"

"Yes," he voiced barely audible. "He ordered James to . . . ."

"To do what?"

"They got Pancho and Miguel!"

"Who's got the kids?" I asked, picturing the five-year-old boys.

"James took them," he offered curtly.

"How do you know?"

"Saw him."

"Where did James take them?"

"The school."

Why there, of all places? I wondered. "What does the man want?"

"He wants the CDs."

I said nothing but listened to his heavy breathing. Then I heard a man yelling obscenities.

"Ms. Samuels, are you still there?"

"Yes, I'm here, Mario. Can he hear what I'm saying?"

"No," he said with some relief. "He just walked away to talk to someone."

"Do they have William also?"

"I don't think so," he whispered.

"When did this happen?"

"About twenty minutes ago."

"Why didn't he have you call sooner?" I asked.

"He was smacking me around and then he ordered James to tie us up in the basement."

"Who hit you?" I asked, fuming.

"The man," he answered.

I heard fear in his voice again and knew instantly that the man was coming back. "Listen to me carefully; I'm going to get all of you out of this mess."

"Uh-huh."

"Tell him I have another call coming in." I pushed the mute button and walked into the kitchen. I quickly explained the situation to the group.

Jack took the phone and began talking to Mario.

Thomas followed him out of the kitchen and so did Doc.

"Henry, I need the keys to the old pickup."

"Sam . . . ."

"Henry! I need them now," I demanded, giving him an unyielding look.

"Let Jack take care of this, Sam," he pleaded.

"I can't, Henry," I stated, watching his coloring diminish. "If something happens to those kids, I will never forgive myself. Now, give me the keys, Henry!"

Reluctantly, he dug into his pants pocket. "Please reconsider this, Sam!"

"Henry, I don't have time to play games. Give me the damn keys now!" I demanded emphatically, raising my voice to him for the first time. I could see the hurt in his eyes when I snatched them from his hand.

"Sam, please don't do this," he pleaded as I grabbed the CDs and my gym bag from the counter top.

"I love you, Henry." I bolted out the door before he could stop me.

Thomas rushed into the kitchen when he heard Peter's old truck roar to life as the boisterous geese started screeching. "Henry, where's Sam?"

"She's gone."

"What do you mean, she's gone?" Thomas asked, furious. He stood there waiting for an answer from the man he viewed as a father figure.

"Thomas, she . . ." began the distraught older man.

"She what, Henry?!" Thomas shouted in a harsh manner, immediately regretting his tone when he saw Henry wince.

"She went to save the kids," Henry revealed.

"You didn't have to give her the keys!" snapped Thomas, mortified.

"Thomas, you . . . ."

"God damn it! Henry! You just stood there and let her go!" barked Thomas.

"Thomas, I . . ." Henry tried to reason with him, meeting his stony gaze.

"Do you have any idea who she's going to meet?" Thomas retorted, growing more alarmed. "James Hill, a murder suspect, Henry!"

"You dismissed the murder charges against him!" Henry countered, incensed.

"That's below the belt, Henry!" Thomas declared. "You know that wasn't my call."

"I'm sorry, Thomas," he said. "But you're wrong if you think either one of us could have stopped her."

"God damn it! Henry!" Thomas yelled again, forcefully. "Why didn't you call me?"

"Thomas, I . . ." Henry tried again to reason with him.

"I just can't believe you handed her the damn keys . . . ."

"I didn't . . . ."

Hearing the loud argument, Jack reentered the kitchen with Doc right behind him. "Thomas, we need to go now!"

Thomas grabbed his jacket and followed Jack out the door, fuming.

"Henry, did she take the CDs?" asked Doc.

"Yes. She took the copies from the counter top."

"You're sure?"

"Yes," Henry groaned, worried about the young woman he regarded as a daughter.

"Good; that means she's thinking clearly," Doc smiled.

"Doc, I . . . ."

"Henry, Thomas knows you couldn't have stopped her. Sam isn't stupid. She'll be okay. It's the rest of us that may not survive her tenure as principal of Madison," commented Doc, who was slowly putting on his jean jacket.

Henry stood there, not knowing what to do. He was usually a man of decisive action, but now he was overcome with fear, floundering like a fish out of water. He called Marge and alerted her of Sam's impulsive actions. And then he told her about his own part in this chaos.

When he ended the call, Doc asked, "Ready now?"

"Yes. Let's go."

Wednesday: 8:30 P.M. at My Home

The dark sky greeted me as I stormed out of the house. Once inside the old truck, I grasped the steering wheel with one hand and fired up the engine with the other. Grateful that Henry was religious about keeping the battery charged, I shifted into gear and peeled out of the driveway, leaving a cloud of dust and squawking geese behind.

I drove down the back roads to school, surprised by the faint odor of Peter's musty cologne. It was odd that his scent still clung to the truck after all this time. It made me think about the last morning when he left for work. Peter had hesitated for a moment before saying something to me. His words were on the tip of my tongue, but I just couldn't remember.

He had been difficult to live with for the most part, but I still couldn't believe he would fake his own death. If he had, why write those letters now? Better yet, if he was dead, who else would know where to plant them?

Somehow, it seemed easier to deal with the kidnapping crisis than with Peter's mysterious disappearance. Was I miscalculating? I hoped not. I wanted a future with Thomas, but I still had a nagging feeling about Peter.

I had to stop this and concentrate on getting the kids out of the building safely. The kidnappers had Mario and the boys but not William. Questions just kept popping up. Who was the man in the background? Were there others involved? Why did Mario let his guard down? Where was William? Or, worse yet, were the boys co-conspirators in this mess? Either way, I needed William's help to rescue them.

Glancing down at the truck's gauges, the gas tank registered nearly empty. I pulled into a self-serve station two blocks from Madison School and parked behind a maroon Chevy. Jumping out, I shoved my credit card into the pump, pulled it out, and then stashed it in a pocket as I flushed ten dollars' worth of gas into the tank.

I looked around as I pumped. Two cars approached the station. One entered the freeway ramp and sped away; the other, a yellow Mustang, slowed down on the frontage road. Once the driver of the maroon Chevy finished pumping his gas, he drove off.

I was left alone at the station as I replaced the pump's hose. A gust of wind covered my face as lightning crisscrossed the veiled sky. This August night seemed to have all the elements of an eerie Halloween Eve—stormy weather, lives at stake, and Peter coming back to haunt me.

I climbed into the driver's seat, quickly slammed the door shut, and locked it. Hunching over the steering wheel, I pretended to fiddle with the radio but, instead, I scanned the area. Once I made sure no one was around, I released the brake, drove around to the back, and parked behind the dark dumpster.

Lightning lit up the area again as I scrunched down in the truck to pull off the pink tank top and put on a black, long-sleeved tee that I had retrieved from my gym bag. I searched the sack and found several loose bobby pins. Then, carefully pulling my hair back, I jabbed the pins into four strategic spots.

I had never removed Peter's gear from the truck. Hopefully, that meant that his raid bag was still hidden underneath the bench seat. I smiled when I lifted the heavy sack onto the seat. Inside the bag, I found a black baseball cap, disposable latex gloves, a Kevlar bulletproof vest, a knife, and his loaded gun. Not many lawyers needed raid bags, but Peter had.

When I was ready, I drove to Madison School and circled the area, taking note of all the parked cars on the streets. But when I saw the yellow Mustang again, butterflies bombarded the pit of my stomach.

I parked on a side street for a quick exit. Then I put on my windbreaker over the Kevlar vest and shoved the CDs and gun into the pockets. After that, I locked the truck and jogged toward the walkway connecting the chapel with the school.

The wind had picked up and the temperature was descending rapidly. This was the normal precursor to a monsoon storm. Bolts of lightning creased the eclipsed sky, and thunder crackled in the distance. The brewing storm would soon make its appearance and, hopefully, move on just as quickly.

I caught a glimpse of a shadow creeping among the trees near the school's playground.

A voice yelled out as the wind conveyed his words. "Ms. Samuels, is that you?"

It's funny how things work. I thought I'd freeze at the first sign of danger, but didn't. My hand went automatically to the gun and I pointed it in the direction of the voice. Eerie flashes lit up the sky as the shadow hid behind a tree. In a moment of covered darkness, I sprinted to the church's entrance and hid behind the stairwell, hoping no one saw me.

Unfortunately, the voice kept repeating my name over and over again. The howling wind carried his muted cry. I was terrified. My hands were sweating profusely, but I was still able to hold the revolver as I scanned the area, trying to track this mysterious voice. The shadow weaved through the trees and bushes, heading straight toward me. I crouched down with my back against the wall and waited quietly.

As I stared at the tall, black shadow in front of the church, beads of sweat broke out. He began pacing back and forth. Finally, he stopped and whispered my name again. This time, I recognized the teenager's voice. Hesitating a moment, I replaced the gun back into a pocket. "William—over here."

He scurried behind the stairs as thunder shook the ground.

"Are you okay?" I asked nervously.

"Yeah," he said in a soft whisper.

"What happened?"

"We were playing tag with Maria Gonzales' son and nephew," William said anxiously. "DeMorgan knocked Mario down and James grabbed the kids. That weird man—the one we told you about the other night—was yelling at them . . . telling them what to do . . . and so was that security guy that got shot the other night. He threatened to shoot the kids if Mario didn't do what the man said."

"Do you know where they took them?" I asked, knowing the answer.

"They're in the school's basement."

"Anyone else involved?" I demanded, recalling Doc's information on Rob Stone.

"Don't think so," he stated hesitantly. "I didn't see anyone else."

"Wait a minute; how do you know all this?" I solicited, seeing the fear in his eyes.

"I was inside the church getting some water. I was real quiet coming out 'cuz I didn't want the kids to notice me. That's when I heard the man order James to take the kids to the basement. After they left, the man punched Mario around until the security guard stopped him."

"Why didn't they grab you too?"

"I guess they didn't see me," he surmised, shrugging his shoulders and then rotating his neck, trying to release the tension.

I cringed as his neck went crack, crack, and pop. "William, I saw the yellow Mustang. Does it belong in the neighborhood?"

"No, Ms. Samuels."

"We need to find the cars that don't belong here. And, if the owner's registration isn't from this area, we need to make sure he or she can't leave."

"Okay, Ms. Samuels."

We jogged back to the old pickup. Once there, I opened the truck's door and grabbed what I needed: a knife, a pair of pliers, and disposable gloves from Peter's raid bag. Then I got lucky and found a coat hanger underneath the seat.

Gear in place, we walked down the neighborhood streets with menace in our hearts. As we approached the first unfamiliar car, I put on one pair of latex gloves and handed William the other set. Then I gave him the hanger. It only took William two seconds to quietly jimmy open the car door. Somehow, I knew he'd be able to do that.

Smiling, I questioned which one of us had acquired "the better" education. Once inside the car, he rummaged through the glove compartment and found the registration. The car belonged to R. Stone and his address was on the other side of town. He popped the hood latch, slid out of the car, and relocked the door.

The wind had increased its velocity and strangely acted as a silencer. I lifted the hood and held it while William yanked the battery cables out and stashed them under the car. Afterwards, we shut the hood.

But when I touched the yellow Mustang, it still felt warm. According to the registration, the Mustang belonged to DeMorgan Beaker. Once William had efficiently disabled the sports car, we moved on to the last car. It was a Cadillac, parked in front of the Mustang. The name José Santos appeared on the registration. I lifted the cold hood, and William went to work.

Afterwards, we walked back to the church, discussing our next move. Somehow, I felt invigorated, but William thought I was crazy.

"William," I solicited, "how can I get into the building without anyone noticing?"

"The boys' bathroom," he replied.

He had destroyed my hopes of an easy entrance. "Which one?"

"The one in the east hall, Ms. Samuels," he declared, still anxious. "But it's weird, though."

"What is?"

327

"James just keeps repeating what the man tells him."

"Do you think he's scared?" I posed, watching him nod his head yes.

As we made our way toward Madison, lost in our own thoughts, we watched the random flashes streaking across the distant skyline and heard the echoing roar of thunder. We froze in mid-step and, immediately, dropped down behind an irrigation berm, watching a familiar Lincoln Continental slowly pull into the school's parking lot.

I wasn't surprised when RJ Beaker stepped out of the car. But when Ruth staggered out of the passenger's side, I was shocked. She seemed to be drugged. Her appearance was a far cry from her public image. Her hair was in disarray and her blouse and pants were ripped to shreds. She appeared to have been in a violent struggle.

William and I traded glances and then just watched them.

"Shut up, asshole!" Ruth shouted hoarsely.

"Ruth, I don't see why you had to come," RJ stated, clearly upset. He helped her regain her balance as she held onto her purse.

"Someone has to make sure things are put right!"

"Santos isn't going to like it."

"Shut up, you sniveling piece of shit! I don't give a damn what that thug wants!"

"But, darling . . ." her husband began in a belittling tone, trying to get control of his wife before she'd . . . .

"Don't patronize me," she retorted, her voice quavering.

RJ tried to push Ruth toward the entrance again, but she pushed him away.

The front door opened and a small man wearing a well-cut black suit emerged. He appeared irritated as he eyed Mrs. Beaker. "RJ, what the hell is she doing here?"

"There's been a change of plans, Santos," Ruth yelled at the man, who was fingering a thin mustache.

"What do ya mean?" he challenged arrogantly.

"You're taking orders from me now," Ruth ranted, waving her arms emphatically as her eyes appeared red and somewhat glazed.

"WHAT?!" he shouted in dismay, staring at the unsteady woman. Turning to RJ, he asked, "What's wrong with her?"

"Don't talk to him! TALK TO ME!" she shouted. "He's nothing but a piss-poor imitation of a man. Bill protected his son, not like you," she sneered, pointing her finger at RJ and then at the small man. "I'm in charge now! Any problems with that?"

"Well, yes," Santos declared. "The boss ain't gonna like this."

Suddenly, Ruth pulled out a gun with a long black silencer from her purse. She shouted, "Who cares what that BASTARD thinks!" Her whole body shook as she held the gun at her side. "He had Bill killed!"

"So what—he got in the way!" Santos snickered. He just stood there laughing at her until he noticed she was lifting the weapon up. "RJ, do something!"

Ruth was fixated on the little man. He backed away from her as she pointed the weapon at his chest. His gun was visible now, pointing right back at her.

"Ruth, put the gun down," RJ pleaded in a loud, desperate tone.

Santos ordered, "Put that thing away before you hurt someone!"

When she didn't, he squeezed the trigger. The bullet grazed her left arm and Ruth screamed out in pain with blood trickling down her limb.

"RJ, control your demented wife or else!"

Ruth staggered a bit before firing blindly at Santos. The bullet struck him in mid-torso, spraying his blood outward into a gust of wind. Stunned, she absorbed the blood splatter as she watched Santos' crumple to the ground.

RJ shrieked, "What have you done?! Are you insane?!"

"Of course I'm insane. I married you, didn't I? I've put up with your whining for years, haven't I? And you didn't even protect me when that bastard raped me. You destroyed DeMorgan's and Lisa's chances of having a normal life! SO SHUT THE FUCK UP, YOU FUCKING BASTARD!" she screamed, now turning the gun on him.

"Calm down, Ruthie. You're shaking."

"Don't you touch me, you fucking bastard!" she slurred, stumbling. "You think I don't know about you and that bitch."

"You've got it all wrong, Ruthie, sweetheart," he cooed smoothly.

"Save it for the fucking bitch. I'm tired of all your lying, you fuck-head."

Stunned by the enormity of what Ruth had just done, I almost let out my own blood-curdling scream when Thomas touched my arm. I hadn't heard him arrive, but William had. Still upset with me, Thomas moved his finger to his lips. Our eyes shifted back to the entrance of the building when we heard the front door slam shut.

Rob Stone stood, scowling with his hands on his hips. He shouted angrily at the hostile couple, "What's going on? Do you want the sheriff to come out here and bust us all?"

No one said anything as the wind picked up again.

Rob clutched a weapon at his side when he saw Santos' body lying face down in the dirt. When he looked up from the corpse, he was stunned to see Ruth Beaker holding a gun, now aimed at his chest. "What the hell happened?"

"Shut up, you cretin! Let me think," Ruth demanded, rubbing her head.

Ignoring Ruth, RJ asked, "Did you find Jane's CDs yet?"

"No. Santos had that Mexican kid call the Samuels bitch to bring the CDs here," declared Rob in an irate tone.

"What CDs?" Ruth demanded. She stumbled forward, holding onto the gun tightly for protection.

"Honey, it's nothing. Why don't you sit down on the bench?" her husband suggested. This time she let him help her.

"What's wrong with her?" Rob demanded.

"She's been upset ever since Austin was killed. Fred gave her some Ambien and something else with vodka to calm her down," RJ reported.

"I don't think it's working," Rob asserted sarcastically.

"Now that's rich," hissed RJ through his clenched teeth. And then, he glanced at his wife. He saw her clutch her abdomen and then retch the last remnants of food from her stomach. When she looked up at him, she was sweating profusely and looked awful.

He snorted, "She thinks Santos killed her precious Austin—isn't that ridiculous?"

Rob looked around, making sure they were alone. "Well, he did."

"You're joking, right?"

"Do I look like I'm joking, you idiot?"

"Why would Santos kill Bill?" demanded RJ, stunned.

"How the hell should I know? He was probably just following orders."

"Let me get this straight. Santos shot Bill on the boss' orders?"

"What's your problem now?"

"I didn't realize . . ." RJ asserted, suddenly worried. He ran a hand through his thinning blond hair, exposing a distended potbelly that hung over his designer jeans.

"Cut the crap, you moron," Stone ordered. "You'd better get that gun away from her before she shoots us."

"Go ahead; be my guest," RJ taunted, hoping he would take the bait.

They just stood there. Neither one of them wanted to confront Ruth. Instead, they bent down and moved Santos' body behind a hedge.

"What are you doing now?" Ruth muttered, slurring her words.

"Nothing, dear," said RJ as he quickly went through all of Santos' pockets.

"You killed him, you son of a bitch!" Ruth exploded, clutching the gun at her side.

"Who are you talking about now?" Rob confronted, walking away from Santos' body. "You're the one that killed Santos."

"Bill! You killed Bill, you son of a bitch! And now I'm going to kill you."

RJ was slowly walking toward his wife as Rob engaged her in a dialogue.

Thomas tapped me on the shoulder. "The SWAT team just arrived." He moved back into the shadows to join the sheriff, who was conferring with his men. Once they were in their positions, the sheriff would give the signal to begin the rescue.

The wind whipped the surrounding trees with vengeance as William and I watched Ruth Beaker disintegrate into madness . . . ranting about Bill's murder, RJ's embezzlement, and tonight's rape.

Five minutes later, I knew something was amiss. So I made my move, knowing Thomas would be beyond furious with me.

Wednesday: 9:15 P.M. at Madison

backed away from the berm and William followed suit. As soon as we were out of sight, we ran to the back of the building and crawled through the basement bathroom's open window. Once inside the boys' bathroom, we waited a moment to listen for movement in the corridor.

William opened the door and felt a slight breeze. "It's clear," he whispered.

"Okay, let's go." To my surprise, the corridor was dark, except for a few night lights plugged into wall sockets. Muffled voices emanated from the storage room, which served as Madison's elephant graveyard. As we approached the entrance, the slight breeze seemed to grow stronger. Hopefully, that meant there was a possible escape route for the boys.

We peered into the shabby den of disarray. A dim fluorescent light illuminated the room. I could see James pacing behind DeMorgan, who was working on a laptop midway down the south wall of the huge room. Mario and the kids were barely visible sitting against the back wall. A myriad heap of broken furniture and textbooks lay scattered everywhere. It looked like someone had tossed everything aside to make room for the large wooden crates piled almost to the ceiling in front of the partially open window.

My plan was simple: I handed William a knife and gave him instructions to free Mario and the kids and then escape through the window while I distracted James and DeMorgan. If they couldn't get out, they were all to hide behind the piles of crates. I knew he had a weapon and would do whatever was necessary to protect his best friend and the kids.

I whispered, "Are you ready?"

William nodded as he disappeared behind the crates. I followed him a moment later and then stopped behind the first crate. My focus was now on the captors. Just by listening to James, I knew he was frightened. He had reverted to immature speech patterns.

"Why are you doin' this, James?" demanded Mario, creating a distraction. He had seen us enter.

"The big man says . . . ."

"What are you, his slave boy?" taunted Mario, angering James further.

"Shut up, you motherfucker! You don't know nothin' bout nothin'."

"What's taking them so long?" DeMorgan declared, looking around the room. "I'm getting pretty nervous."

"Hey De, you thin' somethin' wrong, don't ya?"

"Shut up. My dad said he'd be here, and he will," he assured James, checking his cell phone again. "I'm going up to see if he's here yet."

I froze behind the crate, crouching in the shadows as DeMorgan left. He had been only inches away from me.

"Well, hurry back, fucker!" screamed James at his back.

"Come on, James; my wrists hurt," whined Mario, seeing James approach slowly. "Untie me and let the kids go."

"I can't. They'll hurt my mama," he revealed softly.

"Sure you can. Ms. Samuels won't let anyone hurt you or your mama."

"Shut the fuck up, Mario." James began pacing back and forth directly under the light fixture. He stopped, hearing a noise, and then stared at DeMorgan's laptop sitting on a table.

Concerned that I was too visible, I slithered closer to the second crate. An odd, acrid odor hit me. I was sure that these wooden boxes didn't contain school supplies—maybe illicit drugs? Was this the reason Bill was killed and the boys kidnapped?

Those thoughts definitely didn't make me feel safe. So I peeked between the stacked crates and saw that Mario and the kids were still sitting against the wall, but I couldn't see William. I turned back to James who was gawking at the laptop's screen.

"Okay, don't untie me, but let the kids go," Mario asserted, worried. "Man, you know how sick that DeMorgan dude is. He hurts all kinds of animals and laughs when he kills them. Come on, James; let them go."

"I need 'em for insurance."

"What insurance, man? You know that, when they get what they want, they're gonna waste everybody, including you and your mama."

"I gots the big man's word; no one gets hurt."

"And you believe him?"

"Sure do," he said, but not quite as confidently as before. Droplets of sweat sprung on his upper lip. Doubt seemed to be slowly creeping into his mind.

"I can't believe you're that dumb. He's gonna kill all of us. So how good is your insurance gonna be then?"

"Shut up, man! Let me think. The big man sez he gonna give me lots of money for me and my mama to get out of here."

"Man, oh, man. Are you stupid?"

"I ain't stupid, you fucker!" shouted James, growing more incensed.

"Yes, you sure are. Even if he doesn't kill you and your mama, guess who's left holding the bag?"

"What chu mean?"

"He's pimpin' you to take the fall. It's their word against yours. Don't you know that blood is thicker than water?"

"He ain't neither! He sez he gonna take care of us."

"Come on, James; think. Let the kids go at least. Ms. Samuels will help you."

"Man, I don't need no help. Nothin' gonna happen to me," he declared, looking around the room as if sensing someone else's presence.

"How do you know that, James?"

"Cuz the big man sez so; he got me out of jail for that murder charge. He knew I didn't kill that man," he yelled angrily. Frustrated, James picked up a wooden chair and slammed it against the wall.

I finally put all the pieces together and knew who the head of the snake was—it was Fred Monti, our county attorney. He was responsible for this mess. My heart pounded as I gripped the weapon at my side. I stepped out of the shadows. "Didn't he frame you for the Hernandez murder?"

James turned to face me, suddenly discovering me with an agonizing look of shock. "Miz Samuels. How did you get in here?"

"I crawled in."

"Damn, I forgot all about the boys' bathroom window."

"James, let them go."

"I can't, miss; the big man sez no," James said in a helpless tone, frowning.

"He is gonna burn you, man," warned Mario.

"He won't . . . he be my friend. He let me go free."

"You know he's going to kill us. Let us go!" Mario pleaded.

"I can't."

"Well, then, we have a standoff," I declared.

"A what?"

"A standoff. I have something you want, and you have something I want."

"Like a draw," Mario explained.

"James, let the kids and Mario go, and the CDs are yours to give to your boss."

"I can take them from you."

"You might, but you won't, James." Noisily, I cocked the revolver to let him know I was armed. William was now exposed, inching his way toward Mario and the kids.

James shook his head; sweat began to run down his face. "You think I'm dumb."

"No, James, you're not dumb. You need to do the right thing and let them go."

"You're full of it, miss."

"James, I know you don't like to hurt people. Do you remember telling me that you wanted be somebody important like your uncle?" I asked, watching him closely.

"Yah, so what about it?" he snapped, standing a little straighter.

"Your uncle was killed in Afghanistan fighting the terrorists. He was a brave man who believed in doing the right thing."

"Yah."

"Well, this is your chance to do the right thing. Let these kids go. I'll make sure your mama isn't harmed and that you're treated fairly."

"You can't help her," he cried out nervously. "He's got my mama! He never gonna let her go if I don't do as he sez."

"James, do you know what the word *duress* means?" I asked.

"No."

"It means that someone is making you do something against your will. It's illegal and that's what he's doing by holding your mama and forcing you to do things. You're not going to be in trouble with the sheriff if you do the right thing now."

"I can't . . . he gonna hurt my mama."

"Honey, your mama wants what is best for you no matter what."

"He'll hurt her bad. Like he did De's mama."

"What do you mean?"

"He said De was history if she didn't do what he said."

"How do you know that?"

"His mama told us to get out, but we saw him tear her clothes off and hit her when she cried out. The big man's mean. He made me go to jail so I'd learn to keep my mouth shut," he revealed, wiping his brow nervously.

"James . . ." I uttered gently.

"He laugh at me and sez I'm no good."

"James, you are a good person. Remember what your mama told me at our last parent conference?"

He shook his head.

"She told me how proud she was of you." I saw him smile as the memory resurfaced.

DeMorgan's voice startled all of us as he entered. "James, how did she get in here?"

"Don't know. I thought you told her to come here. Besides, you the one who went up to check on things," James countered, scratching his head.

"Yeah," he sighed. "My mother and dad are arguing."

"Your mama is here?" James asked as hope appeared on his face. "Did you see my mama?"

"No."

William had reached Mario. Crouched down beside them, he cut the duct tape binding Mario's hands. When Mario was free, William handed him a gun and crawled over to the kids signaling them to remain quiet.

To my relief, the two five-year-old boys obeyed soundlessly. They had been sitting still this whole time, listening.

A bolt of lightning momentarily lit the room as it struck nearby. The thunder's loud explosion left us stunned. The monsoon had announced its arrival.

DeMorgan turned toward the laptop and watched the screen flicker. Then, he snapped his focus back to me. "Did you bring the CDs?"

"Yes and no," I uttered, feeling the effects of the cooler air.

"What do you mean?"

"I have one with me," I said as I stood my ground. "You get the other one once the kids and Mario are safe."

"Give me the damn CD!" he demanded in a boorish tone.

I placed the case on the concrete floor and kicked it. The case scooted across the surface, like a hockey puck, directly toward him. DeMorgan grabbed the case and took it to his work station. He inserted the disc and waited for the data to appear on the screen.

William cut the tape binding the two boys together.

I held my breath as I watched them inch their way to the crates. Once they were behind the barrier, I let out a long deep breath. Then taking a quick look around, I realized why Monti and his associates wanted Madison closed. It offered the perfect setup for a drug distribution center. Dealers would have unrestricted access to the building and the freeway. Just like I had suspected all along . . . .

I knew Fred Monti was the front man in control of these minions. But the real question remained: Who was the power behind this—a local drug dealer or a major cartel?

Wednesday: 9:35 P.M. at Madison

stepped back into the shadows. From my vantage point, I could see both a pathway behind the crates, as well as DeMorgan and James. DeMorgan, engrossed in retrieving data from the CD, remained totally unaware that William and the hostages were quietly making their way to freedom. Thankfully, James appeared just as oblivious. He kept pacing back and forth, constantly checking the computer screen and muttering to himself.

It took three long minutes for the boys to reach the window.

Relieved, I checked on DeMorgan and James. They were now both focused on the laptop. Turning back to the boys, I noticed William with the two five-year-olds but Mario was nowhere in sight. Looking up, I suddenly spotted him climbing up the wooden crates.

Once at window height, Mario anchored himself on the edge of the third crate. He pulled the escape lever, but nothing happened. The partially opened window was stuck. He re-adjusted his position and, with one swift move, forced the jammed window wide open.

A loud screech filled the room. He flattened his body against the large box as William signaled to the little boys to remain quiet. The shrill noise made me cringe as I hoped that their captors hadn't noticed.

"What's that?" James blurted out, scanning the room for the strange noise.

Dammit! James had noticed, but DeMorgan still remained absorbed with the data flashing across the screen. Then there was another screech.

This time, DeMorgan heard it. He turned toward James. "What was that?"

James shrugged his shoulders but his eyes had widened, staring at the wall of crates.

I screamed as DeMorgan stood up.

"What are you screaming about?" DeMorgan pressed.

"Rats scurrying about the crates!" I cried with an edge, hoping to distract them long enough for the boys to escape.

DeMorgan chuckled, digesting this information. He returned to the keyboard, dismissing the rustling sounds in the background.

"Whatcha doin', Miz Samuels?" James asked, focusing his attention on me.

"James, I need to sit down," I stated, looking around for an unbroken chair. With none in sight, I shoved one of the haphazardly strewn boxes aside as I pretended to fall forward.

"You needs to be more careful, miss," James said with concern.

"Why aren't you watching her?" DeMorgan complained, irritated by the commotion.

"Cuz . . . ." As James lumbered over to help me up, William gave me the thumbs-up from outside the window and then vanished into the night. They were all out safely as I collapsed onto the box.

"Just watch her, James!" DeMorgan demanded, pulling a document up on the screen. Suddenly, he lashed out furiously, pounding the keyboard, "Oh shit!"

"What's wrong, DeMorgan?" I asked, distressed. He had just scared the living daylights out of me.

"It's this stupid laptop. It's frozen again!" he retorted, escalating into a rage. He stood up abruptly and almost dumped it onto the floor. "I can't do anything on this piece of shit!"

"Can you fix it?" I prompted, trying to redirect his energy.

"Yes," he admitted, calming down some. "I can just reboot."

"Do you think you lost your data?"

"I shouldn't have . . . but this is an old notebook," he declared, sitting back down.

"What if it did?" I asked, holding my breath.

"No problem. The data is still on the CD. I can download it on the computer at home and work with it there."

"The fancy computer?" declared James nervously. His eyes were almost bulging out of their sockets.

"Yeah, the new one my dad bought," he remarked for my benefit, looking over his shoulder at me and then at James.

"You think he'll let you touch it?" he asked hesitantly.

"Sure. Why not, James?"

"I don't know . . . the last time you and me wuz there he got real mad that you wuz messing with his stuff."

"Yeah, well, that was then and this is now. Besides, he needs me to retrieve the information on the CDs."

"And what information is that?" I asked.

"None of your business," he sneered.

The room grew quiet, except for the clicking sound of the keyboard and James' shuffling movements. Softly at first, footsteps drifted through the hallway, adding their rhythm to this strange medley. Then angry voices rose and a woman screamed out in pain.

James backed away from DeMorgan. Recognizing the woman's voice, he asked, "Hey De, what's wrong with your mama?"

"What?" whined DeMorgan, concentrating on the screen. "I don't know."

My heart was racing, realizing that I was on my own. No one was coming fast enough to rescue me. RJ and the others didn't know I was here but, better yet, I had the advantage of surprise and a weapon. Now, I needed to disappear from their view.

The computer froze and DeMorgan began swearing again. James watched me slither behind another box but kept quiet. I held my breath, praying that I wouldn't have to shoot anyone.

Wednesday: 9:53 P.M. at Madison

RJ entered the dimly lit storage room, oblivious to my presence. Irritated, he flipped on the light switches but nothing happened. The room remained dimly lit.

"That damn Samuels bitch didn't show up!" he bellyached. "This is all Jane's fault. How could she lose those damn CDs?"

"Jane said that damn bitch took them," shouted Rob.

"Maybe the bitch didn't take them and Jane has had them all along," RJ suggested, beginning to sweat. "Do you think she's setting us up to take the fall?"

"Shut up, you moron! Jane wouldn't dare because she's in this too deep. Besides, we still have the kids as hostages. That bitch won't let anything happen to them," Rob chuckled, turning to check on them. Then, suddenly horrified, he yelled, "James, where are they?!"

"Who choo mean?" James asked, looking over at the empty space.

A stench of fear washed over his body and mine. I gripped my gun with both hands. My heart was pounding so loudly that I was surprised they didn't hear it.

"DeMorgan, where are the kids?" Rob demanded as he wiped his clammy face with a shirt sleeve.

"I don't know, Rob," DeMorgan retorted defiantly, turning to face the nasty piece of work. "You're the one who tied them up."

"Well, they're gone now, you idiot!" Rob shouted in a condescending tone.

"Don't you call him an idiot, you son of a bitch!" Ruth yelled, defending her son. She staggered forward into the light as RJ held on to her.

"Shut her up or I'll do it permanently!" Rob snarled, turning to RJ and waving the gun at him. "You get my drift, asshole?"

"What's your problem, Rob?" DeMorgan groused, glancing at his disheveled mother. "We got the CD."

"How?" he demanded.

"Ms. Samuels gave it to me."

"Samuels was here and you let the kids go?"

"No!" he protested irritably. Then, gritting his teeth, he gave Rob an insufferable glance. All he wanted to do was get back to his laptop. "Shit, I don't know what happened to the kids. Anyway, what difference does it make? I have what I need to make the transfers."

"Where is she?" Rob insisted, glaring at the computer geek, who was still fiddling with his blasted computer.

"Who?" DeMorgan questioned absentmindedly.

"Samuels, you jackass!" Rob shouted again to deaf ears.

I was relieved that neither boy had given me up. Maybe DeMorgan had forgotten I was there, but James hadn't. He glared at the man, shouting at his friend. He stood there as if debating what to do. Then, quietly, he moved into a position between me and Rob Stone.

RJ let go of Ruth's arm. She staggered aimlessly, walking in circles between piles of broken chairs and boxes. As she turned in my direction, she caught a glimpse of me crouching behind the box.

First, she looked at her son and then at James. "Oh my God, I can't believe this!" she muttered in a low voice as a look of horror contorted her features.

I bit my lower lip, knowing all too well that she was about to tell RJ where I was hiding.

She started to speak, but RJ cut her off. "Honey, please be quiet. If you don't, you're going to make matters worse."

She hesitated and then focused on her son. "Why is DeMorgan here?"

"He's working on something important for me."

"Oh my God!" she gasped, finally seeming to grasp the fact that her son was involved in this mess. "Bill was right and I didn't believe him! This all has to do with . . . ."

"Shut her up!" Stone instructed in a loud voice, shifting his gun from one sweaty palm to the other. He pointed his weapon at her head as he walked over to check on DeMorgan's progress.

"Hey, man, leave my mother alone!" DeMorgan screamed, jumping up.

"Shut up, you twit!" Rob directed, shoving him back into the chair. "I let you get away with shooting me the other night, but tonight I'm in charge!"

"So what?" DeMorgan challenged, standing back up to face him. "What are you going to do . . . shoot us in cold blood like Santos shot Austin?"

"James, shut him up!" Rob ordered frantically as he walked away, looking rather ill. "I'd kill you right now, but we need you to finalize the money transfer."

347

"Come on, De. Take it easy, man," began James in a soft tone as DeMorgan sat down.

The tension in the room was chilling.

Rob paced back and forth near the back wall and then stopped, shoving the gun into the back of his jeans. Drenched with sweat, he unbuttoned his shirt and pulled the collar away from his perspiring neck, as if trying to cool down.

A split second later, we felt the terrifying vibrations of another nearby lightning strike and then the deafening roar of thunder ripped through the room.

Rob covered his ears. Sweat continued dripping down his ashen face as he glanced at the Beakers. He retrieved the gun from his waist and shouted angrily, "RJ, if you don't keep your fucking family in check, I'll shoot first and ask questions later."

"Where's Mr. Santos?" asked James nervously.

"She killed him," Rob sneered, pointing his weapon at Ruth.

"Mom, why?!" gasped DeMorgan. His face had turned white.

Tears ran down Ruth's face. "I don't know why."

No one said anything but just stared at her. She quietly wiped the tears, drifting toward her son. "I don't know why I'm here."

"What do you mean, Mom?" DeMorgan said gently, coming to her side.

"The last thing I remember is Jane fixing me a drink."

"Why were you drinking?"

"I was upset, and the pills Fred gave me weren't working. So I thought a drink would help but, instead, I felt funny."

"YOU FUCKING BASTARD!" DeMorgan roared at his father. He was no longer pale, but his face was burning red. "You let them drug her!"

"Look, son, it's not . . ." RJ croaked, backing away from Ruth and his son.

"Not what I think? Is that what you were going to say, Dad?" he charged, taunting his father. "You've made James and me the fall guys? Didn't you?"

"De, give me a chance to explain," RJ moaned.

"Explain what? That you've fucked everyone over! No, Dad, you're a pathetic asshole!" yelled DeMorgan as a stream of tears rolled down his face. He stumbled over a broken chair, wiping his face with the back of his hand as he glared at his father. "Face it, Dad; the only things you worship are the almighty dollar and scoring."

"RJ, what's he talking about?" Ruth interjected, barely able to stand as she clung to the side of a crate for balance.

"How long have you been drugging her?"

"I'm not going to dignify that insult with an answer."

"I bet you started drugging her when she wouldn't cooperate— the same way you did me!" DeMorgan revealed, now beyond furious. He returned to his seat and stealthily ejected the CD from his laptop.

"Shut up, all of you!" Rob shouted, holding his pale head with both hands.

"You shut up, you fucking doper," DeMorgan ordered, exchanging glances with James.

He walked over to his mother and moved a box so she could sit down. Before he turned to face the others, he kicked the CD toward me. Once Ruth was seated, he protectively put his arm around her shoulders.

James sat on another box with his back to me. He raised his shirttail and removed the gun from the back of his waistband. He held it in his lap, watching the drama.

"De, honey, I'm really okay," Ruth whimpered. She began shaking as if she was going through withdrawal.

"Are you okay, Mom?" DeMorgan challenged, disgusted as he took note of his mother's torn clothes. "He turned you into a fucking whore!"

"Shut up, De!" RJ demanded. His face had turned purple with rage and the veins in his neck protruded against the blotchy skin.

DeMorgan stood up straighter and puffed out his chest in defiance. "Grandma would be so proud of you, Dad. You're nothing more than a fucking PIMP!"

Rob became restless again. He turned away from the family drama and began opening boxes one after another. Disappointment showed on his face each time he didn't find his drug of choice. In a clammy sweat, he seemed to be growing more agitated by the second.

I heard him muttering over and over again, "Where's the damn cocaine?"

I gripped the revolver with both hands to steady my aim. I could tell that Rob was not only jonesing for a fix, but also becoming a dangerous liability. I glanced toward the others. DeMorgan looked ready to explode. RJ appeared furious. And Ruth, a woman whom I'd always thought of as a snob, apparently had become a victim of physical and sexual abuse and was barely holding it together.

"De, please, don't do this," she whispered as he walked away from her.

DeMorgan turned to face his mother in a lethal rage. He shook his head and then waited a moment. "Mom, you think he can hurt me like he hurts you? He can't, 'cause he's not man enough." He glared at his father with scorn. "He can't hit me the way he does you or fuck me the way he does Lisa. My big sister is so scared of him that she lets him have his way with her, but I'm not afraid of the BASTARD ANYMORE!"

RJ had heard enough. He was no longer concerned about his own flesh and blood, or with the movements of his pathetic wife. When DeMorgan walked back to the laptop, he aimed his gun at his own son's back.

Ruth picked up the leg from a broken chair and charged.

Rob hollered, "RJ, WATCH OUT!"

RJ spun around aiming at Ruth as DeMorgan threw the laptop, striking his father's arm just as he fired. The bullet went astray.

Rob began firing at both of the Beakers. A bullet barely missed RJ as he dove behind a large box, but a second shot struck Ruth's left shoulder. Still enraged, the agitated man muttered that he was going to kill DeMorgan for shooting him. In less than five seconds, he reloaded a new magazine into his weapon, aimed the barrel of the gun, and pulled the trigger just as DeMorgan vaulted over a crate. The shot struck the crate as James followed suit and hid behind another large wooden container.

Thankfully, Thomas had taught me how to shoot. Still squatting behind the box, I carefully aimed the revolver at Rob. "Put your weapon down!"

Laughingly, he resumed shooting at DeMorgan and James.

I yelled again, "Put your gun down, Rob!"

He swung his gun toward me, smiled maliciously, and fired. The bullet whizzed by my head, missing me by inches.

351

I discharged my weapon, watching the bullet tear through his upper right shoulder. Blood sprayed everywhere as he screamed out in pain. Keeping my voice steady, I demanded, "Drop the weapon, Rob!"

He switched hands as blood ran down his right arm. The gun was now pointing directly at me. He glared at me with pure hatred in his eyes.

"Please, put the gun down!" I ordered forcefully.

"Go to hell, bitch!" he screamed, targeting me. He fired as I moved aside. The bullet struck the crates next to me as Rob aimed his weapon at James. An instant later, he pulled the trigger again. James fired back, striking Rob in the chest.

My heart was about to explode . . . .

Shocked, Rob dropped the gun, stumbled, and fell to the floor as James held his aim. In that moment, DeMorgan ran to his mother and cradled her as she lay on the floor bleeding. Once James was sure the bastard was dead, he went over to help his friend.

RJ stood up with a deranged look in his eyes. Without warning, he shifted the barrel of the loaded gun directly at his son.

"Drop the gun, RJ," I ordered.

"Or what?" he smirked.

"I'm not going to let you hurt them," I stated. My heart was beating so fast that I thought I'd start hyperventilating, but I didn't . . . I kept my focus.

As RJ fixated on me, James moved away from DeMorgan and his mother. He crouched beside a crate near Rob's body, ready to spring into action.

"Right, bitch," RJ sneered mockingly. "This is all your fault!" He pointed the gun in my direction.

"I mean it, RJ. Drop the gun," I ordered, holding my weapon with both hands.

Just as he was about to pull the trigger, James threw a broken chair limb at him. The bullet went awry and hit another wooden crate.

I fired back. The bullet hit RJ just above his left knee, shattering the bone as James took him down to the floor.

Stunned for a moment, RJ became silent. Then he began to utter a litany of obscenities directed at Ruth and me. DeMorgan jumped up from his mother's side, took the gun from his father's hand, and held the muzzle to his father's head.

"Don't De!" I yelled at the top of my lungs, watching him shaking as he held the gun steady with both hands. "He's not worth it, De. Your mother is going to need you."

He stood there with hatred in his eyes, glaring at his father. He was breathing hard as tears ran down his cheeks, fingering the trigger.

"Don't De," James pleaded, moving out of the way. "Miz Samuels is right!"

I didn't want to shoot DeMorgan. *Oh, God. Please, make him listen*, I begged. "De, please, put the gun down."

He looked up and saw me pointing the gun at him. "You won't shoot me."

"De, I won't let you kill your father. Please, put the gun down," I demanded as evenly as I could with my heart racing. "I'm not going let you destroy your life."

He just stood there glaring at his father.

"De, what's happened here isn't your fault. Lisa and your mother need you. Please don't throw your life away because of him. Put the gun down."

He looked over at his almost unconscious mother. Wiping away tears with his shirt sleeve, he placed the gun down on the floor.

"Thank you, De. Please kick the gun away from your dad."

He did and walked over to his mother and knelt by her side.

I lowered my weapon and then went to over to them. I took off my jacket and carefully applied pressure on Ruth's wound to stop the bleeding. Her breathing was unstable and her coloring had left her face. She appeared on the verge of going into shock.

Not trusting De's father, James stood on guard, glaring at him. RJ lay there groaning in pain, still muttering obscenities, as James gave him his shirt to stop the bleeding.

Suddenly, Jack and his men entered the storage room with their police-issued hardware drawn. He ordered us to drop our weapons.

I wasn't sure of anything, except that James had saved my life! He had saved all of us. He slowly placed the gun on the floor. And I did the same.

After an all-clear sign was given, Thomas entered the room. He walked over and picked me up in his strong arms. I clung to him for dear life as tears appeared.

Once I stopped shaking, I lifted my head from his now damp shoulder and surveyed the chaos. A detective bent over Rob's body while a deputy removed yellow index cards from his breast pocket and began systematically folding them in half, like small tents. After making over a dozen, he carefully placed them next to the scattered shell casings on the floor.

The paramedics worked feverishly on stabilizing Ruth and addressing RJ's wound. DeMorgan and James, both in handcuffs, stood at the entrance of the room. Crime scene techs snapped pictures of the violent aftermath while the K-9 Unit waited to enter the storage room.

"James saved our lives," I informed the sheriff. "If he hadn't pulled the trigger, Rob would have killed all of us," I asserted as Thomas put me down.

Jack spoke softly. "I know. The SWAT team was about to enter when the shooting started. They reported that you and James shot Rob Stone in self-defense, and you were only defending yourself when you shot RJ Beaker in the leg. Is that true, Sam?"

"Yes, she did," DeMorgan insisted before I could say anything. He was standing by the doorway. "She was trying to protect us."

"De's tellin' the truth, Mr. Policeman. She fired after they'd be pullin' the trigger," shouted James defiantly.

"Thank you for your help," Jack said quietly to James.

"Sheriff, do you want me to take Ms. Samuels downtown for questioning," asked a deputy.

"No," the sheriff replied.

I was still trembling as I came to grips as to what just happened. It had been a terrifying evening—and one that was still far from over.

Wednesday: 10:45 P.M. at Madison

"Please, may I speak with the boys for a minute?" I asked Jack. The sheriff nodded his approval. No one interfered as I approached them.

"Thank you for not giving me up," I said, as the deputy guarding the boys stepped away to allow us some privacy. "James, I'm going to find your mother."

He stood quietly with his head down and nodded his acknowledgment.

"Ms. Samuels, I'm sorry about the phone calls and smearing shit in your office," DeMorgan confessed in a somber tone.

"Why did you do that?"

"I thought you were trying to hurt us. My dad said that you were a threat because you were the new principal. He wanted me to scare you off."

"Just a minute, De. I need the sheriff and Mr. Ryan to hear this."

Turning around, I called both men over to hear our discussion. When they came over, I told them what DeMorgan had said and that the boys wanted to tell them what had happened.

They agreed to listen, but Thomas was still uneasy with the situation. He made sure the boys understood their constitutional rights. They had the right to remain silent and to have an attorney present while they were being questioned. Once he was satisfied that the boys comprehended the pros and cons of speaking with law enforcement, he stepped aside.

Jack had a deputy record him reading the boys their Miranda warnings, the boys agreeing to the constitutional waivers, and the interview.

"De, why did you need the CDs?" I asked as James shifted his weight from one foot to the other, looking uncomfortable.

"Ms. Fuller needed me to transfer the district's funds."

"Why didn't she just do it?"

"Mr. Monti thought it was better that I did it."

"Why were you helping them?" I asked, seeing concern in his eyes.

"I had to," DeMorgan replied, looking directly at me. "If I didn't help them, he would hurt my mom again and maybe go after Lisa."

"Who hurt your mom?" the sheriff pressed.

"Mr. Monti did," he whispered, turning red. His moist eyes fell to the floor.

"Are you sure Mr. Monti assaulted your mother?"

"Yes, I know who the jerk is," he declared angrily. "I saw him slap my mother when she told him to leave our house."

"Did you see anything else?" Thomas asked, seeing him breaking out into a sweat.

"I saw him rip her clothes off as she yelled at him to stop."

"Did your mother consent to having sex with Mr. Monti?" the sheriff asked, focused on the young man standing in front of him.

"He forced her to have sex with him," DeMorgan revealed, breathing heavily. "After the bastard finished using her, he slapped

357

her so hard that she had a swollen black eye for weeks. He told her that if she didn't cooperate, she'd regret it."

"What would she regret?" Thomas asked, watching him closely.

"Mom made a deal with Mr. Monti so I'd get probation . . . and if she didn't cooperate, I'd go to jail," DeMorgan disclosed.

"Where was your dad during the sexual assault?"

"He just sat there and watched him hurt her."

Jack and Thomas exchanged glances and then focused again on the boys.

"Why did you take Dr. Austin's briefcase?" the sheriff asked, knowing that DeMorgan's fingerprints were all over it and the documents inside.

"I got scared when I saw his body lying on your desk," he confessed, looking over at me.

"Why were you there to begin with?" I asked.

"Mom knew something was wrong when Dr. Austin didn't return her calls Sunday evening. She kept calling his house, but Mrs. Austin got really mad at her. So in the morning, Mom sent me to check on him. Then I called her and told her what I saw."

"How did she know something was wrong?" inquired Thomas.

"Dr. Austin told her he was looking for evidence at Madison that he could take to the state Attorney General's Office," DeMorgan disclosed, meeting Thomas' gaze for a split second. "I guess someone didn't want him to find the proof."

"Did you enter the principal's office?" Jack pressed, looking up from his notes.

"No, sir," he replied in a respectful tone. "I stood just inside the doorway."

"Could you smell anything?" the sheriff insisted.

"Yes, sir, it was awful," he stated, scrunching his face. "That's how I knew Dr. Austin was dead."

"Was the door open or shut when you got there?" the sheriff questioned.

"The door was open and then I shut it."

"Why close it?"

"It really stank!"

"Where was the briefcase originally?"

"It was on a chair by Mrs. Campbell's desk," DeMorgan reported.

"Were you alone when you went to Madison?" Jack pressed, glancing at DeMorgan and then at James.

"Yes, sir, I came alone."

After Jack and Thomas traded glances once more, the sheriff nodded for me to continue interrogating my former students.

"Was it your car I saw leaving the school Monday morning?"

"Yes," DeMorgan admitted.

"Why bring the briefcase back to Madison?"

"Well, Dad got a call and told me to vandalize your office. I knew I had to get rid of Dr. Austin's briefcase so I put it there . . . kind of like a red herring so the police would think that you were responsible for the murder and not my mom." He paused a moment. "Dr. Austin treated me and my mother with respect."

"But that doesn't explain why you shot Rob," I insisted.

"He kept pushing me around and telling me that I was stupid," he volunteered in a louder voice, "But what really made me mad was that he kept waving a gun in my face, telling me he was going to shoot me. So I grabbed it."

359

"What happened then?"

"We struggled for control and it went off. I knew I was in big trouble when I saw his blood spurting everywhere. So I got the hell out of there," DeMorgan said nervously, looking over at his friend. "I just didn't know who to trust. James kept telling me to go see you, Ms. Samuels, but I couldn't."

James had been listening quietly. "De's sick, Miz Samuels. His dad be givin' him drugs with he medicine. De don't mean to hurt people, but he only gits real mean when he gits drugs."

"James, do you know who killed Dr. Austin?" I asked, seeing his troubled eyes.

"No," he insisted, breaking out into a sweat.

"Rob said Santos did it on orders from the boss," DeMorgan asserted, coming to James' defense.

"Do you know who the boss is?" Jack posed thoughtfully.

"It's Mr. Monti," DeMorgan sneered, sticking a hypothetical knife in the county attorney's back with a vengeful smile. He watched the sheriff and the chief deputy county attorney stop breathing for a moment.

"De, exactly how is Miss Fuller involved?" I prompted.

"She's Mr. Monti's bookkeeper," DeMorgan confided in a snide voice. Then he fell silent as he watched the paramedics wheel his parents out of the room.

"Thank you, DeMorgan. And James, thank you for saving my life," I said, meeting their soulful gaze. They mustered a smile as they stood stiffly handcuffed, embarrassed at my show of gratitude.

Wednesday: 11:00 P.M. at Madison

As I watched DeMorgan and James disappear from my sight, I knew I had to help them. I looked over at Thomas. "We need to get them an attorney."

"Sam . . . ."

"I mean it! They saved my life. Besides, they're not the dealers."

"So you believe them."

"Yes, for the most part," I declared, meeting Thomas' worried gaze.

"Sam, what are you suggesting?" Jack demanded.

"I believe that Fred Monti is manipulating the investigation."

"How?" asked Thomas.

"James indicated that Monti framed him in the Hernandez case."

"Fred wouldn't do that. He's the county attorney," Thomas stated.

"Why not?" I challenged, seeing a flash of doubt in his eye. "He's in the position to control people's lives."

Jack had been listening to our exchange. "Monti is the state's 'Drug Czar.'"

"You're right, Jack, he really is . . . instead of stopping the drug infestation, he is running it," I asserted sarcastically. "Think about it; it all fits."

"Even if Monti did frame James, we don't have enough evidence to link him with the drugs," Jack said, narrowing his eyes.

"That's true, Jack. But Peter suspected Monti of illegal activity and wanted to catch him in the act," I declared.

"Here again, Sam, this doesn't connect him to the drug trade."

"Yes, it does. On the day Peter left for D.C., he read an article in the morning newspaper about the Olivier case. He blurted out, 'Now, I've got that son of a bitch!' None of this made any sense to me until right now."

"Tell me about the Olivier case," inquired Jack.

"From the very beginning, Olivier seemed to know that nothing was going to happen to him, except maybe a slap on the wrist," I said, recalling Peter's rant.

"Why would that upset Mr. Samuels?" Jack pursued.

"Olivier was a repeat offender with violent tendencies," Thomas said, seeing Jack arch a brow. "He got caught red-handed transporting over 800 pounds of marijuana. Peter had pushed hard to send him to prison, but Fred walked him back to the streets. Within a year, Olivier had killed a rival in a drug rip-off and then shot his father."

"Oh."

"Peter blamed Fred for the deaths," declared Thomas.

"When did the article come out?" Jack probed.

"January 22, the day of the plane crash," I reported.

"What did Mr. Samuels do after his outburst?" Jack inquired, adding new information to his notebook.

"He left and probably made several phone calls. One had to be to you, Thomas."

Stunned, Thomas stood there for a moment. "Yes, Peter did call that morning. He left me a message that he needed to speak to me about something important, but that was it. He never called back or left me any information."

"Where were you that day, Thomas?" I asked softening my voice.

"I was in trial and didn't get the message until after the plane crash," he said.

"Who else would he have called, Sam?" Jack asked.

"He would have called his handler," I said, recalling how distant he'd become.

"Who was it?" Thomas pressed, watching me closely.

"I don't know, Thomas," I stated. "He never mentioned his handler's name."

"Fred inherited money just before Peter died," asserted Thomas. "He didn't need to be involved in a drug-smuggling operation."

"That's what Fred led us to believe, because he was already involved. He needed to conceal the money he was making in the drug trade—in other words, he had to cover his ass—so he came up with this inheritance story. Remember all those juvenile busts on the south side of town five years ago?"

"Peter's cases . . ." Thomas reflected thoughtfully as he rested his gaze on me for a moment, and then went on to explain to Jack what we were talking about. "Fred had overridden Peter's decisions concerning drug-smuggling cases that dealt with juveniles who came from wealthy families—one of them was Bill Austin's son. None of these kids were prosecuted," Thomas remembered. "It was the main reason why he quit his job at the county attorney's office and went to work for the Justice Department."

"Sam, do you know what type of cases your husband had been working on at the Justice Department?" Jack probed.

"He was working on drug cases," I stated.

"If Mr. Samuels had to make contact with someone he didn't trust, where would he meet this individual?" Jack pressed.

"In a public setting," I asserted. "Peter was no fool. He'd cover his back."

"Are you sure?" he challenged.

"Yes; Peter would have wanted witnesses around," Thomas stated.

"Would he have used a backup?" pressed Jack.

"Probably, if he'd had time to arrange it," Thomas responded.

"Let's say, for the sake of argument, that this is all true. How does this relate to what's happening now?"

"I think Peter faked his death to catch Fred," I asserted, watching Thomas stiffen.

"Why do you think that?" Jack asked, bewildered.

I reminded them about the letters Doc found in Peter's desk that weren't there two weeks ago. I also told them about the faint aroma of Peter's cologne in his truck and finding his old raid bag under the seat with a loaded gun. Then I added my suspicions regarding the cover-up of the plane crash—Carlo Santini's odd behavior when I questioned him about Peter's death, and the strange man sitting at the bar.

Both men stood quietly, listening to my narrative.

I waited a moment, knowing they were filtering my theory into what they already knew. "Fred Monti and Jane Fuller wanted to use

Madison as a drug distribution center. They were slowly putting all the pieces together."

"Sam, I can't believe this . . . I would've known something was going on," Thomas asserted, taken aback.

"He betrayed you, Thomas. Monti played on your feelings about Peter's death."

"Maybe, but that was over three years ago," he remarked.

"True. But, then, Maxie was diagnosed with leukemia."

Thomas just stood there, evidently upset that he could've been so naïve.

"He must have thought that was the luckiest break of them all," I said, watching him. "He knew how you felt about me. And I was too worried about Maxie to care about the investigation into Peter's death."

"Sam, that doesn't mean Fred's involved with Bill Austin's murder."

"Yes, it does, Thomas. Bill knew that something was going on, especially when Jane started working at Madison."

"Okay, but that still doesn't prove anything."

"Jane knew she was in trouble when the bank manager called Bill about the missing $100,000. She had to do something to save her ass."

"So she implicated you in her ruse," Thomas declared, furious.

"That's true. I don't think the CDs were missing; she'd just made that up," I asserted, seeing their doubtful expression. "She always used a flash drive to work on my computer so none of the data would be compromised, and she is savvy enough to have another backup."

"What kind of backup?" Jack asked, rubbing his head.

"The computer in the lab," I said. "She downloaded her files from the flash drive and burned the CDs in case something went awry. I bet she has copies of everything in a safe place."

"Now, that's interesting," declared Jack thoughtfully. "Sam, did you catch James' hesitation when I asked him about Dr. Austin's murder?"

"Yes, I think he saw Bill confronting Jane in my office Sunday evening," I asserted. "But, I don't think James saw her kill Bill."

"Why did Santos admit to killing him?" Thomas asked.

"Prestige, I guess," I said. "After she killed Bill, she called Fred and he sent Santos to take care of things. This was a win-win situation for Fred. He now had leverage on both Jane and Ruth."

"How so?"

"Jane for killing Bill, Ruth for protecting her son, and even RJ for embezzling money from his family's business," I asserted. "Fred had to protect his investment. Bill's murder and the second break-in created an unsafe environment at Madison."

"So the school would be forced to close," Thomas stated. "And what about RJ?"

"He's Fred's pawn."

"Sam, even if what you're suggesting is true, it is pure speculation and, at best, circumstantial. There is no drug evidence to support your theory."

"Tell that to those kids, Thomas, "I countered. "They'll testify and so will Ruth. I'm sure there are other victims that Fred has harmed. You should be able to charge him on something."

"Sam . . . ."

"Then let's talk about the abuse of power. Fred Monti targeted Bill Austin because he knew that Bill wouldn't allow drugs in any of the district's schools, much less distribute them," I asserted, as both men frowned. "Monti is responsible for his cohorts running me off the road, but now this sadistic scumbag is endangering my students."

"Sam, don't you get it? We don't have any direct drug evidence," stated Jack, exasperated and losing his patience.

"Yes, you do!" I pressed. "These boxes are filled with illegal drugs ready for distribution."

As Jack pondered this, an entire K-9 Unit entered the room. Two black Labs and a giant schnauzer ran around the room once and then directly to the crates.

The female Lab became so excited that she piddled right in the middle of the floor. Her handler smiled when a fellow officer opened the crate and found bags of cocaine. In another corner, the smaller Lab located another store of cocaine. Right in the middle of the room, the schnauzer found a crate filled with marijuana.

I smiled inwardly. I'd been right.

"Sam, you may be right about the drug operation, but that doesn't mean that Peter is involved," Thomas stopped. He had a nagging feeling that I was right about Peter being alive.

I saw doubt in his eyes and then sadness. I felt awful for Thomas.

"Jack, there are only two questions left that need to be answered. Where is Fred Monti? And what has he done with James' mother?" I asserted.

Silence was his answer.

Wednesday: 11:20 P.M. at Madison

As Thomas and I approached Madison's front door, he told me that Marge and Nora were waiting outside. They'd arrived just as the shots rang out from the basement storage room. He had seen the terror on their faces.

Once outside, I realized the downpour had stopped. I inhaled the wonderful scent of rain and felt so much better. In a funny way, it gave me hope. I surveyed numerous people moving about the grounds. Ambulances, fire engines, and law enforcement vehicles were scattered everywhere. And finally, my focus went to the four individuals behind the crime scene tape.

Thomas stopped to speak with a deputy while I approached the small group. Mario and William were positioned next to the still frightened women. Marge stood rigid with Bear sitting next to her as she took in everything. Nora appeared petrified while she cradled Miss Paws in her arms.

I made eye contact with my mother-in-law. She seemed to relax a bit when I smiled, but she still appeared worried. From her stance, I knew she was prepared to defend me. I gave her a hug as she held me tightly while Bear rubbed his nose against my hand gently, checking me out. It was as if, in some weird way, he'd sensed the danger that I had just witnessed. I was so glad that Marge had brought my big guy with her. I bent down and embraced Bear.

Turning toward the boys, I asked, "How are the kids?"

"They're fine," Mario reported, relieved to see me alive.

William chimed in, "As the paramedics checked them out, they were telling their mothers about the new game they had played with James."

"They can't wait to play with him again," Mario added, grinning. "Pancho said, 'It was a real cool game just like real TV.' Just so you know Ms. Samuels, James tried to protect the kids. He kept telling them that he was really sorry."

That made me smile. "I'm glad the boys aren't too traumatized." Reaching out to them, I hugged each teenager and then stood back, realizing that they were no longer children but young adults. "Thank you for your help."

"It was nothing, miss," they echoed, embarrassed. A detective came up to debrief them, so off they went as heroes.

I turned to Marge who was still concerned. I said, "I'm fine."

"Are you sure?" she asked, wiping tears.

"Yes," I declared. "How did you know I was here?"

"Henry told me what had transpired at the house. When he couldn't reach you, because you had turned off your cell, Doc called us," Marge revealed, griping my hand.

"So where's Henry?" I asked, meeting her anxious gaze.

"He's with Doc," Marge admitted, as she avoided answering my direct question.

"Marge, where are they exactly?" I bit my lower lip.

"They're at Fred Monti's cabin in Meadow Hills."

"Why are they there?" I gasped, now beyond frightened when I saw her flinch.

"They wanted to keep an eye on Monti."

"Fred has Sheila Thompson," Nora blurted out nervously.

"James' mother!" I interjected.

"Yes," she sputtered. "He has her tied up in a chair in the back bedroom."

"Nora, how does Doc know James' mother?" Thomas asked, coming over to join us.

"Sheila was his vet assistant years ago," she replied.

"Is there anyone else there besides Fred and Mrs. Thompson?" Thomas inquired.

"Unfortunately, yes," Marge disclosed in a sober tone. "They saw Ruben Santa Cruz and Jane Fuller there."

"That's not good!" I declared, observing everyone's somber gaze.

"Thomas, Doc told us to find you and Sam," Nora asserted in a high squeaky voice. "He said that you would know what to do."

"If I am right about Fred's involvement, he must know by now that something has gone terribly wrong," I declared as Jack joined the group.

Thomas introduced the sheriff to Marge and Nora. Afterwards, he briefed him on the latest development.

Stunned, Jack inquired, "Do you know where Monti's cabin is?"

"Yes," Thomas remarked, giving Jack the exact location of the cabin.

"Marge, does Henry still have his cell on?" I asked.

"Yes. Why?"

"I'm worried—and I don't need any more surprises." Praying that they weren't kidnapped, I pulled out my cell from my back pocket and sent Henry a text message. A few anxious minutes later, my phone rang.

"Henry, are you two all right?" I questioned, hoping they weren't still hanging around the cabin.

"Sort of," he said, huffing.

"What do you mean, 'sort of'?" I demanded, knowing that somehow they were injured.

"We were walking away from the cabin when Doc slipped in the mud and hurt his left knee. And I pulled a groin muscle helping him into the Expedition. Other than that, we're fine."

"Henry, did they see you at the cabin?" I asked, feeling a bit uneasy with the situation.

"I don't think so," he stated.

"Where are you now?" I asked.

"We're in the truck driving to Corky's Bar to nurse our wounds."

"I'll meet you there," I asserted, relieved that they were somewhat safer than I thought.

"Sounds good to me," Henry chuckled. "Tell Marge and Nora that we're okay and that we love them."

"I will. Please be careful. If anything goes wrong, hit the 911 button."

"Will do, Sam," Henry said, hearing anxiety in my voice. "Honey, don't worry."

"Love you, Henry."

"Love you too." As he ended the call, I could hear Doc grumbling in the background. "Screw the Golden Years! I wish I had a bottle of scotch in this old truck?"

Wednesday: 11:50 P.M. near Corky's Bar

The members of the Sheriff's Department knew the location of Fred Monti's cabin all too well. While that was something to be grateful for, Monti's apparent association with the Santa Cruz family was not. The Santa Cruz organization controlled a powerful and dangerous group of thugs, with tentacles everywhere. Not only were they involved in successfully laundering money, but also in the transportation of cocaine and other illegal drugs for a Columbian cartel and other interested groups. Anyone who crossed them usually ended up dead.

It certainly looked like Fred Monti was their *consigliore*. And that thought made me shudder as Thomas put his arm around me and pulled me closer. We waited silently for the sheriff and his squadron to arrive at the rest area a mile away from Corky's Bar.

Within a few minutes, Jack and his force parked next to us. Using an engine hood as a table, he outlined the operation on a topographic map: The SWAT team would surround the cabin, determine who was inside, and negotiate the release of James' mother. Once she was safe, they would take Mr. Monti, Miss Fuller, and Mr. Santa Cruz into custody.

While I listened to the end of Jack's briefing, I was terrified.

As part of the plan, Thomas drove me to Corky's Bar and unceremoniously dropped me off. He didn't want me anywhere near the action. Once he saw me open the front door, he sped off in Jack's Tahoe to join the others, leaving a cloud of dust in the parking lot.

The Country-Western band blasted its music out into the parking lot. Nervously, I ran a hand through my chin-length hair, giving it a tousled look before entering. The dimly lit, jam-packed room reeked of sweat, alcohol, and tobacco and the stench was disgusting.

I stopped near a table to get my bearings as I scanned the room for Henry and Doc and spotted them in a corner by the stage. They were seated near a bearded man jabbering on a cell phone while watching the crowd. Doc waved me away as he yelled for the barmaid. So I made my way to the bar and ordered a beer.

The bartender handed me the bottle. "*Es todo, linda?*"

"*Si, gracias,*" I acknowledged, as I gave him some money. Suddenly, I felt apprehensive. I knew I was tired, but the bartender's voice sounded familiar. Then, looking more closely at the man with bulging muscles and a bushy mustache, I realized who he was— Pepito, the eldest son of Maria and Pepé Martinez.

When he handed the change back, he slipped me a note. Quickly, I shoved both the money and note into my jeans. I walked over to the kitchen area and sat at a table where I could view the entire room. Nursing my beer, I wondered why Pepito was working as a bartender in this grimy dive. This was not coincidental; he must be working undercover for the Sheriff's Department.

Pungent smells emanating from the kitchen made my stomach rumble almost as loudly as the music from the Country-Western band. I wasn't really hungry, but I was nervous. So I sat watching people drinking, smoking, and staggering around.

Ten minutes later, the barmaid came to take my order. I ordered a large bottle of water and nachos and handed her a twenty-dollar bill. After she left, I slowly straightened the crumbled note Pepito had given me. It read, "*Peligro*." I knew that meant "danger."

And just then, Fred Monti sauntered through the front door without a care in the world.

My jaw dropped, now fully comprehending the real danger. Somehow, Jack's operation had gone awry. Now, I was worried about Thomas. Henry and Doc saw Fred and exchanged glances with me. Pepito and the bearded man had also seen him enter.

I reached for my phone but stopped when the bearded man made eye contact with me. Those haunting brown eyes were more than familiar. As I blinked to get a better look, he disappeared into the crowd. Did I just see Peter, or had I imagined him? My hands turned ice cold instantly . . . I needed to warn Thomas.

Getting up, I strolled down the dimly lit hallway and accidently stumbled into the men's bathroom. Luckily, no one was in there. I locked the door and sent Thomas a text to alert him that Fred was here. I waited for his response.

"Thanks," he texted back quickly.

I left after washing my hands several times. Scanning the room, I took my time walking back to my table, taking in the now edgy feel of the tavern. Fred drank at the bar. Doc and Henry lingered at their table, nursing their drinks. "Brown Eyes" was still missing. Just thinking of him as Brown Eyes felt easier than admitting the bitter truth of Peter's treachery.

The nachos waited on the table. Nervously, I ate one chip at a time.

Fred checked his watch for the third time and then looked around the hazy room. He spotted Henry and Doc in the corner. Then he ordered another shot of whiskey and a beer as a chaser. Grabbing his shot, he downed it in one gulp and took his beer in hand. He went straight to their table and sat down.

This was not good, I thought, as we all sat around sipping our drinks.

Still reeling from the shootout at Madison, I wasn't about to make a move. Mercifully, the band took a break, but then someone dropped money into the jukebox, which ratcheted up the tension in the room with honky-tonk blues.

The bar's phone rang. Pepito answered the call as he continued mixing drinks for his waiting customers. I noticed that Fred had been watching him too. I had no doubt we were both wondering the same thing: Who called—a friend or foe? Maybe the phone call had nothing to do with what was going on.

Fred sipped his drink, and I ate my nachos.

Suddenly, two burly drunks started yelling about the Diamondbacks' chances of making it back to the World Series again. Their disagreement escalated into a fistfight. Both men were swinging and punching one another and, if that wasn't bad enough, they fell on tables, knocking down people who got in their way. In a funny way, the fight looked staged. One man landed across the table where Doc and Henry sat while the other brute landed on Fred.

Fred became infuriated. "Get off me!" he yelled. "Don't you know who I am? I'm the county attorney! Now get the fuck out of here!"

Apparently, they didn't care because the fight continued. Fred was shoved aside landing on his rump. A bouncer appeared out of nowhere and grabbed one man by the front of his shirt and the other by the collar. He started to escort the drunks out the door when Fred kicked the brute. The man took offense and went after Fred. Two huge men jumped off their barstools and went to help. They held Fred while the brute used him as a punching bag.

Then the room erupted into a war zone as sirens wailed in the distance.

When I didn't see Henry and Doc at their table, I searched the room and spotted Carlo Santini escorting them to the entrance of the bar. My mind raced with questions. Where was he taking them? And what was he doing here?

I pinched myself to make sure I wasn't dreaming. No, I was wide awake and this was a living nightmare. And where had Brown Eyes gone . . . back to my imagination? I didn't think so! He was here, hiding somewhere.

At the front door, Santini shoved Doc and Henry out into the parking lot. Then he turned back toward me. Unfortunately, he didn't get very far. He was blindsided with a punch and knocked to the floor.

Fred had managed to get to the bar and screamed for the bartender who was gone. He tried to escape out the side doors. But chains were now blocking that exit. I knew that was a fire safety violation and wondered when the doors had been chained, because they hadn't been when I'd first arrived. The county attorney headed toward the kitchen's exit but, he tripped over a chair and landed on my nachos.

Lucky me; I came face-to-face with the bastard. At first glance, he didn't recognize me. But I couldn't resist commenting, "Is this your new style of campaigning? Barroom brawling?"

A look of horror crossed his face as he realized who I was. He reached out to grab me, but I moved my chair back. He looked like a fish thrashing out of water.

My heart stopped when I saw Brown Eyes closing in on us. *Damn you, Peter!* I watched him bring his index finger to his lips, signaling me to remain quiet. That instant of distraction cost me the advantage of surprise.

Fred yanked me out of the chair onto my feet as I tried to get away. He pulled out a gun and ordered me to walk toward the kitchen. But, I couldn't move; I was petrified. My feet felt like they were glued to the floor. Using his height and weight, Fred spun me around like I was nothing more than a rag doll. Aggressively, he pressed the barrel of his gun against my shoulder and forced me toward the kitchen exit.

I knew I was in real danger and had to break free. I racked my brain trying to remember all the martial arts demonstrations I had seen on television. For some strange reason, I ceased being afraid and thought . . . . Timing was crucial. I imagined a huge clock painted on the floor as we walked in a straight line toward the kitchen doors, heading for twelve o'clock.

When someone bumped into Fred, I made my move. I stepped toward the one o'clock position with my left foot and spun clockwise to face the sadistic bastard. I grabbed his right hand and pushed it upwards with both hands. And then, without thinking, I used the heel of my right hand to strike his nose with enough force that it started to bleed. Stunned, Fred dropped the gun.

Before he could recover, I grabbed his shoulders and pulled him toward me as I raised my knee, smashing it into his groin with everything I had. He staggered back and fell to the floor, screaming out in pain.

A deputy promptly secured the gun from the floor and placed it into an evidence bag. Pepito picked up Monti and shoved him into an empty chair and then cuffed him as Sheriff Peterson read the county attorney his Miranda rights.

When I finally caught my breath, I couldn't help smiling. Fred Monti was in custody. And not surprisingly, he "lawyered up" immediately, spewing out that his constitutional rights were being violated as Peter Samuels disappeared into the shadows.

Thursday

August 18

Thursday: 1:25 A.M. at Corky's Bar

I had just finished my interview with the sheriff's deputies, DEA agents, and FBI representatives. During the interrogation, I answered each question to their satisfaction and had the pleasure of watching Fred Monti taken out in handcuffs.

I walked out of the smoky bar, searching for Thomas. I spotted him at the north end of the parking lot next to a huge RV command post. He was listening to Carlo Santini and Jack conferring with the FBI agent-in-charge.

As I turned to locate Henry, I heard Thomas call out. "Sam, wait up!"

I turned back around and waited.

His posture was rigid when he stopped a foot away from me. "Are you all right?"

"Yes," I whispered, looking into his clouded eyes. "Are you?"

Thomas pulled me into his arms and whispered hoarsely in my ear, "I just want you to know that I love you. And that I'm always here for you."

"And I love you, too," I declared, worried. "Thomas, are you all right?"

"No." He kissed the top of my head gently as if it was for the last time.

We were at a crossroad, and my heart was pounding. "Thomas, I saw him."

"I know; I saw him too," he reported tersely.

"This doesn't change anything between us, Thomas," I asserted, looking into his wary eyes. "You have to believe me."

"Mr. Ryan, the sheriff needs you," interrupted a deputy.

"I've got to go, Sam," he uttered with a grim look.

"I'll see you later, okay?" I asserted, wanting desperately to hold on to him. There was no response. He turned his back and walked away. "Thomas, please don't do this," I cried out, fearing that I'd lost him again.

I couldn't believe he would step aside without giving us a chance. I wanted to chase after him, but this was not the time or place. Tears cascaded down my face as I stood frozen in the same spot. The anguish I felt was unbearable and yet, somehow, I'd make him understand that he was the only one I loved. I wanted him, not Peter. The problem was . . . would he listen?

He stopped when he heard me cry out. Glancing back at me and then at Peter, who was now standing next to Jack, he quickly retraced his footsteps.

I tried to suppress my grief.

"Damn it, Sam!" he declared, wiping my tears with his fingertips. "I just want to say one more thing."

"What is it, Thomas?" I solicited anxiously. He took a step back. I had never seen him so conflicted.

He looked into my uneasy watery eyes. "We're still getting married!"

"Really, Thomas," I declared, breaking into a smile.

"Do you need time to think about this?" he asked, taking a step toward me.

"No, I don't, Thomas," I replied. Then I saw that amazing twinkle in his eyes.

"Are you sure, Sam?" he whispered, relaxing a bit. "It's a lifetime commitment."

"Oh, yes, I'm sure," I said as he took me into his arms. This was where I belonged.

"What about Peter?" he pressed, pulling away.

"I'll file for divorce immediately and that will take about sixty days to finalize. Afterwards, Mr. Ryan, we're getting married," I proposed, still beaming. I squeezed his hand as his lips brushed against my forehead.

"So that's the plan," he teased, looking down at me.

"Yes, it is," I asserted, not wanting to let go of him. "Henry saw Peter."

"Yes, he did, and so did Doc."

"What do I say to Henry?"

"Nothing for now," he stated. After looking over his shoulder at Jack, he pulled me closer once more and kissed the top of my head. "I've got to go back to work, Sam."

"Thomas, please wait a minute," I said, lifting my head off his chest. "How do we tell Henry and Marge about us?"

"I think they already know, Sam," he revealed, looking into my gaze. "But, right now, they have to deal with Peter's betrayal. Besides, I want to keep our plans to ourselves," he stated in a masterful tone.

"Are you sure, my lord?" I teased.

"Yes, my lady," he chuckled, tightening his embrace. "Now, I really have to go. And I'll definitely want to see you later."

"That certainly works for me," I beamed blissfully, looking up at him. "Thomas, don't you think that gleam in your eyes will give us away?"

"And your smile won't?" he countered smugly.

"Then we have a problem," I said seriously. Standing on my tiptoes, I looked up into his eyes. "I love you and only you. And I don't care who knows!"

"Really, Sam," he acknowledged, pulling away for a moment. "There is just one more thing . . . ."

"What?" I mused, seeing a lofty grin spread across his face.

"I've been thinking . . . ."

"Yes?" I wasn't sure where he was going with this thought.

"I know you want to have children . . ." he asserted thoughtfully, taking a second to focus on my face.

"Yes, that's true," I declared, hesitating a little.

"You know that I want a large family. And I've been thinking . . . how does twelve children sound?" he declared mischievously.

"Twelve kids!" I gasped.

"Just think of the fun we'll have," he promised.

As I started to protest, he kissed me with a passion that left my whole body tingling. A second later, he released me and walked away.

Oh my gosh, he took my breath away. Now I was even considering having his twelve children. Maybe we could negotiate the number . . . . Oh damn, I didn't care how many children we had. Nothing mattered so long as I was with him. I turned around with a silly grin on my face and sprinted toward Henry. He was standing by Doc's Expedition, sipping coffee.

When Doc saw me approaching, he nudged his cousin. Henry gave Doc his cup and opened his arms to welcome me. I hugged him tightly, shaking like a leaf.

Doc spoke to the deputy standing next to us in order to get permission for us to leave. Before the reporters could swarm around us, Henry helped me into the back seat of the Expedition and Doc started the engine. Once in the passenger seat, Henry turned toward me.

"Sam, Thomas said Monti held a gun to your back—is that true?" Henry demanded while Doc drove off the lot.

"Yes, he did."

Both men grimaced as they traded glances.

"When Fred came out of the door, he was covered in blood and told anyone in earshot that you had assaulted him. Is that true?" Doc asked, still trying to keep his anger in check.

"Yes," I replied, sensing their fury.

"What exactly did you do?"

"I broke his nose and kneed him in the groin."

Henry turned toward me with a smile. "The damn bastard deserved what he got!"

Doc chuckled, "I agree!"

No one spoke for a while until I asked, "Why was Carlo Santini at the bar?"

"Santini and his partner were following Ruben Santa Cruz for days. When Santa Cruz drove to Monti's cabin, they knew something was going down," volunteered Doc carefully, avoiding the name of Santini's partner.

None of us wanted to discuss the fact that Carlo's partner was Peter Samuels—apparently now very much alive. We all knew that discussion would come later.

"They were also monitoring the situation at Madison," added Henry with a strange hoarseness in his voice.

"What did Fred want when he sat down at your table?"

Doc and Henry exchanged glances before Henry answered my question. "He wanted to know why we were there."

"What did you tell him?"

"Nothing," Henry revealed. "The next thing we knew a fight erupted and Carlo shoved us out the front door."

"I told him that you were sitting at the table next to the kitchen," Doc stated, checking his rearview mirror to make sure we weren't being followed. "He said not to worry and that he would get you out of harm's way."

"Do you know what started the fight?" Henry asked.

"Sort of," I disclosed, recalling what I'd seen. "There was an argument between two baseball fans that escalated into a fight. As the bouncer escorted them to the door, Fred kicked one of the guys. Then all hell broke loose."

"My dear, that is an understatement," Doc smirked while he drove up the driveway and parked in front of Henry's home.

Thursday: 1:55 A.M. at the Samuels' Residence

Marge and Nora met us at the front door with Miss Paws and Bear barking. They had been following the breaking news. Fred Monti had been arrested. Several reporters had made the connection between the county attorney and the recent crime wave at Madison School. One reporter speculated that Mr. Monti might be charged with Dr. Austin's murder.

Listening to the late coverage for a few minutes, I was grateful that the media did not have a clue to my whereabouts. Reporters made reference to my recent appointment as acting principal of Madison but then went on to discuss the recent shooting at the school.

Yawning, I stood up and said goodnight. I was glad Doc and Nora were staying the night. I knew how upset Henry and Marge were about Peter faking his death.

Bear followed me down the hallway to Peter's old room, which I used whenever I spent the night at their home. Marge had already turned down the bed for me. I stripped off my sweaty clothes and placed them in the hamper. Then I took a long hot shower to scrub away the night's violence. Once I was dry, I put on a pair of pajamas that she had left for me on the bathroom counter.

I set the alarm clock on the nightstand and climbed into bed, thinking about the man I loved. I was profoundly grateful to be alive and have a future with Thomas. I smiled when Bear jumped up onto the bed, stretched out and, promptly, fell asleep. He'd had a very stressful evening too.

I fell asleep listening to him snoring. The next thing I knew, I heard an irritating blast of noise coming from the nightstand. Smiling, I answered my cell. "Good morning, Thomas," I gushed, looking out the darkened window. "What time is it?"

"It's almost four-thirty. I just wanted to update you before I catch some sleep."

"What is going on?" I asked, sitting up. My exhaustion had instantly been replaced with a burning curiosity.

"Carlo took Fred into federal custody, and it seems that he's going into the Witness Protection Program."

"In other words, he's copped a deal and is now an informant."

"You got it. But he may still be facing state charges. We've brought in two special prosecutors. One is dealing with Fred, and the other is working on the cases against the Beakers and the kids."

"The Beakers?" I asked, wondering about their medical condition.

"They're both in stable condition. RJ is cooperating with the authorities after working out a deal where Ruth gets a free pass. He said she wasn't responsible for anything that happened."

"How magnanimous of him," I commented sarcastically. "What exactly does that deal mean?"

"She will go to a rehab center for domestic violence counseling and then do community service in the barrio," he reported.

I'd told him often enough how I felt about this woman, but now my opinion was different. I just felt so sorry for everything Ruth had endured. "What about the kids?"

"Well, I've been busy. I had David Williams appointed to represent James, and you know he's the best defense lawyer in the state," he asserted. "So, together with DeMorgan's attorney and Jack's help, we hammered out a plea deal with the special prosecutor. The boys will remain under the Juvenile Court's jurisdiction until they complete their GEDs, counseling, and community service. We're hoping to finalize everything by eleven this morning."

"Thank you, Thomas—I mean, Sir Galahad," I acknowledged gratefully, stunned by what he'd accomplished overnight.

"You're very welcome, my lady," he proclaimed warmly.

"Who is going to take physical custody of the boys?"

"Michael Beaker will be their guardian."

"Wow, he really is a take-charge kind of guy."

"He really is, Sam, and he's going to help RJ too."

"And what about James' mother?" I reminded him.

"She's in the hospital undergoing a psych evaluation and David Williams is also going to represent her. This way she won't fall through the cracks in the system. Oh, I almost forgot—Ruth wants to see you," he announced, stifling a yawn.

"Why?" I gasped, surprised.

"I don't know. She just asked for you."

"That's odd," I thought. "What about Bill Austin?"

"He was an innocent victim and has been cleared of all suspicion," he said.

"How were you able to establish this?"

"Jane confessed that she was working undercover for the Justice Department," Thomas said, yawning. "She gave us all of her documentation, including the CDs and flash drive, which proved that Dr. Austin wasn't involved in the conspiracy to import and sell narcotics. Apparently, Fred ordered her to set him up as the fall guy because he wouldn't play ball."

"Wow! This is an amazing turnabout," I declared, relieved that Jane wasn't a crook, more for Patty's benefit than mine. "I'm assuming then that she didn't kill Bill. So who did?"

"Santos did," he declared. "Sam, she wasn't manipulating the district's budget or the money transfers either."

"Who was it then?"

"One of Fred's minions in our Fraud Department," he reported.

"Did Peter know about Jane?"

"No, not until tonight," he disclosed. "They were working on separate cases."

"What about Paul Mendoza's money problems?"

"He does have some money issues, but nothing like the rumors you heard, and he's taking care of them. When we questioned his wife, she admitted to starting the gossip."

"Why would she do that?" I asked.

"She wanted to ruin his reputation in order to get a better settlement in the divorce action. And, as it turns out, he doesn't have a zipper problem—but she does."

"Oh my," I uttered, relieved. "What was Fred's connection to Sheila Thompson?"

"She was his live-in housekeeper."

"No wonder James was frightened," I said softly, running a hand through my rumpled hair. "He was just trying to protect his mother."

"That's right," Thomas asserted.

"Do you think Fred would have killed her?"

"In a heartbeat," Thomas declared with disgust in his voice. "Only he would've had someone else do the job."

"Is that why she was at the cabin?"

"Probably," Thomas surmised. "It would be easier for him to dispose of her body in the woods." Stifling another yawn, he said, "Honey, I have to get some sleep."

"Pleasant dreams, sweetheart. Love you," I said, ending the call.

It was time to greet the day. Before our run, I slowly rolled out of bed and began my morning exercises as Bear did his workout too. After I found a pair of my old sweats and put on my running shoes, we were ready to go. The two of us quietly left the house and began our run.

It felt good. The gentle breeze from the southwest created a welcome fanning effect as the sun's rays released a blast of energy. Soon beads of sweat formed on my face and torso as Bear ran alongside me. After thirty-minutes, we started our cool-down jog back to the house.

I couldn't keep the secret any longer. I had to tell someone. So I told Bear about Thomas' proposal. He jumped around and wagged his tail excitedly. He felt the same way I did about Thomas. Then, I swore him to secrecy. Bear barked in agreement and pranced all the way back to the house. When we arrived home, Bear went to his water bowl and drank greedily. Eventually, he followed me to the bedroom.

Conscious of the day ahead, I went through the clothes that I'd left in the closet after Maxie died. I needed to look professional and selected a navy blazer, matching trousers, and a classic white lace cami. Once I'd showered and dressed, I added gold earrings and my locket.

Bear led the way to the kitchen and I followed him. I heard Marge, Henry, Doc, and Nora rehashing last night's events as they watched the news on television. When they saw us enter, they fell silent.

I saw Fred Monti being booked into the county jail. It was shocking to see him; he looked terrible with his broken nose. I smiled.

"Did you have a good run, Sam," Marge asked as Bear went over to sit next to her. She covertly slipped him a piece of toast.

"Yes," I declared, smiling as I greeted everyone else.

"Good morning," the others replied, not wanting to discuss last night's events in front of me. They turned their focus back to the newspaper.

I made a tofu shake with a fresh batch of blueberries and strawberries that Marge had set out. Afterwards, I took the shake and sat next to Henry.

He poured me a cup of coffee and handed me the front page of the Old Pueblo paper.

I quickly scanned it. Thankfully, the media was still in the dark as to what had transpired over the past few days. "How is everyone today?"

"Fine," they all mumbled at once, looking up from the articles they were reading.

"Jack called and wants to debrief us this morning," Henry stated.

"I can't do that," I disclosed, putting the paper aside. "I have a mandatory principals' meeting. Tell Jack that I can make it later today, and he can call Blanche for the time."

"Okay."

"How did you sleep?" Marge asked, seeing the sparkle in my eye.

"Really well and, strangely enough, I feel energized. But I wore Bear out on our run."

Marge looked down at Bear and patted his head. "Don't worry, Sam. We'll take care of him." Then she got up and made a fresh pot of coffee.

Looking up at the kitchen clock, I realized that I needed to go if I wanted to see Ruth first. Henry handed me the keys to the Avalanche.

"Are you sure?" I asked.

"Yes, honey."

We said our goodbyes. Marge gave me a funny look as I headed out the door.

"Henry, has Thomas proposed?" Marge probed, sipping her cup of tea.

"Why would you ask that?" posed Henry smugly.

"Her smile," Marge answered knowingly. "She's positively glowing. I've never seen her more at peace."

"Well, if he did, it's about time!" her husband declared, raising his coffee cup to toast the possibility.

Thursday: 7:30 A.M. at University Hospital

arrived at the hospital and went directly to the Intensive Care Unit to see Judge Ryan. To my surprise, I ran into Thomas just outside the unit. "Is your dad all right?"

"Yes," he replied, giving me a hug. "There was a change in the schedule and the doctors moved Dad's procedure up. Right now, they're prepping him."

"Where's your mum?" I asked, concerned.

"Ben took her to get something to eat."

"I'm staying," I said, pulling out my cell phone. "I'll let Paul know what's going on."

"No. I think we have it covered. Marge and Henry will be here while I'm in court. And Ben is going to be with Mum this afternoon."

"Why didn't Marge or Henry tell me about this?"

"Sam, I just called them," Thomas asserted, kissing the top of my head.

"I still think I should stay," I stated.

"Dad's going to be fine. I promise you."

Looking up into his loving eyes, I asked, "Are you sure?"

"Yes," he replied, noticing the packages in my bag. "What's in those boxes?"

As I handed him the gifts for his parents, I answered his question, "A book of one of your dad's favorite mystery authors and a puzzle book for your mum."

"You're not going to tell me which author are you?" he declared, chuckling.

"No." I smiled mischievously. "Were you able to get any sleep?"

"An hour's worth," he replied, stifling a yawn. "So have you seen Ruth?"

"No. That's my next stop . . . are you sure I shouldn't stay?"

"Yes," he confirmed, smiling. "You'd better get going. You need to see Ruth now so you won't be late for the superintendent's meeting."

"Say hi to Ben for me and give your parents my love. Please let me know about your dad," I stated, squeezing his hand.

As he brushed his lips against my ear, he whispered that he would.

~~~~~

After I left him, I was still concerned about the judge's outcome. I wanted to be with them but, went to the fourth-floor nurses' station instead, where a nurse directed me to Ruth's room. "Mrs. Beaker is expecting you."

I knocked on the door, still wondering why Ruth wanted to speak with me. An emaciated young woman in baggy jeans and a university sweatshirt opened the door.

Lisa gave me a hug. "Thank you for coming. And thank you for helping DeMorgan and my mother last night."

"You're welcome, Lisa," I stated, meeting her worried eyes. I was stunned at her frail appearance. "How's your mother doing this morning?"

"Better," she indicated, glancing at the woman in the hospital bed. "Mom wants to speak with you privately, but the doctor has limited visitors to just a few minutes."

"I understand, Lisa."

"Okay then. Mom, I'm going to get something to eat," she declared and then left.

"Hi Ruth," I said, walking toward her bed.

"Thanks for coming, Sam," she stated hoarsely, closing her eyes for a moment.

"I hope you're feeling better," I asserted, observing the fragile woman whom I had once considered to be my rival. I took a seat next to the bed and waited for her to open her eyes.

"I am," she admitted slowly, giving me the once over. Then she hissed, "I'm lucky to be alive, no thanks to Fred Monti. He'd been giving me cocktails laced with downers . . . no wonder I've been so out of it."

I sat erect as I quietly listened to her relive the nightmare she'd experienced. When she finished, I said, "I'm sorry you had to go through this, Ruth."

"My attorney told me that you stopped De from killing his father," she sighed. "He also said you were instrumental at stopping the bleeding in my shoulder. Is that correct?"

"Yes, it is."

"Then I want to thank you for saving our lives."

"You're welcome, Ruth."

"Bill was right about you. I should've taken your advice regarding De years ago, but I was caught up in a fit of jealousy."

"Jealousy?" I sputtered, truly surprised. Ruth Beaker was every man's dream—she was blonde and had a gorgeous face and a body to die for.

"To be honest, I was furious that Peter married you," she confided.

"Well, that makes us even, because I always thought you were the love of his life."

"Really," she asserted with a wistful expression. Then she admitted, "You were Lisa's favorite teacher, and she loved being in your class. I should have been nicer to you and tried to include you in our social functions."

"Ruth, I had very little in common with Peter's friends. You were all older than me, so I understood that his friends took their cues from him," I declared, trying to ease her mind. "Besides, I was still in school and then I had Maxie."

She remained quiet for a while. "Paul has it in for you, because of me," she warned, meeting my eye.

I sat there speechless, feeling very ill at ease. Lisa reentered the room with a breakfast burrito in her hand. "Ruth, if I can help you or the kids in any way, please let me know."

"I will, Sam. Thank you again for all you've done," she murmured, drifting off to sleep.

Thursday: 8:15 A.M. on the Way to the District Office

My mind was racing about my conversation with Ruth as I drove to the district's Administration Building. I felt so sorry for her and wished that I had made the effort to get to know her better . . . maybe things would have turned out differently.

The parking lot was filled so I found a spot on the street. I scurried into the building as I heard administrators buzzing about last night's events at Madison. Paul called out my name as soon as he saw me enter the crowded conference room.

He ushered me into his office and shut the door. He took a seat behind the oak desk as I sat down. "Sam, I want you to know that you have my full support and that Madison will remain open for this school year. If you are able to accomplish your goals, the school will remain open for the following year."

"Thank you, Paul," I declared, stunned with the turn of events. "I'm looking forward to working with you."

"I'm glad to hear that," he said, measuring his words. "This morning I watched the news channels and was stunned to hear about what happened last night. I was even more astonished that you hadn't called me."

"Paul, I'm sorry, but I'm not allowed to discuss anything that happened last night."

"So you can't tell me anything?" he questioned, clearly upset.

"The investigation is still ongoing. I can tell you that Ruth Beaker is stable and seems to be doing better. Her daughter is with her."

"That's it?!"

"Afraid so, Paul," I declared, as he seemed to understand. "My hands are tied."

When we returned to the conference room, all eyes were on us.

Paul took the podium. He made sure everyone knew that he was now the man in charge. For the next two hours, he went on at length about the changes in our policies. At the end of his sermon, he wanted us to develop the district's new educational mission statement.

Everyone squirmed in their seats. Now I remembered why I'd resisted becoming a principal. Scanning the room, I noticed that the majority of my colleagues were stifling yawns. It was all I could do to contain myself when he asked for volunteers. Repressing my urge to scream, I politely said, "Our mission is to help each child reach his or her potential."

Others chimed in as well and we debated each and every suggestion. Apparently, Paul had learned something at the parents meeting the other night. I was stunned when they adopted my suggestion. Finally, Paul finished his agenda.

A principal asked, "What happened at Madison?"

Glaring at all of them, he curtly said, "There is an ongoing investigation and there will be no further comments."

The room fell silent.

"Lunch is served in the dining room," he announced.

Luckily, I was able to beg off. Blanche needed me back at Madison.

Thursday: 11:55 A.M. at Madison

Thomas sent me a text as I arrived at school. "Dad's procedure went well. James cleared of Hernandez murder."

I responded, "Thanks. How's your mum? What about the plea agreements?"

"She's fine. Still talking to the attorneys," he wrote.

I entered the building to background music which made me smile. Blanche had found the CDs that I'd left on her desk yesterday afternoon. Grateful for her emergency call, I'd brought her a treat. She had gone to lunch so I left her a note where she could find her sundae.

I didn't know what the crisis was about but, after the days I'd had, I felt I could handle anything, or at least I hoped I could. Then, sitting down at my desk, I began going through the paperwork that had piled up in my in-box.

Blanche knocked. "Thanks for the sundae."

"You're welcome." I asked, "What is the emergency about?"

"The sheriff called and asked if you could be at the county attorney's office at one-thirty."

"That's funny. Thomas sent me a text earlier and didn't mention anything about going downtown," I stated, wondering why Jack wanted to debrief me there. Was I going to be charged for the shootings last night after all?

"Is there anything else?"

"Well, sort of . . . ."

"Blanche?" I questioned, now concerned, because of her tense posture.

"The teachers need your assurance that Madison is going to remain open—considering what happened last night. And they're also concerned about you quitting."

"Everyone is that uneasy?" I commented, drumming my fingertips on the desk.

She nodded.

It was twelve-thirty and the staff had gone to lunch. "Okay, set up a staff meeting for one-fifteen. Then call Jack and Thomas and tell them that I will be available at two-thirty."

"Will do, boss," she teased.

"How did things go this morning?"

"Okay," she said with bit of hesitancy. "The custodians cleaned out the storage room after the sheriff gave them the go-ahead."

"Okay," I stated. "What are you not telling me?"

"Henry and Doc Simpson were here too."

"Now, that is interesting," I said, smiling. "What are they up to?"

"They want to create a learning center in the storage room for you to use."

"Really?" I said aloud. "As long as I have tables and chairs, blackboards, and areas to display the kids' work, they can do whatever they want to the room."

In a serious tone, Blanche volunteered, "Mario and William told me some of what happened last night."

"It was scary," I said, then changing the subject. "Anything else?"

"No. I'll let you know when everyone is here."

"Thanks, Blanche."

I spent the next fifteen minutes shuffling papers from one stack to another. The projected enrollment stats were off, but there was nothing to be done until Monday, when we would have an actual count. A brown folder caught my eye.

It contained the registration numbers for our special programs. As I glanced at the list, I was surprised to see we had enrolled over thirty GED students. Some of them had also signed up for government, reading, and English as a Second Language courses. I knew everyone on the list but one name stood out: Henry Samuels. *What are you up to, Henry?* I thought, grinning.

The phone rang. "Good afternoon, Madison School. How may I help you?"

"Hello, my lady," Thomas greeted softly.

"Hello yourself, my lord," I said, smiling. "Did you get my message?"

"Yes, and I was wondering if you could come down any earlier?"

"I'll do my best, but the staff is a bit uneasy. I need to reassure them that the school will remain open and answer some of their questions."

"Remember, Sam, this is still an ongoing investigation."

"I know, Thomas; I can't discuss the events from last night. I'm telling them that Madison will remain open and that, hopefully, the crime wave is over."

"Sam, I hope that is true."

My heart sank with a strong air of dread about Madison's future.

Thomas heard the change in my breathing pattern. He quickly added, "At this point, as far as Madison School is concerned, we know of no other problems."

"Any progress with the plea agreements?" I wondered, worried.

"Still working on them," he said.

"Thomas, how are your parents doing?" I asked as I heard his call-waiting signal beep.

"Sam, they're fine. Dad's resting and she passed her physical with flying colors. I've got to go. See you when you get here. Love you."

I looked at my watch again. I had just enough time to check on the basement. I knew the sheriff had impounded the suspicious boxes and crates.

Going back down stairs was scary. The custodians had placed the broken chairs and desks out into the dimly lit hallway. I carefully maneuvered through the litter as I heard voices emanating from the storage room.

Mario and William stood inside my future classroom, staring at a sheet of paper.

"Hi, guys."

"Hi, Ms. Samuels," they echoed together.

"Ms. Samuels, can you read Mr. Samuels' writing?"

"Sometimes," I commented, shrugging my shoulders. "Let me see if I can."

Mario handed me the sheet. I had no clue what Henry had written. He had definitely missed his calling and should have been a doctor. "Sorry, Mario, I can't. Did he say anything when he handed this to you?"

"Not really, except that he wanted the room cleaned out."

"Well, nothing can be done until the district hauls the debris away. As to his list, I guess we're going to have to wait until he comes back and deciphers his scribbling for us," I stated, watching the boys smile.

"No lie, miss."

"Mario, I'm setting up a committee to oversee an honors project. I would like you to design the murals for the hallways."

"No problem, Miss," William volunteered, answering for his friend.

"Like what we did in our classroom?" Mario asked, giving William a look.

"Yes, but a little different," I asserted. "I want the kids to think about honor—integrity—and the choices they make. Do you think you can do this?"

"No problem," William repeated as Mario and I turned to face him. William was wearing one of the biggest smiles I'd ever seen.

"I'm glad to hear that," I commented, beaming.

"Me too," Mario declared, grinning.

"Mario, could you have a draft on my desk by Monday morning?"

"Yes, he can," William declared as Mario and I suppressed our laughter.

"Thanks for the opportunity, Ms. Samuels," Mario said.

"You're welcome. One more thing—thank you both for your help last night," I asserted, hoping they understood that what we had witnessed was nothing but sheer greed and a complete lack of respect for human life. "If it wasn't for your courage, the results may have been very different."

Embarrassed, they looked away.

"Miss, what's going to happen to James and DeMorgan?" solicited William.

"James has been cleared of the Hernandez murder, but I'm not sure about anything else."

"Do you think James is going to jail for kidnapping the boys?"

"I hope not. He was a victim in this mess and, for that matter, so was DeMorgan. They have good attorneys, and I will help them as much as I can."

As I left them behind, I went back upstairs to the sound of Latin music. It created a warm and upbeat environment. I hoped the teachers were also enjoying the serenade. I peeked into several classrooms and was relieved to see them coming to life.

Smiling, I entered the teachers' lounge a few minutes before our meeting. I poured myself a cup of coffee. Taking a sip, I was pleasantly surprised that it tasted like real coffee instead of sludge.

The teachers already there seemed pleased by my reaction.

"Gina made the coffee," said Ray, smiling.

"Well, she gets my vote for preparing the best coffee of the year," I declared with a wry smile as she entered the lounge. "Thank you, Gina, for making this wonderful pot of coffee."

"You're welcome. We thought you needed a break today and not the . . . ."

"Sludge," I confirmed with a smile. "I can't tell you how much your thoughtfulness means to me." Tears welled up in the corner of my eyes. "The past couple of days have been enough to try the patience of a saint and, since I'm no saint, you can well-imagine my need for this extraordinary cup of coffee."

Everyone began to laugh.

Taking another sip, I noticed Blanche and the stragglers had entered and taken their seats.

"Good afternoon. Thank you for coming to this unscheduled meeting. First off, Dr. Mendoza assured me that Madison will remain open and the district will honor its commitments. As for the future, that depends on how well we do this school year. Mr. Samuels has also indicated that the foundation will continue to give us any assistance we need," I confirmed, stopping for a moment to catch my breath.

"I have an update on the condition of Mr. and Mrs. Beaker. They are both stable and are expected to recover fully. However, Rob Stone died during the night," I stated, seeing the horror in their eyes. "Blanche, does the school have funds to send flowers or food to the family?"

"No, Sam. We generally do it by donations."

"Would someone like to volunteer to chair this? It would mean collecting money to send flowers and coordinating a food drive for the Stone family. Ned Tomer is the head of the district's Security Department and Rob was his son-in-law."

Ray raised his hand. He informed the group that a sign-up sheet for food would be placed by the check-in board in the office.

"Blanche, could you find out when the service is and if there is anything we can do to help the family?"

She nodded, saying that she would take care of it.

"By the looks on your faces, I know you have questions to ask."

"What happened last night?" Gina probed, leaning forward.

"That's a good question. I'm sorry but I cannot comment on what occurred last night because it might jeopardize the ongoing investigation."

"Sam, are you being pressured by the district not to speak to us?" Gina huffed.

"No, Sheriff Peterson and the special prosecutors have directed me not to speak to anyone about the facts in this case until after the trials have occurred," I stated, seeing everyone's frowns. "I think the prosecutors are worried about witnesses sharing information because that could cause a mistrial or, worse, the defendants would walk away from the charges—scot-free."

"In other words, they don't want cross-contamination," Ray surmised.

"That's it exactly, Ray."

"As far as Madison is concerned, everything is still a go?" Gina pressed.

"That's right, Gina. If there are any other questions pertaining to the school that I can answer, please ask away." As I scanned the room, no one seemed to have any.

"I have a two-thirty meeting at the county attorney's office downtown. So, if you need something, call me tonight at home."

Everyone nodded.

"Have a good evening," I stated and then asked Gina and Ray to walk with me as I told them about the Honors Committee.

"That's a great idea, Sam. I would love to help," Ray offered as we entered my office.

"Thanks, Ray." Then, turning to Gina, who sat down, I solicited, "What are your thoughts?"

She seemed intrigued with my idea but thought it through. Finally, she answered, "I agree with Ray. It's a good way of teaching ethics."

"I asked Mario to utilize the themes that we used in our classroom—like self-respect, being responsible for your choices, working together, tolerance, etc."

Ray agreed to chair the committee, and I told them where they could find the boys.

On my way out of Madison, I could feel that Blanche wanted to ask me about the investigation, but she decided against it. It was a wise move on her part, since I was all nerves.

Thursday: 2:25 P.M. at the County Attorney's Building

parked in the visitors' section and walked into the building as Thomas sent me a text. "Plea agreements for Ruth, De, and James finalized."

"Thanks." I wrote before I took the elevator up to the ninth floor. I couldn't imagine why I needed to go downtown—I still had a nagging feeling that I was going to be arrested for shooting Rob Stone or RJ Beaker. I shuddered just at the mere thought of going to jail.

A receptionist at the front desk greeted me warmly and directed me to a conference room at the end of the hall. A second later, a badge wearing Jane Fuller stepped out of an office and came over to me.

"Sam, I'm sorry for what I put you through," she said softly, as we walked down the corridor.

"Why did you tell them I'd taken your CDs?"

"Fred wanted them immediately, and I panicked."

"I can understand that," I asserted. "But why?"

"Fred had become paranoid over the past few weeks. I knew he would search every inch of my house and car, as well as Madison. If he thought I'd double-crossed him, he'd kill me," she stated. "Just so you know I'm still working undercover. I had to protect those files at all cost. If he had access to them, a lot of innocent people would be hurt."

"What about Ruben Santa Cruz?"

"Fred wanted him to distribute the drugs but he refused," she asserted.

"Why?"

"He thought Fred was a liability."

"Oh." I uttered.

"I never thought that Fred would have those kids kidnapped."

"But he did," I said, meeting her worried gaze.

"I'm grateful that you were able to protect them," Jane stated. Her pager went off.

"Thank you," I replied, then watching her leave. Still stunned, at Jane's statements, I took a moment to focus before I knocked on the conference room's door.

"Come in," a man answered in an authoritative voice.

I was surprised to see Marge and Henry sitting next to an empty chair.

Douglas White, Peter's boss at the Justice Department, stood behind a large desk. He pointed to the only empty seat.

It was then that I noticed that Nora and Doc were there. Thomas and Jack weren't invited to this meeting. Now I was terrified.

"Mrs. Samuels, thank you for coming," Mr. White announced as I sat down. "Special Agent Santini reported your concerns about the lack of information regarding your husband's death. Mr. Samuels also made a call to one of my associates. First, let me tell you that Washington has been following this situation very closely since the beginning. In order to protect the integrity of the investigation and to save lives, it has been necessary to keep all information classified." He took a moment to make sure that I understood what he said.

"Mr. White, I have only a few questions to ask," I stated in a somber tone. I looked over at Henry and Marge as she took my hand.

"Go right ahead," he directed, sitting down behind the desk. "That is the purpose of this meeting, in light of the recent events."

"Does Mr. Ryan know about your investigation?" I asked, needing to know Thomas' involvement.

"He does as of this morning when I briefed both him and the sheriff."

"I see. Did Mr. Monti know?"

"No. We kept everything under wraps, waiting for Mr. Monti and his associates to make their move. When Agent Santini reported the school district's budget problems, coupled with the money transfers into the Santini Construction Company's bank account, we knew our long wait was coming to an end."

I felt drained but still needed to know the reason why. "Who ordered the hit on my husband?"

"We think Mr. Monti did."

"Based on what?" I demanded impatiently.

"Information your husband sent us before he died," he revealed, giving us a small nugget.

Everyone was on edge. I took a deep breath and let it out slowly. "Why were we led to believe that Peter was dead?"

Marge stiffened at the mention of her son's name. She'd always suspected something was awry when we received his death notification. Evidently, she was still processing what Henry had told her about the ghost we had all seen last night. Poor Henry paled at the question. Doc bowed his head as Nora sat perfectly still, grappling to understand Peter's deception.

As we waited patiently for the answer, I could see Mr. White struggling with the truth. The question was . . . what would he do with it?

"I'm afraid I can't answer that question," Mr. White stated tersely. "As you well know, Mrs. Samuels, we are still in the middle of this investigation."

Tears sprung from my eyes, but my voice was steady. "Why?" I demanded, staring down this petty bureaucrat. "Our daughter was gravely ill and we needed a bone marrow donor. Because of your ongoing investigation, my daughter died."

His face remained immobile.

So I added, "You do know that I saw Peter last night at the bar."

"That is an unfortunate development," he declared harshly. His face had reddened, comprehending the fact that their cover had been blown. He went into damage-control mode. "That doesn't change our position. We need to protect the integrity of the investigation at all costs."

"Really, Mr. White, even when the dead man in question is very much alive?" I countered in a matter-of-fact tone.

"You know where we stand on this issue, Mrs. Samuels. Now, if there are no other questions, we are done here," he stated dismissively, closing his file.

"I do have another question, Mr. White. Who was his handler in Washington?"

"A woman named Sarah Stein," he reported.

I stopped breathing and just stared at the man. Nothing else mattered; I now knew where Peter had been hiding all this time. He had been with Sarah. I was ready to go. "I have no further questions. Thank you for your time."

Marge had been holding my hand tightly during this terse exchange. We traded glances and then stood up. Together, we helped Henry up. Then, arm-in-arm, we walked out of the conference room with Doc and Nora following us.

Thursday: 2:45 P.M. at the County Attorney's Building

Thomas turned toward us the moment he heard our footsteps. His bloodshot eyes narrowed and the lines on his face deepened. He had been waiting down the hallway, with his broad shoulders drawn tightly together. He gripped a folder firmly in his hand. The navy tie was slightly off center—an unusual sight for him.

When we approached him, I took his hand. He escorted me away from the family for a private conversation. Thomas told me that he had Peter's documents authenticated earlier in the day. He explained each legal piece of writing he handed me and clarified all of my questions. Then, quietly, he told me that Peter had executed the divorce papers weeks before his disappearance.

"Why didn't he just tell me he wanted a divorce?" I declared, infuriated with my former husband. "I would have gladly given him one."

"Maybe he was trying to protect you and Maxie," Thomas said in Peter's defense.

"That's bull, Thomas!" I asserted, feeling the awful sting of betrayal. "He was having an affair with Sarah."

"Who is Sarah?" he asked, puzzled by my anger.

"Sarah Stein is Peter's handler. She is also my first cousin," I informed him, measuring my words carefully. "I never told you that my mother's parents disowned her when she married my father. Sarah sided with my grandparents and never forgave my mother for leaving her behind. She has hated me with a vengeance ever since my birth."

"That's awful," Thomas declared.

"Yes, it is," I asserted, looking into his eyes. "Peter and Sarah have been living in Mexico with my mother's parents, the Steins."

Thomas took a deep breath, now fully comprehending Peter's betrayal. "Sam, are you all right?"

"Yes," I uttered, taking his hand again. In that moment, I realized that I was relieved. I would always be grateful to Peter for giving me Maxie and his family. But now, I was free of him and this living nightmare.

"Sam, you have a funny look on your face," Thomas commented, concerned. "Are you sure you're okay?"

"I've never been better, sweetheart," I beamed. Looking up into Thomas' loving eyes, I knew how lucky I was to have him in my life. He was the man I had always been in love with. And now, we were moving on together.

Epilogue

People Matter

Children matter. They need to be respected and valued, aside from who they are and where they come from. Their journey in life may take them beyond their dreams.

Parents matter. They are their children's first teachers and set the bar for their future.

Sam made sure that Maxie felt safe and had fun during her life. RJ Beaker taught his son to be a bully. Mario's mother showed her son how to stand up and help others.

Teachers matter. They help children develop their potential and a passion for learning.

Sam made sure that the children came first and failure was never an option.

Leaders matter. They have a fiduciary responsibility to collaborate with one another to make the right decisions.

And readers matter. They pass the torch on to the next generation. Thank you for caring and for taking the time to read this book.

How we conduct our lives matters. The choices we make determine who we are and who we can become. By working together, we help our children thrive and give them hope for a better future.

Diana Taylor Hart

About the Author

Diana Taylor Hart

Diana Taylor Hart writes page-turning suspense novels laced with intrigue and romance that also carry underlying messages of hope and inspiration for our time.

Hart has taught in the elementary schools in Arizona's barrios and loved every moment. There she found students bright and eager to learn and came to love them, as well as their families. They taught her lessons in humility and made her a better teacher, she weaves this theme into her books to emphasize that children really matter.

Hart writes about teaching in the barrio to address sorely neglected issues that impact young lives, generate excitement about learning, and prompt students to think.

She earned her bachelor's and master's degrees at the University of Arizona.

Hart lives in the beautiful state of Arizona where she and her husband enjoy sunset strolls with their dog.

Going Home

By Diana Taylor Hart

Do Sam and Thomas make it to the altar?

And what secrets still remain for her to unravel?

The action continues!

Readers who enjoyed Sam's adventures in *Moving On* and crave more suspense and romance will love *Going Home*, another action-packed mystery laced with more drama and intrigue than ever before.

Sam is mysteriously summoned to her estranged grandparents' estate. Upset after a vicious confrontation with them, she receives an urgent message from Madison Elementary School regarding a withdrawn kindergartener whose behavior indicates signs of possible abuse. Worried and distraught, Sam needs answers.

This leads her down a pathway lined with horrifying secrets and spine-tingling danger that hits too close to home.

For more information about her upcoming books, visit dianataylorhart.com, like me on Facebook, and follow me on Twitter.

Made in the USA
San Bernardino, CA
26 June 2013